"Time to show them that there's a new sheriff in town," Kirk said. "Mister Chekov, fire warning shots across th᠎ ᠎ bows."

"Yes, Captain."

Chekov acted w᠎᠎᠎᠎᠎᠎᠎᠎᠎᠎᠎᠎᠎᠎᠎᠎᠎᠎᠎᠎᠎᠎᠎᠎᠎᠎ accuracy. Within moments, a᠎᠎᠎᠎᠎᠎᠎᠎᠎᠎᠎᠎᠎᠎᠎᠎᠎᠎᠎᠎᠎᠎ between the racing ships, forci᠎᠎᠎᠎᠎᠎᠎᠎᠎᠎᠎ ᠎᠎᠎᠎ply alter course to avoid flying into the᠎᠎᠎᠎᠎᠎᠎᠎ay which cut through the vacuum like a flaming s᠎᠎᠎᠎᠎ before harmlessly impacting with the planet's atmosphere where it turned some high-altitude clouds into steam.

"You came rather close to the prow of the Andorian vessel," Spock observed, "for a warning shot, that is."

"Just trying to make them listen to the captain, sir."

"I admire the enthusiasm, Ensign," Kirk said, "but let's not get carried away. We want to show our teeth, not actually bite anyone . . . if we can avoid it."

"Aye, aye, sir," Chekov answered. "Understood, sir."

The ensign's sharpshooting got the other captains' attention. Both the Tellarite and the Andorian reappeared upon the main viewer, looking even more irate than before.

"Have you lost your mind, Kirk?" the Tellarite bellowed.

"You had no call to fire upon my ship!" the Andorian said. *"That beam missed my ship by meters!"*

STAR TREK®

THE ORIGINAL SERIES

THE ANTARES MAELSTROM

Greg Cox

Based on *Star Trek*
created by Gene Roddenberry

GALLERY BOOKS

New York   London   Toronto   Sydney   New Delhi

G

Gallery Books
An Imprint of Simon & Schuster, Inc.
1230 Avenue of the Americas
New York, NY 10020

This book is a work of fiction. Any references to historical events, real people, or real places are used fictitiously. Other names, characters, places, and events are products of the author's imagination, and any resemblance to actual events or places or persons, living or dead, is entirely coincidental.

™, ® and © 2019 by CBS Studios Inc. All Rights Reserved. STAR TREK and related marks and logos are trademarks of CBS Studios Inc.

This book is published by Gallery Books, a division of Simon & Schuster, Inc., under exclusive license from CBS Studios Inc.

All rights reserved, including the right to reproduce this book or portions thereof in any form whatsoever. For information, address Gallery Books Subsidiary Rights Department, 1230 Avenue of the Americas, New York, NY 10020.

First Gallery Books trade paperback edition August 2019

GALLERY BOOKS and colophon are registered trademarks of Simon & Schuster, Inc.

For information about special discounts for bulk purchases, please contact Simon & Schuster Special Sales at 1-866-506-1949 or business@simonandschuster.com.

The Simon & Schuster Speakers Bureau can bring authors to your live event. For more information or to book an event, contact the Simon & Schuster Speakers Bureau at 1-866-248-3049 or visit our website at www.simonspeakers.com.

Manufactured in the United States of America

10 9 8 7 6 5 4 3 2

Library of Congress Cataloging-in-Publication Data

Names: Cox, Greg, 1959– author.
Title: The Antares maelstrom / Greg Cox.
Description: First Gallery Books trade paperback edition. | New York :
    Gallery Books, 2019. | Series: Star trek: the original series |
    Identifiers: LCCN 2019004508 (print) | LCCN 2019009130 (ebook) | ISBN
    9781982113216 (ebook) | ISBN 9781982113209 (paperback)
Subjects: | BISAC: FICTION / Science Fiction / Adventure. | FICTION / Science
    Fiction / Military. | GSAFD: Science fiction.
Classification: LCC PS3603.O9 (ebook) | LCC PS3603.O9 A85 2019 (print) | DDC
    813/.6—dc23
LC record available at https://lccn.gov/2019004508

ISBN 978-1-9821-1320-9
ISBN 978-1-9821-1321-6 (ebook)

To our old home in Oxford, Pennsylvania,
where I began working on this book,
and our new city of Lancaster, where I finished it.

Historian's Note

The events in this story take place in the latter years of the U.S.S. *Enterprise*'s five-year mission (2265–2270).

Prologue

Baldur III

"What's taking so long?"

"Gimme a minute. I'm getting some screwy readings."

Pierre Fremont squinted at the readouts on his secondhand Starfleet-surplus tricorder, which, honestly, had seen better days. His partner, Belinda Sharikh, sat in the driver's seat of the mobile phaser drill they had leased for the day in order to dig a new well for their homestead. Looming evergreens bordered the clearing as he walked ahead of the drill, methodically scanning the ground for a suitable aquifer to tap into. Moss, rocks, and old stumps, the latter waiting to be dug out, carpeted the outdoors. Sweating beneath the afternoon sun, Pierre cast a longing glance at the shady forest before turning his gaze back to the squirrelly readings on the tricorder's display panel. The data on the screen kept fluctuating. Visual static obscured the graphics.

"Screwy how?" Belinda asked. Like him, she was wearing a practical coverall suitable for a hard day's work. Heavy-duty treads supported the open cab of the drill conveyor while the actual phaser mechanism was suspended on a crane in front of her. A transparent aluminum windshield failed to conceal her worried expression.

"I'm not certain," he confessed. "I'm getting some kind of interference that's making it hard to get a precise reading, or maybe this old piece of junk is just on the fritz again." He smacked the device with his palm in hopes of knocking it back into proper working order. "I swear, I'm tempted to trade this thing in for an old-fashioned dowsing rod."

"A what?"

"An archaic bit of Earth folklore." He recalled that offworld history, let alone superstitions, were hardly among Belinda's interests. They were both third-generation colonists, born and raised on Baldur III. Earth, and the Federation, for that matter, were about as remote from their daily lives as Romulus was. They were Baldurians, through and through. "Never mind. Doesn't matter."

"Just tell me where to drill," she insisted. "We need get this monster back to town before nightfall or we'll be charged another day."

"Trust me, I'm well aware of that."

Ever since their old well had gone dry, they'd been reduced to hiking a quarter mile to the nearest creek just to keep themselves properly hydrated. A new well would make their lives much easier and free up more time to concentrate on building their fledgling lumber business, maybe even work up enough funds to get one of those fancy plasma-powered, automated sawmills. Belinda had big dreams of going into handcrafted custom carpentry as well.

Assuming we don't have to spend half our time toting water.

Despite the annoying (and inexplicable) interference on the tricorder, he kept probing beneath the surface until he was almost at the edge of the clearing, about twelve meters from their rustic log cabin, which was composed of equal parts timber and thermoconcrete. Solar paneling shared the roof with a chimney and a bare-bones communications array. Erratic though they were, the tricorder readings indicated that the water table was relatively accessible at this location, plus or minus a reasonable margin for error.

This will have to do, he decided. As Belinda had reminded him, they needed to get the drill back by nightfall and the town was a good fifty kilometers away. *We don't have time to search for the ideal spot to drill.*

He unclipped a paint canister from his work belt and sprayed an X on the moss, marking the spot. "Here you go."

"Right on it."

She positioned the drill directly above his mark and donned a pair of protective goggles to protect her eyes from the glare of the phaser beam. Pierre did the same, backing away from the site as she fired up the drill, slowly at first to avoid digging too deep. The last thing they wanted to do was punch a hole in the bedrock for the water to drain away into.

A ruby-red beam issued from the tip of the drill, burning down through the rocky soil toward the water table, forming a hole approximately fifteen centimeters in diameter; they could widen the hole later once they were certain they were in the right spot. A high-pitched whine accompanied the beam, which steadily increased in intensity, going from red-hot to blue to a brilliant white that, despite the goggles, made his eyes water if he looked directly at it for too long. He could feel the heat from the beam even from several paces away. Smoke and steam rose from the pit as the beam drilled through dense layers of dirt, clay, and stone. Pierre grinned. So far, the drill was worth every credit.

This is saving us hours, maybe even days, of heavy labor.

"How am I doing?" Belinda shouted over the whine of the phaser as well as the hissing steam. Gloved hands worked the control panel.

"Right on track!" He monitored her progress with the tricorder. "Just a few more meters . . . hang on, what the—?"

A sudden energy spike, coming from deep beneath the surface, registered on the device, blanking out the data on the screen. A warning siren sounded. A red light flashed.

"Watch out!"

An underground explosion rocked the ground beneath his feet. A shock wave burst from the pit, sending rocks, Pierre, and other debris flying. Barely missing one of the nearby trees, he landed flat on his back on the forest floor, the wind knocked out of him. He lay there dazed for a moment, catching his breath, before adrenaline—and concern for Belinda's safety—gave him the strength to scramble to his feet.

"Belinda?"

"Over here!"

The shock wave had toppled the drill platform and thrown her from the cab, but, to Pierre's relief, she appeared to be okay as she got up from the ground. If anything, she looked more concerned with the damage to the drill. The windshield was cracked, while the phaser itself had broken loose from the crane and was now an inert mass of mangled steel that, for better or for worse, was no longer capable of firing a beam. *Probably just as well,* he thought, *given that it's not pointed at the ground anymore.*

"Damn it," Belinda swore. "There goes our deposit!"

"At least we're still in one piece," he pointed out.

"There's that," she conceded, brushing herself off. "But what just happened?"

Pierre wanted to know that too. He glanced around the clearing, which was now strewn with dirt and debris. He noticed that certain rocks appeared to be glowing faintly, as though permeated with some kind of luminous material. He scanned one such fragment after recovering and resetting his tricorder. His eyes bulged as the device identified the targeted substance.

"Ye gads. These rocks are laced with pergium!"

The rare mineral was valued throughout the quadrant for its ability to power life-support systems. Pierre assumed that the phaser beam had accidentally energized a deposit of raw pergium, setting off a chain reaction, but just how big a deposit were they talking about?

A different kind of excitement kept his heart racing even as the initial jolt from the explosion subsided. He cautiously approached the gaping pit forged by the explosion.

"Careful there!" Belinda said.

"Uh-huh," he murmured, but his gaze remained glued to the tricorder's readouts. No longer set to detect the presence of water, the device scanned for pergium instead.

His jaw dropped at the results.

"Yikes, this is trashed." Belinda circled the capsized drill platform, shaking her head in dismay. "You don't think they're going to expect us to replace the whole thing, do you?"

"Forget the drill." A grin stretched across his face. "Forget the well. Forget the whole darn lumber business. Turns out we're sitting on top of a huge vein of raw pergium, just waiting to be mined."

She turned away from the battered drill as the full implications of their discovery sunk in. "You mean . . . ?"

"We're set for life . . . and then some!"

He realized then and there that their lives were never going to be the same.

This changed everything.

One

Captain's Log, Stardate 6162.1 *The discovery of vast quantities of pergium on a previously obscure frontier planet has set off an old-fashioned "gold rush." Would-be prospectors from across the quadrant stampede toward Baldur III in hopes of striking it rich, resulting in a crisis situation as neighboring planets and way stations are ill-equipped to cope with the flood of ships competing to get to the planet in time to stake their claims. Although Baldur III is not technically under Federation jurisdiction, being an independent colony, the* Enterprise *has been diverted to respond to the crisis and render whatever assistance it can to overwhelmed local authorities, such as those running the nearest deep space station . . .*

"Well, I'll be," McCoy said. "Talk about no room at the inn."

"An apt allusion, Doctor," Spock stated, contemplating the startling image on the viewscreen. "For once, I must agree with you."

At least a dozen spacecraft of varying sizes, designs, and origins swarmed Deep Space Station S-8, which was clearly never intended to accommodate so many visitors at once. A few of the smaller vessels were docked at the station itself, but most were orbiting the structure or were jockeying to get into position to do so, approaching the station from every conceivable angle and orientation. The overcrowding posed an obvious haz-ard in its own right; just watching from his chair on the bridge of the *U.S.S. Enterprise*, Captain James T. Kirk witnessed at least one near collision when an impatient Arcturian cruiser tried to squeeze in front of a slower Therbian transport, which wasn't about to make way for it. The former "blinked" and decelerated only moments before the ships would have plowed into each other.

"Remind me to raise our shields before we get too close to the station," Kirk said. "Looks like they're badly in need of a traffic cop . . . or twelve."

"Aye, aye, sir," Lieutenant Sulu said from the helm. He shook his head at the crush of competing vessels ahead of them. "You'd think it was Wrigley's Pleasure Planet."

"Or St. Petersburg in springtime," Ensign Chekov chimed in. The young Russian was seated beside Sulu at the navigation station.

Both of which destinations, Kirk reflected, could easily ac-commodate such crowds, unlike the besieged space station. Gazing at the chaotic scene, he understood more fully why the *Enterprise* had been dispatched to deal with the situation. And this was just a rest stop on the way to Baldur III; Kirk could only imagine what things were like on the planet. Tales of the lucky strike on Baldur III—some more exaggerated than others—had been spreading across subspace for weeks now. "Pergium fever" had broken out in sector after sector.

"Lieutenant Uhura, hail the station. Notify them of our approach."

"Aye, Captain."

McCoy leaned on the cherry-red guardrail surrounding the command circle. "Any idea where we're going to park?" he asked wryly.

Good question, Kirk thought. He hoped the station's manager, one George Tilton, would have some suggestions regarding that.

He swiveled his chair toward the communications station behind him. "Uhura?"

"My apologies, Captain, but I'm having trouble getting through to the station. Between S-8 trying to communicate with the other ships, and those ships also hailing each other, the channels are jammed." She fiddled with her earpiece. "And from the sound of things, I'm not the only one encountering difficulties. People are frustrated . . . and tempers are getting frayed."

"I see." Kirk appreciated her assessment of the climate they were flying into. "Use the priority channel. Starfleet override."

"Aye, sir," she replied. "Transmitting override now."

That should do it, Kirk thought. He was not above pulling rank when the circumstances called for it. They had not come all this way, diverting from their ongoing survey of the Enkidu Nebula, just to be put on hold. "Thank you, Lieutenant."

In theory, Tilton was expecting the *Enterprise* after appealing to Starfleet for assistance. The remote space station had been established to serve as an all-purpose rest stop for travelers crossing what had been a relatively untrafficked region of space. Seen from head on, it resembled any number of other deep space stations scattered throughout the quadrant. Holding a fixed position in space, as opposed to orbiting any star or planet, it rotated on a vertical axis. A habitation cone at the "top" of the station held most of the living and leisure facilities. The cone rested above the core of the station: a large saucer that consisted primarily of storage and engineering compartments holding most everything visiting ships might need for repairs or refueling. Three tubular arms radiated from the core, with docking facilities and smaller habitation cones at the end of each arm. A fully equipped shuttlebay was located at the bottom of the station, beneath the central saucer. Interior lights, shining through multiple viewports, indicated that the station was very much occupied at present.

"Looks like a feeding frenzy," Kirk said. "With S-8 at the middle of it."

"Indeed," Spock said from his science station. "The discovery of pergium on Baldur III is a welcome development, given its utility and relative scarcity, but I confess I find this disorderly rush to profit from the development somewhat unseemly, not to mention uncivilized. All this tumult simply because of naked avarice?" His stoic Vulcan features and level tone managed to register his disapproval nonetheless. "I would have thought that even humans would have evolved beyond such primitive motivations by now."

"And you've lived among us for how long now?" McCoy said with a smirk. "Never underestimate the human desire to get rich quick, no matter the era. And before you lecture us from your high-and-mighty perspective, what's that Vulcan salutation you're so fond of? 'Live long and prosper,' isn't it?" He nodded at the screen. "Those folks are just looking for a little prosperity, that's all. Can't really fault them for that."

As ever, Spock rose to the debate.

"Prosperity and profit are not necessarily the same thing, Doctor, particularly once a society has developed to the point that material need is no longer a matter of survival. When you have eliminated poverty and hunger, the pursuit of wealth becomes illogical."

"Logic." McCoy snorted. "Only a Vulcan would expect people to behave logically when there are fortunes to be made."

"You, Doctor, are a cynic."

"No, just a realist," McCoy insisted. "Particularly when it comes to the less 'civilized' corners of the galaxy."

"He has a point, Spock," Kirk said, joining the discussion. "You're right that on Vulcan or Earth or any of the more advanced worlds at the core of the Federation, people are less likely to succumb to 'gold fever' because their lives are already rich and satisfying in different ways, but out here on the frontier? That's a whole other story. Existence can be much rougher around the edges this far out, so you still have plenty of hardscrabble miners, colonists, adventurers, and, yes, opportunists who might be tempted by the prospect of a big score."

"Even if there is no guarantee of riches?" Spock asked. "It stands to reason that many of those en route to Baldur III are already too late to capitalize on the discovery, and may not achieve enough profit to justify the expense and effort of their expedition."

"A reasonable prediction," Kirk said, "which is probably why I'm not spotting any Vulcan vessels in that traffic jam ahead, but never underestimate the allure of a treasure hunt. It's not logical, but it's potent regardless."

"I confess," Chekov said, "if I was not in Starfleet, I might consider striking out for Baldur III."

Spock raised an eyebrow. "Is that so, Ensign?"

Chekov gulped and began to backpedal furiously. "*If* I was not in Starfleet, and was not, of course, fully committed to my duty as a Starfleet officer, which I absolutely am, to the very marrow of my being . . ."

"At ease, Ensign." Kirk let Chekov off the hook. "No need to explain why an adventurous young soul might be tempted to seek his fortune on a far-off world of riches, especially if everyone else seems to be doing so." He chuckled indulgently. "It may seem like a primitive impulse, Spock, but it's a natural one, and we're a long way from more 'civilized' climes."

Spock looked unconvinced. "Perhaps, Captain, but—"

"Forgive me for interrupting, Mister Spock," Uhura said, "but I have Mister Tilton for you, Captain."

"Thank you, Lieutenant," Kirk said, tabling any further discussion of the psychology of gold rushes until later. "Put him through."

"Aye, sir."

Tilton appeared on the viewscreen, supplanting the live image of the station. He was an older Earthman of British descent with gaunt features and receding silver hair. A simple tan jumpsuit indicated that he was a civilian, reporting to the Federation rather than to Starfleet. Kirk put Tilton in his midsixties, possibly older.

"Sorry to keep you waiting, Captain. I've got my hands full, to say the least."

Kirk noted the weariness in the other man's voice as well as the puffy circles under Tilton's eyes. He could tell at a glance that the station manager was overworked and under stress. Tilton was showing definite signs of strain. His shoulders sagged.

"So it appears," Kirk said. "I appreciate you taking the time to talk to me."

"No more than I appreciate your arrival," Tilton said. *"To be honest, I've been counting the days until you showed up."*

"We're actually en route to Baldur III," Kirk reminded him. "But I understand that you've requested Starfleet assistance as well?"

"Whatever you can spare, Captain. The situation here is becoming . . . well, untenable."

"Understood," Kirk said. "I'd like to beam over and assess the situation firsthand, but the congestion around the station poses a problem. I'm not certain we can get close enough to get within transporter range, so perhaps I should take a shuttlecraft instead."

"I wouldn't advise that, Captain. I'm afraid our hangar bay is already packed to capacity. I suppose I could order a civilian vessel to clear room for you, but they're not going to be happy about it, and tensions are mounting as is."

Kirk sympathized with the manager's situation. "No need to put you in an even more difficult position." A possible solution occurred to him. "Are your transporters working?"

"Overtime," Tilton said, *"but, yes, they're still fully operational, despite being employed around the clock to transport visiting crews and cargo."*

"Good," Kirk said. "So we'll fly a shuttle close enough for you to beam us aboard, leaving a pilot at the helm, of course."

"*That works,*" Tilton said, nodding. "*I'll instruct the transporter operators to prioritize your request.*" He keyed something into a console. "*That's bound to provoke some grumbling as well, but it's better than trying to displace a vessel or two.*"

"I'll see you shortly, then. Kirk out."

Kirk flicked a switch on his chair's right armrest to end the transmission. Tilton's image vanished from the viewscreen, restoring the image of the space station. Kirk surveyed the bridge crew, assembling a landing party.

"Spock, Sulu, Chekov, you're with me." Kirk glanced at McCoy. "You interested in tagging along as well?"

"If you need me," the doctor answered, "but I've got a whole slate of physicals lined up for this afternoon, plus some routine surgery on Ensign Singer's busted knee. If you can spare me . . ."

"Tend to your patients, Doctor." Kirk recalled that Singer had taken a nasty spill down a Jefferies tube earlier that day. "As far as I know, this isn't a medical emergency." He activated the ship's intercom to contact engineering. "Mister Scott, please report to the bridge."

Scotty could hold down the fort while he checked out the station.

"Welcome aboard, Captain, officers."

Tilton met them at the station's main transporter room, which was located in the central habitation cone. As he stepped off the transporter pad, Kirk noted a long line of people, representing myriad humanoid species, waiting impatiently to be beamed back to their own vessels, while another crowd loitered farther back in a lobby area, perhaps waiting to meet up with some expected new arrivals. Kirk found himself on the receiving end of more than a few scowls and dirty looks from folks who were plainly unhappy about the Starfleet party cutting in line ahead of them. Dissatisfied muttering reached his ears.

Sorry, Kirk thought. *Starfleet business.*

He introduced Spock and Sulu to Tilton; Chekov had remained at the helm of the shuttle, awaiting their return. He had been instructed to maintain a reasonable distance from the station until summoned back to retrieve the boarding party.

"Thank you for coming, gentlemen," Tilton said. "We can talk more freely in my office." He indicated the exit. "If you'll kindly follow me."

Only a single security officer accompanied Tilton. "Coming through," she said, raising her voice to be heard over the general chatter. "Make way, please."

She cleared a path through the jostling crowd, many of whom took advantage of the situation to vent their frustrations at the station's manager:

"Tilton! My ship is still waiting to be refueled!"

"What happened to my flight clearance?"

"Why are the Rigelians getting special treatment?"

"The sonic showers on Level Six are malfunctioning again!"

"I'm filing a complaint about you not responding to my previous complaints!"

"What is Starfleet doing here?"

Tilton sported a pained expression as he attempted to fend off the barrage of grievances and questions being thrown at him. Ducking his head and avoiding eye contact, he murmured vague, noncommittal replies.

"Sorry, I'm otherwise occupied at the moment. Please direct your inquiries to my office. The station computer is processing them as fast as it can . . ."

"That's not good enough, Tilton!" a malcontent bellowed. He was a scruffy-looking, pink-skinned humanoid whose origins Kirk couldn't immediately place, given how many sentient species were indistinguishable from humans at first glance. His clothing and accent hinted at possibly Izarian roots. "I need to get to Baldur III while the getting's good!"

More voices, chirps, and growls added to the unhappy chorus. Just as Uhura had reported, things were getting ugly aboard the station. Kirk resisted the temptation to place a hand on his phaser, concerned that might be seen as provocative. Sulu looked to him for direction, clearly worried about the mood of the crowd as well. Kirk discreetly signaled him to let Tilton and his security detail take the lead here.

Let's play this by ear, he thought. *Steady as it goes.*

"Please, everyone calm down," Tilton entreated the discontented travelers. "We're fully aware of your concerns and are doing our best to address them. As you can see, Starfleet is on hand as well. Please be patient while I sort this out with Captain Kirk and his people."

"I don't have time to be patient!" somebody shot back, but Tilton's appeal seemed to keep matters from boiling over. Or perhaps it was the presence of Kirk and the others that appeased the crowd to a degree. Kirk winced inwardly; he hoped that both Tilton and the frustrated travelers weren't expecting too much from the *Enterprise,* which could not stay long before continuing on to Baldur III. There was a limit to how much they could alleviate the crisis.

Exiting the transporter room brought them to a bustling promenade that appeared only slightly less packed than the lobby they had just left. A diverse assortment of sentient species— mammalian, reptilian, avian, amphibian, insectile, and some less immediately identifiable—squeezed past each other as they headed either clockwise or counterclockwise down a wide, curved corridor that, based on Kirk's familiarity with other deep space stations, probably circled around to meet itself. Automated walkways assisted pedestrians, while antigrav lifters carried assorted luggage, equipment, and storage bins. A babel of voices, vocalizations, and languages tested the station's automatic translators.

"It appears this so-called fever is not just endemic to humans," Spock noted.

"More's the pity," Kirk said.

He took in the scene as Tilton led them toward his office. Shops and services lined the promenade, offering food, lodgings, supplies, grooming facilities, information, communications access, entertainment, and other necessities and luxuries. Directional signs indicated the way to the hangar deck, infirmary, cafés, spas, recreational options, and so on. As was standard aboard such stations, some of the facilities were operated by the station, as a public service, while others were commercial operations leasing space on the promenade. The rush toward Baldur III appeared to be a godsend for the local merchants and restaurateurs, although Kirk had to wonder how well they were holding up under this unexpected flood of potential patrons. Too much traffic might almost be more of a hardship than too little. The frenetic ambience reminded him less of a well-ordered space station than of an Argelian bazaar. All that was missing were belly dancers and a fortune-teller or two.

"Talk about a circus," Sulu said quietly.

"My thoughts exactly," Kirk said, "and I don't envy the ringmaster."

For a circus, however, the scene was definitely lacking in high spirits. Most everyone struck Kirk as in a rush and out of sorts. Baldur III was where the action was; these people wanted in and out of the space station as quickly as possible—and everyone else out of their way.

"Fascinating," Spock observed. "Alarming, but fascinating." He surveyed the commotion with detached amusement. "I find myself somewhat grateful that Doctor McCoy stayed behind on the *Enterprise*. He would no doubt find this venal stampede confirmation of his rather jaundiced view of humanoid nature . . . and I would have difficulty refuting that."

"Venal is rather harsh," Kirk said. "These people are just eager to improve their lives, on worlds where a healthy bank account still makes a difference."

Spock remained dubious. "If you say so, Captain."

They soon arrived at Tilton's office, where a diamond-shaped doorway slid open to admit them. The office itself was fairly modest, being only slightly larger than Kirk's personal quarters back on the *Enterprise*. Furnishings included a desk, a computer terminal, and a circular meeting table. A viewscreen dominated one wall, while an actual porthole offered a view of the (congested) space around one of the station's radial arms. A schematic diagram of the station currently occupied the viewscreen. A potted fern, a 3-D backgammon set, a few old-fashioned codex books, and a scale model of the ill-fated *U.S.S. Shenzhou* provided some personal touches. Microtape disks were piled high atop the desk.

The manager sighed in relief as the door closed behind them, cutting him off from the crowds and their demands. He wiped his brow with a handkerchief.

"You see what I'm up against, gentlemen."

"I'm getting the general picture," Kirk said. If nothing else, the brief walk from the transporter room to Tilton's office had given him a snapshot of conditions aboard the overtaxed station. "You're essentially a modest roadside inn that suddenly finds itself along a major trade route."

"That's one way to put it," Tilton agreed. "Can I offer you some refreshments? I'm afraid we ran out of genuine coffee some time ago, but I can still muster a synthesized substitute. Or perhaps you'd prefer tea?"

"Tea will do fine," Kirk said, "and may even be preferable to my companions."

"Indeed," Spock stated.

"Tea works for me too," Sulu said. "Thanks."

A food slot dispensed the beverages, which Tilton handed out as the men took their place around the table. A triscreen viewer, similar to those found in the *Enterprise*'s briefing rooms, occupied the center of the table.

"Let me show you the problem in a nutshell," Tilton said. "Computer: display regional star chart."

"*Displaying*," the computer replied.

A chart of the sector appeared on the viewscreen. Dominating the map was an amorphous, cloud-shaped region of space, delineated in red, which lay directly between the station and the Baldur system. A label identified the highlighted region.

The Antares Maelstrom.

"I assume you're familiar with the Maelstrom?" Tilton said.

"Not from personal experience," Kirk answered, "but I know of it. It's a dangerous region of space that no vessel has ever crossed successfully, due to violent energies and possibly hostile life-forms as well."

"To be more precise," Spock said, "the Maelstrom is home to immense, violent currents and eddies of supercharged plasma, whirling at exceedingly high velocities around a heavy mass at its core. The destructive forces at work are such that no vessel or unmanned probe is known to have withstood them long enough to make the crossing. Even obtaining reliable data on conditions within the Maelstrom has proven challenging, due to the difficulty of transmitting signals in and out of the vortex. It is, in many ways, opaque to conventional sensors and communications channels."

Kirk appreciated the concise summation. He expected nothing less from Spock.

"And no survivors means no firsthand reports on the Maelstrom's depths?"

"Precisely, Captain."

"What about the hostile life-forms said to prowl the Maelstrom?"

"Unconfirmed," Spock said, "and largely conjectural. Theories regarding dangerous entities dwelling within the Maelstrom are largely based on rumors, folklore, and, at best, fragmentary, indistinct, and sadly ambiguous images transmitted by probes shortly before they were destroyed or lost contact with outside observers." His tone indicated that such reports were to be taken with a sizable grain of salt. "Given that unusual life-forms have been discovered in any number of seemingly inhospitable environments throughout the galaxy, one cannot rule out the possible existence of unknown entities thriving within the Maelstrom, but neither can one assume their existence. It may also be that the Maelstrom's well-earned reputation for consuming ships has simply spawned legends of lurking menaces lying in wait for unwary travelers."

Kirk got the idea. "Here there be monsters."

"Which is not to say," Spock pointed out, "that all monsters are imaginary."

As we've learned only too well, Kirk thought.

"In any event," Tilton said, "this station is the last stop before the long detour around the Maelstrom. In the past, we rarely got more than two ships a month, if that. Truth be told, when I accepted the post as manager, I was expecting a rather quiet, low-key job without a lot of excitement or drama, but ever since pergium was discovered on Baldur III . . . well, it's been anything but."

"I thought some ships *had* made it across the Maelstrom," Sulu said. "Or so I've heard."

"Tall tales and rumors," Tilton said, waving away such reports. "There are indeed stories about a shortcut through the Maelstrom—the Antares Passage, it's called—but you'll never meet anyone who has actually taken it. 'I knew a fellow who knew a fellow who heard about a ship that made it through in one piece' . . . that sort of talk. But it's just a myth . . . and a dangerous one."

"Dangerous how?" Kirk asked.

"In the present climate, it's only a matter of time before somebody tries to take a shortcut through the Maelstrom in order to get to Baldur III ahead of the competition. I've been doing my best to strongly discourage this, even placing a warning buoy at the border of the Maelstrom, but—"

Before he could say more, the office door slid open and a tall, muscular woman in a navy-blue station security uniform burst in. Her face was sweaty and flushed and her short blond hair disheveled. She had a wrestler's build, worthy of a Capellan warrior, and a stern, no-nonsense expression. Kirk immediately got the impression that she was not somebody you wanted to get on the wrong side of.

"Sorry I'm late," she said. "Had to break up an altercation on Level Three."

"Anything serious?" Tilton asked.

"Nah. Just some pushing and shoving over energy vouchers. My people and I shut it down before it got out of hand." She shrugged. "The usual . . . these days."

"A sorry state of affairs, as I was just telling our guests." Tilton turned to introduce the newcomer. "Max Grandle, my head of security."

"Pleased to meet you," the woman said gruffly to Kirk and the others. "Don't get the wrong idea, though. I've got things under control."

"No criticism intended," Tilton assured Grandle. "It's not your fault that we lack the resources and personnel to deal with the current crisis."

"Just saying we're managing so far," she insisted. "Security-wise, at least."

"We're not here to step on anyone's toes," Kirk said diplomatically. "But I imagine you wouldn't refuse a helping hand or two . . . just until things settle down."

"I suppose not," Grandle conceded. "Not trying to get all territorial here. Just wanted to make sure my people get the credit they deserve."

"Duly noted," Kirk said.

He considered his options regarding the station's situation. He couldn't make gold fever go away or triple the station's capacity overnight, and like the throngs of fortune hunters overrunning the premises, he also needed to get to Baldur III as soon as possible. Still, it was obvious that the station was seriously shorthanded, and he *did* have more than four hundred well-trained Starfleet personnel back on the *Enterprise*. He could probably spare a few dozen crew members for the time being.

"Here's what I can do," Kirk said. "I can loan you some of my crew to tide you over until the Federation can provide you with additional personnel of your own. From the looks of it, you need—or could benefit from—additional security, engineering and technical support, and perhaps some medical staff as well?" Kirk asked on McCoy's behalf, knowing that Bones would raise the issue if he were present. "How is your infirmary coping with the increased traffic through the station?"

"Doctor Trucco and her staff are managing," Tilton said, "but I'm sure they'd be grateful for some backup as well."

"I suspected as much," Kirk said. He couldn't spare McCoy, but it sounded as though Doctor M'Benga was needed more on this station than aboard the *Enterprise* for the present, especially with the wide variety of species passing through S-8; M'Benga specialized in xenomedicine. "Let me loan you a doctor and a few nurses as well, if only to ease the load on your own people."

"That's very generous of you, Captain," Tilton said.

"Hang on," Grandle said. "Who are all these new people going to report to? I don't have time to train a whole new crew."

"We're talking Starfleet personnel, Mister Grandle," Kirk pointed out. He appreciated that the security officer didn't like asking for help on her turf, but Kirk didn't have time to tiptoe around Grandle's ego. "They hardly require training to do their jobs. And as for supervising them, I believe Lieutenant Sulu is more than up to the task."

Sulu did a double take. "Me, sir?"

"I can't think of anyone better suited to the job, Mister Sulu," Kirk said. In fact, the idea of leaving Sulu in charge of matters on the space station had been brewing at the back of Kirk's mind since he'd first assembled the landing party. He was going to need Spock and McCoy and Scotty when he got to Baldur III, but Sulu had enough command training and experience to oversee the Starfleet team on loan to the station, and it would be a good preparation for the day when Sulu was given command of a ship. "Lieutenant Sulu is one of my top officers," Kirk assured Tilton and Grandle, "who at times has taken command of the *Enterprise* in my absence. He has my total confidence."

"I agree, Captain," Spock affirmed. "A logical choice."

To his credit, Sulu maintained a poker face, displaying no sign of doubt or trepidation at this unexpected assignment. "Thank you, Captain." He nodded at the station's administrators. "I look forward to working with you to keep this station running smoothly."

Kirk noted with approval Sulu's diplomatic phrasing. Not "restore order" or "get things under control," but "keep this station running," as though Grandle and company were already on top of things. *Nicely handled, Hikaru.*

"Wait a minute," Grandle protested anyway. "Just who is going to be in charge of who here?"

Kirk held back to see how Sulu dealt with the woman's attitude. He and Grandle were going to have to work together after all.

"Let's keep it simple," Sulu said. "Your people report to you, my people report to me, and we collaborate, along with Mister Tilton, to deal with any issues that arise. We all have the same goal after all: making sure that this station remains operational despite the excess number of travelers passing through."

"I suppose," Grandle said grudgingly, "but you're fooling yourself if you think it's going to be that easy. What about when we're not on the same page, or when your people get in my people's way?"

"We're all professionals here," Sulu said firmly. "We'll manage."

"And, ultimately, this is my station," Tilton reminded all concerned. "I can settle any disputes that might arise, although I'm convinced that won't be necessary." His tone made it clear that he considered the debate over. "Thank you again, Captain Kirk."

"Glad to be of service," Kirk said. "I'll have a full roster drawn up. And I'll want your input when it comes to selecting your team as well, Mister Sulu."

"Of course, Captain," Sulu replied. "I may already have some ideas along those lines."

"I'd be surprised if you didn't, Lieutenant." Kirk could tell that Sulu was anticipating the challenge ahead. "Sorry you won't be going on to Baldur III with us, but I need you here, doing what needs to be done."

"You can count on me, Captain." Sulu grinned. "Just pick me up a postcard or two, and try not to forget where you left me."

"Trust me, I'm not giving up my best helmsman. Don't get too comfortable."

"Honestly, Captain, I don't see that happening."

Two

Baldur III

"And I thought that space station was being overrun," McCoy said. "Looks like that was just a preview of coming attractions."

Kirk knew what Bones meant. After taking the long way around the Antares Maelstrom to arrive at Baldur III, they'd found the same congested conditions they'd encountered back at Deep Space Station S-8, but on a much larger scale. Scores of ships orbited the planet, with the geosynchronous space above the colony's home base, now called "Jackpot City," particularly in demand. Some ships were attempting to land at the planet's only spaceport, while others were beaming down to remote areas of the planet in hopes of staking a claim to a rich vein of pergium before anyone else. Most of the activity was centered on a northern continent in the eastern hemisphere, where the initial discoveries had been made, but some of the newer arrivals were striking out for less picked-over climes. Viewed from the bridge, Baldur III resembled a greenish-blue orb attracting a swarm of flying insects. As Kirk understood it, more ships and prospectors were arriving every day.

"Get us a place in orbit," Kirk ordered, "within transporter range of the city."

"Aye, sir," Lieutenant Rick Painter responded. A slender, brown-haired man of European descent, he had taken Sulu's place at the helm for the duration. "Might be a tight squeeze, though."

"Try not to bump anyone's fenders." Kirk was anxious to beam down to the colony and meet with the local authorities. "Uhura, hail the colony and notify them of our arrival. Tell them I'm eager to assess the situation on the ground."

"Actually, Captain," she replied, "I'm afraid we may already have a situation on our hands. I've been monitoring the chatter between the ships and the spaceport, and tensions are running hot. Too many ships demanding permission to land at one time." She gave him a worried look. "Matters are escalating."

Kirk trusted her judgment; she wouldn't call this to his attention unless there was serious cause for concern.

"Let me hear."

"Aye, sir. Here's the most pressing dispute at the moment."

Heated voices sounded across the bridge:

"Please, Captains. You need to be patient. We're trying to accommodate everyone as efficiently as we can, but our spaceport is only so large . . ."

"To blazes with being patient. We haven't come all this way just to stay stuck in orbit for days. There's pergium to be mined!"

"Wait your turn, you bullying lout. You think you can squeeze in ahead of the rest of us? My ship got here before yours. If anyone has been waiting too long to be cleared for landing, it's me."

"We'll see about that. We hailed the colony first. That gives us priority!"

"Nonsense! You can't reserve a landing pad in advance. First come, first served!"

"Please, Captains, you both need to be reasonable about this. Our facilities are overtaxed. We're doing the best we can."

"That's not good enough! I demand to be allowed to land. And you, in your pathetic excuse for a spacecraft, don't even think about trying to land before us."

"Or what? I'll have you know I don't respond well to threats."

"Is that supposed to intimidate me? I'll put my ship up against yours any time."

"I've heard enough," Kirk said. "Patch me into that frequency."

Uhura nodded at her post. "Done, sir."

"Attention, Captains. This is Captain James T. Kirk of the *U.S.S. Enterprise.* You'll forgive me for breaking into this discussion, but matters are obviously getting out of hand. Please refrain from any further saber rattling and comply with the directions from the spaceport, which, frankly, would be in their rights to turn both of you away at this point." He closed the channel.

McCoy chuckled as he leaned against a railing. "Not mincing words, are you, Jim."

"I am being the very model of diplomacy . . . under the circumstances."

"They're responding, Captain," Uhura alerted him. "And they're not happy."

"Why am I not surprised? On-screen."

"Aye, sir."

An orbital view of Baldur III was replaced by a split screen displaying the head and shoulders of both the feuding captains. On the left: a jowly male Tellarite visibly bristling with indignation; on the right: a female Andorian with a look of icy disdain on her pale blue countenance. Her antennae quivered irritably.

"Oh, brother," McCoy muttered.

Just our luck, Kirk thought. Despite being founding members of the United Federation of Planets, Tellarites and Andorians mixed about as well as matter and antimatter. He should have known he'd find a couple of them locking horns in this competitive atmosphere.

"Mind your own business, Enterprise," the Tellarite said, wasting no time going on the offensive. *"Starfleet has no authority here."*

"To the contrary," Kirk replied. "We are here by express invitation of the Baldur III colony to help maintain order during the current influx of new arrivals. And exchanges like I just over-heard are not making my job any easier."

"*Inconveniencing you is hardly our concern,*" the Andorian said. "*These delays were unacceptable to begin with, and are not made less so by certain other parties attempting to barge ahead of us. We may not be as boorishly bellicose as a Tellarite, but we will not be shoved aside with impunity.*"

"*Who are you calling a boar, you stuck-up icicle,*" said the Tel-larite. "*You can take your Andorian attitude and—*"

"Captains!" Kirk interrupted. "Squabbling like this is not going to land either of your ships any faster."

"*It will get my ship down to the surface before hers.*" The Tel-larite stamped a hoof audibly. "*That's good enough for me!*"

The Andorian's antennae recoiled in disgust. "*Spoken like a snout-faced ruffian accustomed to trampling over anything resem-bling proper manners and decency.*"

"That's quite enough, both of you," Kirk said. "Get control of your tempers and let the space-traffic controllers down on the planet do their jobs."

"*Thank you, Captain Kirk,*" a voice from planetside said. "*We appreciate your intervention. We ask that all visitors abide by our rules and protocols—*"

"*Or what?*" the Tellarite said with a snort.

"Don't test me," Kirk said. "If I have to play traffic cop, I will."

He wondered how many vessels in orbit around the planet were listening to the exchange. This wasn't exactly a secure channel. He could well be playing to a sizable audience, which meant he couldn't afford to back down.

"*This is getting me nowhere,*" the Tellarite said. "*I'm landing now, with or without anyone's permission.*"

"*Not before me,*" the Andorian shot back. "*Enjoy choking on my thrusters!*"

Both captains abruptly cut off their transmissions, vanishing from the viewscreen.

"Uhura," Kirk barked. "Get them back."

"I'm trying, sir, but they're not responding."

Spock looked up from the scope at his station. "The Tellarite vessel is indeed breaking orbit, as is its Andorian counterpart."

"Show me."

The ships in question appeared on the screen. Both were civilian vessels, considerably smaller and less impressive than the *Enterprise*. Kirk's blood pressure rose as he watched them descend toward the planet's surface, weaving back and forth and leapfrogging past each other in their haste to get to the surface first, despite frantic injunctions from the spaceport to return to their original positions. Kirk had no idea where they thought they were going to land unless they thought that the spaceport would somehow find room for them if they had to. Or perhaps they intended to touch down on the first available plain or clearing? As Kirk understood it, most of the vicinity around Jackpot City was densely forested.

"Time to show them that there's a new sheriff in town," Kirk said. "Mister Chekov, fire warning shots across their bows."

"Yes, Captain."

Chekov acted with commendable speed and accuracy. Within moments, a coruscating azure beam zipped between the racing ships, forcing both of them to abruptly alter course to avoid flying into the incandescent ray that cut through the vacuum like a flaming sword before harmlessly impacting with the planet's atmosphere, where it turned some high-altitude clouds into steam.

"You came rather close to the prow of the Andorian vessel," Spock observed, "for a warning shot, that is."

"Just trying to make them listen to the captain, sir."

"I admire the enthusiasm, Ensign," Kirk said, "but let's not get carried away. We want to show our teeth, not actually bite anyone . . . if we can avoid it."

"Aye, aye, sir," Chekov answered. "Understood, sir."

The ensign's sharpshooting got the other captains' attention. Both the Tellarite and the Andorian reappeared upon the main viewer, looking even more irate than before.

"*Have you lost your mind, Kirk?*" the Tellarite bellowed.

"*You had no call to fire upon my ship!*" the Andorian said. "*That beam missed my ship by meters!*"

"If anyone is acting irrationally here, it's not me," Kirk said. "And, from now on, this is very much my call. Now get back in line before I have to demonstrate exactly what a *Constitution*-class starship is capable of."

In a very real sense, he was holding a winning hand here. Neither of the two transports stood a chance against the *Enterprise* and they both knew it. The only question was whether one or both of the rebellious captains were defiant enough to push their luck regardless.

"Don't think I'm bluffing," he advised. "I'm more than willing to disable both your vessels if necessary."

And that went for anyone else listening in.

"*This isn't over, Kirk.*" The Tellarite gnashed his tusks. "*Just wait until my government hears about this!*"

"Object all you want. I'm sure they'll be delighted to hear all about how you threatened a vessel registered to another member of the Federation. And that goes for you too," Kirk said, addressing the Andorian captain. "Your hostile transmissions are a matter of record."

"*No need to make a galactic case out of it,*" she said. "*There wouldn't even be a problem if the authorities on Baldur III weren't so woefully unprepared.*"

"*Exactly!*" the Tellarite blustered. "*Straighten this sty out, Kirk, if that's what you're here for!*"

They signed off abruptly, racing to get the last word.

"Congratulations, Jim," McCoy said. "You just got an Andorian and a Tellarite to agree with each other. Will wonders never cease."

"Sensors confirm that the rival ships are returning to their original orbits," Spock said. "Somewhat surprisingly, the other ships are allowing them to do so rather than seizing the opportunity to claim those positions for themselves."

"I'm not surprised," McCoy said. "Seems to me the captain just made quite a first impression. I wouldn't want to cross him either."

"I can vouch for that," Uhura stated. "I'm picking up lots of chatter about the way you handled that situation, Captain."

"Good," Kirk said. "Let's hope that impression sticks."

It occurred to him that the rancorous captains may have done him a favor by providing him with an opportunity to lay down the law right away. With luck, that altercation would pay off in the long run, discouraging any other ships from taking matters into their own hands.

"One has to wonder, though," McCoy said. "If it's this bad up here, what it's like down there?"

"That's what I'm worried about," Kirk confessed.

Three

Deep Space Station S-8

A full-on brawl was underway in a general store on the promenade. Rival space travelers and prospective prospectors had turned the mercantile establishment into a melee. Fists, fur, and feathers flew as an impressively diverse mob of upset customers tore into each other, making Sulu glad that unauthorized phasers and disruptors were not allowed in the public areas of the station. He and Grandle and their respective security teams arrived on the scene only moments after receiving an alarm. Sulu had six crew members backing him up. Grandle had two.

"Welcome to my life these days," the security chief said. "You ready to get your hands dirty?"

"Lead the way," Sulu replied.

Even though his team outnumbered Grandle's, Sulu deferred to her in the interests of collegiality. The way he saw it, he and the crew members from the *Enterprise* were here to provide backup and support, not to butt heads with the station staff.

Let Grandle call the shots for now.

The mixed security force waded into the fray, intent on separating the combatants, which proved easier said than done. The mere arrival of the authorities did nothing to abate the pandemonium, which continued as though nothing had changed. Bodies slammed into counters and shelves and display cases, many of which, Sulu noted, looked woefully picked over. A few less bellicose customers were squeezed into corners, trying their best to stay out of the brawl while waiting for an opening to dash out of the store. Hand-to-hand combat was the order of the day, with some prehensile tails, trunks, and tentacles added to the mix. Sulu ducked as a small gold-skinned Ithenite flew over his head after being flung by a red-faced bruiser who looked big enough to have some Vegan blood in him. The Ithenite crashed into a force field protecting a case of valuable merchandise, causing the field to flash and crackle from the impact. Slams, crashes, grunts, and curses competed with the Antarian muzak playing in the background. Exotic profanities blistered Sulu's ears.

"That's enough!" Grandle shouted over the hubbub. She clambered onto a large circular counter at the center of the store the better to be seen and heard. "Break it up!"

Her commands fell on deaf ears and antennae, forcing Sulu and the others to resort to more physical forms of persuasion, while dodging punches and blocking blows thrown in their direction. Sulu was half tempted to stun the whole mob and sort them out later, but that would be unfair to any innocent bystanders caught up in the chaos. An angry Bolian, his blue face flushed all the way to indigo, hurled a can of unsequenced protein at Sulu, who ducked just in time to avoid a broken nose. The can crashed into a bare display case behind him.

"You heard the woman!" Sulu said loudly. "Stand down!"

A head popped up from behind the central counter. Mint-green skin and elaborately coiffed orange hair identified the man as a Troyian. "Thank the stars you're here, Grandle!" he exclaimed. "Stop these barbarians before they wreck my store!"

"That's the idea, Naylis." Grandle jumped off the counter into the fracas, landing between two furious shoppers who were doing their best to batter each other senseless. She shoved them apart, trying to keep them at arm's length from each other. Her fierce expression would have done an ancient Greek Fury proud. "Get a hold of yourselves! What do you think this is, the twentieth century?"

More force fields, guarding shelves and displays, crackled as brawlers collided with them. A stack of self-heating rations was knocked over, spilling onto the floor. An irate Tellarite, wielding a steel thermos as a bludgeon, charged at Sulu for no reason in particular. His attack boasted more enthusiasm than finesse, so Sulu deftly employed a judo move to hurl the porcine brawler out of the store into the hallway, only to gape in surprise as a burst of energy jolted the Tellarite as he passed over the threshold. The thermos slipped from his grasp as he collapsed onto the floor.

"Shoplifting precaution," Naylis explained, noting Sulu's confusion. "Nobody leaves without paying."

Good to know, Sulu thought. As the security teams pulled more and more people away from the brawl, restraining them as necessary, he headed into the thick of the commotion, hoping to defuse it at its core. His eyes zeroed in on a hooded figure, wearing a poncho-like garment, who appeared to be at the heart of the donnybrook, holding its own against three other brawlers despite being outnumbered. Rapid-fire kicks and punches sent the figure's opponents reeling. Sulu was impressed even as he saw a problem to be dealt with. The hooded one had serious moves.

"Whoa there!" He seized the furious fighter from behind. "Let's just take a moment to chill out here."

The fighter struggled to break free, making Sulu wish he knew how to administer a Vulcan nerve pinch. He narrowly avoided an elbow to the gut. An angry voice accosted him.

"Get your hands off me, you grabby slime devil!"

He recognized the voice and accent immediately. Startled, he released her.

"Helena?"

She spun around to face him. Her hood fell away, revealing

the unmistakable features of Helena Savalas. Her striking brown eyes widened.

"Hikaru?"

Fond memories surfaced, but the middle of a brawl was no place for reminiscing. One of her opponents barreled at her, intent on mayhem, so she leaned forward, bracing herself against Sulu, as she delivered a solid backward kick to the other brawler's solar plexus, staggering him. Looking past Sulu, over his shoulder, she calmly alerted him to another threat.

"Behind you."

He appreciated the warning. Spinning around, so that he and Helena were back to back, he found a wild-eyed Saurian swinging a scaly fist at him. Sulu deflected the blow and kicked the reptilian backward.

"What are you doing here?" he asked Helena.

"Ferrying a load of would-be miners to Baldur III." She grabbed a hostile Trill by the arm and swung him into a wall. "You?"

"Trying to contain disturbances like this." Sulu drew his phaser and stunned another attacker at short range. "Mind making my day easier . . . for old times' sake?"

"Well, since you asked so nicely . . ."

By now, the combined security forces had largely gotten things under control, having broken up the fights and restrained the most combative participants. Tempers were still running hot, but there was more glowering and muttering than actual bodily harm going on. Split lips and black eyes suggested that there was about to be a run on the infirmary. A Ktarian spit angrily onto the floor. Naylis scowled at the offense, but let it pass.

"All right, then," Grandle said, laying down the law. "That's enough of that. This is a Federation station, not an Orion slave market. Disperse peacefully, if you don't want to end up in the brig . . . or have your station privileges revoked."

Sulu understood why Grandle was giving the brawlers an opportunity to avoid arrest; besides the danger of re-igniting the violence, if they tried to run them all in, they would find the station's detention facilities already near capacity. Better to just let everyone go their own way. *I would have made the same call.*

"But she started it!" a spiky male Nausicaan protested, pointing at Helena. A mane of greasy brown hair framed his irate features. A vertical row of thorn-sized horns creased his forehead, giving him an intimidating appearance that didn't seem to cow Helena one bit.

"Like hell I did!" she shot back. "You and your brutish cohorts literally yanked that last universal translator unit out of my hands just as I was paying for it, and laughed when I demanded it back." She reached into her poncho and drew out the item in question: a baton-sized translator. "Who's laughing now, Tuskface."

"You human pestilence—" The Nausicaan lunged for her, but was held back by Ensign Banning, a burly Canadian security officer who had won more than his share of arm-wrestling matches in the *Enterprise* rec room. Sulu drew his phaser on the Nausicaan for good measure.

"I don't care who started it," Grandle insisted. "I'm ending it. Anybody else got a problem with that?"

People griped under their breath, but nobody seemed inclined to push their luck. Grandle nodded in satisfaction.

"That's more like it."

"Excuse me." Naylis rose to his feet after hiding behind his counter. He was a slight individual who looked to be middle-aged, by Troyian standards. His double-breasted violet tunic had a satiny sheen. A sculpted hairdo rose fin-like on both sides of his scalp, with nary a strand out of place despite the recent violence. His features had a vulpine cast. "Who is going to pay for the damage to my store, not to mention the lost business?"

Sulu glanced around. Aside from the general disarray, he didn't see much in the way of actual damage, thanks to the protective force fields shielding much of the merchandise. He assumed that Naylis had activated the shields as soon as the fighting started.

"File a claim with the station manager," Grandle advised, "unless you want to press charges against anyone in particular?"

Naylis mulled it over for a moment, then shook his head. "It's a shortsighted shopkeeper who jails his own customers." He looked over the mess and sighed. "I don't suppose you can loan me some of your people to help clean up?"

"Sorry," Grandle said. "We're security, not maintenance."

"Can't blame a fellow for asking," Naylis said with a shrug. "In any event, thank you for your timely intervention, Mister Grandle. And you too, Lieutenant Sulu."

Sulu was mildly surprised that the shopkeeper knew his name. "You're well informed."

"That's putting it lightly," Grandle said. "Naylis probably knows more about what's going on in this station than I do, most of the time. He can also get his hands on just about anything . . . for the right price."

"*Legally*," the shopkeeper stressed. "Of course."

"Uh-huh," Grandle said, sounding skeptical. "Anyway, Sulu, I hate to admit it, but you and your people handled themselves well in that ruckus. Probably couldn't have shut it down as quickly without your help."

"That's why we're here." Sulu accepted her olive branch, despite being more than a little distracted by Helena's unexpected presence. Although most of the disgruntled civilians were making themselves scarce, she lingered a few meters away, clearly waiting for him. He assured himself that the brawl was well and truly over before stepping away from Grandle and Naylis. "If you'll excuse me, I see an old . . . friend I need to catch up with."

"Friend" was not entirely a euphemism. They had certainly parted as friends, even if their history was a bit more complicated than that. He joined her as she was tucking her hard-won translator wand back into an interior pocket of her poncho. She looked up as he approached, her face again eliciting many warm and warmer memories. A purple bruise, left over from the brawl, discolored her chin, but otherwise she looked much as he remembered her.

"Fancy meeting you here," he said. "It's been—what? A couple of years?"

A chance encounter at the worlds-famous botanical gardens on Arden VI had led to coffee, dinner, and, eventually, one of the best shore leaves ever. Although they each had their own lives and careers, they had always tried to make the most of it on those rare occasions that their paths had crossed.

"Something like that," she said. "You're still with the *Enterprise*?"

"Chief helmsman, temporarily reassigned to help things run smoothly despite the sudden increase in traffic."

"Really? Has that caused any turbulence?" She massaged her chin. "I hadn't noticed."

"You'd be surprised," he quipped back. "And what's new with you?"

"First officer and communications specialist aboard the newly rechristened *Lucky Strike*, a commercial vessel far less impressive than a *Constitution*-class starship. We've been chartered to ferry a load of impatient prospectors to Baldur III, which is a booming business these days."

Sulu could believe it. "How long you going to be in this neck of the woods?"

"Depends on how quickly we can get some minor repairs done and stock up on enough provisions. We're also hoping to pick up a few more passengers, since we've still got room for more."

"And every vacancy represents a lost fare?"

"Bingo," she said. "Our skipper wants a full ship before we set out. In fact, I suspect he's out trying to poach some passengers from the competition as we speak."

Sulu didn't like the sound of that. One ship stealing fares from another sounded like another brawl in the making. Still, he refrained from complaining to Helena about it, since he didn't want to spoil their reunion. *Something to share with Grandle instead,* he decided. *Just to give her a heads-up.*

In the meantime, running into Helena again was a pleasant surprise.

"I hope you won't hold it against me," he said, "if I'm crossing my fingers that the *Lucky Strike* doesn't depart too quickly."

"Are you kidding? I'd be offended if you *weren't* wanting me to stick around for a while." She casually placed a hand upon his arm. "So, want to get a drink or something?"

"Sounds good to me," he answered. "I hear there's a cozy little bar on Level—"

His communicator chimed urgently, as did Grandle's a few meters away. The interruption was as unwelcome as the news Sulu received when he answered the hail. Grandle sprang into action immediately, heading toward Sulu.

"Break time's over," Grandle announced. "Got another disturbance, this time at the customs center on Arm B."

"So I hear." Sulu gave Helena an apologetic look as he lowered his communicator. "Looks like I need to take a rain check on that drink. Duty calls."

"Duty has lousy timing," Helena snarked. "But what are you going to do? Go. We'll have to catch up another time, if we get a chance."

"Thanks," Sulu said, summoning the rest of his security team. "Try not to start any more brawls until then, okay?"

She smirked at him. "No promises."

"You coming, Sulu?" Grandle called from the hallway.

"Right behind you."

He was already anticipating whatever uproar awaited them, and hoping that there weren't too many frustrated travelers involved. One free-for-all a shift was already one too many.

We're going to need a bigger brig.

Four

Baldur III

"Welcome to Jackpot City," the mayor said.

The landing party, which consisted of Kirk, McCoy, and Yeoman Martha Landon, materialized in the town square, where they were greeted by a delegation of community leaders. Kirk's arm itched where McCoy had administered a tri-ox compound right before they beamed down; Baldur III's atmosphere was thinner than that found on most M-Class planets, being somewhere between Vulcan's and Earth's. It was breathable, but humans could benefit from a boost, just to avoid getting lightheaded or short of breath. Kirk took a deep breath of the crisp fall air. So far the injection seemed to be doing the trick.

"Thank you," he replied. "We got here as soon as we could."

He took in the sights. The once-obscure colony had turned into a sprawling, ramshackle boom town almost overnight. Older buildings made of wood and stone and brick were surrounded by newer structures, including prefabricated steel barracks, several temporary shelters composed of quick-setting thermoconcrete, and more than a few grounded shuttles and spacecraft that had been repurposed as lodgings, trading posts, dance halls, and whatnot. Glancing around, Kirk was amused to see a vintage Kazarite escape pod being used as a sandwich shop. Twilight was falling in this corner of the planet, but the din of new construction continued even as the outdoor lights came on. Throngs of people, sporting the attire of many different worlds, roamed the bustling cobblestone sidewalks while groundcars cruised the streets. An air-truck zipped by overhead. Snow-capped mountains and wooded hills loomed in the distance.

"Soon as you could beats the alternative, in my book," Mayor Margery Poho said. She was heavyset, bordering on chubby, with an easy smile, shrewd brown eyes, and graying dark hair. Creases around her eyes and mouth gave her face extra character. Casual attire indicated a preference for comfort and durability over pomp. A rumpled overcoat protected her from the elements. "We're glad of any help we can get from the Federation."

"Within reason," an elderly member of the delegation muttered. He eyed the landing party warily. Appearing to be in his seventies, the man had a bushy walrus mustache, a ruddy complexion, and leathery features that suggested a lifetime of exposure to wind and sun, despite the wide-brimmed hat currently keeping his head covered. He walked with a cane, but showed no sign of infirmity. "And only up to a point."

Kirk wondered what his issue was.

"Allow me to introduce two of my most valued advisors." Poho indicated the old man with the cane. "This is Boyd Cahill. His family was among the original settlers on Baldur III."

"And don't you forget it," he said. "And with no help from the Federation, I might add."

Poho introduced her other advisor: a tall, rangy man clad in a faded burgundy jumpsuit. Long, unruly brown tresses escaped a tightly wound gray bandana. "And this is Navvan, who has emerged as a spokesman for our newer citizens."

He dipped his head. "Welcome."

"Pleased to meet you," Kirk said. "Excuse me, but you're a Troglyte, aren't you?"

"That's right," he said. "Many of my fellow miners have

migrated to Baldur III in search of greater opportunities . . . and less prejudice against our people."

Kirk couldn't blame them. Back on their homeworld of Ardana, the so-called Troglytes had labored in the zenite mines, scorned and exploited by an elite class of cultured aristocrats. Kirk liked to think that the miners' situation was improving, thanks in some small part to his own intervention a few years ago, but he also knew that it was unrealistic to expect generations of prejudice and discrimination to be overcome easily.

"And is the label 'Troglyte' still acceptable to you?" Kirk said.

"We are reclaiming the name, defining it not as a slur but as something to be proud of," Navvan said. "There is no shame in laboring deep beneath the surface. We only insist on doing so for ourselves, not to benefit those who despise us."

"Can't argue with that," McCoy said. "From what little I saw of Ardana."

"Before or after the Federation meddled in its internal affairs?" Cahill said. "No offense, Navvan. I get that your people got a raw deal there, which you were dealing with on your own terms even before Starfleet stuck their nose into your business."

Kirk chose to confront the man's attitude head-on.

"You have a problem with Starfleet and the Federation, Mister Cahill?"

"Not at all," the man said. "Long as they keep their distance."

Poho sighed.

"You have to understand, Captain, that Baldur III has always been an independent colony, founded in part by people who wanted to forge a new life away from the Earth and its allies. There's some concern that our recent windfall might make Baldur III more attractive to the Federation, which has largely let us be until now."

Kirk valued her honesty.

"I won't lie," he replied in kind. "The Federation would be happy to have Baldur III join the UFP, and there's a case to be made that this would be to our mutual advantage, but the choice as always is yours."

"I knew it," Cahill harrumphed. "Starfleet's so-called aid is just a ploy to get their hands on our pergium. Once they get their foot in the door, we'll never be rid of them." He shrugged at the landing party. "Nothing personal."

"That's not the case at all," Kirk said. "We're here at your invitation."

"For now," Cahill said ominously. "But what happens when it's time for you to leave?"

"Hush, Boyd." Poho rolled her eyes. "Don't be a crank. This is no way to greet our guests." Changing the subject, she turned the collar of her overcoat against a chilly breeze. "Hope you don't mind beaming down to the square instead of directly to my office. I wanted to show off Jackpot City: past, present, and future."

She gestured broadly at the nascent metropolis, before calling their attention to the tall wooden building facing the square. Upright wooden logs supported the roof of the portico shielding the front door. Windows looked to be genuine glass instead of transparent aluminum. A clock tower, complete with a traditional analog clock face, topped the venerable-looking structure.

"Take a gander at Town Hall. It was the first permanent public structure erected on this colony, more than two generations ago. It's still the center of the colony, even if we've also done our best to upgrade its tech over the years. That's Baldur III in a nutshell: proud of our past, but looking forward to our future."

"Spoken like a politician," Cahill said. "Give me the past any day. Before all this craziness."

"More like a pragmatist," she retorted. "Baldur III is changing, whether we like it or not. The smart thing is to make the most of it, while preserving what really matters."

"The promise of a new and better future is precisely what drew so many of my people to Baldur III in the first place," Navvan said. "Some aspects of yesterday are best left in the past."

Kirk had witnessed firsthand the way the Troglytes had been treated on Ardana. That past was nothing to hang on to.

"In any event," the mayor said, "it's getting a bit nippy out now that the sun's going down. How's about we move this indoors?"

"Don't mind if I do." McCoy massaged his arms to keep warm. "These Starfleet uniforms are good for most climates, but I'm kind of wishing I'd brought a sweater."

"At least you're not wearing a skirt, Doctor," Landon quipped.

The blond young yeoman, who had been with the crew for three years, was along to record the meeting for posterity, while also being on hand to help out as needed. Kirk knew that she could hold her own in a fight, just in case a brawl broke out in the overcrowded boom town. Not that he expected violence, for certain, but you never knew. This was the frontier, after all.

"Always preferred trousers myself," Poho said, "but to each their own."

She led them into the building. An antique cage elevator brought them to the fourth floor, where a conference room proved a mixture of old and new. Handcrafted wooden furniture, which Kirk assumed to be carved from lumber native to the planet, was supplemented by a modern computer terminal, a viewscreen, and a convenient food slot. The latter quickly produced several mugs of steaming hot cocoa.

"To take the chill off," Poho explained as they all sat down at the conference table. "By the way, Captain, I liked the way you handled that standoff in orbit earlier. Thanks for backing up our folks at the spaceport . . . and giving those hotheaded captains a good talking-to."

"You heard about that?" Kirk asked.

"Don't let my good looks fool you," she joked. "I stay on top of things. Listened to that recording a couple of times, to be honest. Did my heart good." She blew on her cocoa to cool it down. "Seriously, just having the *Enterprise* up there to keep the peace goes a long way toward stabilizing the situation up above."

Kirk had left Spock in command aboard the ship for that very reason. Considering how volatile matters were beyond the planet's atmosphere, he'd wanted the coolest head he knew keeping watch over the overcrowded orbits.

"Glad you approve," Kirk said.

"I did and do," Poho said. "Here's hoping you can make a difference down here too."

She shot a warning glance at Cahill, who refrained from comment. Foaming cocoa discolored his snowy-white mustache.

"That's what we're here for," Kirk said. "Perhaps you can begin by telling us where you're most in need of—"

The overhead lights dimmed for a moment before coming back on. The computer terminal beeped as it powered up again. Poho sighed in exasperation.

"Did I mention the brownouts?" she said wryly. "Our power grid is strained to the breaking point, what with all the new buildings and people, or so our engineers tell me. We've even had a few blackouts here and there. Nothing too serious yet, but folks are already getting tired of the random fluctuations and outages."

"I don't understand," McCoy said. "Isn't pergium used for generating energy?"

"Down the road, sure," Poho said. "But first the raw ore needs to be refined and processed, power plants need to be built, the necessary infrastructure put in place." The lights flickered again, earning a dirty look from the mayor. "Eventually, we'll have energy to spare, but right now we're still playing catch-up, and the sudden influx of newcomers is outpacing energy production."

"Wasn't a problem before all these offworld prospectors started pouring in," Cahill said.

"Because you were just a backwater," Navvan said. "Times are changing."

"Who asked them to? Maybe some of us liked being a backwater." He swept his gaze over all the assemblage, as though daring them to challenge him. "I was born and raised on Baldur III, and three generations of my family are buried here." He nodded at the Troglyte leader. "How long have you and yours been here?"

"Does that matter?" Navvan asked.

"It does to me," Cahill said, "and plenty of others I could name."

"But not to everyone," Poho said firmly. "Don't forget, Boyd. My roots here are dug just as deeply as yours, and I don't think we need to keep Baldur III frozen in amber just to keep things exactly the way we remember them. Tomorrow tends to kick yesterday out the door, which is the way it's supposed to work, and, as long as I'm mayor, everybody's opinion matters, no matter whether they were born in these parts or not."

Navvan nodded. "Which is why you can count on my support, Mayor, and the rest of us 'offworld prospectors.'"

"Nothing personal," Cahill assured him. "Just have to speak my piece, is all."

"Of course," Poho said. "Why else do you think I keep you around?"

Kirk sat back and observed the dynamics in play. Listening to Poho manage her advisors, he was getting a much better sense of the divisions among her constituents, particularly between the newcomers and the descendants of the original settlers. At the rate people were arriving, the former would soon outnumber the latter; Kirk didn't envy Poho having to try to keep both populations happy.

I need to avoid taking sides, he thought. *If possible.*

"My chief engineer, Lieutenant Commander Scott, may be able to assist you with your power issues," Kirk said. "I'll have him beam down to take stock of the situation. Knowing Mister Scott, he's bound to have some suggestions . . . and will probably want to take a hands-on approach to the problem."

"And I'd like to find out more about how your medical facilities are coping with this crush of potential patients," McCoy said. "I can't imagine they're any less overextended than your spaceport or generators."

"You imagine correctly, Doctor," Poho said, "although I wish I could tell you different."

"So let me get this straight," Cahill said. "The solution to having too many new people is to beam down even more new people to manage our affairs? Am I the only one who realizes how crazy that sounds?"

"And what do you suggest?" Navvan asked. "That the rest of us pack up our bags and leave? That the mines be shut down so you and your fellow nativists can all go back to logging and farming or whatever? That you just pretend the pergium was never discovered?"

"Well," Cahill hedged, "I'm not sure I'd go that far, but . . ."

"But what?" Poho asked. "The genie is out of the bottle, Boyd. Captain Kirk and his crew are just here to help us get a handle on it."

"Just saying that we need to make sure that handling the genie doesn't mean turning the whole works over to the Federation . . . indefinitely."

"Would that be so bad?" McCoy asked. "The Federation is an alliance, not an empire. What's wrong with joining together for the common good? Plenty of other worlds are thriving as members of the Federation."

"Good for them," Cahill said. "But they're not Baldur III."

"Baldur III is not the Baldur III you remember," Navvan replied. "Not anymore."

"My point exactly!"

Kirk let the men argue among themselves, while silently hoping that the fractures in the community wouldn't pose too much of a challenge in the days to come. From the look of things, he was going to have his hands full as it was.

He finished off his cocoa.

Five

Approaching the Antares Maelstrom

"Hailing Karisian vessel! You are placing your ship and passengers in extreme jeopardy. Turn back at once!"

Sulu piloted the *Allegra*, a compact ship he had commandeered from the deep space station. He was in hot pursuit of the *Tigris*, a commercial freighter registered out of Karis Prime, under the command of a Captain Anwar Dryyde. The ship, which had more than sixty passengers listed on its manifest, had deviated from its flight plan and was heading straight for the Antares Maelstrom despite the warning buoy, just as Tilton had feared a ship was bound to do eventually.

Risking dozens of lives for the sake of a shortcut.

"Hailing *Tigris*. This is Lieutenant Hikaru Sulu, representing Deep Space Station S-8. Please respond!"

"Mind your own business, Starfleet!" the other ship responded. The transmission was audio only, so Sulu could only imagine the speaker's surly expression. *"I know what I'm doing . . . and I don't need your permission!"*

Captain Dryyde, Sulu presumed. "I beg to differ, Captain."

In fact, the jurisdictional issues here were a bit murky. The Antares Maelstrom had been declared hazardous by all sensible spacefaring civilizations and coalitions, but Sulu wasn't sure if, strictly speaking, he had the authority to prevent foolhardy vessels from daring it. That being said, he wasn't about to stand by while dozens of lives were on the verge of being thrown away out of greed and impatience. Let the bureaucrats sort the legalities out; he knew what Captain Kirk would do.

"Hold on tight," he advised Ensign Peggy Knox, who was riding shotgun beside him in the copilot's seat. Fresh out of the Academy, the redheaded crewman was young and energetic. A constellation of freckles gave her face character. The rest of his security team was back on the station, still providing backup for Grandle and her people.

A sudden burst of acceleration overcame the inertial dampers, throwing Sulu and Knox back against their seats, as *Allegra* sped after *Tigris,* pushing its engine to the limit. The other ship had a head start on them, but Sulu was determined to catch up with *Tigris* before it entered the Maelstrom, even if that meant exceeding the ship's recommended cruising velocity. Warning lights flashed on the flight controls, a fact that did not escape Knox's notice.

"Lieutenant . . ."

"I see them, Ensign. Just think of those as suggestions."

"Understood, sir."

The race was on, not just against *Tigris,* but against time as well. Sulu could see the Maelstrom up ahead: an immense, kaleidoscopic region of swirling plasma currents many parsecs across, too vast to easily circumvent. Luminous streaks and swells, varying widely in hue and intensity, produced an almost psychedelic effect. Viewed from sectors away, Sulu knew, the Maelstrom was basically an enormous pinwheel, rotating so fast on its axis that it appeared to be a blurry sphere; this close, it filled up the horizon for as far as the eye could see. And long-range sensors fared no better than the naked eye; surging energies hid whatever dangers and mysteries might be hiding within the Maelstrom's perilous depths.

"Damn it, Dryyde," Sulu said, losing his temper. "Do you

want to kill your passengers and crew? Change course before it's too late. Baldur III will still be there if you take the long way around."

"*Sorry,*" the captain replied. "*Not getting paid to take the scenic route, but you're free to turn back if you haven't got the nerve.*"

"This isn't about courage." Sulu feared he was wasting his breath. "It's about being responsible for the passengers in your care!"

Dryyde snorted over the channel. "*Whose idea do you think it was? See you on the other side, Starfleet, if you can find the Passage!* Tigris *out.*"

"Dryyde? Dryyde?" Sulu tried to restore the transmission, but his hails went unanswered. Empty static taunted him. "Hailing *Tigris*. Please respond!"

"Seems like he's done talking, sir," Knox commented.

"Agreed."

Knox's assessment of the situation was dead-on. Sulu realized that common sense and persuasion were not going to be enough to save *Tigris* and the lives aboard her.

"Let me know when we're within target range of the *Tigris*," he instructed Knox.

"Will do, sir." She monitored the sensor readouts. "Are we thinking tractor beams?"

"I wish," Sulu said. *Allegra*'s tractor beams were strong enough to tow a disabled vessel if necessary, but not enough to capture a speeding ship that didn't want to be detained. "At best, our beams could only slow *Tigris* down a little. Arm the phasers instead."

Knox nodded. "Aye, sir."

They were gaining on *Tigris,* which was nonetheless getting way too close to the outer fringe of the Maelstrom. This was going to be close.

"Do we follow them into the Maelstrom if we have to?" Knox asked.

Good question, Sulu thought. "We're not going to let it come to that, Ensign."

The ship was equipped with a basic phaser array for self-defense. No photon torpedoes, as on the *Enterprise,* but Sulu didn't need that kind of firepower anyway. He wasn't out to repel a Klingon battle cruiser, just to stop a reckless captain from committing suicide along with the lives in his care.

"Coming within phaser range, sir," Knox reported.

Sulu gave Dryyde one last chance to come to his senses. "Sulu to *Tigris.* This is your final warning. Return to your original flight plan or face the consequences."

He kept the threat vague—for a reason.

"Back off, Starfleet!" Dryyde responded, breaking his silence.

"Lieutenant!" Knox said. "He's firing up his weapon batteries."

"Figured he might," Sulu said coolly. "Raise shields."

"Aye, sir."

A violet disruptor blast, fired from the stern of the *Tigris,* rocked the ship. Sulu smiled slyly. "And there it is. Good."

Knox gave him a puzzled look.

"They fired first," he explained, "on a Federation vessel no less. Think we're entitled to defend ourselves now."

So much for the legal niceties.

"Damage?" he asked.

"Nothing serious," Knox stated. "Yet."

Sulu wasn't surprised. He suspected that Dryyde just wanted to discourage his pursuer, not destroy them; that had been more of an angry outburst than an attack. Still, Sulu had no intention of taking any further fire. *Tigris* got one free shot, that was all.

"Taking evasive action."

He yawed sharply to port, then oriented *Allegra* so that it presented a smaller target to *Tigris.* He scrutinized the other ship, guesstimating the range and sweep of its disruptors. Sulu wasn't one hundred percent familiar with this particular model of freighter, but he'd studied enough similar vessels to have a pretty good idea where its limits were in terms of its weapons and targeting capacities. Swooping in toward the *Tigris,* he maneuvered the ship into a sweet spot where the freighter's disruptors couldn't be aimed unless Dryyde did some tricky maneuvering of his own.

We're the itch you can't quite reach, Sulu thought.

He gambled that Dryyde had no real desire or stomach for a fight; the other captain was in flight—not fight—mode. *Tigris* just wanted to get to the Maelstrom unobstructed.

Sulu wasn't going to let that happen.

Not that there was an easy way to stop *Tigris.* No matter how surgical a strike, phasers were destructive and violence always carried risks. Sulu didn't want to destroy the freighter in order to save it. He needed to minimize any chance of casualties.

"Scan that freighter," he ordered Knox. "Find me a vulnerable spot that won't trigger an explosion or compromise life-support."

"Aye, sir." She quickly summoned the necessary graphics. "We could target one of its warp nacelles."

Sulu shook his head. "Too much danger of triggering a catastrophic plasma cascade." An idea occurred to him. "What about its external sensor array?"

She scanned the schematics. "That could work. They're not tied directly into the life-support or propulsion systems."

"Target that specific area," he ordered. "High-intensity beam. Narrow focus." He carefully stayed within the sweet spot, trying to maintain a consistent distance and position with regard to *Tigris.* "And, Ensign, precision counts."

"Understood, sir."

A single crimson beam shot from the ship's nose to strike *Tigris* at the sensor bulb atop the freighter's prow. Azure energy flashed where the phaser beam collided with the freighter's shields, which successfully deflected Knox's initial blast. Reacting to the attack, *Tigris* veered away, attempting evasive action of its own, while remaining on course for the Maelstrom, which stretched before them like a galactic barrier. This close, it loomed ahead regardless of any evasive zigs or zags.

"Again," Sulu ordered. He had never expected a single shot to do the trick. The ship zoomed after *Tigris*, matching its twists and turns as Sulu worked the helm, determined to keep the freighter's external sensors in Knox's sights. "Keep it up!"

"Yes, sir!"

The phaser beam battered *Tigris*'s shields as Knox did a good job of keeping it focused on the desired area, despite the moving target. Sulu appreciated the challenge facing her in that she needed to hit *Tigris* hard enough to penetrate her shields without punching a hole all the way through the freighter's hull.

"Nice shooting, Knox."

"Nice flying, sir, if you don't mind my saying so."

A final flash of bright-blue energy signaled the collapse of *Tigris*'s shields. Vapor issued from the sensor bubble as the ship's phaser reduced it to slag. Knox ceased fire before breaching the hull. She studied the scanner readings.

"Their sensor array is toast," she reported. "They're flying blind."

"What a shame," Sulu quipped. He could readily imagine the panic on *Tigris*'s bridge right now as their viewscreens went blank along with their navigational readouts. He hoped Captain Dryyde was ready to see reason, now that he couldn't see anything else.

"Sulu to *Tigris*. Do you require assistance?"

Static garbled the reply, suggesting that the phaser attack had damaged *Tigris*'s communications equipment as well. *"Blast you, Starfleet! This was none of your business!"*

"Your shields collapsed after only a few sustained blasts from our phaser," Sulu pointed out. "How long did you think they were going to survive the Maelstrom?"

"The Passage," Dryyde insisted, perhaps a bit defensively.

"We're still on course for the Passage. We just need to stay on track and we'll be fine . . ."

"Seriously?" Sulu couldn't believe how stubbornly irresponsible the man was. "You were willing to stake your ship on flimsy, substandard shields and a tall tale about a mythical safe passage!"

"It's not a myth!" Dryyde ranted. *"My passengers paid good money for the coordinates. They swear they're legit!"*

Sulu rolled his eyes. Dryyde was irresponsible *and* gullible, it seemed, and Sulu, frankly, was tired of dealing with him. *I'm missing my dinner date with Helena for this?*

"Ensign Knox, hit them with a reverse tractor beam. Just enough to spin them around a bit."

"Will do."

Switching to the tractor controls, Knox did as instructed. A rippling amber force beam slammed into the unshielded freighter, causing it to tumble end over end. Sulu got dizzy just looking for it; he hoped, for its passengers' sake, that *Tigris's* artificial gravity was still working properly, otherwise they were likely to be experiencing some serious space-sickness.

"Stick to your previously plotted course," Sulu challenged Dryyde. "You don't even know which way you're going anymore. Shut down your engines and let us tow you back to the station . . . unless you'd prefer to fly blindly without any sense of direction. Space is a big place, Captain. Pretty sure your passengers aren't paying to get lost between the stars."

A long pause preceded Dryyde's reply. *"You win, Starfleet. But you'll be hearing from the Karisian Shipping Authority. You had no right—!"*

Sulu cut him off. He glanced at Knox. *"Tigris?"*

"Powering down, sir." She beamed in triumph. "You did it, Lieutenant. Saved all those people, whether they liked it or not."

"We did it, Ensign. I'll be requesting a commendation for you."

Unlike Knox, he couldn't bask in their victory without

worrying about future crises. Tilton's warning buoy was clearly not enough to discourage folks from braving the Maelstrom, especially with rumors of a safe passage circulating. They had managed to intercept *Tigris* before it entered the Maelstrom, but next time they might not be so lucky.

We're going to have to patrol the border full-time, he realized. There was no way to truly block the route to the Maelstrom in three-dimensional space, short of employing a fleet of ships or an entire field of automated mines, but keeping *Allegra* on patrol between the station and the Maelstrom would prevent any future ships from getting a head start like *Tigris* had. Deploying the ship would leave the station a ship short, but Sulu didn't see any way around it if they wanted to avoid another near disaster like this one. *Now I just need to talk Tilton into it.*

"Locked onto *Tigris,*" Knox reported.

"Music to my ears, Ensign. Let's head back to port."

Six

Baldur III

"Oh my gracious, talk about a stunning view."

Margery Poho gazed at her planet from the bridge of *Enterprise*. Kirk had invited her to visit the ship after their meeting in Jackpot City. Her advisors had declined the invitation, with Navvan citing a previous obligation and Cahill, somewhat huffily, insisting that he preferred to stay put on Baldur III, thank you very much. This suited Kirk, who hoped to have a private discussion with the mayor, away from her fractious subordinates, while returning her hospitality.

"Would you believe," she said, "that I've never actually set foot off-planet before?"

"Better late than never."

Kirk enjoyed sharing the moment with her and McCoy. He had orbited so many planets, visited so many far-flung worlds, that it had almost become routine. It was refreshing to be reminded, once in a while, just how astounding it was to be able to admire an entire world from the heavens. He let her savor the view before introducing her to Spock, who rose from the captain's chair to confer with them.

"I trust your visit to the surface was fruitful, Captain."

"It was informative," Kirk said. "We've got our work cut out for us, but I'm certain our crew, working in conjunction with

Mayor Poho and her people, are up to the task. How goes it up here? Any more problems with impatient new arrivals?"

"None worth troubling you about," Spock replied. "Congestion and delays remain an issue, to the frustration of all concerned, but the various captains and passengers are, for the most part, not letting their emotions get the better of them. I confess I am uncertain whether to attribute such restraint to the lingering effect of your own actions earlier, or to acknowledge that even non-Vulcans can behave logically. It is almost enough to give one hope for humanity."

"That's the spirit, Spock," McCoy chimed in. "We'll make an optimist of you yet."

"I am neither an optimist nor a pessimist, Doctor, merely a scientist. I take the universe as it is and do not attempt to impose my own attitudes on it."

"Speaking as a politician," Poho said, "there's something to be said for that approach. In my experience, you can't effect real change unless you face reality head-on. Mind you, I also have to take my fellow citizens' attitudes into account."

"In any event," Kirk said, "I'm glad to hear that nothing too interesting happened in my absence."

"Actually, Captain," Spock said, "there is a matter you should be aware of . . . and perhaps the mayor as well. It is not immediate, but it is important."

Kirk instantly went on alert. He knew Spock well enough to understand that whatever the Vulcan was referring to was serious.

"What is it?" he asked.

Spock surveyed the bridge. "It might be best to discuss this in the briefing room."

"It's that delicate?" Kirk asked.

"Not necessarily, but it requires some explanation. I merely suggest that the briefing room might be a more conducive environment in which to conduct the discussion."

"I'll take your word for it, Mister Spock." Kirk turned to Poho. "Well, Madam Mayor, it sounds as though the rest of your tour will have to wait."

"Lead on, Captain," she replied. "I'm sure a starship conference room is *much* more fascinating than the earthbound variety."

McCoy cleared his throat. "Ahem."

"Feel free to join us, Doctor," Kirk said, "unless you're needed in sickbay?"

"Already checked with Chapel. No immediate fires to put out."

"Very well, then." Kirk walked over to use the intercom on his chair. "Captain to Mister Scott. Please report to the bridge."

He'd be dispatching Scotty down to the planet shortly, to grapple with Jackpot City's power shortages, but in the meantime Scott could man the bridge while Kirk was getting briefed by Spock on whatever new issue had arisen.

"I don't suppose you can give us a hint, Mister Spock, as to what this is all about?"

Hinting was not exactly the Vulcan way, but Spock attempted to oblige.

"Are you familiar with a planet called Yurnos, Captain?"

Poho certainly recognized the name. Her face fell immediately. "Oh, crap."

———

A short turbolift ride brought them to the *Enterprise*'s main briefing room, where Spock elaborated on the topic at hand.

"Yurnos is a Class-M planet located only one solar system away from Baldur III. It is inhabited by a humanoid species that is still centuries away from developing space flight. The Federation has long been aware of their existence, but has been careful not to interfere in their development, per the Prime Directive."

"Our ancestors did the same," Poho said. "History tells us

they briefly considered settling on Yurnos, but chose to move on to the next system once they discovered the planet was inhabited. Baldur III had barely any animal life at all, let alone any sentient species, which made it much more attractive."

Kirk nodded. "Go on."

"Until recently," Spock continued, "the Yurnians have been largely undisturbed, unaware of even the existence of Baldur III, let alone the existence of life beyond their planet. There are now indications, however, that their proximity to Baldur III might be threatening that isolation. To be more precise, there is apparently evidence that some of the newcomers flocking to Baldur III have been trading covertly with the nearby Yurnians."

"Nearby" being a relative term, Kirk realized. To the primitive Yurnians, Baldur III might as well be on the other side of the galaxy, but to a warp-cable vessel it was just down the road. Four or five light-years was either near or unimaginably far, depending on your technology.

"And we know this how?" McCoy asked.

"For some time, a team of trained Federation observers have been studying the Yurnians and their culture," Spock explained, "dwelling undercover among them in order to avoid detection. They claim to have detected definite signs of extraplanetary cultural contamination by parties unknown. With the *Enterprise* already in the vicinity, they have requested our assistance in this matter."

McCoy lifted his eyebrows. "Popular these days, aren't we?"

"The crises are not unrelated, Doctor. All stem from the recent rush to Baldur III."

"True enough, Mister Spock," Kirk said. "Nevertheless, our dance card is filling up."

"But there's no pergium on Yurnos, is there?" McCoy asked. "So what could any gung-ho prospector be after there?"

Poho sighed.

"I think I know the answer to that. It's called *nabbia*."

"*Nabbia*?" Kirk echoed. "What's that?"

"A leafy plant, Captain, native to Yurnos," Spock said. "Its roots are commonly used to brew tea, I believe."

McCoy regarded Spock with amusement. "And you just know that off the top of your head?"

"I was not idle while you and the captain were visiting Jackpot City, Doctor. Upon receiving word of the problems on Yurnos, I naturally reviewed all relevant Starfleet files on the planet."

"Naturally," McCoy said.

"But what's so special about this plant," Kirk asked, "that it's worth violating the Prime Directive for?"

"Besides the fact that it's all but impossible to grow anywhere else?" Poho asked. "The tea that Mister Spock mentioned promotes oxygen absorption in the bloodstream, for reasons that Doctor McCoy could probably explain better than me. On Yurnos, the tea is just a mild intoxicant, but on Baldur III, it can help folks cope with the thin atmosphere."

"Like tri-ox," McCoy said.

"Which is pricey and hard to come by in these parts," Poho said. "*Nabbia* tea is a viable alternative, particularly for newcomers. Makes hard labor easier for miners from offworld."

Kirk frowned at the mayor. "And you knew about this?"

"I was aware that there was a black market for *nabbia* tea," she admitted, "but, honestly, I've had bigger issues on my hands than folks indulging in a little herbal medicine. My ancestors relied on *nabbia* when they first settled here generations ago, and it's always been possible to get your hands on some if you really want to." She shrugged. "Not too surprising, I suppose, that the trade is ramping up as our population does."

"Despite the possible effect on the Yurnians?" Kirk asked.

"Nobody is conquering or colonizing the planet," she insisted, "or providing them with phasers or warp drives. No ships from other worlds are landing in plain sight of the Yurnians or offering them tours of the sector. We don't encourage people to traffic in *nabbia*, exactly, but folks have always been discreet in their dealings with the Yurnians . . . at least until recently."

Kirk appreciated her honesty, if not her rather *laissez-faire* attitude toward the practice. He couldn't help wondering if she had her own stash of bootleg tea tucked away in a cupboard somewhere. Or had her own family been settled on Baldur III long enough to acclimate to the thin atmosphere?

"With all due respect, Mayor, I think you may be taking this too lightly. In my experience, even the most harmless contamination can sometimes have profound effects on a developing civilization."

Sigma Iotia II came immediately to mind. There were times, granted, when one had to bend the Prime Directive for the greater good, but ensuring a steady supply of invigorating tea did not strike Kirk as one of them. The potential risks far outweighed any minor rewards.

"What about those Federation 'observers,' then?" Poho asked, a bit defensively. "Why aren't you getting on your high horse about them?"

"*Trained* observers," Kirk stressed, "with a very different agenda. They're experts in blending in with pre-warp civilizations without arousing suspicions, and their express mission is to observe without interfering. Somehow I doubt that your entrepreneurial tea smugglers place quite the same priority on protecting the Yurnians' culture from outside influences, particularly if business is indeed booming these days."

Kirk had firsthand experience when it came to discreetly studying naïve civilizations from within, going back at least as far as his first planetary survey on Neural many years ago, so he knew just how tricky such operations could be. In the end, he reflected ruefully, not even the best of intentions had kept Tyree and his people untouched by the universe at large, to their lasting detriment. He didn't like the idea of something similar happening to the Yurnians.

"Precisely, Captain," Spock agreed. "If the illicit tea trade is expanding in concert with the 'gold rush' on Baldur III, it is all the more imperative that we take action to prevent any further contamination on Yurnos, before its people's future is irrevocably altered."

Poho scowled. "Just wait one minute, gentlemen. You're here to help us out on Baldur III, not crack down on some minor smuggling operation on Yurnos, just because of some abstract principle of noninterference. We've got *real* problems down on the surface, Kirk, or have you forgotten that?"

"The Prime Directive is more than just an abstraction," Kirk argued, "even if it's open to interpretation at times. I'm sorry, Mayor, but we can't simply ignore this, no matter how pressing matters are on Baldur III right now." He held up a hand to forestall any further objections from Poho. "We're just going to have to manage both situations with the resources and personnel available to us."

Too bad they were already shorthanded with Sulu and his team on loan to the space station, over on the other side of the Maelstrom. Kirk didn't have a whole lot of people to spare.

"A suggestion, Captain," Spock said. "Perhaps I might lead a small mission to investigate the situation on Yurnos, the extent of which remains to be determined, while you and the remainder of the crew address the known issues here on Baldur III, which, as the Mayor correctly observes, are both real and substantial."

"Makes sense," Kirk said. "At this point, we don't know enough about what's happening on Yurnos to gauge what sort of actions might be required. A simple fact-finding mission is probably in order. But why you, Spock?"

"I have already familiarized myself with the available data on the planet," Spock reminded him. "Moreover, the Prime Directive issues *are* serious enough to warrant the deployment of a senior officer. Mister Scott's talents are best applied to the challenges on Baldur III, and this is hardly a medical matter," he added, glancing at McCoy. "Therefore, I am the logical candidate."

"Correct me if I'm wrong," McCoy said with a smirk, "but did you just conclude that you're expendable?"

"Not at all, Doctor. I am merely pointing out the most efficient division of labor."

Kirk couldn't fault his reasoning. "How small a mission are you thinking about, Spock?"

"The smaller the landing party, the less risk of exposure," Spock said. "Perhaps only one other crew member, in addition to the Federation observers already on the planet." That this was an unusually small complement for such an expedition did not appear to concern him. "If necessary, we can always request further personnel from the *Enterprise,* depending on what we discover on the planet."

Kirk wondered if Spock was also keeping his proposed team to a minimum in order to avoid leaving Kirk any more shorthanded than absolutely necessary.

"Who do you have in mind?" he asked.

"Ensign Chekov strikes me as suitable to the task," Spock said. "Despite his youth, he has an inquisitive mind, has taken part in numerous landing parties, and copes well under pressure. I am also quite familiar with his strengths and weaknesses, eliminating a number of variables from the equation. Chekov is a known quantity."

"High praise indeed," McCoy quipped. "Coming from a Vulcan, that is."

"Applied to a mere human, Doctor, that *is* high praise."

Kirk approved of Spock's suggestion. He needed Scotty and McCoy and Uhura here on the *Enterprise,* as well as below on Baldur III, but he could spare Chekov. And he felt better about sending Spock off to Yurnos with the stalwart young Russian to watch his back—and vice versa.

"You convinced me, Spock. Brief Chekov on the mission and take a shuttle to Yurnos at your earliest convenience."

"Yes, Captain. Before I go, however, I have a favor to ask of the mayor."

Her eyes narrowed. "And what is that, Mister Spock?"

"Would it be possible to obtain a sample of the *nabbia* sold on Baldur III? Possibly from your law-enforcement agency?"

McCoy smirked. "Thinking of trying it yourself, Spock?"

"Negative, Doctor. I am Vulcan. Thin air does not trouble me. I merely seek a sample of the contraband product for forensic purposes. It may aid me in my investigation on Yurnos."

"A perfectly logical request, Mister Spock, as one might expect." Kirk looked to Poho. "Well, Mayor. Do you think this can be arranged?"

"I suppose so," she said. "Cracking down on *nabbia* use is hardly a priority, but we do occasionally confiscate some bootleg tea in the course of maintaining law and order. It's an additional charge we can throw at some rowdy who was raising hell anyway." She shrugged. "I'll have a small quantity beamed up to you."

"Thank you, Mayor," Spock said. "That would be most helpful."

"Least I can do."

He rose from the table and exited the conference room, leaving Kirk and McCoy alone with the mayor. Her body language unclenched somewhat.

"Well, I guess two crewmen and a shuttle won't make that much difference in terms of the big picture," she conceded. "But I hope this business on Yurnos won't end up being too much of a distraction from your actual mission here."

Her blasé attitude toward trade with the Yurnians still troubled Kirk, but he reminded himself that she was simply prioritizing the needs of her people, which was her job, after all. She was responsible for the safety and welfare of Jackpot City, so perhaps she could be forgiven for having tunnel vision in that regard. He knew what it was like to have large numbers of people depending on you.

"Don't worry," he assured her. "The *Enterprise* is not going anywhere as long as we can make a difference here."

"Don't let Boyd Cahill hear you say that," she joked. "He'll have a fit."

Kirk chuckled, but the laugh hid deeper concerns. Despite his confident words just now, he was concerned about spreading his crew too thin. Spock and Chekov were setting off for Yurnos, Sulu was still back at S-8, and he'd barely begun to tackle the problems down on Baldur III.

Was he juggling too many balls with too few hands?

Seven

Baldur III

"Get me some more plasma substitute!" McCoy barked. "On the double!"

A local nurse threw up his hands. "We're all out of the right type, Doctor."

"Damn it." McCoy stepped away from the operating table where he had just finished reattaching an arm that had been all but severed during some sort of grisly mining accident. The surgical support frame mounted over the bed hummed as it generated a sterile field; it was an older model that McCoy hadn't seen in years, but seemed to be holding up for the time being, thank goodness. The operation was a success in that the victim—an underage Bolian—was likely to keep her arm, but she had lost a lot of blood while being rushed to Jackpot City from a mining camp in the mountains. McCoy put a protoplaser down on a cluttered counter and flipped open his communicator. A dedicated channel, previously set up by Uhura, immediately connected him to sickbay and Nurse Christine Chapel.

"That's right," he told her. "I need you to beam down more artificial plasma, type H-slash-three. Get me at least forty liters, even if you have to break into our emergency reserves . . . again."

"Message received, Doctor," Chapel replied. *"I'll see to it immediately."*

"Good. At this rate, I may need you to set up an old-fashioned blood drive on the *Enterprise* to replenish our stores."

"*Whatever you need, Doctor. Are you sure you can't use me down on the planet?*"

"Could I ever," McCoy replied, "but with M'Benga off with Sulu and his troops, I need you minding the store in sickbay."

"*You can count on me, Doctor.*"

"Never doubted it for a moment. McCoy out."

He put away the communicator and turned to the waiting nurse, whose name was Sinclair.

"More plasma should be arriving at the beam-down site shortly. Make sure this woman gets at least a pint as soon as possible." The surgical frame monitored the patient's blood pressure and circulation, but McCoy checked her pulse the old-fashioned way just because. It was weaker than he would have liked, but steady enough that he judged that she could go a little while longer without a fresh infusion of sera. He took out a hypospray and administered nine cc's of benjisidrine to stabilize her in the meantime, noting with concern that even his personal medkit was running low and needed to be restocked.

"That's that . . . for now."

He turned off the surgical frame to save power, as well as to extend the outmoded mechanism's life-span, then wiped his brow with a swab. He had been on his feet for longer than he wanted to think about, volunteering at the town's only medical facility, and he was starting to feel short of breath to boot. He was overdue for a tri-ox injection, but felt obliged to try to ration the valuable compound, especially after hearing about how relatively difficult it was to come by on Baldur III. Leaning against the nearest convenient wall, he wearily contemplated his surroundings.

Jackpot City's "hospital" scarcely warranted the name, being more of a clinic, in reality. It was only slightly larger than McCoy's sickbay back on the *Enterprise* and nowhere near as well equipped or supplied. In some wards, cots and even mattresses on the floor supplemented a newly inadequate supply of beds. Temporary structures erected behind the modest brick building served as both a triage center and spillover areas. McCoy had barely begun his inspection of the facilities, hours ago, when a collapsed mine had flooded the hospital with a slew of new patients, urgently requiring varying degrees of care. McCoy had rolled up his sleeves to help deal with the crisis and hadn't stopped working since.

"Who's next?" he asked Sinclair.

"I think we're caught up for the moment, Doctor."

"Thank heavens for that. And Doctor Burstein?" McCoy asked, referring to the town's regular physician.

"Doing his rounds, I believe. Shall I page him?"

"No bother. I can find him on my own. Just keep an eye out for those fresh supplies from the *Enterprise*."

Sinclair nodded. "Will do."

McCoy departed the surgical ward, hoping to finally get a chance to discuss the colony's medical situation with Burstein before another emergency demanded his services. Given the modest size of the clinic, McCoy quickly located Burstein in the main recovery ward, which was filled beyond capacity. Wayne Burstein was making his way from bed to bed, checking on his patients. He looked up at McCoy's approach.

"Doctor McCoy," Burstein greeted him. The boyish young physician looked as though he was fresh out of med school, making McCoy feel even older than he actually was. A mop of unruly black hair and a bad case of five-o'clock shadow hinted at a long shift, with little time for personal grooming. Burstein's smooth, youthful features betrayed signs of fatigue as he paused in his rounds. "How did that last surgery go?"

"Well enough," McCoy said. "We saved the arm, barring any unexpected complications." He held out an open hand. "Barely had a chance to introduce myself before they started carting in the broken bodies."

"Good thing you were on hand." Burstein tucked a data slate under his arm before shaking McCoy's hand. "I really appreciate you pitching in. That was a zoo even by recent standards, although I wish I could say it was all that unusual."

"You get a lot of accidents these days?"

"More than I'd like," Burstein said. "Problem is, pergium mining is new to these parts, so you've got a lot of eager would-be miners who don't really know what they're doing, and the same applies to many of the newcomers flocking to Baldur III in hopes of striking it rich. They're learning on the job, taking shortcuts, rushing things, which is a perfect recipe for accidents and injuries. Throw in overwork, dehydration, poor living conditions, and new and exotic germs from all over the quadrant, and the recipe just gets more toxic. You've got to understand, this wasn't a mining planet before a few months ago. When I was growing up here, the major industries were logging and homesteading." He cocked his head toward a bandaged patient lying in a bed. "Cecil here was the town barber before he took it into his head to go digging for pergium."

"So?" the patient replied. "I'm supposed to keep sweeping up hair clippings while other folks are out there making a fortune?" He shook his head, then winced at the motion. "Not a chance, sonny. Soon as I'm back on my feet, I'm heading back out to my claim."

"How about you just take it easy for now?" Burstein said. "Doctor's orders."

"Says the kid I gave his first haircut," Cecil said. "And who could use a trim and a shave, if you don't mind me saying."

"Whose fault is that?" Burstein turned to McCoy. "See what I mean?"

McCoy nodded. He knew all about stubborn patients. He'd treated James T. Kirk.

"So you're from around here, I take it?"

"Born and raised," Burstein said. "Left to study medicine

on Earth, with a residency on Mars, before coming home just in time for the 'gold rush' to turn everything upside down. So much for my plans to become a simple colony doctor." He shook his head. "There was a brief time when I knew all my patients' names by heart, but with new people arriving every day, it's a struggle just to keep track of what planets they're all from."

"How are you coping?" McCoy asked.

"Not going to lie." Burstein continued on his rounds while McCoy tagged along. "It hasn't been easy. Besides the increased workload, a more diverse population means we need a wider variety of resources when it comes to treating everyone from Aurelians to Zellorites."

An injured Hydrathi recovering on the next bed, receiving a transfusion of eggplant-colored fluids, demonstrated his point. As McCoy well knew, the Hydratha were severely allergic to several standard medications and so required versions specifically tailored to their body chemistries. He couldn't imagine that Baldur III had required much in the way of species-specific pharmaceuticals prior to recently.

"Any chance of expanding your facilities," McCoy asked, "what with the booming economy and all?"

"Eventually." Burstein paused to compare the Hydrathi's vitals to the data recorded on his slate. "I've put out feelers to various medical associations and academies in hopes of attracting qualified professionals to Baldur III, which may pay off in time, but at the moment we're in an awkward, if not positively dangerous, period of transition. The population is burgeoning, but the infrastructure to support it isn't there yet, since the vast majority of the new arrivals are prospectors, not doctors or nurses. Heck, I've even lost a couple of my own orderlies to the mines."

They moved on to another patient, who occupied a cot squeezed in between two genuine biobeds. Pillows propped her up into a seated position as she sipped on a mug of some steaming beverage. Burstein consulted his slate as he briefed McCoy on the particulars of her case.

"Did I mention that our thin atmosphere doesn't help when it comes to treating our newest residents? Take Yelsa here. She fainted while working her claim the other day, nearly fell off a ravine up in the hills outside the city. I'm holding her overnight for observation until I'm confident that she won't collapse again." Since her cot lacked a proper diagnostic monitor, Burstein scanned her with a medical tricorder instead and downloaded the results to his slate. "How you feeling, Yelsa?"

"Much better, Doctor," she wheezed. A pronounced Meraki accent indicated that she was indeed new to the planet. She gripped the mug with both hands. "This tea you prescribed is really helping. I'm not feeling nearly so light-headed anymore."

Tea? McCoy arched an eyebrow.

"Glad to hear it," Burstein said. "You drink every drop, and I'll be back to check on you later if I can."

"Thank you, Doctor."

McCoy held his tongue until they were safely out of earshot of Yelsa and the other patients. He kept his voice low. "About that tea . . ."

"Yes, McCoy, it's *nabbia*." Burstein lifted his gaze from his slate. "I know what you're thinking, but before you judge me, consider the circumstances. This isn't Earth or Alpha Centauri. Tri-ox compounds and other such palliatives are in short supply and need to be shipped in from the other side of the Maelstrom. In the meantime, I've got more and more patients like Yelsa in need of relief, which the tea provides." He looked McCoy in the eyes. "I ask you, Doctor, what would you do?"

McCoy didn't have a good answer for that.

"I'm not sure," he admitted. "But you do know where the *nabbia* comes from, right, and what's at stake there?"

"Of course, and I choose to look the other way for the sake of my patients." Burstein faced McCoy unapologetically. "The question is, McCoy, are you willing to do the same, now that you've had a chance to see what I'm dealing with?"

McCoy had to think about that. In the long term, of course, the Yurnians needed to be allowed to make their own future, without risk of outside influences or contamination, which meant shutting down the black-market trade in *nabbia*, but he could hardly blame Burstein for treating his patients to the best of his abilities, using whatever limited resources were available to him. McCoy had heard Yelsa's lungs whistle when she spoke; if the bootleg tea made it easier for her to breathe, and there were no better options available, why let her suffer as a matter of principle?

"I'm not judging you," McCoy said. "Hell, if I was in your place, I might quietly prescribe a little tea myself. I'm not going to report you, if that's what you're worried about, or insist you turn over whatever secret store of *nabbia* you've got stashed away. That tea's already been smuggled over from Yurnos, so you might as well put it to good use. But you should know that the tea trade's days are numbered, at least if my captain has anything to say about it, so you probably shouldn't plan on—"

The lights dimmed overhead, distracting McCoy. Patients and orderlies blurted out exclamations. Diagnostic monitors reset themselves. Burstein swore under his breath before muttering in annoyance.

"Not again." He glared at the lights as though trying to power them up through sheer force of will. "As if we don't already have enough *tsuris* to cope with . . ."

McCoy was disturbed to see that the periodic brownouts extended to the hospital as well. Suppose the clinic had lost power entirely while he was reattaching that one patient's arm? In theory, the surgical support frame could run on battery power as a backup, but considering how old and outdated that particular unit was, McCoy had to wonder just how well its batteries were holding up. He guessed that the hospital's backup generators, if they had any, were also probably insufficient to the increasing demands on them.

Everything on this planet seems to be running on fumes, he thought. *Including its healers.*

The lights returned to full strength, but some worrisome flickers mitigated McCoy's relief. He regarded the lights with a certain lack of confidence. For all he knew, the next brownout could be only minutes away.

"That's better," Burstein said, "until the next outage. A planet full of pergium, and we can't even keep the lights on with any reliability." He looked at McCoy. "I don't suppose you've got a spare power plant tucked away in your medkit?"

"No," McCoy said. "But for what it's worth, I've got an associate looking into the problem . . . and he's something of a miracle worker."

"I'm telling ye, Captain, we need to shut this down."

Chief Engineer Montgomery Scott was not happy, as evidenced by the way his Aberdeen accent grew more pronounced as he addressed Kirk and Mayor Poho at Jackpot City's new power plant, which just happened to be a mothballed starship that had been repurposed to provide energy to the rapidly expanding boomtown. Scott had urgently requested the meeting in the grounded ship's old engine room, where a bare-bones matter-antimatter assembly was now yoked to the city's laboring EPS relays. A crew of local technicians operated the control consoles while the reactor itself could be seen through a clear EM shield grating. The assembly chugged in the background, a bit more roughly than the comforting hum of the *Enterprise*'s own engineering room. It was less of a purr than a gargle.

"Shut it down?" Kirk didn't like the sound of that and, judging from her expression, neither did the mayor. He felt another headache coming on, both figuratively and literally, despite the fact that the ship's old life-support system provided more Earth-like air quality than was found elsewhere on Baldur III. "Explain yourself, Mister Scott."

"Honestly, Captain, I hardly know where to begin. This entire jury-rigged setup breaks practically every reasonable safety precaution I know of, not to mention most principles of sound engineering." He looked regretfully at Poho, acknowledging her presence. "If you'll pardon me for saying so, Mayor."

"Go ahead, Mister Scott." Poho crossed her arms atop her chest. "Speak your mind."

She and Kirk had beamed down directly from the *Enterprise*, where they had been coordinating their joint efforts to manage the unprecedented rush on the planet, but Kirk was aware that the converted vessel occupied a park near the center of the city, not far from Town Hall, actually. He remembered noticing it on maps and schematics of the evolving community. According to Poho, it commemorated the colonists' original landing site and was therefore off-limits to the new construction rising up all around the park.

"Well, for one thing," Scott said, "this ship's . . . power plant . . . whatever you want to call it . . . is practically a museum piece."

"No surprise there, Mister Scott," Poho said. "Up until a few months ago, it *was* a museum. *Thunderbird* is the ship that carried the first party of settlers to this world generations ago. In those rough early years, when the colony was just getting off the ground, it provided both shelter and energy to the original pioneers."

Kirk nodded. "Not an uncommon practice on frontier worlds, even today."

"Eventually, *Thunderbird* was retired from active service, preserved as nothing but a historical exhibition, until the current power crunch forced us to fire it up again just to keep the lights on. Our technicians worked around the clock to adapt the old engines to our present needs. Figured the reactor that once propelled us across the galaxy could now power Jackpot City's bigger and bolder future."

Scotty appeared unimpressed by the history lesson.

"That's all very well and good, ma'am, but, in my professional estimation, you're taking a major risk here. It's not just that the hardware is old and past its prime, you're putting it to a use it was never designed for and, frankly, doing so in a rather hasty and slapdash manner."

Poho bristled at the accusation. "The situation here was and remains urgent. We didn't have time to waste on any extended planning and review process. We needed to get the job done, and we needed to get it done yesterday."

Kirk sympathized. He had occasionally been known to order Scotty to throw out the rule book in the interests of saving the ship in a timely fashion. The dour engineer often protested pushing his precious engines too far, but usually managed to make it work anyway, despite some grumbling. Could he do the same here?

"But you've cut too many corners," Scott said. "Just taking a quick tour of the premises, I spotted more serious safety violations than I have fingers to count them on, and a troubling lack of backup systems to boot. Put bluntly, none of this . . . farrago . . . is up to code."

"Is there anything we can do about that?" Kirk asked. "Can you and your people address the most dangerous of these violations?"

"We can try, Captain, but we'd just be adding lifeboats and a fresh coat of paint to the *Titanic,* if ye take me meaning. It wouldn't change the fact that this entire operation is a catastrophe waiting to happen." His dour tone and expression conveyed the gravity of his reservations. "And I'm sure I don't have to tell you, sir, that a potential matter-antimatter mishap is nothing to take lightly."

"Neither are the pressing needs of this community," Poho

said. "We're on a razor's edge here, what with the frequent outages and brownouts. Even with *Thunderbird* picking up much
of the load these days, we're barely holding on by our fingertips.
You have no idea how much pressure I'm under regarding these
power glitches. My constituents are demanding results, so the
last thing I want to do is lose ground on that front."

"Better to disappoint your citizens than blow them up," Scott
said. "At the very least, I strongly recommend shutting down
this power station until the proper backups and emergency-
control systems can be installed."

"And what do you suggest we do in the meantime, Mister
Scott?" Poho dug in her heels. "We're not just talking about friv-
olous creature comforts and conveniences. We need *Thunderbird's* output for basic communications, transportation, security,
sanitation, and other fundamental services, including the police
department, the fire department, the hospital . . ."

She has a point, Kirk conceded. McCoy had already reported
on the strained conditions at the city hospital, including the
sporadic energy issues. Nevertheless, Scotty's objections seemed
to go beyond his usual grumbling whenever vital machinery
was not being treated with the proper respect. Kirk gathered
that Scott had good reason to be worried by what he had discovered here.

"I understand your concerns, Mayor, but Mister Scott is one
of the finest engineers in Starfleet. If he says this setup is unsafe,
we should listen to him."

"Unsafe by Starfleet standards, maybe," Poho said. "But here
on Baldur III, we don't have the luxury of doing everything by
the book. We've learned to improvise and get by with whatever's
available."

"Improvisation is one thing," Kirk argued. "Inviting disaster
is another."

She remained unconvinced. "You want to talk safety? Disasters? Worst-case scenarios? Emotions are already running high

in these parts, as you've seen for yourself. Particularly between the newcomers and the old-timers. You want this city to come apart in a major blackout? We could be talking riots, looting—"

"Losing an election?" Scotty said archly.

"Belay that kind of talk, Mister Scott," Kirk chided him. "We're guests here."

Poho's voice took on a frostier tone. "Thank you for remembering that, Captain."

"You'll have to forgive Mister Scott," Kirk said. "He's an engineer, not a diplomat, and he's not one to mince words when he sees something out of order, which is probably why the *Enterprise* is still in one piece."

"Well, I did ask him to speak his mind," Poho recalled. "Don't get me wrong, Captain. I'm not questioning Mister Scott's expertise. I'm sure this operation is far from ideal, by his exacting criteria. But I have to weigh the risks in light of the bigger picture, and I'm putting my foot down. *Thunderbird* is staying on for as long as it takes to get some new-and-improved power plants up and running."

"With all due respect, then," Scott said, "you are doing so against my strong recommendation. On the record."

Kirk could tell the mayor's mind was set, but felt compelled to press the point anyway. "There's nothing we can say to change your decision?"

"I'm afraid not, Captain. Shutting down *Thunderbird* is off the table, I'm sorry."

Kirk understood where she was coming from, but feared she was making a big mistake. His hands were tied, however. He couldn't simply pull rank and trust his own instincts, which were to follow Scotty's advice, but he couldn't in good conscience walk away from a potential disaster either. To his frustration, he could only do what he could.

"You heard the mayor, Mister Scott. Do whatever it takes to make this power plant as safe as you can manage. Bring down as many of your people from the *Enterprise* as you need. Hold this place together with spit and glue if you have to. Do you read me?"

"Aye, sir," Scott said. "I'll do my best."

Now that the matter was settled to her satisfaction, Poho unfolded her arms and adopted a more conciliatory tone.

"This is my call, Kirk, Mister Scott," she assured them. "Anything goes wrong, it's on my head, not yours."

Kirk found that small comfort.

Eight

Yurnos

"Approaching the planet, Mister Spock."

Chekov piloted *Galileo* toward Yurnos, which was clearly visible through the shuttlecraft's forward ports. Spock had been engaging in silent meditation in the copilot's seat, but roused himself as they neared their destination. The planet—which even from a distance appeared much less arid than his native Vulcan—appeared to grow in size as the shuttle headed toward it at sublight speed, slowing as they passed a solitary moon. A polar aurora illuminated the planet's higher latitudes; Spock recalled that Yurnos had an unusually dynamic magnetic field.

"Thank you, Ensign." Spock cleared his thoughts for the mission ahead. "I assume you have fully briefed yourself on the planet during our transit."

"Of course, Mister Spock." He recited what he had learned with the enthusiasm of a student anxious to impress his teacher. "Yurnos is a Class-M planet inhabited by a primitive humanoid species that look much like, well, yours truly. From what I gather, their technology is roughly equivalent to that of, say, eighteenth-century Europe or Russia. They are still a long way from developing a warp-capable civilization and are therefore protected by the Prime Directive. The plant that concerns us, *nabbia,* grows only in a certain region in the northern hemisphere of the planet. Efforts to cultivate it elsewhere have proved problematic; it's theorized that *nabbia* thrives only under very specific environmental conditions, related to the climate, the atmosphere, the native flora and fauna, and certain rare nutrients in the soils, including—"

"That is sufficient, Ensign. I commend your diligence."

Spock was already familiar with all relevant data concerning Yurnos and *nabbia,* but was pleased that Chekov had educated himself on the topics. Spock considered the young ensign a protégé of sorts. Despite his youth and unfortunate emotionality, Chekov had the makings of a fine Starfleet officer. Doctor McCoy had once accused Spock of being a bad influence on Chekov, but Spock preferred to think that he was training Chekov to achieve his full potential by encouraging him to think like a scientist.

"Thank you, Mister Spock."

Spock scanned the planet as they approached its atmosphere. The Yurnians' modest level of technological development could be seen by the absence of radio waves and other electromagnetic transmissions, as well as the lack of any artificial satellites in orbit around the planet. He easily detected a homing signal coming from the Federation observers who had alerted the *Enterprise* to the problem on Yurnos. He locked onto the signal and transmitted the coordinates to Chekov before hailing the source of the signal.

"*Galileo* to Federation outpost. We are approaching your location. Anticipate landing in approximately three-point-seven minutes."

"*Received,* Galileo," a female voice replied. "*We're ready for you.*"

Spock had been in prior communication with the observers, a husband-and-wife team of cultural anthropologists, so they were anticipating *Galileo*'s arrival. There was no danger of the Yurnians intercepting the transmissions, as they had yet to even

discover electricity, which made communicating with the observers relatively uncomplicated. Similarly, there was little risk
of *Galileo* being spotted above a certain altitude, although Spock
intended to exercise extreme caution anyway.

"You may begin your descent," Spock instructed. "Take care
to avoid coming within view of any large population centers."

"Understood, Mister Spock. We will sneak in quietly like
thieves in the night."

"I would have preferred a less larcenous comparison.
Proceed."

They angled down into the atmosphere, *Galileo's* shields and
sturdy duranium hull protecting them from the heat of reentry.
The desired coastline was cloaked in darkness as it came into
view. Spock had deliberately calculated their course and speed
so that they would arrive at the observers' location late at night,
the better to elude detection by anyone gazing up at the sky. As
they exited the cloud cover, Chekov switched off the shuttle's
running lights and navigated by sensors alone. As they had been
told, a homing signal led them to a small mill on the outskirts of
a nearby seaport. Spock's keen eyes made out the mill and various adjoining buildings, including a farmhouse, a silo, a stable,
and a large stone barn. Temporary landing lights flared in the
darkness, guiding them toward the latter. Spock glimpsed a pair
of tiny figures on the ground, peering up at the shuttle.

The anthropologists, Jord and Vankov, he assumed. *Formerly
of the University of Catulla.*

The barn door was open to receive *Galileo.* Spock estimated
there was sufficient clearance to allow the shuttle to pass
through the entrance, but it would be a tight squeeze. With all
due respect to Chekov, he found himself wishing that Sulu was
piloting instead.

"Would you prefer me to take control of the helm?" he asked.

"*Nyet,* Mister Spock." Chekov confidently steered *Galileo* into
the barn. "Just like entering the hangar deck."

The shuttle touched down on the packed-dirt floor of the barn. Spock and Chekov emerged from the spacecraft into warm, muggy air and the pungent odor of manure. Oversized rodents, the size of horses or cattle, occupied nearby stalls. They rose up on their hind legs and chittered in alarm at the shuttle's arrival. Spock knew from his research that the beasts, which were taxonomically akin to ground squirrels, albeit of much larger proportions, were a common form of domesticated livestock in this region. Silky fur, ranging in color from russet to gray, coated their slender bodies. Large eyes and bushy tails no doubt made them appealing to most humanoid sensibilities. Federation files labeled them megamarmots, frequently abbreviated to simply "marmots," which was the closest translation of the actual Yurnian name for the species. Prominent incisors indicated a tendency to gnaw.

"Hush now! Go back to sleep!" Jord quieted the animals by stroking their tufted ears. "There, there, nothing to worry about. Just some visitors, that's all."

Spock recognized the tall, middle-aged woman from the Federation database. A pair of archaic bifocals rested atop her nose. She wore simple linen garments that had presumably been sewn by hand. She turned toward her husband, who was similarly clad. He was busy collecting the portable landing lights, shutting them off one by one as he did so. Somewhat shorter than his wife, he had the beginnings of a pot belly. A missing tooth hinted at the barbaric dentistry of the planet. Apparently Vankov had sacrificed the tooth in order to maintain his cover among the Yurnians.

"Vankov!" she said. "Hurry up and close that barn door before somebody sees!"

"It's four in the morning, and the nearest neighbor is kilometers away," he observed. "Who's going to see?"

"Never hurts to be cautious."

"Fair enough." Vankov stowed the lights in a wooden barrel

before tugging the barn door shut from the inside. Hanging lanterns, smelling faintly of fish oil, illuminated the spacious stone structure. "Wouldn't want anyone to know we're hiding a spaceship in our barn, even if they wouldn't know a Starfleet shuttlecraft if they saw one."

"Indeed," Spock said. "Too early exposure to spacefaring beings and civilizations is exactly what we are here to prevent."

He introduced himself and Chekov to the couple. Jord looked him over. Worry creased her brow.

"We're going to have to hide those ears as well," she said.

"All in good time," Vankov said. "Why don't we take this into the house and let the livestock get back to sleep."

Spock was inclined to agree. Vulcans possessed an acute sense of smell, more so than most humanoids, so the earthy aroma of the barn did not encourage him to linger. He made certain *Galileo* was fully powered down and secure before allowing their hosts to escort them out a side door, where a short walk brought them to the farmhouse: a simple wooden structure with a slate roof and a brick chimney. After the long voyage from Baldur III, Spock appreciated the opportunity to stretch his legs and was almost disappointed when they entered the home moments later.

Perhaps there will be time for a stroll later.

Oil lamps lit a parlor on the ground floor, where they settled around a polished wooden table in front of a large empty hearth. The window shutters were drawn for privacy's sake, despite the seasonal heat, which was far more humid than the invigorating warmth of Vulcan, at least as far as Spock was concerned. A carpet bearing a colorful geometric design protected the floor. A mechanical timepiece ticked regularly on the mantel; Spock noted that the Yurnians divided their day into ten equal hours. This struck him as admirably decimal.

"Sorry for the summer swelter," Vankov said, "but at least

you missed the rainy season. I swear, this whole place turns into mud for months at a time. I hope your flight was a smooth one?"

Spock deduced that Vankov was the more gregarious of the pair. "It passed without incident, thank you."

"Can I help you to some chilled tea from the icebox?" Vankov asked.

Spock raised an eyebrow. "*Nabbia* tea?"

"Naturally."

Chekov looked uncertainly at Spock before replying to Vankov. "Er, well, that's very generous of you, sir, but—"

"At ease, Ensign," Spock said. "*Nabbia* is not contraband here on Yurnos, where it is a natural part of the planet's ecosystem, so no ethical or legal issues attach to partaking of it in this context. We may accept our hosts' hospitality with a clean conscience."

Chekov shrugged. "In that case, some tea would be most welcome, sir."

"But not to excess," Spock cautioned, recalling that the tea was said to be mildly intoxicating. He judged, however, that courtesy outweighed temperance in this instance, and one small cup apiece would do neither him nor Chekov any harm. And it *had* been a long trip from Baldur III.

"Stay where you are," Vankov said. "I'll be right back."

A sample of bootleg *nabbia*, provided by Mayor Poho's police force, currently resided in a storage compartment aboard *Galileo*. Spock had already made a cursory examination of the tea, taking note of its chemistry and genetics, but had yet to actually experience it brewed as a beverage. He was mildly curious to see what drew the smugglers to Yurnos.

True to his word, Vankov quickly returned with the refreshments. Spock found the notorious tea slightly sweeter than his taste, but not unpleasant. There was little documentation on the effects of *nabbia* on copper-based blood, so he wondered if he would benefit from its oxygenating effect. A medkit, complete with a hand scanner and reader tubes, resided in *Galileo*'s stores; it might be informative to compare his and Chekov's blood-oxygen levels later on.

"A bit stuffy in here," Vankov said. "Perhaps I should open a window."

Jord shook her head. "What if a carriage happens by and wonders what we're doing up so late, entertaining strangers?"

She eyed Spock's ears again, but refrained from commenting on them. Not for the first time, Spock regretted that Vulcan ears were relatively uncommon in the Alpha Quadrant. He was proud to have inherited his from his father and his father's fathers, but they did occasionally pose a problem when visiting worlds where Vulcans and Romulans were unknown.

"I suppose you're right," Vankov said to his wife. "Forgive the lack of interior temperature controls, gentlemen. We avoid using advanced technology except when absolutely necessary, even when we have no reason to believe we're being observed. If we allowed ourselves modern conveniences, it would be too easy to fall into the habit of using them too often and imprudently. One stray Peeping Tom spies me using an antigrav lift to lift a bale of hay, and the jig would be up. Chances are, we'd find ourselves on trial for sorcery."

"And that would be the best-case scenario," Jord stressed. "Better we be hanged as witches than exposed as aliens."

"Better in the larger sense," Vankov clarified. "Not so much for us, personally."

Spock approved of their caution. "I understand that you have been dwelling here for sixteen years?"

"Eighteen by the local calendar," Vankov said. "We've made a home here in order to study the Yurnians up close and personal. It's been an amazing opportunity to observe a barely industrial society as it develops in real time. We're confident that our work will someday lead to a fuller and more nuanced understanding of Hodgkin's Law."

"Eighteen years," Chekov said. "Doesn't it get lonely?"

"We have each other." Vankov reached across the table to take his wife's hand. "And it's not as though we're hermits spying on the natives from behind a camouflaged duck blind or something. We're on good terms with our neighbors, the folks in town, our customers, and so on. We enjoy their company, even if we have to hide the fact that we're not actually from this planet."

"And, to be clear," Jord added, "we take pains to stay out of local politics and community affairs, always erring on the side of caution for the sake of the Prime Directive. We won't even take a stand on a new tax or tariff for fear of interfering with the natural evolution of their society."

"Which is not always easy," Vankov said. "It can be hard— very hard—sometimes to just sit back and watch these people, whom we've come to know so well, make grave mistakes or endure injustices. Or to watch them suffer and die from medical issues that could easily be treated by modern science. Or even to just hold your tongue when you see them doing things the hard way, when a simple technological innovation would make their lives so much easier." He sighed ruefully. "But . . . you're in Starfleet—you know exactly what I'm talking about."

"Indeed," Spock said. "The temptation to intervene can be a powerful one, but logic dictates that primitive cultures must be allowed to develop in their own way and at their own pace. My own people have understood that for millennia."

Chekov nodded. "Although the Prime Directive, as we know it today, was first written in Russian."

"Come again?" Vankov looked at Chekov as though wondering if the tea had gone to the younger man's head. "You can't be serious."

"You must forgive Mister Chekov," Spock said. "His pride in his heritage sometimes gets the better of him." He gave Chekov a warning look. "It is a human eccentricity. Some, I believe, find it amusing."

"Never mind," Chekov said sheepishly. "We were saying . . . ?"

Vankov let it pass. "In any event, it is good to have visitors with whom we can speak freely. I'm sorely tempted to keep you up the rest of the night talking galactic affairs. Do you really think that the Organian Peace Treaty is going to hold? And is it true that Baldur III might join the Federation?"

"Both interesting topics," Jord said, "but not what these men are here to help us with."

"You are correct," Spock said. "We should address the matter at hand . . . unless you would prefer to wait until morning?"

"Don't worry about that," she said. "We keep our own hours, and this has been brewing long enough." She rose from the table. "If you're done with your tea, please follow me."

A stairway in the kitchen led to the basement, which was packed with belongings suitable to the planet and its current level of civilization: baskets, barrels, glassware, winter attire, a broken spinning wheel, a snow shovel, and other accoutrements. Cobwebs clustered in the corners, but the dirt floor and stone walls were dry rather than damp. A cooler temperature prevailed than upstairs.

"It is rather more comfortable down here," Chekov said. "I approve."

Jord approached a framed oval mirror that was mounted to a wall. She paused in front of it. "Requesting access to nerve center. Identity code: five-jay-five-zee-five-delta-nine."

The silvered mirror lit up as though enchanted. A luminous green beam scanned Jord to confirm her identity.

"Access granted," an automated voice replied.

A panel slid open in the "dirt" floor to reveal another stairway leading to a hidden subbasement. Jord started toward it.

"Move briskly," she advised. "The hatch will close behind me in exactly three minutes."

It was like stepping through a time portal from the past to the twenty-third century. They soon found themselves squeezed into a compact control room that looked as though it belonged on the *Enterprise* instead of buried beneath a rustic farmhouse. A computer station boasted a large rectangular viewscreen while a secondary work station presumably allowed both Jord and Vankov to make use of the nerve center at the same time. Glazed enamel walls and a tile floor provided a clean, sterile environment, although Spock noted that some local form of arachnid had managed to spin a web in one corner of the ceiling anyway. Intended for only two people, the control room could barely accommodate four.

"This whole setup is rigged to self-destruct," Jord assured them, "should anyone besides Vankov or I find their way in here. Explosive charges will reduce the entire place to atoms, leaving no trace of evidence behind, just to be safe."

Vankov winced at the picture she painted. "Like I said, we're strict about abstaining from modern technology in our every-day lives, but we do need the proper equipment to conduct our work and to stay in touch with the universe beyond Yurnos, as when we contacted the *Enterprise* for instance. We're not going to preserve our data on parchment."

"Naturally," Spock said. He recalled having been marooned in Earth's past without access to the tools and materials he was accustomed to. "One can hardly expect you to make do with stone knives and bearskins."

"Technically, there are no bears on Yurnos," Vankov said, "but, yes, exactly."

"I take it, however, that this equipment is not the cultural contamination you were concerned about," Spock said. "You have something else to show us."

"I'm afraid so." Jord removed a box from a storage compartment. "Take a look at this."

The box contained an eclectic assortment of objects: a tin can, a safety razor, a matchbook, a Klingon dagger with a stainless-steel blade, a trillium bracelet, a three-bladed Capellan throwing star, a vial of some unspecified tablets, and an unopened bottle of Antarian glow water, albeit with the identifying label peeled off. It went without saying that the more exotic items were not native to Yurnos, and he suspected that the same applied to the more mundane artifacts. He inspected the razor.

"I take it that these objects are not consistent with the present technology of this region?"

"Not one of them," Vankov confirmed. "Granted, things could be worse. We haven't found evidence of anything ridiculously egregious, like a phaser or a communicator, which suggests that the smugglers are showing *some* restraint, perhaps in order to keep a low profile?"

"Nevertheless," Jord said, "I'm sure I don't need to tell you that even the most seemingly harmless bit of contamination can yield serious consequences. Minor changes snowballing into major shifts in culture and technology."

"Mind you, nothing cataclysmic seems to have occurred yet," Vankov said, "but you can see why we were worried enough to contact Starfleet, especially when we got word that the *Enterprise* was already in the vicinity."

"I concur with your assessment." Spock put down the razor and inspected the matchbook instead. He noted that only three matches remained. "May I ask how you obtained these objects?"

"By hook and by crook, mostly," Vankov said. "Traded for some of them, outright stole some of the others. We've been keeping our ears to the ground, alert to gossip and rumors about unusual 'foreign' objects turning up." He glanced at the box. "Spotted a local bravo showing off that Klingon blade in a tavern. Won it off him in a game of chance." A smirk lifted his lips. "I cheated, of course."

"He had no idea of its true origins," Jord explained. "He thought it was simply from some exotic faraway land on the other side of the world. Fortunately, Yurnos is a large enough world, travel-wise, that distant lands might as well be on another planet, as far as the average resident is concerned."

"Lucky for us *and* them," Chekov said. "As long as no ambitious trader decides to set sail across the ocean in search of more trillium or glow water. They would be in for a big disappointment."

"Which is exactly the kind of unintended consequence we need to avert," Jord said, "by stopping the influx of such items before the Yurnians' future is irreparably altered in ways impossible to foresee."

Spock considered the problem. "And you believe this contamination is related to the illegal trade in *nabbia*?"

"So we assume," Jord said. "That's the only thing smugglers from other worlds have ever really wanted from Yurnos. It's always been minor concern in these parts, but ever since Baldur III suddenly became a major port of call, the problem seems to have escalated to an alarming degree." She gestured at the box of contraband. "We've collected all these items in just a matter of months."

"A reasonable supposition," Spock said. "We spoke with the leader of the Baldur III colony, who reluctantly confirmed that the ongoing flood of new arrivals to the planet has spurred a commensurate increase in the demand for *nabbia*."

"And what do they intend to do about it?" Jord asked indignantly. "I don't begrudge Baldur III their windfall, but the Yurnians shouldn't have to pay for their new prosperity. Baldur III is a system away from Yurnos; these people shouldn't be affected by what happens there for centuries at least. Can't they—or Starfleet—do something to shut down the black market for *nabbia*?"

Spock chose not to mention that Mayor Poho had other priorities. "That is what we are here to investigate."

"Do you know who is behind this?" Chekov asked.

Jord shook her head. "People like to show off their new toys, but tend to get tight-lipped when you ask where they came from. We suspect that the folks who actually received the contraband from the smugglers liquidate them quickly, converting the rare 'foreign' oddities to the local currency as soon as they can via the black market, possibly through a variety of middlemen. In short, they're covering their tracks well."

"There's a thriving underground economy hereabouts," Vankov elaborated, "mostly devoted to avoiding various taxes, including those on foreign and imported goods."

"To the extent," Jord said, expanding on the topic, "that most people prefer to look the other way when it comes to smuggling and under-the-counter trading."

"And we're reluctant to blow our cover," Vankov added, "by poking around and asking too many questions. We run a mill and mind our own business, at least as far as Yurnians are concerned. We can't run around interrogating people like constables or tax collectors, at least not without attracting unwelcome attention."

Spock understood the delicacy of their position. They had invested a good portion of their lives to embedding themselves in this community without violating the Prime Directive. It would be unfortunate, if not tragic, if years of work were undone by their efforts to curb the illegal trade between the two planets.

"Let us take the lead in the investigation," he suggested. "As strangers, we are bound to attract a degree of attention regardless, so we have less to lose if we appear too inquisitive." He noted Jord's worried brow. "Not that we intend to behave in too conspicuous a manner. Subtlety and stealth are called for under the circumstances. Isn't that correct, Ensign?"

"Absolutely, Mister Spock. This is not our first undercover mission on a primitive world. We will be nothing, if not discreet."

"I hope so," Jord said.

Spock considered the logistics of smuggling items on and off Yurnos. "You do not have a spacecraft of your own, correct?"

"That's right," Vankov said. "This was always intended to be a long-term study, so we were dropped off here by a research vessel many years ago. The idea was always that we would arrange to be picked up by another ship if and when we chose to leave Yurnos at the completion of our work."

Jord frowned. "You weren't suspecting us of being involved with the smuggling, were you?"

"That would be illogical, given that it was you who alerted us to the problem in the first place." Spock examined the primary computer station, noting that its functions included various sensor controls. "No, I was merely reviewing the number of known space vessels coming and going from Yurnos. Have you a means of detecting any ships approaching or departing the planet?"

"In theory." Vankov indicated the console. "We've been monitoring Yurnos's orbits for signs of the smugglers' vessels, but have been unable to detect any traffic within transporter range of the planet, let alone any ships or shuttles coming in for a landing."

Chekov scratched his chin. "Are you certain your sensors are functioning properly?"

"They picked up your shuttle's approach with no problem," Jord insisted. "But, as far as we can tell, *Galileo* is the first spacecraft to visit Yurnos in months, if not years."

Spock made a mental note to inspect the observers' sensor array in the near future, but it was entirely possible that the equipment was as fully operational as Jord maintained. The smugglers could hardly count on the observers' sensors being out of order, provided they were aware of the anthropological team's presence on the planet at all.

"Logic dictates, however, that the smugglers must have a

means for transporting goods back and forth between Yurnos and Baldur III, and that those means would necessarily involve one or more ships. The question that then arises is how precisely have the ships eluded detection all this time."

"What can I say?" Vankov threw up his hands. "It's a mystery."

"So it appears," Spock stated, "but one which I intend to solve."

Nine

Baldur III

"Any word from Spock and Chekov?"

McCoy joined Kirk on the bridge, where the captain was reviewing some requisition requests on a data slate while Yeoman Landon stood by waiting for him to sign off on the documents. Frequent trips to the planet's surface to consult with the mayor and her advisors had put Kirk behind on his paperwork, so he was taking the opportunity to catch up while he could. He looked up from the slate to reply to McCoy.

"They've arrived on Yurnos and have made contact with the Federation observers. That's all Spock has reported so far, but their mission is proceeding."

"Well," McCoy said, "let's hope they're having an easier time of things than we are. Although I feel sorry for Chekov, having nobody but Spock for company."

"Captain," Uhura interrupted. "I'm receiving a distress signal from the planet. It's from Lieutenant Baines."

Kirk recalled that Jack Baines was heading a small security team that had been assigned to assist the local authorities in maintaining order on Baldur III. All thought of requisitions and reports fled Kirk's mind as he handed the slate back to Landon and turned toward Uhura.

"Pipe it through, Lieutenant."

"Aye, sir."

Baines's voice emerged from the speakers: *"Hailing,* Enterprise! *Please respond!"*

"We read you, Baines," Kirk said. "What's happening?"

"We're in hot water, Captain. Got called in to deal with a claim dispute between two rival groups of prospectors, both of whom insist the other was trespassing on their turf. Things started out ugly and came to blows fast."

Kirk could hear shouting and commotion in the background, as well as the tension in Baines's voice. He sounded like a man under fire.

"We tried to break it up, sir, but, to be honest, there's too many of them and not enough of us. We could really use—"

A harsh smacking noise, followed by an inarticulate grunt, cut Baines off in midsentence. A metallic clang suggested that his communicator had fallen onto a hard surface.

"Baines?" Kirk asked urgently. "Baines! Do you read me?"

Shouts, screams, thuds, and crashes seconded Baines's report of a violent altercation underway. A sudden high-volume crunch sounded like thunder on the bridge, causing Kirk and the others to wince, but was immediately replaced by static, which Uhura mercifully muted.

"I've lost the signal," she said. "I believe the communicator is no longer operative."

Kirk visualized a heavy boot stomping on the device, or some similar impact. "Did you get a trace on the signal's origin before it was cut off?"

"Captain, I have the location." She consulted the computer. "It appears to be a wilderness area one hundred thirty kilometers outside the city."

Lieutenant Painter looked back at Kirk from the helm. "Perhaps a wide-dispersal phaser blast, set on stun, to pacify the entire site long enough for us to rescue our people and secure the scene?"

"Creative thinking, Mister Painter," Kirk replied. "But pergium mining plus a phaser burst add up to an explosive combination. We're not going to be able to resolve this from on high." He instantly decided on a course of action. "Uhura, transmit those coordinates to the transporter room." His finger jabbed the intercom button. "This is the captain speaking. Dispatch a security team to the transporter room on the double."

He sprang from his chair and started for the turbolift. "Bones, you're with me."

"You bet I am," the doctor said. "Just hope I'm not too late for Baines."

Landon hurried after them. "Permission to accompany you, Captain? To document the incident?"

Kirk remembered how she'd handled herself during that business with Vaal on Gamma Trianguli VI. Come to think of it, a record of this mission might come in handy in the event of any future investigations or legal proceedings regarding Starfleet's intervention in the dispute.

"All right, Yeoman. Just keep a sharp lookout."

"Always do, sir."

Kirk wasted no time getting underway. Less than ten minutes after receiving the distress signal, the landing party took their places on the transporter platform, fully geared up for the mission. A medkit was slung over McCoy's shoulder, while phasers had been issued to all concerned, including the three red-shirted security officers Kirk had found waiting for him in the transporter room. Kirk took a moment to brief them on the situation before reminding the entire party of the probable hazards ahead.

"Chances are we're beaming into a fight, facing an unknown number of hostiles. We need to be on guard and ready to defend ourselves—and others—from the moment we materialize."

Landon patted the phaser on her hip. "I hear you, Captain."

"Be careful with your phasers," Kirk said. "Pergium reacts

explosively when struck by energy beams. Hand-to-hand combat is recommended, but if you must use your phasers, confine yourself to short, targeted bursts, preferably at close range. One stray shot could lead to a big bang. Am I understood?"

"Aye, Captain," Landon said.

"Very well, then." He nodded at Lieutenant John Kyle, who was at the transporter controls. "Energize."

"Energizing."

The familiar sensation of the transporter effect washed over Kirk, then quickly reversed itself, leaving him somewhere else. Within a heartbeat, the landing party went from the calm, orderly environment of the transporter room to chaos.

They found themselves atop what appeared to be one of several corrugated steel cargo containers that had been converted into shelters or storehouses. The endangered security team crouched on the roof of the container, aside from Baines, who was out cold or worse, an ugly bruise discoloring his forehead. The furious shouting and fighting Kirk had overheard before suddenly came from all around and sounded much closer. It was twilight, and a damp autumn wind came as a jolt after the controlled climate of the *Enterprise*.

"Heads down, sir!" one of Baines's team shouted. Ensign Lisa Nichols took the landing party's sudden materialization in stride. "It's not safe!"

A crimson beam, sizzling past Kirk's skull, punctuated her suggestion. He dropped down onto the cold metal roof along with the rest of the landing party. McCoy scurried to check on Baines, his medical scanner already in his hand. Kirk left Bones to his doctoring as he cautiously lifted his head to survey his new surroundings.

The mining camp occupied a wooded clearing on a mossy slope leading down to a wide gully that looked to be a dried-up riverbed, which was where the actual mining had obviously been taking place. An industrial-sized sonic plow was parked in the gully, where it had apparently been employed to remove successive layers of soil and rock in order to expose a thick vein of pergium buried deeper below the surface; unlike a phaser drill, sonic waves were unlikely to set off a chain reaction. Bins and sledges loaded with unprocessed ore waited to be transported. Floodlights mounted on looming tree trunks illuminated the work site as the sun gradually set in the east. A deep pit had been dug near one end of the trench, perhaps to reach an even deeper ore deposit.

At the moment, however, any and all mining had given way to the heated battle being waged in and around the excavation site. A few dozen prospectors, divided into Troglytes and native Baldurians, were going at each other with a vengeance, wielding fists, shovels, picks, crowbars, and other implements. Considering the amount of mined pergium out in the open, Kirk was relieved to see that few of the miners were equipped with sidearms, but, remembering the beam that had just missed his head only moments before, he feared an accidental explosion was only a matter of time. A few fallen miners already littered the landscape, but moans and movements suggested that they were only injured, not deceased. He dared to hope that nobody had been killed yet.

"What's the story here, Ensign?" he asked Nichols.

"Nearly as we can tell, Captain, the river marks the border between two claims. The Trogs—as they call themselves, I believe—detected a rich vein of ore beneath the river and started mining it. Some of the locals objected, insisting that the river itself was theirs by tradition."

"River?" Kirk asked.

"The Trogs dammed the river farther upstream and dug a canal to divert it away from the mother lode. Which just caused more hard feelings, with the locals accusing the Trogs of deliberately moving the border to expand their claim."

Kirk nodded. "So that's why they called you in?"

"Actually, it was the Trogs who called the authorities, when the locals started interfering with their mining operations." Nichols gave Kirk an apologetic look. "We tried to calm everybody down, but . . . things bubbled over anyway. Sorry, Captain."

"No need to apologize, Ensign. I'm sure you did your best." He briefly wondered which side had thrown the first punch, then decided it didn't really matter at this point. "What happened to Baines?"

"We took a position on top of this shelter, to claim the high ground, but the lieutenant got nailed by a rock thrown by one of the rioters. Lost his communicator too."

"Yes, we heard that." Kirk assumed it had fallen to the ground below. He glanced over at the unconscious officer. "How is he, Bones?"

"Took a nasty blow to the head all right," McCoy reported. "No fractures, but a definite concussion." He flipped open his communicator. "One to beam up. Transmitting precise coordinates now. Alert sickbay to expect a patient."

Baines's inert form dissolved into sparkling golden energy before vanishing altogether. The characteristic whine of the transporter was all but lost in the noise coming from the fight. Kirk was confident that the injured man would soon be in good hands.

But what about the rest of them?

Kirk noticed the lack of uniformed Baldurian personnel, either up on the roof with the Starfleet personnel or caught up in the fracas below.

"Where are the local security forces? Why aren't they handling this?"

"They're no-shows, sir." Nichols sounded distinctly aggrieved. "We kept expecting them to show up and reinforce us, and even tried hailing them for backup, but . . . no response. We were on our own, Captain, with no help from the local police."

Kirk scowled. He'd have to look into that later. "You getting all this, Landon?"

The yeoman was stretched out on the rooftop, recording the scene below with her tricorder. "Affirmative, sir."

"What are your orders, sir?" Nichols asked.

Good question, Kirk thought. He was tempted to beam Nichols and the others to safety, letting the prospectors work out their differences on their own, but their mission here was to help keep the peace. He wasn't about to abdicate that responsibility the first time things got messy. Retreat was a last resort.

And talking was always the first way to go.

"Give me your communicator, Ensign."

"Yes, sir."

Nichols handed her communicator over to Kirk, who dialed its audio output up to maximum. Holding it out before him while speaking into his own communicator, he rose to his feet and used Nichols's device to amplify his voice like a loudspeaker.

"THIS IS CAPTAIN JAMES T. KIRK OF THE *U.S.S. ENTERPRISE.* PUT DOWN YOUR FISTS AND WEAPONS AND CEASE HOSTILITIES IMMEDIATELY. LET'S WORK THIS OUT WITHOUT VIOLENCE!"

His words fell on deaf ears, ignored by the warring prospectors, aside from a single, red-faced Baldurian who drew a vintage laser pistol from his belt and fired wildly at Kirk.

"Who invited you here anyway?"

The crimson bolt missed Kirk by a meter, but he ducked down regardless, just in case the angry miner's aim improved.

"I think they're past talking to, Jim," McCoy said.

Kirk was inclined to agree. "Can't say I didn't try."

The doctor viewed the violence with obvious distaste. He shook his head in reproach. "Talk about a sorry spectacle. Have they lost their damn minds? Looks to me like there's enough pergium to go around."

"Careful, Bones," Kirk said, "you're starting to sound like Spock."

"I'm going to pretend I didn't hear that."

Kirk pondered his next move. Even with the addition of the

landing party, the Starfleet contingent was significantly outnumbered and on unfamiliar terrain. He could beam down even
more reinforcements, but that might just add fuel to the fire. He
needed to defuse this donnybrook, not escalate it.

"Captain! Look over there!"

Landon called Kirk's attention to a specific altercation taking
place several meters away. A Troglyte was loading a small bin of
pergium onto a floating antigrav sledge, much to the outrage of
the hot-headed Baldurian who had taken a shot at Kirk.

"Don't even think about making off with that ore, you offworld claim jumper! That belongs to us!"

He fired recklessly at the Troglyte, who threw herself out of
the line of fire, tumbling down the slope away from the floating
sledge, which was struck by the crimson bolt instead—with immediate results.

A deafening explosion shook the camp. The shockwave
struck the shelter Kirk and the others were perched on, toppling
it from its moorings and onto its side, spilling the Starfleet crew
members onto the damp, spongy ground below—and into the
thick of the fray. His ears ringing, Kirk scrambled to his feet in
time to see a snarling miner charging at him, swinging a shovel
at Kirk's head.

That's it, he thought. *I'm all out of patience.*

He ducked beneath the shovel and retaliated with a kid-
ney punch that sent the other man staggering backward. Kirk
wrested the shovel from the miner's grip and rammed its handle
into the man's chest, knocking him flat on his back. He started
to look around to check on the others, when a burly Troglyte
grabbed him from behind, pinning Kirk's arms to his sides.

"Let me go!" Kirk protested. "You called us, remember?"

"Like that did any good!"

At this point, Kirk realized, neither side was thinking
straight. He smashed the back of his head into the Trog's nose,
causing the prospector to cry out in pain. The shock loosened

the Trog's grip enough for Kirk to elbow him in the gut . . . hard. The Trog let go of Kirk, who spun around and smacked the flat of the shovel into the side of the miner's head, dropping him. Surprisingly, the Trog tried to get back up again, but a karate chop to the man's neck put him down for the count.

Not as elegant as a nerve pinch, Kirk thought, *but I'm only human . . .*

"Are you all right, Captain?"

Kirk turned to see Landon heading toward him. A snarling Troglyte lunged at her from behind. His fists were locked together above his head.

"Landon!" Kirk shouted. "Watch out!"

A deft judo move flipped the Troglyte over Landon's shoulder and onto his back in front of her. Before he could figure out what had happened to him, she drew her phaser and stunned him at point-blank range. He went limp at her feet.

"You were saying, Captain?" she said with a smirk.

"Never mind, Yeoman. Carry on."

Kirk recalled that Chekov had briefly dated Landon for a time. *Lucky Chekov,* he thought before taking in the damage from the explosion. A smoking crater was surrounded by strewn rubble, while another shelter was badly dented by the blast. Kirk counted themselves fortunate that only one small bin of pergium had been set off. Suppose an energy beam had hit the mother lode instead?

"You all right, Jim? Landon?"

McCoy staggered toward them, limping, while Nichols and the other security officers took up defensive positions around the captain, grappling with the out-of-control prospectors, who were lashing out at every stranger in sight. A miner broke through the guards' rank, only to run into a flying kick from Kirk. The soles of the captain's boots struck the miner squarely in the chest, bowling him over. Another close-up burst from Landon's phaser stunned the man senseless. Kirk climbed to his feet.

"Nothing broken, Doctor," he said, "although I'm not sure we're doing much good—"

The roar of a heavy-duty engine drowned out Kirk's words, competing with the general cacophony of the battle. The noise drew his gaze to the sonic plow, which was no longer sitting idle in the gully. With a Baldurian miner in the driver's seat, the powered-up machine started up the slope toward what was left of the Troglyte mining camp, no doubt intent on demolishing it. A cone-shaped sonic agitator, designed to break up packed dirt and rock, was mounted above a wide steel scraper blade durable enough to move large quantities of earth. A suction funnel sprayed any excess soil and gravel off to one side like an old-fashioned snowblower. Industrial-strength treads carried the hijacked plow up the hill, tearing apart the mossy slope in the process. Panicked combatants dashed out of its path. Crimson beams scorched the surface of the steel blade as a few miners risked firing at the plow. A frantic prospector scrambled up the trunk of a nearby tree, a move that struck Kirk as strategically unsound.

Unless . . . ?

Kirk spotted another tree rising along the plow's path, a floodlight mounted among its upper branches. Metallic rungs had been secured to the tree trunk to provide easier access to the lights. If it stayed on its present course, the rogue plow would pass by the tree momentarily.

"Cover me!" he ordered.

Dashing across the ravaged clearing, he clambered up the side of the tree and out onto a (hopefully) sturdy branch, where he crouched, waiting for the plow to come closer. The tree was not directly in the path of the destructive sonic wave projected by the agitator, but even the outer ripples were enough to shake loose the floodlight so that it crashed to the ground many meters below. Vibrations threatened to dislodge Kirk, who hung on to the branch for dear life until the open cab of the plow was directly beneath him. Letting go, he dropped onto the startled miner in the driver's seat, who yelped in surprise. Kirk flung the man from the cab and seized control of the plow.

His first instinct was to shut down the machine before it could do any more damage, but perhaps there was some way he could use the plow to cool down the feuding prospectors, many of whom were still fighting riotously in the contested gully? The problem echoed in his brain.

Cool them down?

He smirked as an idea occurred to him.

The controls for the plow were admirably user-friendly. Kirk took advantage of this to make a swift U-turn and steer the machine back down into the dried-up riverbed, where he headed upstream as fast as the heavy industrial device could manage. A few moments of experimentation taught him how to raise the blade so that it wasn't scraping the ground before him, thereby increasing the plow's speed by a significant degree. Within minutes he came within sight of the dam, an impressive structure that the Troglytes had economically fashioned from the materials at hand: logs and rocks, mostly, with a bit of thermoconcrete mortar.

Can't fault them for their industry, Kirk thought.

He drove the plow straight toward the dam, while dialing the sonic agitator up to its maximum setting. Intense vibrations buffeted the structure, pulverizing the packed lumber and stone. The smaller pieces shook loose first, but then the larger components began to crumble as well, setting off a slew of miniature avalanches. Logs turned into splinters. Heavy stones and mortar were reduced to gravel. Water spurted through newly formed gaps in the dam.

Yes, Kirk thought. *It's working!*

The closer the plow got to the dam, the more the agitator dismantled it. Kirk kept up the sonic barrage until he was certain that the dam was on the brink of collapse. At the last moment, just as the plow was about to smash into the disinte-grating dam, Kirk steered it hard to the right, lumbering up and out of the increasingly muddy gully onto a rocky bank. Jets of cold mountain water sprayed Kirk as he drove away from the dam, which came apart with the sound of cracking logs, tum-bling stone, and a rushing river.

Kirk switched off the agitator and looked back over his shoul-der. Foaming water, no longer diverted from its accustomed course, flooded the gully on its way downstream toward the mining site. He flipped open his communicator.

"Kirk to landing party! There's a flood on your way!"

———————

"Let me through," McCoy barked. "Can't you see? I'm a doctor, not a prospector!"

He limped across the ravaged slope overlooking the mine, where the plow's rampage had left a trail of torn-up earth, caus-ing him to wonder just what had become of Kirk anyway. He'd twisted his ankle after having been thrown from the roof of the cargo container, but he ignored the pain as best he could. Try-ing to attend to the injured, McCoy dodged angry miners, who didn't seem to care whose skull they wanted to crack anymore. Landon and Nichols did their best to run interference for him, while trying to avoid becoming casualties in their own right. The remaining Starfleet personnel were busy trying to break up fights and defend themselves at the same time.

"Where's the captain?" Landon delivered a high kick to a fe-male Troglyte's jaw. "Where's he gone?"

"Your guess is as good as mine, Yeoman."

McCoy felt like a combat medic, trying to treat wounded men and women under less than ideal conditions. An anguished groan drew him to a fallen miner lying not far from the crater left behind by the explosion. Kneeling down beside the man, McCoy recognized the troublemaker who had taken a shot at

Kirk and later set off that bin of pergium in the first place. A bad burn on his left side suggested that he had been too close to his own accidental handiwork. McCoy dosed the scorched miner with a general anesthetic before using a spray applicator to apply a topical compound to the burnt areas. The compound, which contained both a coagulant and an antibiotic, would prevent any bleeding or infection until the man could be treated at a proper sickbay or planet-bound clinic.

"Just hang on," McCoy said. "We'll get you fixed up soon."

An electronic chirp stepped on his bedside manner. He heard Landon's communicator chirp too. He plucked his communicator from his belt.

"McCoy here."

The captain's voice came over the device:

"Kirk to landing party! There's a flood on your way!"

"Come again?"

McCoy needed only a few words of explanation before he sprang to his feet and ran down the hill to shout at the people still fighting it out in the gully.

"Everyone out of the riverbed! The dam's busted!"

A handful of combatants, including a few Starfleet officers, registered what he was saying and raced to get out of the gully in time, but McCoy's warning went largely unheeded in the tumult—until the returning river came roaring back into the mining site, knocking both Troglytes and Baldurians off their feet. The frothing water was only chest deep in most parts, but the force of the flood was still enough to break up the fight in a big way. An antigrav sledge loaded with unprocessed pergium was carried away by the river, heading downstream to who knew where. At least one miner, safely on the shore, cried out in dismay as the precious ore was washed away.

The wall of water moved past the site, leaving a muddy river behind. Drifting pieces of splintered wood were evidence of the dam's demise. Floundering prospectors found their feet and, fighting the current, dragged themselves onto drier land, sputtering and swearing a blue streak. McCoy swept his medical tricorder over the bedraggled assemblage, but didn't spot any serious injuries, just a mob of soggy, unhappy prospectors whose mother lode was now underwater.

Serves them right, he thought. *Letting greed turn them into—*

"Help! I can't swim!"

A Troglyte had been swept into the deep pit that had been dug into the gully, where the water was now much deeper than elsewhere. He was splashing wildly, unable to get any footing while struggling to keep his head above the water. The other Trogs stood by helplessly, clearly uncertain what to do; McCoy guessed that there hadn't been a lot of pools or water parks in the zenite mines on Ardana.

"It's okay!" Landon ran down the hill toward the drowning man. "I'm coming!"

She kicked off her boots and dived into the river just as the imperiled Troglyte sank out of sight. McCoy watched tensely, holding his breath, until she surfaced moments later, holding on to the man by his shoulders. She swam him to shore, where the other Troglytes helped them out of the gully. The man coughed up plenty of water, but was still breathing, as far as McCoy could tell. He rushed over to examine him more closely.

"Thank you, thank you!" the Trog said, coughing. "I thought I was a drowned man."

A quick medical scan revealed that the man's heart was still pounding and that he had swallowed a fair amount of water, but that his lungs were clear enough, requiring no artificial respiration. McCoy added the grateful Trog to his growing list of patients who would need to be checked out more carefully later. He wondered if Landon's heroics would earn them enough goodwill to bring this whole ugly business to a close.

"You!" A fuming miner pointed at McCoy. He looked Baldurian beneath the mud. "You knew the water was coming! Was Starfleet responsible?"

"You had no right to flood our mine!" an equally upset Troglyte protested. "You owe us for everything we lost, our gear, our profits!"

So much for goodwill, McCoy thought. Surly expressions and harsh voices targeted McCoy and his companions, as the security folks began to assume defensive positions. The doctor feared that Kirk might have ended the strife between the rival prospectors by giving them a common enemy.

Lucky us.

"And where's our plow?" another Trog demanded. "What's become of it?"

McCoy had no idea, but was saved from admitting that by the rumble of heavy treads. All heads turned to see the missing sonic plow come out of the woods into the clearing. McCoy was glad to see Kirk in the driver's seat.

"Right on cue," he muttered. *Leave it to Jim Kirk to make a big entrance.*

———

Well, this is one way to get people's attention, Kirk thought.

He'd made good time cutting through the woods. The sonic agitator was turned off to avoid damaging anything else, but he kept the plow idling, if only to keep the various factions on their toes. From the looks of things, flooding the gully had indeed cooled things down to some extent. Now he just had to keep them from heating up all over again.

"Listen up!" Kirk raised his voice to be heard. "This insanity has gone on long enough. I understand that both sides have their grievances, but bashing each other's heads in isn't going to get you anywhere, or get any pergium mined. Don't you see? There's no profit in fighting . . . for any of you."

"So we're just supposed to stand by while these offworlders steal our resources?" a Baldurian challenged him. "From our river?"

"Who says that river belongs to you?" a Troglyte said. "And you didn't even know that vein was there. *We* found that pergium, not you. We dug it up with our own sweat and skill!"

More voices joined the debate. Kirk was encouraged that they were back to talking, but feared that the argument could all too easily erupt into violence again. At the moment, he cared less about which side was in the right than about keeping the peace. It wasn't his job to play Solomon with regard to a river—or the pergium waiting beneath it.

"Look," he said, "it's not my place to decide who that ore belongs to or where one claim ends and another begins. That's for the local authorities to decide. If you have a dispute, take it to court."

"The courts?" someone jeered. "They're backed up for months. We'd go broke waiting around for some overworked bureaucrat to settle this!"

"And what makes you think we'd get a fair hearing?" a Troglyte asked. "The courts and the mining bureau are packed with old-timers, who think this whole planet belongs to them just because their families arrived here a few generations before we did!"

"So?" a Baldurian said. "You got a problem with that?"

Here we go, Kirk thought. "Gentlemen, ladies! Let's not start this up again!" He held up his hands for silence while counting on the idling plow and agitator to keep the crowd in line long enough to hear him out. "I promise you, I'll speak directly to Mayor Poho about getting this resolved in a timely fashion. And, in the meantime, I'm going to place this site under surveillance. Anyone tries to resume mining this claim, or to abscond with whatever ore has already been mined, before your arguments have been heard, and I'll detonate this entire vein with a phaser blast from the *Enterprise*. Is that clear?"

His statement provoked plenty of complaints and grumbling, but no one took a shot at him. Kirk chose to take that as progress.

"You have my word," Kirk told them. "I'll be talking to the mayor about this right away."

As it happened, he had some pressing questions for her himself.

———————

"What I want to know, Mayor, is why were my people hung out to dry? Where were the local security forces?"

Kirk addressed the mayor via the computer station in his quarters. Uhura had set up a secure channel to the planet so that he and Poho could speak frankly away from the bridge. Her face looked back at him from the small viewscreen.

"My apologies, Captain. The truth of the matter is that we're suffering a serious manpower shortage. It's not just that our population keeps growing, stretching our resources thin, but also that too many of my people have ditched their duties to join the prospectors, making a bad situation worse. If nobody responded to your team's calls for backup, it's probably because there weren't any local officers available to do so."

"I suppose I should have seen that coming," Kirk said. It seemed that even some of the folks running Baldur III were not immune to the lure of pergium. He was proud of the fact that, by contrast, not one of his crew had jumped ship to take part in the madness. Proud, but not surprised. Starfleet attracted only the best.

"And the courts and administrative agencies?"

"Same story, I'm afraid," she said. *"People want to work claims, not process them."*

"Well, we're going to have to do something about that," Kirk said, "unless you want more scenes like we witnessed today. If people can't turn to the proper authorities to resolve their differences, they're going to start taking the law into their own hands more and more often."

Poho looked pained. *"So what do you suggest we do about it, Captain?"*

"First off, you probably need to prioritize claim disputes. Appoint more people—qualified people—to rule impartially on such issues. And make sure that both newcomers and old-timers are represented on such boards, to avoid even the appearance of bias."

"And where am I supposed to find these extra people, when I'm already bleeding personnel as it is?"

Kirk hesitated, worried about mission creep, but spoke anyway.

"We have people aboard the *Enterprise* who are trained in administrative and legal matters. I can also put in a request to the Federation for additional judges and lawyers and, well, bureaucrats, to serve on an interim basis until you can bring your own institutions up to speed."

"Oh, wouldn't Cahill and his cronies love that?" Poho winced in anticipation. *"Federation officials stepping into our courts and agencies, ruling on our affairs. He'd see that as a stealth takeover for sure."*

"I have to say," Kirk said, "maybe you should consider joining the Federation? You're not a small, remote colony anymore and, with all due respect, you may need a lot more organization and support to manage the thriving, well-populated world you're becoming. The Federation can help Baldur III achieve its full potential."

Poho frowned. "Is that what this has really been about all along, Captain? Claiming Baldur III for the UFP?"

"No," Kirk stated. "But it may be your best option . . . because the current state of affairs is not working."

Ten

Deep Space Station S-8

The *Solar Wind*'s departure was extremely short-lived. The chartered spacecraft had barely flown two hundred kilometers from the station before its warp *and* impulse engines failed inexplicably, leaving it adrift in space, beyond the range of the station's tractor and transporter beams. With the station's own ship busy guarding the border of the Maelstrom, Tilton had been forced to respond to the *Wind*'s SOS by dragooning a handful of private vessels to assist in the rescue operation. Some had "volunteered" more readily than others, creating more tense situations for Sulu to handle.

It never rains but it pours, he thought.

Anticipating trouble, a full security team was on hand as the ship's captain and senior officers were the last to be beamed back aboard the station, after the *Solar Wind* was towed back within transporter range. Although no one had been harmed, an angry mob of unhappy customers awaited them, none too happy to find themselves where they started rather than en route to Baldur III.

"We want our credits back!" a rescued passenger demanded almost immediately. He shook his fist at the *Wind*'s captain, Zita Mansori. More voices added to the tumult. "We paid for a working ship, not a junk heap!"

"There's nothing wrong with my ship," Mansori said, bristling. "It passed every inspection."

"Then how come we're not on our way to Baldur III right now?" another displaced passenger challenged her. "Answer me that!"

"Honestly, I smell sabotage," Mansori answered. "Somebody wants to stop us from getting to our destination!"

Not a totally implausible explanation, Sulu thought, looking on from the sidelines. He wanted to dismiss Mansori's accusation as nothing more than an excuse to get herself and her ship off the hook, but, unfortunately, this was hardly the first such incident. Just yesterday, the docking clamps had refused to release a departing Tarkalean shuttle, delaying its exit by several hours, while yet another ship needed to turn back before they could get too far after their food processors turned out to be badly contaminated. None of these freak malfunctions had resulted in any serious injuries or fatalities so far, but their increasing frequency was worrisome. It was possible, he supposed, that the string of mishaps were simply the result of the headlong rush to Baldur III testing the resources of both ships and station, yet he couldn't rule out the possibility of foul play.

"Nonsense!" A colorful figure stepped forward to refute Mansori's charges. "Everyone knows the *Wind* is a worn-out relic that should have never been pressed back into service."

The speaker was a male Midasite with silver skin, golden eyes, a mane of curly gold hair, and a pencil mustache. His flamboyant attire had a piratical flair, complete with a fur-trimmed, jet-black jacket, checkered leggings, and broad-brimmed boots. Spican flame gems, flashy but of little value, studded his wide leather belt and a front tooth. Prominent canines gave him a carnivorous smile.

"Watch your mouth, Dajo!" the affronted captain snarled. "Don't you talk about my ship like that!"

"Fine," Dajo said. "I'll talk about my ship instead." He raised his voice to be heard over the general chatter. "The name's Mirsa Dajo, for those that don't know, and I still have a few berths left aboard my own ship, the *Lucky Strike*. You want to get to Baldur III, talk to me, although the seats are going fast so I wouldn't advise you to dither."

The *Lucky Strike*?

That's Helena's ship, Sulu realized. *And that must be her captain.*

A few of the *Wind*'s former passengers succumbed to Dajo's sales pitch and started shoving their way toward him, much to the dismay and outrage of Mansori.

"You!" she accused Dajo. "This was your doing all along! You sabotaged my ship in order to poach my passengers!"

He laughed out loud. "Keep telling yourself that, Zita."

Sulu signaled his team to get between the quarreling captains, even as Mansori and her officers surged toward Dajo, possibly looking for a fight. Complicating matters, Helena emerged from the crowd to stand beside her captain.

This is getting awkward, Sulu thought.

"Everyone cool down," he ordered. "Let's not start throwing wild accusations around, or rushing to judgment before the facts are in." Good thing he had enough security on hand to back up his authority. "Captain Mansori, I suggest you see to your ship and its repairs. Captain Dajo, if you could try to be a little less provocative when it comes to lining up customers . . ."

"Of course, Lieutenant," Dajo said amiably. "It was never my intent to stir up trouble. Just trying to come to the assistance of anyone inconvenienced by the *Wind*'s unfortunate lack of space-worthiness." He guided a collection of potential customers out into the promenade. "Now you understand that, due to the last-minute nature of the bookings, I need to charge a premium—"

Mansori glared at Dajo as he departed with many of her passengers, but thankfully limited herself to giving him the evil eye. Sulu admired her self-control as he made his way toward

Helena, who had lingered behind in the lobby of the transporter room.

"You have a moment?" he asked her.

"Sure. You up for that drink at last?"

"If only." He led her to a quiet corner where they could converse more privately. He glanced around to make certain they couldn't be overheard. "I don't want to put you on the spot, but I have to ask: Could there be any truth to Mansori's accusations?"

She stiffened, obviously taken aback by the question. Her inviting smile vanished faster than a Romulan bird-of-prey activating its cloaking device.

"Wait. Are you actually asking me if my captain is a saboteur?"

"Nothing personal," he insisted. "But I wouldn't be doing my due diligence if I didn't at least try to investigate any possible threat to the security of this station."

"And I wouldn't be much of a first officer," she countered, "if I went around gossiping about my captain."

"That's not a yes or a no."

He hated to press Helena like this, but if there was any chance that Dajo was sabotaging his competition, he needed to ask the hard questions, even if it meant risking their friendship—and spoiling their reunion.

"No!" she said emphatically. "Mirsa is no saint, and not above taking advantage of the *Solar Wind*'s bad luck, but he's no saboteur. You think I'd be working for him if he was capable of that?"

"Probably not," Sulu said, immediately regretting the "probably" part. "I mean, no, of course not, but is it possible that he could be up to something without you knowing? Can you think of him doing or saying anything suspicious lately?"

"Oh, so now you're implying that I'm simply clueless or a bad judge of character?" Her dark eyebrows dived toward each other to form a V that signified trouble for whoever had just got on her bad side. Her nostrils flared along with her temper. "Way to dig yourself out of a hole, Hikaru."

"This isn't about you . . . or us. I'm just asking for your help, in a professional capacity."

"Tell you what," she said. "I see anything 'suspicious,' I'll let you know. In the meantime, I'll thank you to not take the word of a disgruntled rival over my captain."

"Fair enough," he said, hoping to resolve the friction between them. Glancing about, he saw that the crowd had dispersed to some degree, even though there were still plenty of people waiting to use the transporters. With any luck, he had a few moments to kill before the next crisis demanded his attention. "I don't suppose you're ready for that drink now?"

He knew he was pushing his luck, but . . .

"Another time," she said, her tone frostier than Alfa 177 after sundown. "After all, I wouldn't want to get in the way of your 'professional' duties."

She turned and strode away from him without a backward glance.

Sulu sighed.

Saw that coming.

Eleven

Baldur III

"The skies are green and glowing, where my heart is, where my heart is . . ."

It was open-mic night at the Pergium Palace, one of Jackpot City's most popular night spots, or so Lieutenant Nyota Uhura had been informed. She enjoyed the spotlight as she sang out on an elevated stage at the center of the nightclub's bustling ground floor. The stage, which was roughly the size of the command circle on the bridge of the *Enterprise,* projected her voice and image all over the establishment, from a towering three-story-tall hologram to numerous viewscreens mounted about the club, above the bar, and throughout the gambling parlors on the mezzanine. As venues went, Uhura had to admit, it was rather more impressive than the rec room back on the ship.

The crowd was much bigger too. The club was packed with prospectors, both homegrown and otherwise, eager to unwind, along with plenty of busy workers—hosts, bartenders, servers, and dealers—ready to relieve them of any excess credits. The Pergium Palace, which, contrary to its name, was not actually made of pergium, was just one of several happening new watering holes that had sprung up in the wake of the colony's new-found prosperity, none of which came as any surprise to Uhura, who appreciated the importance of downtime. All mining and no play didn't sound healthy to her.

"Somewhere beyond the stars, beyond Antares . . ."

Enthusiastic cheers, whistles, and applause greeted the final chorus of her song. Gratified by the audience's response, she took a bow and descended a short ramp to the carpeted red floor, ceding the stage to the next hopeful performer. Her mouth was dry and she felt a bit out of breath, even though she'd heard that the Palace pumped extra oxygen into the air to keep its clientele hale and in high spirits, the extravagance paid for by the steady stream of credits flowing into the club's coffers everywhere she looked. Automated assayers, scattered through the premises, converted small quantities of ore into credits, to be spent on food, drinks, gambling, and recreation, not necessarily in that order. Uhura suspected that the real fortunes to be found on Baldur III these days came from making money off the miners instead of actually mining.

Probably safer and easier too.

Her red Starfleet uniform matched the Palace's vibrant carpet, tablecloths, and trimmings. Compliments on her singing trailed her as she scoped out the scene with a strategic eye. Although she appeared to be on leave, and had every intention of enjoying herself, she was actually on a mission for Captain Kirk, who had assigned her the task of taking the temperature of the colony by mingling with its residents in a more relaxed, less formal setting than, say, an administrative meeting or briefing. He wanted the real scoop from the ground, not just the "official" story. And if, in the process, she boosted the *Enterprise*'s standing in the community by launching a bit of a charm offensive . . . well, public relations were a form of communications, after all.

Hailing frequencies open, she thought. *Let's make some new friends.*

Booths and tables radiated outward from the stage in concentric circles, tiered so that most folks had a good view of the

entertainment, which currently consisted of a slightly intoxi-
cated prospector who was trying, with distinctly mixed results,
to wow the audience by combining juggling with Edosian hula
dancing. Uhura averted her eyes and checked out the crowd
instead. The majority of those present looked Baldurian to her,
but there were a decent percentage of new arrivals as well. Her
fellow crew members, easily spotted thanks to their bright red,
blue, and gold uniforms, were also well represented, socializing
with the civilians in the interest of winning their trust. Lieutenant Frank Hamm waved at Uhura from a nearby table, where
he appeared to be the life of the party. She returned the greeting
with a smile, but did not join him. She was not here to hang out
with her friends and colleagues from the *Enterprise*; she wanted
to get to know the people of the planet—and to let them get to
know her.

So where best to go about it?

She wove through the crowd, looking for a nice mix of locals
to engage with. There was some self-segregation going on, with
Andorians sitting with Andorians, and Troglytes sitting with
Troglytes, and so on, but not as much as one might fear, the con-
vivial atmosphere encouraging folks to interact with each other.
If there was not infinite diversity in infinite combinations, there
was at least reasonable diversity to a promising degree. Smiling,
she headed in the general direction of the bar.

"Brava! Brava! The songbird herself!"

A deep, jovial voice called out to her, coming from a grinning
stranger who appeared to be holding court in a crowded booth
up ahead. He was an older fellow of Falstaffian proportions,
who looked a bit like her favorite uncle back in Mombasa. An
embroidered silk caftan screamed both money and style. He had
one arm draped over the shoulder of an attractive younger man
sitting next to him. *Yep,* she thought. *Just like Uncle.*

"Why, thank you," Uhura replied. "That's one of my favorite
songs."

"I can see why," he said. "Your voice complements it exquisitely." He beckoned her toward the booth. "Would you care to join us for a drink or two?"

She considered his invitation. Although his attire suggested that he was a native Baldurian, she noted with approval that he had both locals and newcomers in his party. No Starfleet personnel yet, however. *Just what the captain ordered.*

"Don't mind if I do."

She looked in vain for an open space.

"Squeeze over, everyone," the man exhorted his companions. "Make room for the lovely chanteuse."

Uhura managed to squeeze into the booth across from her fan.

"Nyota Uhura," she introduced herself, omitting her rank to better blend in with civilians. "Thanks for having me."

"The pleasure is all ours. Oskar Thackery," he offered in return. "And this handsome lad is Rixon."

"Hi," his companion said rather languidly. His enticing green complexion suggested an Orion somewhere in his family tree. "Nice song."

"And as for the rest of these miscreants," Thackery continued, "I'm far too lazy to rattle off all their names. You'll pick them up as we go, I'm sure."

"Not to worry," Uhura assured him.

"You must be thirsty after that magnificent rendition," Thackery said. "Allow me to get you a drink." He called out to a teenage server a few tables away. "Flossi, my dear! We have a parched singer in need of your services!"

"Brake your thrusters, you demanding old reprobate," Flossi shot back lightly. "You're flush enough these days you can afford a little patience."

Thackery chuckled in response.

"Don't let her fool you. It's obvious I'm her favorite customer."

"That's what they all say." Flossi finished up at the other table before strolling over to the booth with exaggerated leisure. A blond beehive hairdo, a short turquoise skirt, and knee-high boots indicated that the latest styles had made it to Baldur III despite its remote location on the wrong side of the Maelstrom. "What can I do for you, Oskar?"

"Another round of drinks, if you please." He glanced at Uhura. "What's your poison, Nyota?"

Her throat craved something soothing. "Just some warm tea, with a squirt of honey if that's possible."

"Nothing stronger?" Thackery asked. "Surely you're not on duty?"

Not exactly, she thought. "Tea with honey is easier on my vocal cords."

"Can't argue with that. A true artist takes care of her instrument." He turned back toward Flossi. "One buttermint tea with honey, please. On my tab."

"Um, speaking of tea . . ."

Rixon called the server over and whispered something in her ear. Flossi looked sideways at Uhura, thinking something over, before nodding. "I'll be right back with your orders."

Uhura was pretty sure she knew what that exchange was about. She had been briefed regarding *nabbia* and its effects with reference to Mister Spock's mission to Yurnos. *I'm going to go out on a limb,* she thought, *and guess that the Palace serves a tea that isn't listed on the menu.*

Apparently *nabbia* use was indeed pervasive; something to report to the captain the next time she saw him, not that she intended to bust anyone's chops over a contraband beverage tonight. She was here to listen and learn, not judge.

"So," Thackery said. "Tell us about yourself, Nyota."

"Oh, my uniform speaks for itself. You all know what brings me to Baldur III." She deflected the query back toward her host. "I'm more interested in hearing your story. Looks like you're doing well for yourself these days."

"I cannot lie," he said. "Fortune has been kind. Mere months ago, I was barely eking out a living as a fungus farmer, cultivating specialty mushrooms while moonlighting as a notary to keep the wolf from the door. Then it turns out that my humble cabin is sitting on top of a king's ransom in pergium and, *voilà*, no more spores and fertilizer for me. And the best part is, I don't even have to dig up the ore myself. I just lease the mining rights out to interested parties and collect an equitable share of the profits."

"Some people get all the luck," a woman sitting next to Uhura groused. A sour expression made her look older than her years. Loose brown hair hung down to her somewhat bony shoulders. A khaki coverall clothed her frame. "We haven't all struck it rich, you know. Haven't found enough pergium on my property to power a small household fabricator."

"Take heart, Levity," Thackery consoled her. "Your ship may still come in. But don't think that I take my good fortune for granted. Rest assured, I'm more than grateful for the way the fates have smiled on me."

"Long as you keep picking up the tab," said Levity, whose name seemed at odds with her attitude. "Can't complain about that."

Flossi returned with their orders.

"Your prompt service impresses as always." Thackery produced a small metal canister from beneath his jacket and shook a pellet-sized nugget of pergium onto the table. "Don't forget your tip."

Flossi unclipped a microassayer from her belt and scanned the nugget. She whistled at the results before pocketing the tip. "Seventy-nine percent pure. Thanks, Oskar. You're not so bad sometimes."

"Music to my ears," he replied. "Just keep the libations coming."

Uhura observed Rixon enjoying his tea, although she tried not to be too obvious about it. "This is quite the establishment," she said of the Palace. "It always been this hopping?"

"Hardly!" Thackery said. "Before the boom times, Baldur III had no nightlife to speak of, aside from a handful of rustic taverns. This place was barely half the size it is now and nowhere near as lively. We called it Pioneer's Pavilion, and it mostly hosted the occasional dance, swap meet, holiday social, wedding, funeral, or community potluck. Maybe, if you were lucky, you could get a decent card game going upstairs." He mimed a yawn, before gesturing expansively at the teeming club surrounding them. "Now look at us! Jackpot City is livelier than Argelius on a Friday night."

"I don't know." Levity nursed some fizzy blue concoction, which didn't seem to be lifting her mood any. "My dad keeps saying things were better before the boom. Quieter, less hectic."

Thackery shrugged. "More boring, you mean."

"And then there's all the new people," Levity said. "Maybe too many." She glanced at Uhura. "Present company excluded, of course."

Uhura didn't take it personally. She sat back and listened attentively. This was just the kind of chatter she'd been hoping to tune in to.

"Beats the old days," Thackery insisted, "when all you ever saw was the same old faces, week after week, year after year. You could go ages without ever meeting anyone new, whereas nowadays we have a genuine Starfleet officer sitting at our very table."

"Happy to oblige," Uhura said. "Meeting new people and visiting new worlds is my job description."

"You're a breath of fresh air!" Thackery said effusively. "Reminding us that the universe is far bigger than this one little planet."

"That's what they tell me," Uhura replied, as Flossi returned to clear away some empty cups and plates. "Can't wait to find out for myself."

Uhura took advantage of the moment to get the young server's perspective. "What do you think of the recent changes, Flossi?"

"Oh, I'm making out like a bandit," she said, "and putting most of it away, unlike some big spenders I could name." She smirked at Thackery. "I'm saving up to see the galaxy, and not just on a viewscreen. No way am I going to stay glued to this gravity well for my whole life. I want to experience everything the quadrant has to offer, from the ruins of Camus II to the dragons on Berengaria VII."

"The dragons are definitely worth checking out," Uhura said. "My advice, go in springtime just as the babies are hatching."

Flossi gaped at Uhura. "You've actually been there?"

"Once or twice." Uhura was pleased to discover that, contrary to initial reports, not all of the original Baldurians had chips on their shoulders regarding new arrivals and the rapid changes to the colony. "You ever consider applying to Starfleet?" she asked Flossi.

"Is that even possible?" the teenager asked. "Considering we're not part of the Federation?"

"Definitely. There's probably some extra paperwork involved, but that's all. Why, I had a Betazoid roommate back at Academy."

"Not that it matters," Levity said. "The Feds are going to gobble us up soon enough."

"You think?" Rixon asked. The tea seemed to have perked him up some.

"Bound to happen eventually," Thackery said with a shrug.

"And that doesn't bother you?" Levity replied. "Baldur III losing its independence and becoming just another cookie-cutter Federation planet? No different than hundreds or thousands of others?"

Uhura felt compelled to speak up.

"Joining the Federation doesn't mean sacrificing your individual culture or the character of your community. The UFP isn't about homogeneity or conformity; it's about a wide variety of spacefaring civilizations, each with their own distinctive ways and customs and beliefs, working together in harmony and cooperation. I mean, look at how different Vulcans are from Tellarites, or humans from Kelpiens. Trust me, I've been to Andor and Izar, and the local cultures there are nothing alike. Why, even back on Earth, you would never confuse New Orleans with Baghdad or Havana, even though the planet has been unified for centuries. The only thing most Federation worlds really have in common is a shared commitment to peace, progress, and the Prime Directive."

She hadn't intended to make a speech, but she felt strongly about the subject.

"Well, you'd have to say that, wouldn't you?" Levity replied. "You're Starfleet. Starfleet and the UFP are pretty much the same thing."

"That's a common misconception," Uhura began, "but actually—"

"No more politics, please!" Thackery placed his hands over his ears. "This is a nightclub, not town hall. I hereby decree that any talk of politics be banished from earshot. Tonight is for fun and frivolity and good company."

Levity scowled. "Well, I was just saying—"

"Hush," he said. "Let's just enjoy ourselves."

"No problem." Uhura leaned toward Flossi and quietly addressed her. "Feel free to ask me about Starfleet some other time."

"Thanks," the server said. "I may take you up on that."

An excruciating aria from the stage, where a new performer was hitting notes that possibly only a Caitian could hear, elicited hisses and boos. Uhura felt sorry for both the singer and the audience. She spotted a few customers heading for the exits.

"Our ears are going to need soothing after this infernal caterwauling," Thackery said, wincing. He looked to Uhura. "Perhaps you can redeem the night by treating us to an encore?"

She judged that she was definitely making inroads when it

came to ingratiating herself with the locals. She looked forward to sharing what she'd learned with Captain Kirk as she polished off her tea, which was just as restorative as she'd hoped. She figured she had another song in her . . . for the sake of the mission, of course.

"Well, if you insist."

Twelve

Yurnos

"You don't think the smugglers might have a cloaking device, Mister Spock?"

Chekov and Spock had set up shop in the underground nerve center beneath the farmhouse, Jord having entered their biometrics into the automated security system. *Galileo* remained hidden in the nearby barn, where it would hopefully evade discovery for the duration of their mission. It occurred to Spock that a cloaking device would be convenient on undercover missions such as this one; alas, they were not standard issue on Starfleet shuttlecraft and were unlikely to ever become so.

"We cannot eliminate that possibility," he replied, "but I strongly doubt it. A Romulan-quality cloaking device is vastly more valuable than a cargo of bootleg tea, as well as being far beyond the reach of a mere smuggling operation. They are advanced military technology, not something one expects to find at the disposal of tea smugglers."

"I suppose," Chekov said, "but then how are the traders getting the *nabbia* on and off the planet without being detected? We inspected the observers' sensor equipment, and everything was in order. They should be able to detect any visiting vessels."

His accent rendered that last phrase "wisiting wessels," but

Spock was well accustomed to Chekov's occasionally Russian-flavored pronunciations. He barely noticed the peculiarity.

"That, Ensign, remains a puzzle to be solved."

The whoosh of a concealed panel sliding open heralded visitors.

"Hello, down there." Vankov descended the stairs, bearing a lightweight wooden carton, which he laid down on a counter. He paused to wipe the perspiration from his brow. "Took me the better part of the day, but I managed to obtain tea samples from pretty much every merchant in the province, to go along with the samples we provided you earlier. Thank goodness you only needed a pinch of each variety, or our household budget would be in tatters."

Spock could tell from the man's flushed features and sweaty aroma that he had indeed been out riding in the muggy weather for some time. He appreciated Vankov's strenuous efforts on their behalf.

"A 'pinch' will suffice for our purposes," Spock said. "I trust that you took note of where each sample was obtained and that they are each carefully labeled."

"Naturally, Mister Spock, just as you instructed." He gestured at his purchases. "See for yourself."

Spock rose from his seat at the primary workstation to inspect the contents of the carton. As promised, the box was filled with several small paper envelopes, each of which had been labeled in a neat and legible hand. A robust aroma confirmed that the envelopes contained samples of *nabbia* tea obtained from a variety of sources. Vankov reached beneath his jacket to produce a written document, penned in parchment and rolled into a scroll. He handed the scroll over to Spock.

"I made a list of where each sample came from as well."

Spock unfurled the scroll and examined the list, which appeared to be quite meticulous, even if he found the crude medium more inconvenient than quaint. It would be necessary to scan the document in order to transfer its content to the computer library. This was less than efficient, albeit unavoidable, considering the circumstances. He could hardly expect Vankov to roam the countryside with a data slate or tricorder in hand.

"Well done," Spock said. "Let us hope your labors prove fruitful to our cause."

Vankov looked pleased to be of use. He glanced around the control room. "So, any progress so far?"

"That depends on how you define progress," Chekov said. "We are getting nowhere very fast."

"Patience, Ensign. We are in fact making progress by eliminating possibilities via a methodical scientific approach to the problem."

Chekov sighed. He had been assiduously at work at the auxiliary station for some time. "Aye, Mister Spock. I did not mean to imply otherwise."

Spock opened one of the envelopes. Inside was a "pinch" of fresh tea, consisting of very thin shavings of *nabbia* root, each less than two millimeters in width. This particular batch appeared to have been aged for several weeks, giving it a darker color and more pungent odor than some other varieties. He noted with a twinge of disappointment that its color and scent were slightly different than the sample of bootleg *nabbia* they had obtained on Baldur III before departing for Yurnos, although he reminded himself that such superficial differences did not necessarily mean that they were not a match genetically; as he had learned, the manner of preparation could have a substantial effect on the tea's final appearance and properties, which was why a more rigorous analysis was mandated.

"To be more specific," he explained to Vankov, "we are attempting to determine the source of a specific variety of *nabbia* known to have been sold on Baldur III, in hopes that it will lead us to the smugglers. Variations in color and taste are inconclusive, so we are relying on DNA instead, searching for a genetic match to the contraband *nabbia*."

"Interesting," Vankov said. "That would have never occurred to me. Then again, as an anthropologist, I'm more interested in social evolution than genetic drift."

"You would not have been able to pursue this avenue of investigation in any event," Spock pointed out. "Not without a sample from Baldur III."

"True enough," Vankov conceded. "We weren't in a position to pop over to another planet to pick up some illicit tea. You needed to bring that incriminating evidence with you."

"Precisely," Spock said. "At present we have compared the bootleg tea to most of the samples from your pantry and personal stores without finding a match." He sealed the envelope and placed it back in the carton. "This larger selection of samples increases our chances of success."

He contemplated the many new samples to be tested. Although Spock liked to think that he worked more efficiently than most, he was glad that Chekov was on hand to share the workload and allow them to process the samples twice as fast. Despite his impatience, the young human had been both careful and diligent in his work.

"I should leave you gentlemen to your labors. Shall I prepare you a light repast? Jord usually frowns on eating in the nerve center, but we can probably make an exception in this case." He directed his attention to Spock. "I assume that, being Vulcan, you are a vegetarian?"

"That is correct," Spock said. "I hope that does not pose a—"

"*Bozhe moi!*" Chekov blurted. "Mister Spock! We have it!"

His obvious excitement caused Spock's own pulse to quicken although his stoic features displayed only curiosity. "A match?"

"Affirmative, sir!" Chekov reviewed the readings on the tricorder he had been using to analyze the samples on a genetic level. "This particular sample is genetically identical to the *nabbia* confiscated on Baldur III, right down to the last chromosome and base pair."

Vankov shared Chekov's emotive reaction. "Are you positive, Ensign?"

"Absolutely!" He hopped out of his seat and handed the tricorder to Spock. "Look, Mister Spock. Tell me I'm wrong."

Spock had no reason to doubt Chekov's findings, but he reviewed the readings on the tricorder's display. A side-by-side comparison of the samples' genomes confirmed that they were indeed identical beyond even a reasonable margin of error. It appeared that this tea came from the same source as the tea confiscated on Baldur III, which might be able to point them toward the identity of the smugglers.

"Excellent work, Mister Chekov." Spock called Vankov's attention to the sample Chekov had just scanned, which had come directly from the household's pantry. "Where was this tea obtained?"

Vankov examined the tea and its label. He held the dried flakes up to his nose and sniffed them. A grin broke out across his face.

"Oh, I'd know this tea anywhere. It's one of Eefa's."

Spock did not recognize the name. "Eefa?"

"A local tea merchant," Vankov explained. "She has a shop a few towns over." He sniffed the tea again. "Yes, this is definitely one of her more popular wares. Goes by the name of Suffusion." He shrugged modestly. "I fancy I've become something of a *nabbia* connoisseur in our years here."

Spock took his word for it. He preferred hard evidence to Vankov's nose, but it would be simple enough to verify the tea's provenance.

"I believe I should meet this Eefa."

Thirteen

Deep Space Station S-8

"Here she is, Lieutenant! The saboteur!"

Sulu hurried across the station's main shuttlebay, which was located at the "bottom" of the station's core, relative to its artificial gravity. Two security officers, Knox and Johann, accompanied him. He had responded quickly to a report of attempted sabotage to one of the shuttles parked in the hangar, but was careful to manage his expectations when it came to solving the mystery of the ongoing accidents and malfunctions. A certain degree of paranoia was running rampant on the station, resulting in an uptick of false alarms and red herrings that had taxed the already overworked security teams. Sulu wanted to think that an actual saboteur had been nabbed at last, but he knew better than to get his hopes up.

"Lieutenant Sulu?" a male Vernalian addressed him. A thick exoskeleton supported his invertebrate anatomy. "I'm Pilot First-Class Uco. I caught this individual snooping around my ship!"

His upper pincers had a tight grip on the arm of . . .

Helena?

"Let go of me!" she fumed as additional members of the Vernalian crew stood by, glowering at her. She fought to extricate her arm from the pilot's pincers. "For Athena's sake, I keep telling you, I was just looking to barter a spare transfer coil for a subspace radio control circuit. I was only eyeballing your ship because it looked like its basic components were compatible with the *Lucky Strike*."

Sulu glanced around, but didn't see Helena's ship in the hangar. As far as he knew, it was currently docked at one of the station's outer arms. He sighed wearily.

Another false alarm, he realized, *and Helena in the middle of it.*

"Everybody calm down," he said. "Sounds to me like this is just a simple misunderstanding."

"Yes! Thank you, Hikaru. That's what I keep saying."

Sulu wished she hadn't addressed him by his first name. He wanted to avoid even the appearance of favoritism.

"But she was carrying this," Uco insisted, holding up a well-equipped tool belt, which he had apparently taken off her. "And lurking suspiciously!"

"I wasn't lurking," she said. "I was window-shopping. So naturally I had my tools with me, in case I needed to inspect the merchandise."

"Sounds plausible to me." Sulu looked over the ship, which appeared undamaged. "Did either you or your crew find any evidence of sabotage or tinkering?"

"Well, no," Uco conceded. "Probably because we caught her just in time!"

"That's not enough to hold her on." Sulu stepped forward and released her from the pincers; to his relief, Uco did not resist. "But thank you for being on the alert for any possibly suspicious activity. Rest assured, we'll keep a close eye on her from now on."

"Keep a close eye on—" Her jaw dropped. "Seriously?"

He gave her a pointed look. *Just go with it, okay?*

"If you'll please come with me, ma'am."

She hesitated, then came around. "Fine. Whatever. I'm clearly not getting that circuit from these clowns." She snatched her tool belt back and glared at the Vernalians. "Hope you don't need an extra transfer coil at some point."

She took Sulu's arm as he guided her away from the ship, glad to have defused the situation without too much conflict. His security escort tagged along, looking relieved as well. They were heading for the nearest turbolift, when a sudden explosion blew out a small section of the ceiling high above their heads. Dust and debris rained down on the hangar floor as well as on the ships parked there. An emergency klaxon blared.

"Hikaru?" Helena said. "What is it? What's happening?"

"Damned if I know." He could practically feel the adrenaline flooding his system as he went into full alert mode. "Heads up!" he barked to his ensigns before shouting loudly to whoever could hear him. "Is anybody hurt? In need of assistance?"

He heard plenty of shouting and panic, but no immediate cries for help. Peering up at the ruptured ceiling, he assessed the damage; it didn't look as though any life-threateningly large chunks had fallen, nor did he see much in the way of flames. For a second, he allowed himself to hope that they had gotten lucky and there had been no serious casualties.

Then thick purple vapors started gushing from the rupture, hissing like a Regulan eel-bird. Sulu's eyes widened in alarm as he identified the toxic fumes.

"Plasma coolant!"

He knew how dangerous the gas leak was. Plasma coolant could suffocate most humanoid life-forms if they inhaled too much of it. The capacious volume of the shuttlebay bought them all a bit of time, as it would take a few minutes for the fumes to fill the hangar completely, but he could already hear people coughing and gasping in distress. He made a point to breathe through his nose even as the acrid odor of the coolant irritated his nostrils. He felt an itch at the back of his throat. His eyes began to water.

"Why aren't the emergency fans and filters clearing out the fumes?" Knox asked.

"I don't know, Ensign," Sulu replied. *More malfunctions? Sabotage?*

"Should we attempt to evacuate, sir?" Ensign Johann asked him.

"Not going to be that easy," Sulu feared. People were already streaming toward the turbolifts and emergency stairwells, only to find that they'd been automatically sealed off to contain the spread of the gas. It was possible that he could override them somehow, but first he had to keep himself and his team—and Helena—from asphyxiating before they could help anyone else. "Breathing masks. We need breathing masks, pronto."

"Over there." Helena pointed across the hangar while holding her other hand in front of her mouth, muffling her voice somewhat. "I spotted it while I was 'lurking' earlier."

Sure enough, an emergency supply closet, clearly labeled, was located against a bulkhead a few meters away. Sulu pried it open, triggering another alarm, and found maybe a dozen unused breathing masks at his disposal. More than enough, he assumed, for the shuttlebay back before the "gold rush," but not nearly sufficient now. He placed a mask over his nose and mouth, receiving immediate relief, before dealing them out to Helena and the two ensigns. The mask did a good job of filtering out the coolant while providing a limited amount of oxygen, which was generated by a chemical reaction that triggered as needed. Sulu took a deep breath, appreciating the fresher air, even though his eyes were still watering. He wiped the tears away to assess the situation.

It wasn't good.

Panicked people began collapsing onto the floor, while others were running around in distress. He suspected that some species had less lung capacity than others or might be more susceptible to the fumes. The purple vapor was spreading like a fog, filling up the hangar, making it difficult to see what was going on. The space door was in place, sealing the vapor in, and they couldn't open the door to vent the coolant into space without flushing everyone out into the vacuum as well.

Unless . . .

"We need to get everyone into the shuttles," Sulu ordered. The shuttles were airtight and equipped with their own life-support systems; they were the perfect shelters during this crisis even if they couldn't go anywhere yet. "Spread out! Hurry!"

"Aye, sir!" Knox said.

"We're on it!" Helena said, pitching in.

Sulu prayed that would be enough as he rushed toward a fallen humanoid who was gasping for breath like a fish out of water. He placed one of the extra breathing masks over the man's face, then helped him to his feet. Looking around, he saw that the nearest shelter was the Vernalian shuttle Helena had been accused of spying on earlier.

Here's hoping they're not still holding a grudge, he thought.

His arm around the other man, he half dragged, half carried the stricken traveler toward the shuttle's main airlock, which was already sealed against the fumes. Sulu couldn't blame the Vernalians for slamming the door shut, but he was sure they had room for more. He pounded on the solid duranium door with his fist.

"Open!" he shouted. "This is Lieutenant Sulu! I have a casualty!"

He could try to hail the shuttle via his communicator, but first he'd have to find the proper channel. Shouting was probably more efficient, as long as the Vernalians didn't choose to ignore him. He strained to keep his humanoid burden up on his feet. The man was still coughing hoarsely, despite his mask. He was clearly in need of medical attention.

"We have dying people out here! Open up!"

He briefly feared that the Vernalians were only concerned with their own safety, but the airlock hissed and the door slid open, revealing Uco wearing a different-model breathing mask, which Sulu assumed came from the shuttle's private stores. The mask was crafted to fit the insectoid contours of the pilot's features.

"Thanks!" Sulu thrust the shaky victim into Uco's arms. "I'm going back for more. Be ready for me!"

The airlock door whooshed shut behind him as he rushed back out onto the foggy hangar floor, drawn by the sound of coughing and labored breathing. He squinted desperately at the ceiling and saw that an engineering team had somehow managed to shut off the coolant leak, so that no more of the vapor was hissing from the rupture.

About time, he thought.

He fanned at the remaining fumes to see through them and spied several more figures sprawled on the floor, gasping for breath. People were succumbing to the fumes faster than Sulu and his allies could rescue them; even with Helena and the pair of officers backing him up, there was little chance that they could get all the imperiled victims into the shuttles before people started dying, if they hadn't expired already.

I'll just have to keep going and save as many as I can, he resolved. *And hope that Tilton and the others can get the vents and filters working again.*

He plunged into the toxic fog, practically stepping on another choking victim, who had already passed out from the fumes. Hefting her in a fireman's carry, he staggered back toward the Vernalian shuttle, while passing yet another casualty. He needed a lot more backup, but they were cut off from the rest of the station until the hangar could be vented. Sulu wondered if there was any time or point to applying triage to the victims when everyone outside the shuttles was in danger of asphyxiation.

How did he choose whom to save?

The responsibility weighed him down as heavily as the unconscious victim he was toting. His communicator chirped for his attention, but he wasn't about to put the woman down to answer it. He staggered toward the waiting shuttle, breathing hard, when he suddenly heard footsteps pounding the floor around him. Peering through the choking mist, he saw a slew of civilians, equipped with a variety of breathing masks and environmental suits, pour out of their respective shuttles to assist in the rescue operation, picking up the fallen off the floor and hustling them back into the nearest shuttles, which were all being drafted into service as emergency shelters.

Yes! Sulu rejoiced, overjoyed by the number of volunteers. It did his heart good to know that the headlong rush for pergium hadn't completely squashed people's better instincts. His throat tightened, and not from the fumes. *This is more like it!*

With many more hands to assist in the effort, the casualties were brought aboard the shuttles. Airlocks sealed, protecting them all from the leaking coolant. Sulu peeled off his sweaty breathing mask as he joined Helena and Uco in the cockpit of his shuttle, their previous enmity forgotten in the face of the greater emergency. Behind him, on the floor of the passenger compartment, a Denobulan medic was applying field treatment to the most severely affected casualties. His medical tricorder hummed repeatedly. A hypospray hissed.

Sulu trusted the medic to do his work, addressing Uco instead. "Are your short-range sensors operational?"

"No reason they shouldn't be," the pilot said. "Why?"

"Scan the hangar for life-forms." Sulu believed they'd managed to get everyone aboard a shuttle, but he wanted to verify that, especially with the swirling fumes impeding visibility. "I want to make sure we didn't leave anyone out there."

"Good thought." Helena sat down in the copilot's seat. Her voice was slightly hoarse from her brief exposure to the fumes. "If you don't mind, Pilot. At the risk of patting myself on the back, I have a knack for this kind of thing."

"Go ahead." Uco got up and headed back toward the passenger compartment. "I need to check on my people anyway."

Sulu plopped down into the vacated seat. He was feeling slightly short of breath himself, not to mention fatigued. His lungs and eyes burned. He made a mental note to have M'Benga check him out in the infirmary once the more injured patients were seen to. He watched tensely as Helena activated the sensor controls. The sooner they got those patients to the infirmary, the better.

"Well?" he asked.

"Just give me a moment." She deftly adjusted the control panels, then examined the readings. "I'm not picking up any life-signs outside the shuttles. Of course, that could mean—"

"In which case, there's nothing to be done for them," he said grimly. He plucked his communicator from his belt and flipped it open. "Sulu to Station Manager. Repeat: Sulu to Station Manager. Please respond."

Tilton replied almost immediately. Sulu assumed the man was in his office, attending to the crisis. His voice sounded more exhausted than agitated, as though he was nearing the end of his rope.

"Sulu? We tracked your communicator to the shuttlebay. Are you all right?"

"The situation is under control for the moment, but we have casualties in need of immediate medical attention. I need you to open the space doors so we can vent the gaseous coolant out into space."

"But the people in the hangar—?"

"Are secure within their vessels, Mr. Tilton. They'll be fine."

"Understood, Lieutenant. Stand by."

The massive space door retracted, separating into two halves as it opened up. Ordinarily, this would reveal the empty space outside the station, but the dense purple fog obscured the view. Only a force field remained between the hangar and the vacuum beyond. It crackled through the mist, as though fighting the increased air pressure.

"Lowering space door shields," Tilton reported.

The force field dissolved, opening the hangar up to the void. The shuttles themselves remained magnetically fixed to the floor, but the sudden decompression sucked the contaminated atmosphere out into space, along with miscellaneous objects discarded during the panic. Sulu flinched as a random data slate flew past the cockpit, followed by pieces of charred debris from the ceiling. He worried that vital evidence was being lost, but venting the coolant took priority. Investigating the explosion, and trying to determine its cause, would have to wait until later. The view from the cockpit cleared as the thick fog exited the hangar. A paper coffee cup joined the other refuse tumbling out into the vacuum.

No bodies, that he could see.

"Nice work, Hikaru," Helena said. "I hope you're not going to blame this on Mirsa too."

He couldn't tell if she was teasing him or if she was still irked that he had discreetly questioned her about her captain earlier. Maybe a little bit of both?

"That depends." He tried to maintain a light tone. "Just how expendable does your Captain Dajo think you are?"

"Ha-ha," she replied. "Very funny. And the answer, by the way, is not one bit."

"Smart man." Sulu was encouraged by their easy banter. "Seriously, however, I have absolutely no reason to suspect Dajo more than any other visitor to the station. Still, I can't believe this was just another accident. A freak explosion *and* the emergency systems malfunctioning?" He shook his head. "There have been too many accidents and systemic failures. People are getting hurt. Lives are in danger."

And no ship is safe, he thought.

He made a snap decision. "Can you patch my communicator into the station-wide public-address system?"

"Can a Horta burrow through solid stone?" She scoffed at his inquiry. "I'm a communications specialist, remember?"

"Absolutely," he said. "Do it."

"Aye, aye, Lieutenant." She gave him a mock salute and plucked what looked to be a customized earpiece from her poncho. She brushed back her hair and affixed it to her ear. It chirped as she activated it and sparkled like a piece of jewelry. Her fingers fiddled expertly with the cockpit's comm controls until his own communicator chirped in response. She nodded at him. "You're on."

He coughed and cleared his throat before raising the communicator to his lips. A glass of water would have eased his irritated throat and lungs, but there was no time for that. For all he knew, another ship could be preparing to disembark from the station at any moment. He was aware of several planned departures on the schedule.

"This is Lieutenant Sulu, acting commander of the Starfleet personnel assisting in the management of this station. On my authority, I'm instituting a temporary lockdown until certain security issues are resolved. No vessels are allowed to arrive or depart for the time being. We ask for your patience and cooperation. Sulu out."

He cut off the transmission and closed his communicator. Helena gaped at him.

"Hoo boy." She whistled in appreciation. "That's not going to make you any friends."

"I don't expect it to."

He regretted taking unilateral action without consulting Tilton and Grandle, but, in his judgment, every moment had counted. They could debate his decision later. In the meantime, he wasn't willing to risk another ship venturing out into space or arriving at the station, not with a saboteur on the loose. Any vessel could become a death trap.

"I don't imagine your captain is going to be too pleased," Sulu said.

"Oh, he's going to be hopping mad," she said confidently. "The *Lucky Strike* is all booked up, at premium prices, and almost ready to take off for Baldur III."

Sulu suspected that Dajo wouldn't be the only one upset by the lockdown.

"What about you?" he asked Helena. "Do you think I made the right call?"

She paused before answering.

"Honestly . . . I'm not sure."

Fourteen

Yurnos

Wavebreak was a modestly sized seaport about half a day's ride from the mill. A marmot-drawn wagon brought Spock and Chekov to the edge of the town, where Jord dropped them off to avoid attracting too much attention to herself. A country road, running along a rocky coastline, led toward the port, whose outer buildings could be spied in the near distance. Sailing ships, sporting brightly colored banners, were docked at piers roughly half a kilometer away.

"Sorry I can't take you straight to Eefa's shop, but I need to be discreet. I'd rather not be seen chauffeuring a pair of strangers through the middle of town."

"Your caution is well warranted," Spock said. "We can manage from here."

"Just follow the directions we gave you, and you'll be fine. Good hunting."

She turned the wagon around and started back toward the mill as the men set off on foot for the town. It was midafternoon, but the weather was still hot and humid, relieved only by drifting white clouds and a briny breeze blowing off the harbor. Both men had changed into native garb, borrowed from Vankov, their phasers and communicators hidden beneath linen vests and jackets. A stitched leather satchel, slung over Spock's shoulder, held his tricorder. Wide-brimmed hats protected their heads from the sun, while also helping to conceal the tapered points of Spock's ears. He hoped that would be sufficient to disguise his alien origins.

At least the Yurnians do not sport horns, antlers, fur, or scales.

A short hike brought them into the town proper, where the dirt road evolved into a wide city street paved with seashells. Spock noted that shells of various colors and sizes were widely used as decoration throughout the town, often in the form of mosaics adorning the entrances of assorted shops, taverns, and temples. Some such mosaics displayed geometric patterns similar to those displayed on the carpet at the farmhouse— apparently a popular design in this region of Yurnos—while others were less abstract, advertising the nature of the various shops and businesses by depicting cups, baths, cakes, candles, and so on. Townspeople strolled the sidewalks, largely ceding the streets to carts and wagons. Harnessed marmots padded down the streets, occasionally leaving their droppings behind. He and Chekov drew a few curious looks, but no one appeared particularly startled or alarmed by their presence. It occurred to him that a seaport would likely be accustomed to travelers and traders from elsewhere. He wondered if that characteristic had attracted the anonymous smugglers to Wavebreak in the first place, on the assumption that they would attract less notice here.

A plausible theory, he thought.

"What do you think, Mister Spock?" Chekov asked, keeping his voice low. "Do you really think this Eefa person can lead us to the smugglers?"

They had already discussed this on the way to town, but Spock had long since accepted that humans were often uncomfortable with silence and felt a need to generate "small talk," even if this meant repeating themselves.

"That the bootleg tea came from Eefa's shop is our most promising lead," Spock said. "I lack sufficient data, however, to estimate any probability of success when it comes to locating the actual smugglers trespassing on Yurnos."

According to Jord and Vankov, Eefa was incontrovertibly a native Yurnian, born and raised in this vicinity, whose family and origins were a matter of record. It stood to reason therefore that she was not one of the actual smugglers, although it remained to be determined whether she was at all aware of where her tea was going. It was entirely possible, he reminded himself, that Eefa was simply an innocent tea merchant who had never heard of Baldur III, let alone the Prime Directive.

"But what if we don't learn anything from Eefa?" Chekov asked. "What then?"

"We will cross that bridge when we come to it, Ensign. In the meantime, we appear to have arrived at our destination."

Eefa's tea shop was located on a quiet side street within sight of the docks. The mosaic above the doorway depicted a *nabbia* bush, denoting the nature of her business. A whistle sounded as they entered the shop, thanks to a small bellows attached to the door's hinges. Spock admired the ingenuity of the simple mechanism.

Very creative.

The robust aroma of *nabbia* permeated the interior of the store, which was relatively cool compared to the heat outdoors. The front of the store displayed a wide selection of pots, cups, saucers, empty glass canisters, and other paraphernalia, while the actual tea was stored in a wall of wooden racks behind a long rectangular counter. A mechanical scale rested atop the counter. An erasable slate announced current prices and specials. Spock noted that Suffusion was among the varieties of tea being offered.

"Cozy shop," Chekov commented. "Very tidy."

The shop was occupied only by a hefty male Yurnian sitting on a stool in one corner, fanning himself with a paper fan bearing the same logo seen above the door. A colored bandanna covered his pate, a fashion choice often adopted, according to Vankov, by Yurnian men who were losing their hair, as they were apparently prone to do as they aged. The man looked the newcomers over, but made no effort to stir from his perch. A single grunt acknowledged their arrival.

Security, Spock surmised. *Not a salesclerk.*

"Hello?" Chekov said.

"Be right with you!" a chipper voice called from a back room. A Yurnian woman emerged to greet them, bustling up to the counter. She was a handsome older woman wearing an apron over her everyday attire. A bun of auburn hair was piled atop her head. Calculating blue eyes struck Spock as possibly out of alignment with her broad professional smile. "Well, well, I see we have some new faces visiting us today. Take off your hats, gents, and make yourselves at home. Let me get a better look at your handsome faces."

"As you wish."

Spock removed his hat, not wishing to offend. A tightly wound bandanna, similar to the one sported by the guard, protected the tips of his ears from scrutiny. Chekov doffed his hat as well; a mop of dark hair explained his lack of a bandanna.

"There now," the woman said. "My name's Eefa. How can I help you fine gentlemen?"

"I am Fultar, and this is Tocas," Spock stated, using names supplied by Jord and Vankov, who had assured their visitors that the aliases were so common as to be forgettable. "We represent a trading company that is interested in purchasing large quantities of *nabbia* on a regular basis."

"Is that so?" Eefa's smile grew even broader, her eyes even more calculating. "Any variety in particular?"

Spock played the next card in his deck. "I understand Suffusion is quite popular."

The name did not provoke a visible response beyond a flicker of avarice. Spock had hoped for a more telling reaction.

"A delicious tea. Very much in demand." She inspected his attire as though assessing his income. "How much are you looking to pay?"

"We have considerable resources," Spock said, "but would prefer to trade in goods rather than local currency."

"Interesting." She leaned across the counter. "What are you looking to trade?"

Spock nodded at Chekov, who produced a felt bag from his vest pocket. Chekov opened the bag and spilled a handful of polished trillium beads onto the table. Their lustrous black gleam attested to their appeal and value.

The gems came from a trillium bracelet in Jord and Vankov's collection of contraband. Spock had judged the Klingon and Capellan artifacts too distinctive to recycle, but hoped that the trillium beads would be less distinctive if no longer in the form of a bracelet. It was a calculated risk, but he had deemed it preferable to introducing yet another offworld item to Yurnos. And if it happened that Eefa *did* recognize the gems . . . that too could be informative.

"There is more where these came from," Chekov stated. "Much more."

Eefa's eyes lit up at the sight of the trillium, but a new wariness entered her face and body language as well. Spock could practically see her go to yellow alert. Her eyes went from wide to narrow. Her smile became more forced.

"Seems to me I've seen beauties like these before." She lifted her gaze from the gems to appraise her visitors once more. "Where exactly did you say you were from again?"

"We did not specify that," Spock said.

He could not even hint at space travel or other worlds without knowing whether or not Eefa was aware that she had sold *nabbia* to aliens.

"You're going to have to do better than that," Eefa insisted. "If you're foreigners, there's legalities to be observed. Taxes and tariffs and duties, all of which need to be carefully recorded so the governor's tax men get their share. And if you're thinking of a serious, long-term business arrangement . . . well, you'll need to be registered as foreign trading partners, times being what they are."

Spock rather doubted that the anonymous smugglers observed such niceties.

"That would be . . . inconvenient for us. We would prefer to keep our transactions off the books, as it were."

"Ah, so that's how it is." She mulled the matter over, as though weighing caution against profit, before addressing the guard. "Woji, I think this business requires some privacy." She glanced at the doors and windows. "If you don't mind . . ."

The guard grunted in assent. Hopping off his stool, he locked the front entrance and pulled some blinds down over the windows. Eefa turned up a lamp to compensate for the sunlight being blocked by the blinds.

"There; now we can speak frankly." She faced Spock and Chekov with her hands upon her hips. "What makes you think that I would be party to such an arrangement?"

"We were drawn by the quality of your wares," Spock suggested, wanting to draw her out. His goal, after all, was to extract vital intelligence from her without compromising his own mission.

"No, there's more to it than that," she said, shaking her head. "I'm not the only tea dealer in this province, let alone this town, and yet somehow these beauties"—she gestured at the trillium—"have found their way to my shop again? Don't tell me that's mere coincidence."

"I would not insult your intelligence by doing so," Spock said. "In truth, we have reason to believe that you have conducted similar transactions with other traders."

"What other traders?" she quizzed him.

She wants to know how much I know, Spock realized, *while*

I seek to discover how much she knows about the smugglers and their operation.

He regretted that Captain Kirk was not at hand to conduct this negotiation. He excelled at such exercises, which he often likened to human card games. Spock preferred chess himself, but had been told he had a good poker face.

"Strangers from afar," he said, "such as ourselves."

"Friends of yours?"

"Let us say that we are in the same business," he said with deliberate vagueness.

"Ah, I get it now." Comprehension dawned on her face. "You're the competition, looking to horn in on their business."

"In a manner of speaking," Spock said, going along with her narrative. "We represent another, larger trading company with an interest in absorbing our colleague's operation, on terms equitable to all, naturally. Perhaps you can arrange an introduction?"

"We can make it worth your while." Chekov scooped up the trillium and placed it back in his bag. "If you're interested."

Her eyes tracked the bag as he returned it to his pocket. She licked her lips, clearly unwilling to part with it. She looked Spock squarely in the eyes.

"Are you willing to put that in writing?" she asked.

"Is that necessary?" Spock asked. He could not imagine that such a contract could be legally enforceable under the circumstances. "As mentioned, we prefer to keep our business off the books."

"This would be just between us," she said, "to jog your memory just in case you suddenly remember this conversation differently once I've fulfilled my part of the bargain." She smirked at them. "You know the old saying, 'Memories fade faster than ink.'"

"Ah, yes," Chekov said, unconvincingly. "That old saying."

"My family came over from the Old Kingdom," she said

proudly. "That was two generations ago, but I learned the old wisdoms on my mother's knee and hold to them to this day."

She drew a parchment and a coral pen from a drawer beneath the counter and hastily dashed off a letter of agreement. "Shall we agree to goods equivalent to, say, two hundred *zeels* in exchange for me facilitating a meeting between you and certain customers, with a ten percent bonus if the meeting yields the desired outcome?"

"Those terms are acceptable," Spock said, declining to haggle over payments he had no intention of making. A contract to enable an illegal conspiracy was null and void by definition, nor did he wish to insert any further non-Yurnian goods into the planet's economy. He took the document from Eefa and briefly reviewed it, having acquired a rudimentary knowledge of the written language while studying Yurnos earlier. "Shall I sign at the bottom?"

He reached for the pen, but she refused to surrender it. She put the pen away and extracted another sharp piece of coral, which she handed to Spock instead.

"Not in ink," she specified. "Blood, as tradition requires for bargains of import. 'Swear by the heart, sign by the blood,' as the saying goes."

Spock found himself wishing that Eefa was less of a traditionalist. Her stipulation posed a difficulty: Yurnians did not boast green blood.

He attempted to pass the coral needle to Chekov. "Would you care to do the honors?"

"What's the matter?" Eefa said, the evasion not escaping her notice. "Your own blood is too good to seal a deal with?"

"I am merely prone to infections," Spock said.

"Don't be ridiculous," she said, frowning. "Nobody ever died of a pinprick." She shared a glance with Woji, who loomed ominously behind them. "Or is it that you don't truly wish to commit to this pact?"

"I am quite sincere," he lied.

"Then why balk at signing the proper way?" She took the parchment back from him and tore it up. "I can't do business with someone I can't trust, and I can't trust anybody who won't spill a few drops of blood as a show of good faith. A pity, truly. I'd thought we might all profit from our acquaintance, but it seems I was mistaken."

"Let's not be too hasty," Chekov said. "Perhaps we can still work this out."

"Too late for that, I think." She pointed toward the exit. "You'd best leave now."

Woji grunted in agreement.

"I disagree." Spock was not ready to depart as they had yet to achieve their aims. To retreat now would leave them no closer to tracking down the smugglers and shutting down their operations. Better perhaps, he concluded, to force a confrontation in hopes of inducing the opposition to show their hands.

"What was that?" Eefa said, bristling. "This is my shop. I decide when it's time for you to go. Isn't that right, Woji?"

The guard massaged his knuckles. Spock ignored him.

"Let us dispense with polite circumlocutions," he said. "We all know that you have been selling your tea—Suffusion, in particular—to smugglers in exchange for exotic goods which you then sell on the black market. We are in pursuit of the smugglers and will not be deterred. You can answer our questions . . . or would you prefer that we summon the local constables?"

She blanched at the suggestion.

"I've done nothing wrong. I'm a tea merchant. I sold tea. Where's the crime in that?"

"That is for your own magistrates to decide," Spock said, "but surely you are aware that your customers have secrets to hide, and that you are abetting them by helping them to conceal their illicit activities."

Spock wished he knew more about her actual dealings with

the smugglers, as well as whatever local regulations she may have bypassed. He could only hope that her guilty conscience would fill in the blanks in his accusations.

"You tell her, Mister . . . Fultar," Chekov said, playing along. He subjected Eefa to a stern gaze. "You're up to no good, and you're not going to get away with it."

"Is that so?"

She drew a flintlock pistol from beneath the counter and aimed it at Spock. It was a primitive firearm, not nearly as sophisticated as a phaser or disrupter, but possibly even more dangerous at close range. Old-fashioned projectile weapons could not be set on stun, as Spock knew from painful experience. He had once been shot—and nearly killed—by an equally crude firearm.

"Stay where you are," she ordered. "You had your chance to leave peacefully, but, no, you had to make trouble." She peered at them above the muzzle of the pistol. "Who are you exactly? And what made you think you could bully me in my own shop?"

"We are no one you want to pull a weapon on," Chekov blustered. "I'll tell you that."

The young ensign's tense body language indicated that his human fight-or-flight reaction was urging him to action. Spock suspected that Chekov was only moments away from drawing his phaser or perhaps springing forward to wrest the pistol from Eefa's grip; as both he and Spock were well trained in various forms of combat, it was likely they could subdue both Eefa and her guard if necessary, but that would not gain them any more information than they already possessed. Allowing Eefa the upper hand for the time being was more likely to yield significant revelations, albeit at some risk to their personal safety.

"We are at a distinct disadvantage," he advised Chekov. "I suggest we comply."

Chekov shot him a puzzled look, as though uncertain why they were not making more of an effort to defend themselves,

only to catch on belatedly. He nodded at Spock, somehow resisting the urge to wink. Spock admired his restraint.

"Of course, Fultar. I understand."

"Now you're talking sense," Eefa said. "Shame it took so long."
Brandishing the pistol, she gestured toward a curtained doorway at the rear of the shop. "Take them in the back while I figure
out what to do with them."

Woji escorted them into a back room behind the wall of tea
racks. The chamber appeared to combine the functions of office
and storeroom. Ledgers were piled atop a desk. Canvas bags and
metal canisters held additional stock that had not yet made it to
shelves. Barrels were tied together by lengths of sturdy chain. A
wastebasket needed emptying.

"Search them," she instructed Woji.

The guard frisked the prisoners, grunting as he confiscated
their phasers and communicators. Despite the logic of letting
themselves be captured at this juncture, Spock flinched inwardly at the loss of the devices, which represented yet another
potential source of cultural contamination. It had been a risk
carrying the items on their persons, but one could hardly go
searching for criminals unarmed and with no means of calling
for assistance. Woji's hands-on search provided an opportunity
for a judicious nerve pinch; Spock relinquished that chance, but
not without reservations. He hoped he would not regret that lost
opportunity later.

Playing it safe, on the other hand, will get us nowhere.

Woji presented his discoveries to Eefa, who did not seem
nearly as confounded by them as perhaps she should have been.
If anything, her eyes widened in recognition.

"I knew it!" she exclaimed. "You're from Collu S'Avala too!"

Chekov blinked in confusion. "Colloo savalla?"

"Don't play dumb," Eefa said. "Collu S'Avala. The mystical
kingdom far across the waves, atop the highest mountains,
where you obviously hail from." She toyed with the phaser in a

way that Spock found somewhat troubling. "Where else could you have obtained these marvels?"

Spock thought he understood. The name had escaped his studies of Yurnos, but Collu S'Avala appeared to be some fabled, supposedly distant realm that was likely more myth than reality, not unlike Shangri-La, Atlantis, or Sha Ka Ree.

"And that is where you believe your mysterious trading partners come from as well?" he asked Eefa. "From Collu S'Avala?"

"None other," she replied. "Some believe it is just a legend, but I always knew it was real."

All became clear to Spock. It was evident that Eefa did not know that her clients were from another world. Instead she had been led to believe that they came from a mythical land embedded in the lore of the planet. Spock greeted this realization with some relief; playing on the local folklore was preferable, from the standpoint of the Prime Directive, to prematurely introducing Yurnians to the reality of interstellar travel and societies. He resolved to do nothing to disabuse her of the notion.

"A logical conclusion," he told her. "I cannot refute it."

"I should think not." She kept the pistol trained on the captives. "Tie them up and gag them," she instructed Woji. "I need to think."

Spock considered resisting, but decided there was still more to be learned about the actual smugglers, so he stood by calmly. Eefa looked to be in no hurry to eliminate them, suggesting that she was merely a greedy tea dealer, not a murderer. This struck him as eminently plausible; furtively selling *nabbia* to smugglers was one thing, committing cold-blooded homicide was another.

Spock was caught off guard, however, when Woji roughly yanked his bandanna off, exposing the Vulcan's ears. Spock assumed that the guard had simply intended to use the cloth as a gag, but the results were far more consequential. Woji backed away, gasping instead of grunting, while Eefa gaped at Spock in a way that implied that she had never laid eyes on a Vulcan before.

"Uh-oh," Chekov said glumly.

Spock shared the sentiment.

"Your ears!" Eefa said redundantly. "Who . . . what are you?"

"An accident of birth," Spock stated, hoping to salvage the situation. "Nothing to concern you."

"Don't tell me what to be concerned about, you . . . whatever you are."

Her voice quavered while becoming shriller as well. She was clearly more agitated by his ears than by the sophisticated electronic devices they had been carrying. Spock was suddenly very glad that she had not been exposed to the sight of his verdant blood, even if his refusal to sign the contract had placed him and Chekov in their present predicament.

"These waters are too deep for me," she lamented. "Finish tying them up while I reach out to our other friends from across the seas. They had better know what to do!"

Woji eyed Spock uneasily, but worked up the nerve to bind the prisoners' arms behind their backs with thick lengths of chain at hand in the storeroom. Metal locks clamped shut, holding the chains in place. Pistol in hand, Eefa observed the procedure even as she retrieved a surprising item from a desk drawer: a modern communicator, not unlike the ones taken from Spock and Chekov.

The plot thickens, Spock thought.

The communicator was notably generic in design, making it difficult to link to any specific world or species. It was a simple civilian model of the sort that could be acquired at any common port of call, such as Deep Space Station S-8 for instance, but not on a world as technologically undeveloped as Yurnos. Spock deduced that Eefa had received the device from the smugglers. It chirped as she switched it on.

"Hello, hello?" she said into the communicator. She paced about the back room impatiently. "Answer me, curse your skins. I need to talk to you at once!"

A blinking violet light indicated that her hail had been received. She stepped away and turned her back on the prisoners, but Spock's keen hearing allowed him to easily eavesdrop on the discussion.

"We hear you," a male voice replied. *"What's so urgent?"*

"We've strangers poking around, asking questions and wanting answers. Strangers of your sort, no less."

"Our sort? What do you mean by that?"

"From your corner of the world, I mean. Well, one of them is. I don't know where the other comes from. He doesn't look like any person I've ever laid eyes on. His ears are pointed . . . like a *whysser* tree leaf."

"Whatever that is." The anonymous voice sounded annoyed at being bothered. *"Just get rid of them. Send them away."*

"It's too late for that. They already know too much for my peace of mind. I've got them wrapped up tight in the back of my shop, but I can't hold them here indefinitely. We need to do something about them!"

"So dispose of them."

"Oh, no," she protested. "You're not sticking me with this. This is your business, your affair, your people. You need to deal with this!"

"What exactly do you expect us to do?"

"I don't know. That's your problem. I just want them off my hands and out of my hair. Do you understand me?"

Spock listened intently. From what he heard, his strategy was working even better than he had hoped. If Eefa had her way, they might soon be face-to-face with the smugglers themselves. Matters were proceeding in a most productive manner.

Aside, that was, from the unfortunate matter of their captivity.

Fifteen

Deep Space Station S-8

Less than an hour after the emergency in the shuttlebay, Sulu emerged from the infirmary, which had been forced to cannibalize adjacent storage areas and a gymnasium in order to accommodate all the new patients. Doctor M'Benga had given Sulu a clean bill of health, more or less, while advising him to get some rest.

Right, Sulu thought. *Like that's going to happen.*

A mob of angry civilians had already gathered outside Tilton's office to protest the lockdown. Grandle blocked the entrance, backed up by a trio of stone-faced station security personnel. She shouted over the frustrated crowd, struggling to maintain order.

"Dial it down, everybody! Mister Tilton is reviewing the situation and will release a statement soon. We appreciate your concerns, but all this commotion isn't helping. The sooner you let us do our jobs, the sooner we can straighten this out."

"And how long is that going to take?" Mirsa Dajo stood out among the protesters. "I have passengers booked for Baldur III. I can't afford to keep them waiting!"

"And I'm one of those passengers," a nameless Tiburonian said, his species evident from his exaggerated earlobes. "I've staked everything on this expedition! You can't strand me here!"

A chorus of voices, from both skippers and would-be miners, added to the tumult. Sulu pined briefly for the (apparently short-lived) teamwork and unity displayed during the crisis in the shuttlebay. It was discouraging to see people clashing angrily again now that the immediate emergency was over for the time being.

"That was my call," he said loudly. "If you have any issues with it, take them up with me . . . after I've had a chance to confer with Mister Tilton and Chief Grandle."

Braving the gauntlet, he strode through the crowd, which grudgingly parted to let him through. Complaints, demands, questions, and curses pelted him, reminding him of the treatment Tilton had gotten when the landing party from the *Enterprise* had first beamed aboard several days ago. Grandle's eyes tracked Sulu's progress toward the office door, her beefy arms crossed atop her chest. Her stoic expression would have done Spock proud, providing no clue as to what kind of reception Sulu could expect from her.

"Sulu," she greeted him.

He nodded at the door. "He waiting for me?"

"What do you think?"

Leaving her people to guard the door, Grandle led Sulu into the office. Tilton was slumped in the chair behind his desk, staring off into space. His eyes were vacant, as though his spirit had already departed his body. He barely acknowledged Sulu's arrival, merely lifting his head to look at the newcomers. The strain of the last few months was obviously getting to him. Sulu regretted adding to his troubles.

"Sorry for setting off that brouhaha out there," he began.

"Don't apologize," Grandle said. "You made the right call."

Sulu was pleasantly surprised by her reaction. "I did?"

"In my book, yes," she said. "We've obviously got a serious problem on our hands, so we can't take any chances. Business as usual is going to have to wait until we can guarantee the safety of this station by finding out who is responsible for these incidents."

"My thoughts exactly." Sulu was glad to find Grandle on the same page. He turned toward Tilton, who had the final say on the matter. "Do you feel the same way, sir?"

"What's that, Lieutenant?" Tilton asked, as though he hadn't been paying attention. He stared out the viewport gazing blankly at the rotating arms of the station and the crowded space beyond. His voice was hollow, affectless.

"The lockdown, Mister Tilton," Sulu prompted. Despite his preemptive action, he had no desire to usurp the manager's authority. It would be better for all concerned if they presented a unified front on the controversial move. "Do we have your okay?"

"I suppose." Tilton shrugged, seemingly worn out. "Do whatever you have to, Lieutenant."

"Thank you, sir."

The man's condition worried Sulu, who wondered if he should have M'Benga discreetly check the older man out. The last thing the station needed during this crisis was an overwhelmed manager who had checked out mentally and physically. Sulu started to turn away from Tilton, to confer with Grandle, when the manager startled Sulu by speaking up again.

"Lieutenant Sulu?"

"Yes?"

"The incident in the shuttlebay?" Tilton roused himself to ask. "How bad was it? How many hurt . . . or worse."

"No fatalities that we know of," Sulu said, although any bodies would have been swept out into space when the hangar depressurized. Short-range scanners were now searching the surrounding vacuum for any possible humanoid remains. "Doctors M'Benga and Trucco have already discharged the majority of the victims, who were just suffering from treatable respiratory problems, but are keeping roughly eleven patients under observation, just to be safe. They expect everyone to make a full recovery . . . eventually."

Sulu's own throat and lungs felt raw and scratchy, but that was the least of his concerns. "It could have been a lot worse."

"Thank goodness," Tilton said. "Thank goodness . . ."

His voice trailed off as his gaze drifted back to the view outside his viewport. His face went slack as his eyes emptied out again. Sulu shared a concerned look with Grandle, who could hardly miss how out of it Tilton was. The security chief shrugged helplessly.

Looks like it's just the two of us for the duration, Sulu thought.

Sixteen

Yurnos

The wagon rolled over a bumpy road, which did not make the ride any more comfortable for Spock and Chekov, who were stowed in the back with the rest of the cargo, hidden beneath a coarse, heavy tarp. Barrels of *nabbia* shared the bed of the open buckboard wagon with the captured Starfleet officers as, unable to see anything, Spock relied on his other senses. The paws of harnessed marmots padded against the road as a team of four pulled the wagon, whose squeaky axles needed oiling. By his reckoning, they had left Wavebreak behind and were now making their way down a lonely, unfrequented road late at night. The smell of brine and the persistent sound of waves crashing against rocks indicated that they were hugging the shore, en route to a clandestine rendezvous with the smugglers, whom Eefa had, with some effort, persuaded to meet with her at their usual spot.

So far, so good, Spock thought, *after a fashion.*

Ironically enough, Eefa was doing precisely what she had originally agreed to do: facilitate a meeting with the smugglers.

Although, admittedly, the conditions were less than ideal.

He and Chekov remained bound and gagged, unable to communicate with each other. Spock tested the chains binding his wrists behind his back, which proved stronger than anticipated. He had to commend Yurnian metallurgy; the chains resisted even his Vulcan strength. It was possible that, with significant time and effort, he could break his bonds, but not without attracting undue attention from their captors, who were at present seated at the front of the wagon, less than a meter away.

"Hurry it up," Eefa urged Woji, who was apparently driving the wagon, while his fidgety employer sat beside him, carrying on a one-way conversation with the guard, who Spock was beginning to suspect was literally mute. "And keep your eyes sharp and your ears pricked. Wouldn't do to run across any pesky revenue agents out hunting for honest smugglers. As far as I know, they haven't caught wind of our favorite cove yet, but you never know. 'No secret stays such forever,' as they say."

The wagon paused, causing Spock to wonder if they'd reached their destination. He heard Woji dismount and lumber to the right side of the road, where, from the sound of it, he exerted himself to move some heavy object, possibly a boulder or log. Brush rustled as well, as though being shifted out of the way. Eefa scooted over and took the reins while Spock attempted to deduce what was happening.

"That's it," she said. "Clear the way."

The wagon turned off the road onto an even bumpier surface. Eefa paused long enough for Woji to replace the obstacle and brush he had moved; Spock deduced that the way to the "cove" she'd mentioned was blocked and camouflaged to avoid discovery.

A logical precaution, he thought.

Woji clambered back onto the wagon, which descended a steep, winding trail that, judging from its uneven terrain, barely qualified as a road. The crashing surf grew louder as the air grew saltier, suggesting that they were nearing the hidden cove. Spock anticipated the end of the ride with some eagerness; beyond encountering the smugglers at last, he had been bounced and bruised by his rough accommodations longer than he would have preferred. Chekov was doubtless of a similar mind.

The road leveled off, and they continued only a bit farther.

"That's far enough," Eefa said. "Lock the wheels."

Woji grunted as he brought the wagon to a halt and engaged a mechanical brake.

"Fetch our unwanted passengers," Eefa said. "The sooner we unload them onto their fellows, the easier I'll rest."

Spock was inclined to agree. He also wished to make the acquaintance of the smugglers as expeditiously as possible. Curiosity and duty spurred a keen sense of anticipation that was nearly as powerful as any human emotion.

Woji followed her instructions. Within minutes, the tarp was yanked back, exposing the captives to the light of a solitary moon. None too gently, he dragged them out of the wagon and onto their feet. Spock's stiff legs, which had been on the verge of falling asleep, welcomed the activity. He appreciated being upright again as he got his bearings.

They had indeed reached a small, rather isolated cove sheltered by rocky slopes and cliffs. Foaming surf lapped against the edge of a pebbly beach, while a warm breeze blew off the water. Spock surmised that the cove was not visible from the road above, making it an ideal spot for maritime smuggling. All that was missing was any sign of the smugglers themselves. He, Chekov, Eefa, and her accomplice appeared to have the remote beach to themselves, nor did he discern any vessels upon the water or in the sky.

Curious, he thought.

"Where are they?" Eefa scanned the horizon. "They should be here by now, curse them!"

Spock shared her concern. He and Chekov had endured considerable danger and discomfort to reach this juncture. He did not wish to think that it had been a wasted effort. What if the smugglers left Eefa waiting in vain?

"Mgggmgg!"

A muffled protest escaped Chekov's gag. If anything, he appeared more discontented than either Spock or Eefa, which was perhaps understandable, considering the circumstances. Spock reminded himself that Chekov was merely human, after all.

"Mmggllggm!"

Chekov clearly wished to be heard, gag or no gag. Eefa shrugged in resignation.

"All right, all right," she said wearily. "Go ahead and take their gags off, Woji. Our foreign friends are surely going to want to question them . . . if they deign to show up."

She brandished her pistol as Woji removed the captives' gags.

"*Da!*" Chekov blurted as the gag came away from his mouth. He took a deep breath of the seaside air. "Are you all right, Mister . . . Fultar?"

"I am unharmed," Spock said. "And you?"

"Well enough, although I'm not fond of being trussed up like a Preebian sponge-hog." He spit the taste of the gag from his mouth. "I've been treated better by—" He caught himself before mentioning Klingons or the like. "Well, by worse characters than you."

"Don't even think about shouting for help," Eefa warned them. "There's nary a soul around for leagues."

"Why would we wish to summon help?" Spock said. "We are precisely where we want to be." He glanced about the deserted beach. "I take it our guests are overdue?"

"You're an icy one, aren't you?" She regarded him with annoyance. "I'd be a good deal more worried if I was in your position. Both of you."

"We will take that under advisement," Spock said.

That they were possibly in serious jeopardy did not elude Spock, yet they were making significant progress in their investigation. Danger was inherent in many Starfleet missions; one simply had to be confident in one's ability to cope with hazardous situations as they arose. Focusing entirely on self-preservation defeated the purpose of visiting new worlds and defending the Federation and its principles.

"You do that," she said, keeping him and Chekov in her

sights. She plucked her generic communicator from a pocket and tried to contact her tardy partners in crime. "Hello? Can you hear me? Where in limbo are you?"

"Patience," a voice answered. *"We're right offshore. You didn't think we were going to show ourselves until we needed to?"*

Eefa risked glancing at the bay. Spock followed her gaze and witnessed a disturbance in the water several meters beyond the beach. The moonlit water frothed and roiled as a large object rose from the deep water farther out. Foam streamed off the object, revealing the metallic hull of a green-tinted vessel roughly the size of a Starfleet shuttlecraft. It rose vertically from the depths, its nose pointed toward the beach.

"A submersible!" Chekov exclaimed, stating the obvious. "That's how they've evaded detection so far."

On the planet at least, Spock mused. The mystery of how the smugglers came and went from Yurnos without being spotted by sensors remained to be solved. "So it appears."

Levitating less than a meter above the water, the smugglers' craft glided toward the beach at a relatively cautious pace, giving Spock ample time to inspect it as it drew nearer. The unmarked craft bore no name or registration number, which was suspicious in itself. Streamlined contours rendered it well suited to both atmospheric and aquatic travel, but a pair of extendable nacelles, currently tucked in on both the port and starboard sides of the craft, indicated that it was space capable as well. Spock estimated that its cargo capacity was sufficient to take on enough *nabbia* to justify a trip to Baldur III and back.

"Don't tell me you're surprised by that remarkable craft," Eefa said. "We all know that such marvels are commonplace where you come from."

"Ah, yes," Chekov said. "Collu S'Avala."

"Precisely." Spock remained conscious of the need to avoid revealing any more to the Yurnians than they already knew. "A veritable land of wonders."

The marmots chittered and pawed the ground as the submersible shuttle approached, their agitation notable but not too extreme. Spock took this to mean that the huge rodents had seen the craft before. Woji crossed the beach to calm them, leaving Eefa to watch over the bound prisoners.

The aquamarine craft touched down on the beach, landing gear extending to cushion its landing. A side door opened and a pair of humanoids emerged. Spock was not surprised to see that they were largely indistinguishable from Yurnians, given Eefa's startled reaction to his more Vulcan characteristics. The duo consisted of a pale-skinned male and a darker-skinned female, both wearing utilitarian olive-colored jumpsuits with no insignia or other identifying markers. The man had a comet tattooed on one cheek; the woman flaunted a trillium pendant and ear studs. Both bore surly expressions. Disruptor pistols clung to their hips.

"Hello, Mars, Venus," Eefa greeted them. "Glad you could join us after all."

Spock assumed those were code names or aliases, much as he and Chekov had been employing. Their etymology suggested, but did not confirm, that they hailed from the Sol system. If so, they were a long way from home.

Then again, he reflected, *so are we.*

"Let's make this snappy," said the woman, who was presumably Venus. "I hope you brought enough *nabbia* to make this trip worthwhile. Some of us have schedules to stick to, you know?"

"Yeah," her partner said. "What makes a couple of snoopy strangers worth all this fuss?"

"You tell me," Eefa said.

She waved Spock and Chekov forward with her pistol, so that Venus and Mars could get a better look at them. Genuine surprise registered on the smugglers' faces.

"A Vulcan?" Venus said.

"Or a Romulan."

"On this side of the Neutral Zone?" She snorted at the notion. "Don't be daft."

Spock could not immediately determine which of the pair was in charge, if either of them were. A third figure—the pilot?—could be glimpsed through the front viewports of the shuttle. Spock noted that the craft had not powered down upon landing but was instead "keeping the motor running," as humans put it. It seemed the smugglers were not planning on staying long—and perhaps wanted to be able to make a hasty exit if necessary.

"Vulcan? Romulan?" Eefa said, understandably at sea. "I don't know what you're saying."

Spock worried that the smugglers were revealing too much about the galaxy beyond Yurnos's gravity well.

"Pardon the interruption, but we should be mindful of the Prime Directive when choosing our words."

The smugglers exchanged a look.

"Yep, Vulcan, all right," Venus said smugly.

Mars conceded the point. "With a human partner, no less."

"Takes one to know one," Chekov said.

"What's that accent?" Mars asked. "Russian?"

"I don't get it," Venus said. "What are a Russian and Vulcan doing here, poking their noses into our business?"

"Stop talking like I'm not here!" Eefa grew ever more agitated. "What in limbo is a Vulcan?"

"One of the forbidden secrets of Collu S'Avala," Chekov volunteered. "Trust me, you are better off not knowing."

Nicely improvised, Ensign, Spock thought. Chekov's "explanation" cowed Eefa to a degree. Looking uncertain, she retrieved their phasers and communicators from the front of the wagon and presented them to the smugglers.

"We took these off them before," she explained. "That's when I knew they weren't just any snoopers. Well, that and the ears on that one."

Mars and Venus took the devices, which they regarded with alarm.

"These are Starfleet issue!" She cast an anxious look at the captives. "Oh, crap, this is not good."

"You're telling me." He ran his hand nervously through his lank, dirty-blond hair. "We've got Starfleet breathing down our necks now? They haven't got better things to do?"

"You were violating the Prime Directive," Spock pointed out. "Starfleet could not overlook that."

"We didn't violate anything!" Mars wheeled about to confront Spock. "It's not like we set ourselves up as gods or anything. We just exchanged some harmless trinkets for tea, that's all."

"'Harmless' is debatable in this instance," Spock said, "and your entire operation is highly questionable. That we became aware of it at all demonstrates that you were not being nearly as careful as you thought."

"I don't need a lecture from you, Vulcan." Mars clipped a stolen communicator and phaser to his belt as he looked to his partner for guidance. "So what are we supposed to do now? Vanish them?"

"And put us on Starfleet's most-wanted list? Are you kidding me?" Venus asked, claiming the other Starfleet devices. "We're not talking about a couple of shady customers moving in on our racket. These are honest-to-goodness Starfleet operatives. You realize what kind of heat 'vanishing' them would bring down on our heads? They'd hunt us across the entire quadrant!"

She was clearly worried more about provoking Starfleet than about infringing on the Prime Directive. While this was personally advantageous to him and Chekov, Spock questioned her priorities.

"Starfleet?" Eefa was lost again. "What is this 'Starfleet' that's got you bothered?"

"Nothing we want anything to do with," Venus said. "Period."

"What are you saying?" Eefa plainly didn't like where this was going. "You're supposed to take them off my hands, deal with them yourselves."

"Forget that," Mars said. "We're not letting them get anywhere near our boat. They've seen too much already." He glowered at Eefa. "You should have handled them on your own and never dragged us into this mess."

"This was already your mess," Eefa protested. "They're your people, not mine. It's your lot they're after, not me!"

"Tough." Venus looked fed up with the entire topic. "We don't have time for this. We need to get that tea loaded and head up north before we miss our window."

"You got that right," Mars said. "Don't want the light show to start without us."

"Loose lips much?" She nodded at Spock. "Pointy ears are listening."

Too late, Spock thought, intrigued by the smugglers' exchange. A theory began to formulate in his brain as he recalled the planet's unusually variable magnetic field.

"You listen here!" Eefa was tired of being confused and dismissed. "Don't think for one minute that you're taking my tea without taking these two as well. I didn't bring them all this way just for you to leave me in the lurch. They're your problem too!"

She swung her pistol at the smugglers and away from her captives. Woji took up an aggressive stance between the smugglers and the wagonful of tea. He crossed his brawny arms across his chest, while keeping an eye on Spock and Chekov as well. A menacing growl rumbled up from his chest.

"Seriously?" Mars said. "You're actually threatening us?"

Eefa stood her ground. "What does it look like?"

"It looks like you're making a big mistake." Venus raised her voice. "You reading this, Mercury?"

An amplified voice issued from the shuttle. "Loud and clear, Venus."

"Then you know what to do," she said.

A scarlet disruptor beam fired from the nose of the craft, striking Woji. The man flared up brightly, briefly becoming an incandescent red silhouette, before dissolving into atoms, leaving only a fading afterimage behind.

His sudden incineration panicked the marmots, which reared up on their hind legs and screeched loudly enough to hurt Spock's ears. Their upper paws smacked their silky chests as a sign of their distress. The animals tugged frantically at their harnesses, but remained anchored to the stationary wagon.

"Woji!"

Eefa stared in shock at where he had been standing only moments before. A few fading red sparks were all that remained of the man and even those blinked out within seconds. Her horrified gaze swung back toward the smugglers. "Fiends! Monsters! You didn't have to do that!"

"Said you were making a mistake." Venus smirked at Eefa's primitive flintlock pistol. "Now put away that toy and let's get that tea loaded before we lose our patience and light you up just as bright."

Eefa's pistol arm fell to her side. "You didn't have to do that," she whispered.

No, they did not, Spock thought.

He mourned Woji's death and regretted that he had not been in a position to save him. The silent Yurnian had not treated him or Chekov kindly, but Spock knew little of the man beyond that. Woji had surely had a life and aspirations of his own, which had just been ruthlessly cut short simply to intimidate others. The waste of life appalled Spock, who noted also that the smugglers were not above murdering random Yurnians, even if they balked at killing Starfleet officers as a matter of self-interest. He suspected that lesson was not lost on Eefa either.

"You coldhearted Cossacks!" Chekov could not contain his emotions. "You had no right to kill that man!"

Mars shrugged. "Just a primitive nobody on a nowhere

planet. The galaxy won't miss him. Just be grateful you two have way higher profiles."

"And yet your 'harmless' smuggling operation has now claimed the life of a native of this world," Spock said. "Does that not call into question whether you should be doing business on this planet at all?"

"Save your breath," Mars said. "I'm not stupid enough to debate ethics with a Vulcan. Folks on Baldur III want *nabbia*. We mean to oblige. End of story."

"Baldur III?" Eefa echoed.

The planet in question was not even visible from Yurnos. Spock resisted the impulse to lift his gaze toward Baldur, which was but one of many stars gleaming faintly in the night sky. He took comfort in the fact that the name meant nothing to Eefa, who appeared deeply shaken by Woji's abrupt incineration. He wondered how close they had truly been.

"Enough chitchat," Venus said. "We've got work to do and a deadline to make."

"Just like that?" Chekov said. "A man was murdered and you're talking about—"

She drew the disruptor pistol on her hip. "I said, no chitchat."

"Shame we vaporized the hired muscle." Mars wandered over to inspect the barrels of *nabbia* waiting in the wagon. "Come along, Eefa. Guess it's up to you and me to get these goods loaded, while Venus and Mercury make sure your new friends don't go anywhere."

Spock and Chekov stood by as the loading got underway. With both Venus's and her vessel's weapons trained on them, Spock saw no purpose in tempting death to prevent a single load of tea from being carted away; he believed he had learned enough about the smugglers' methods and operation for the time being. Antigrav lifts were employed to transport the heavy barrels from the wagon to the shuttle. Eefa took the levitating pallets in stride, apparently regarding them as yet another exotic marvel from Collu S'Avala, akin to a flying carpet or some equivalent fancy. The task was accomplished quickly, and the smugglers' craft was soon ready for departure.

"Just one more thing," Mars said to Eefa. He secured a small wooden crate from the submersible and deposited it in the back of the wagon. "Your payment for the *nabbia*: another carton of sparkly glow juice from faraway. Wouldn't want to welch on our side of the deal."

"And you think that makes up for the rest of it?" Eefa said bitterly. "For Woji?"

Venus shrugged. "Consider that the penalty for expecting us to clean up your mess."

"You soulless piece of tripe . . ."

"Always a pleasure, Eefa." Mars took her hand and kissed it. "Hope this won't put a crimp in our business relationship." He glanced at where Woji wasn't. "I'm sure you can find another hired hand. Maybe even a more talkative one?"

"Curse you," she muttered under her breath.

"Oh, don't be like that," Venus taunted her. "Water under the bridge."

"So that's it?" Eefa said feebly. "You're truly just going to leave me alone with these two Starfleets, whatever that means?"

"Now you're getting it," Mars said. "We're not touching this poison plant. It's all yours."

"But . . . but what am I to do with them?"

Mars's gaze dropped to the pistol Eefa was still carrying limply at her side.

"You're a smart woman. You'll figure it out."

Seventeen

Deep Space Station S-8

"I've known Tilton for years," Grandle said. "Never seen him like this."

With space aboard the station at a premium, Sulu had no choice but to share Grandle's office with her. An extra plasti-form desk had been squeezed up against Grandle's so that they faced each other. It made for cramped conditions, but was only temporary. It also allowed them to discuss the station manager's condition in private.

"He ignored my suggestion that he get checked out by a doc-tor," Sulu said. "He didn't take offense; he just shrugged it off and said he was too busy, even though I'm not sure how much he's actually accomplishing these days. He seems to have shut down, basically, and is pretty much running on automatic pilot."

"Cut him some slack," Grandle said. "He's not a young man anymore, and you've seen the bedlam we've been dealing with for months now. This is not what he signed on for."

"No criticism intended," Sulu assured her. "I'm not passing judgment on his stamina or character; just wondering how to handle the situation. A vacation would probably do Tilton worlds of good, but now's not exactly a good time . . . unless you're willing to step up and fill in as a manager for the time being?"

Grandle scoffed at the notion. "I've got enough on my hands without taking on all that administrative work as well. And who is going to talk Tilton into taking a break during this crisis? You? Me?" She shook her head. "We're just going to have to muddle through unless—" Her eyes narrowed suspiciously. "You're not thinking of declaring him unfit or anything, are you?"

"I'm hoping it won't come to that," Sulu said. He had no desire to file a negative report on the seemingly burnt-out manager. It was possible that Tilton needed to retire or be replaced, especially now that the once-obscure station had become a major interstellar crossroads; Sulu wondered if it would be enough to quietly inform Captain Kirk, who could then discreetly notify Starfleet, instead of going through official channels. "We need to keep an eye on the situation, for everyone's sake."

"He's a good man," Grandle insisted. "He doesn't deserve to be forced out."

"Not saying he does," Sulu said, "but our joint responsibility is to the station and its visitors, not one man. We have to consider the bigger picture."

Just like Captain Kirk would, Sulu thought.

"I know, I know," Grandle conceded. "Doesn't mean I have to like it."

"Ditto," Sulu said.

He went back to what he had been doing before: reviewing data and security footage relating to the near disaster in the shuttlebay. The cause of the explosion had yet to be determined, in part because the station's engineers were too busy working around the clock to repair and inspect the plasma coolant system. In the meantime, the search for bodies sucked into space had been called off; Sulu was now confident that no one had been killed in the incident.

But what about next time?

Determined to track down the source of the accidents, Sulu sipped from a cup of herbal tea as he studied the info on his desk's computer terminal. He squinted at the security footage, examining it from every angle available, but saw only what he already knew. The explosion had blown a small hole in the hangar ceiling at exactly 1500, resulting in the coolant leak. He'd scanned the recordings for hours prior to the explosion, hoping to spot something suspicious, but all he had to show for it was tired eyes, the beginnings of a headache, and a growing sense that time was running out before the next "accident" endangered lives and vessels.

"Computer, replay security recording, starting five minutes prior to the explosion."

"Replaying."

He watched again as shuttle crews, station personnel, and random travelers went about their business in the hangar, blithely unaware of what was about to transpire. No one appeared nervous, or suicidal, or in a hurry to exit the hangar before the explosion. From some angles, Sulu saw himself escorting Helena away from the paranoid Vernalians and their shuttle. He could hear the general hubbub in the shuttlebay: overlapping voices, humming machinery, amplified announcements over the public address system . . . and possibly something else?

"Hmm," he murmured.

"What is it?" Grandle looked up from her own work. "You see something?"

"Not *see*," Sulu replied. "But maybe hear."

Remembering that he had four more senses, Sulu closed his eyes and signaled Grandle to keep quiet. He listened again to the security footage, mentally sifting through the ambient noise to zero in on one specific sound: a high-pitched whine rising in the background. Was it just his imagination or did that sound like . . . ?

Don't jump to conclusions, he cautioned himself. With the computer's help, he meticulously muted every other identifiable sound until all that remained was an unmistakable screech that Grandle also identified immediately.

"That's a phaser on overload!"

"Right on the money," Sulu agreed. "Someone placed an overloading phaser in one of the ceiling panels, leading to the explosion that caused the coolant leak."

Grandle came around their desks to look over Sulu's shoulder. "But how did they manage to smuggle a phaser aboard?"

"And avoid detection while planting it in the ceiling?" Sulu added. "I suppose they could conceivably beam the phaser into the ceiling, but that would require very precise coordinates, not to mention access to a transporter station."

He couldn't help glancing over at the compact, two-person transporter pad installed in the far corner of Grandle's office, near the entrance to the brig. As Sulu understood it, the pad served to help transfer prisoners to and from the brig without having to parade them through the public areas of the station. Site-to-site transporting within a station or ship remained dangerous unless you had a transporter pad at both ends, but it would be conceivably possible to transport a small object like a phaser into a conduit or service tube if you knew what you were doing—and didn't particularly care about damaging anything essential.

His glance at the transporter did not escape Grandle's notice. "Hang on there! You're not seriously thinking that—"

Her own computer terminal beeped urgently. An alert light flashed atop it. Grandle darted back to her own terminal to investigate. Her eyes widened as she viewed the display screen.

"What is it?" Sulu asked.

"An emergency airlock, leading out into space, has been opened without authorization." She scanned the information. "Arm B, Level Nine."

"An unscheduled repair job?" Sulu knew that such airlocks were primarily used for inspections of and maintenance work on the station's exterior.

Grandle's gaze was glued to the screen. "Not seeing any EVA work in progress at the moment. Even if the repairs were unplanned, in response to a newly discovered problem that required an immediate response, there would be a report in the database. And there would also be a log of somebody using the airlock, period." She looked up from the terminal. "Believe it or not, Sulu, people don't just wander in and out of the vacuum on this station. Not on my watch."

"I believe you," Sulu said. "Which means somebody's taking an unsanctioned jaunt outside your station."

He didn't like the sound of that. *Not on my watch either.*

"Computer," Grandle ordered, "show space around Arm B, Level Nine on main viewer."

"Complying," the computer said.

A view of the surrounding space appeared on the large view-screen on the wall opposite Grandle's desk. Sulu had to swivel his chair around to inspect the area, which was far from empty. Smaller spacecraft were docked to the station's outward arm while larger vessels could be seen orbiting in the background between the station and the stars. Sulu winced at the heavy traffic outside, which reminded him of both the ongoing crisis and the multiple opportunities for sabotage available.

So many potential targets.

His eyes searched in vain for one or more figures floating through the void or clinging to the station's hull. It felt like he was hunting for a cloaked Romulan warship.

"Do your exterior sensors include motion detectors?" he asked.

"Of course," Grandle said, "but with all the vessels orbiting the station now, a solitary individual or two are barely going to register. We're not exactly scanning an empty void."

Sulu grasped the challenge. He contemplated the myriad spacecraft on display—and his eyes locked onto one particular vessel: a fairly bare-bones passenger ship about 150 meters in length. Cheap gold plating distracted from the fact that the vessel was clearly at least a decade old. He recognized the freighter from having looked it up days ago, just for curiosity's sake.

It was the *Lucky Strike.*

Helena's ship.

"Zoom in on that Midasite cruiser," he said to Grandle.

"Any particular reason?"

"Just a hunch," Sulu admitted. "Its captain was involved in an altercation with another captain the other day."

He didn't mention that Mirsa Dajo had been accused of sabotage since there had been no evidence to back up that charge. Nor that Dajo had been among those loudly protesting the lockdown.

"That's all you've got to go on?" Grandle asked with obvious skepticism.

It wasn't much, Sulu admitted to himself. "You got a better idea?"

"I wish," Grandle said, giving in. "Here you go."

Magnified, the space around the *Lucky Strike* filled the screen. The ship appeared undisturbed, locked in orbit around the station as it awaited the go-ahead to depart for Baldur III.

"So much for your hunch," Grandle said. "Seen enough?"

"I suppose." Sulu was both relieved and disappointed to find nothing amiss on or around Helena's ship. "Thanks for indulging— Hold on, what's that?"

A flicker of motion against the blackness of space caught his eye before vanishing from sight. It came and went so fast he couldn't be sure he'd seen it.

"What?" Grandle asked.

"Back up a few moments." Sulu got up from his chair and walked over to the viewscreen. He watched intently as Grandle reversed the displayed images until . . . "There!"

Grandle froze the image, capturing what appeared to be a momentary spurt of vapor in the vacuum of space. Sulu pointed at the screen. "You see that?"

"Clear as day," Grandle said. "A vapor jet from a thruster suit?"

"That's what I'm thinking." He squinted at the screen. "Can you go in closer?"

"Try and stop me."

Grandle adjusted the controls, further magnifying the area around the telltale jet. Observed at such close range, a camouflaged figure came into view: an individual in a matte-black spacesuit flying silently toward the *Lucky Strike*'s starboard nacelle, propelled by discreet, intermittent jets of gas.

"I don't recognize the design of the suit," Grandle said. "That's not one of ours."

"Definitely not standard issue," Sulu agreed. Starfleet EV suits were designed to be highly reflective to make their wearers more visible and easier to locate when outside in the vacuum. They were also one size fits all, more or less. The customized suit on the screen, on the other hand, seemed expressly intended to vanish against the blackness of space.

Momentum carried the anonymous figure closer to the nacelle. Another well-gauged puff of gas adjusted their trajectory.

"Any way we can hail them?" Sulu asked.

"Without even knowing who they are?" Grandle threw her hands up. "I'm open to suggestions."

Sulu suspected that Uhura would find a way, but they didn't have time to hail random frequencies in hopes of reaching the mystery spacewalker. He watched with concern as the stranger touched down on *Lucky Strike*'s nacelle. Sulu couldn't imagine they were up to any good.

"Within transporter range?" he asked urgently.

"Locking on now." Grandle operated the transporter controls at her desk, which were tied into the pad across the room. "We may not be able to talk to that suspect, but we sure as hell know exactly where they are."

This wouldn't work, Sulu realized, if the *Lucky Strike* had its shields raised, but there was no reason for the ship to maintain its shields while parked in orbit around the station, which was no doubt what the possible saboteur was counting on as well.

"Energizing," Grandle said, pushing a lever.

Onscreen, the space-suited figure dissolved into a cloud of shimmering energy that vanished from view even as it re-formed above the transporter pad in the office. Sulu drew his phaser, set on stun, in anticipation of the stranger's reaction to being transported without warning and against their will. Even as the sparkling energy coalesced back into matter, Sulu braced himself for fireworks of a different sort.

"Good instincts," Grandle commented, "but the automated filters are intended to screen out any weapons or explosives."

Sulu felt better having the upper hand just the same. "Simply want a peaceful conversation, that's all."

The spacewalker materialized on the platform. A tinted visor concealed their features while the pressurized black suit obscured their species and gender. Their body language conveyed their surprise, however, at suddenly finding themselves in the security chief's office instead of riding the *Lucky Strike*'s nacelle. A muffled curse defeated the universal translator.

"Welcome aboard," Grandle said. "Please identify yourself."

The figure turned toward Grandle. A female voice emerged from her helmet's speaker. *"You had no right—!"*

"You operated a station airlock without authorization," the security chief replied. "That makes it my business."

"If you'd done your job properly, I'd be long gone by now!"

Her voice sounded familiar to Sulu, despite being distorted by the speaker. "Remove the helmet."

The suspect hesitated, but complied with instructions. Air hissed as the seal attaching the helmet to the suit was broken. The helmet came off to reveal the flushed and perspiring face of Zita Mansori, captain of the *Solar Wind*.

"Captain Mansori," Sulu greeted her. "I thought I recognized your voice."

Grandle glanced at him. "You know this individual, Sulu?"

"We've met in passing." He kept his eyes on Mansori. "Care to explain what you were doing on that nacelle?"

"What if I don't?"

Sulu noticed a tool kit affixed to her belt. Without asking, he stepped forward to confiscate it. She bristled at the liberty, but was in no position to object. He cracked it open to reveal a small assortment of compact tools, including a rodinium-tipped drill capable of piercing, say, the casing of a warp nacelle. He showed Grandle the drill.

"Apparently your transporter filter doesn't register this as a potential weapon," Sulu said. "I'd think about plugging that hole with a software patch."

Grandle scowled at the drill. "Consider it done."

"So I have a tool kit," Mansori said. "What's the big deal?"

"So you weren't planning to perform any unauthorized surgery on the *Lucky Strike*'s nacelle?" Grandle challenged her. "Maybe drill a few inconspicuous leaks in just the wrong places?"

"Prove it," she said. "Is there a law against spacewalking?"

"Maybe not," Grandle said, "but it doesn't look good when there's a saboteur afoot and you're caught red-handed."

Mansori's face went pale as she realized just how much trouble she was in. "Slow down. You don't think I was behind *all* those so-called accidents? That's insane. My ship was one of the first to get sabotaged. I was just after a little payback!"

"She has a point," Sulu conceded. "Her ship, the *Solar Wind*, suffered some major malfunctions days ago . . . and she blamed the *Lucky Strike*'s captain, Mirsa Dajo. Minus anything in the way of evidence, that is."

"I told you before," Mansori said, "Dajo's the one you should be looking at, not me."

"Oh, we have reason enough to hold you for the time being." Grandle worked the transporter lever again, dispatching Mansori to a cell in the brig, which, like all the cells, was equipped with built-in transponders to enable one-way beaming. Force fields sealed off the cells once they were occupied. Grandle waited until the transport was complete before calling up a view of the cell on the main screen. She nodded in satisfaction as Mansori materialized in the formerly empty cell. "Figured I'd let her cool her heels a bit while we sorted this out. What are you thinking?"

Sulu lowered his phaser. "Honestly, I think we may have caught *a* would-be saboteur, but not *the* saboteur. What's Mansori's motive for sabotaging her own ship?"

"Misdirection?"

"To what end? The *Solar Wind* would be well on its way to Baldur III by now if its engines hadn't been tampered with. Instead, Mansori is losing passengers and profits to the likes of Dajo." Sulu clipped his phaser back to his belt. "This business with Mansori strikes me as a personal grudge taken to an extreme, nothing more."

Grandle scowled. "Which would mean that the real saboteur is still at large."

"Probably." The more Sulu thought about it, the more he suspected that Mansori was (relatively) innocent when it came to the rash of malfunctions plaguing the station and its visitors. "Just look at how easily we caught her. This was an amateur job; the real saboteur wouldn't have triggered that alarm exiting the airlock, or we would have nabbed them by now."

"Unless she finally got sloppy?"

"After leaving no trace up until now?" Sulu asked. "You really believe that?"

"No." Grandle slumped down in her seat. "Would've made life easier, though."

"Tell me about it."

A disturbing thought pushed its way back into Sulu's brain. What if the real sabotage was an inside job? As Mansori had just demonstrated, it was difficult for a civilian to pull off such a crime without being detected by the station's security systems, let alone do so repeatedly. You'd need to be very familiar with those systems, and have free access to most anywhere on the station, to carry out an ongoing campaign under Grandle's very nose.

Mansori couldn't do that, he thought. *Nor Dajo or another visitor.*

He peered at Grandle, reluctant to share his suspicions with the prickly security chief. Sulu trusted his Starfleet team implicitly, but Grandle was bound to react badly to even a hint of an accusation against her and her staff; Sulu decided to keep his theory to himself until he had more to go on.

"Something on your mind, Sulu?"

Sulu briefly wondered if Grandle could be the saboteur, but that made no sense. She had no reason to disrupt the workings of her own station—and every reason not to.

"Just wondering what you were planning to do with Mansori?" Sulu lied.

Grandle contemplated the prisoner on the viewer. Mansori had shucked the bulk of her spacesuit and was now pacing back and forth in a lightweight, protective undergarment. In a moment of frustration, she flung a discarded gravity boot at the entrance to the cell; azure sparks crackled as the boot bounced off the force field confining her. She ducked to avoid being nailed by the rebounding footwear.

"Tempted to ship her off to a penal colony," Grandle said, "along with half the other troublemakers disturbing my peace, but I'll probably just keep her under wraps until the lockdown is lifted and she can go be somebody else's problem." She flicked a switch to banish the view of the cell and its unhappy occupant. "Beats having to press charges and go through all the rigmarole of a hearing. Case you haven't noticed, we're short on judges and lawyers in these parts as well."

"Works for me," Sulu said. All they really had on Mansori was trespassing and attempted mischief. "You expect Tilton will go along with that?"

"Ordinarily, that would be his call," Grandle admitted, "but . . . what were we just talking about before?"

"Tilton," Sulu recalled, "and the fact that he's not all there."

"Exactly." Grandle stared morosely at the empty screen. "I hate to admit it, but he's just a ghost of his former self."

A ghost, it occurred to Sulu, who could go anywhere he pleased.

Eighteen

Baldur III

"The sooner we wean you off this creaky old rust bucket the better."

Montgomery Scott barely remembered his quarters back on the *Enterprise*. He had been practically living in the *Thunderbird*, trying to keep the rickety refurbished spacecraft up and running. It was well into the night shift and he slugged down a cup of coffee, wishing he had something a wee bit stronger to spike it with, as he conferred with the power plant's manager, Paul Galligan, in an administrative office just off the main control room. The blueprints for a new hydroelectric generator, currently being constructed in the hills outside town, were displayed on a desktop terminal before them. Scotty hoped that this and other such projects would soon get Jackpot City to the point where they could take *Thunderbird* offline for good.

"Someday perhaps," Galligan said. He was a middle-aged family man whose job had become much more demanding in recent months. Worry lines creased his face, while Scotty was pretty sure he had been wearing the same ratty wool sweater for days now. "But that generator won't be operational for weeks at best, unless we cut some pretty serious corners."

"Don't even think about it," Scott said sternly. "You're going to build that thing, you build it right or you're just asking for heartache down the road." He glanced around at his surroundings. "One jury-rigged time bomb is quite enough, if you don't mind me saying so."

"Oh, you've made your opinion of this operation quite clear," Galligan said, shrugging, "and I'll concede that getting our power supply from *Thunderbird*'s old engine room is more of a matter of necessity than preference. As for the hydroelectric plant, I suppose we could try to throw more people and resources at the project, although I'm not entirely sure where we'd get them from."

"Aye, there's the rub." Scott was torn between making *Thunderbird* as safe as possible and helping the colony develop viable alternatives in a timely fashion. The truth was, he ought to concentrate on both, but there was never enough time or people to get it all done, especially if he wanted to keep the *Enterprise* adequately staffed as well. Lieutenant Charlene Masters was currently minding engineering in his absence, but he was reluctant to pull any more technicians away from her to assist him planetside. "We'd be robbing Peter to pay Paul."

"Hard to know what to prioritize," Galligan agreed. "In the meantime, and you're not going to like this, we've been requested to increase our output by another nine percent."

Scott nearly spit out his coffee. "Are ye out of your mind? We should be scaling down, not ramping up!"

"I don't like the idea either," Galligan said, "but demand keeps increasing faster than we can keep up with. You've got the new expansion at the spaceport, which is now operating around the clock; new computers and offices being set to process mining claims and disputes; temporary housing for all the new arrivals . . . all of that requires additional energy, beyond what we're already producing."

"Can't ye tighten your belts some?" Scott asked. "Restrict consumption to what's strictly necessary?"

"You want to be the one who shuts down all the bars and

music halls, or explains to people why their sonic showers and protein resequencers aren't working?" Galligan flinched in anticipation of the flak that such restrictions would generate. "And, honestly, I'm not sure that modest energy-conservation measures would really make a significant dent in the demand. We'd be getting a lot of grief for very little gain."

"I suppose." Scott reminded himself that they were dealing with an unruly civilian population, not disciplined Starfleet crew members trained to sacrifice creature comforts if necessary. "But even still—"

A muffled thump from the engine room caught Scott's attention. He didn't know the geriatric rumblings of the *Thunderbird* the way he knew the *Enterprise*'s every hum and murmur, but that didn't sound right to him. A frown betrayed his unease.

"Did you hear that?"

Before the other man could answer, a junior technician stuck her head into the office. "Excuse me, Mister Galligan, Mister Scott?" Kate Spears said. "But we seem to have an issue."

The young Baldurian, who had previously struck Scott as a good worker, appeared worried, but not panicked. Scott hoped that boded well. Nevertheless, he got up from the desk and headed straight for the control room. Galligan did the same, interrogating Spears all the way.

"What is it, Kate?" he asked.

"There was a blockage in the deuterium stream feeding into the reactor, possibly caused by some unwanted clumping. The system automatically flushed the clog loose by increasing the pressure behind it, but it looks like that might have damaged a valve or two, maybe."

I knew something sounded wrong, Scott thought, wishing he'd been mistaken. They strode briskly onto the floor of the engine room, which was sparsely populated by a mere skeleton crew. He immediately glanced at the primary diagnostic board, specifically the gauge monitoring the reactor's internal temperature, and was relieved to see that it was only running a little hot, not enough to pose a major concern yet. *Thank heaven for small favors!*

Spears sat down at an empty control panel as Scott and Galligan looked over her shoulders. Glancing about, Scott noticed other technicians looking frustrated and anxious as they fought their instruments, which were clearly not cooperating as well as they were supposed to. Despite that reassuring temperature reading, Scott could feel in his bones that this was not going to be a simple fix. His gut churned in anticipation.

"Problem is," Spears elaborated, "we're having trouble controlling the flow of deuterium into the matter-antimatter assembly, so we have to keep compensating with the antimatter to avoid an imbalance, but now the magnetic constrictors governing the antimatter stream are acting up, possibly in response to the rapid fluctuations in the system. One glitch keeps leading to another, like dominoes falling."

Scott didn't like what he was hearing. He glanced again at the core-temperature gauge and saw that it hadn't budged one bit since the last time he'd checked it, despite the erratic variations in the input streams.

That couldn't be right.

Crossing the chamber, he quickly confirmed what he feared: the temperature reading was frozen and had not updated itself for at least six minutes. Fear gnawed at his nerves as he did a forced reset on the monitor. All at once, the temperature reading jumped into the yellow zone, indicating that the reactor core was already way too hot for safety's sake. Warning lights blinked on belatedly.

"Bloody hell," Scott muttered.

The tension in the control room mushroomed as well. Galligan went pale, but managed to keep his composure. "Bring that temperature down," he ordered his workers, "however you can."

"I'm trying," Spears insisted, her eyes glued to the displays at her panel. "But nothing's working. Matter and antimatter are flooding the warp core."

Scott hurried to her side. "Have ye tried compressing the stream before it reaches the injectors?"

"I wish I could," she said, stress tinging her voice. "But the variable compression nozzles seem to have been knocked out of alignment."

Scott recalled seeing an inspection report on those nozzles. They were well past their expected lifetime, by a generation or so. Replacing them had been high on his maintenance team's to-do list, but there had been other components that had needed upgrading first and replacement nozzles had proven hard to come by, considering they were antiques these days. Most everything on the *Thunderbird* was old and obsolete, in fact, meaning that replacement parts had to be fabricated from scratch or more modern units made to adapt to the older systems, with varying degrees of success.

That's coming back to bite us, he thought. "What about the backup dampers?"

Spears did a system check. "Shut down for an overhaul, sir. Supposed to be back online by Monday."

Scott felt his own temperature rising. He had argued against keeping the reactor running while the secondary dampers were being brought up to code, but had been overruled; in theory, the system should be back in place by now, but everything was running behind schedule due to unexpected complications and more pressing emergencies. Scott silently cursed the ancient vessel and the colonists who had thought it was a good idea to drag her out of retirement. On the *Enterprise,* there were any number of tricks he could try to bring the overheating reactor back under control; *Thunderbird* was not the *Enterprise,* however. Even in her prime, she lacked the redundant backup systems and options built into a modern *Constitution*-class starship, which left Scott only one course of action.

"We've got to shut the whole works down . . . while we still can."

Galligan stared at him as though he'd lost his mind. "A total shutdown? You can't be serious. There will be blackouts throughout the city and that's just for starters. It will take days to get the reactor back online if we shut down completely. Longer if we have to inspect and repair the entire assembly!"

"You'd rather risk a warp core breach in the middle of the city?" Scott said. "Because that's what we're looking at if we don't pull the plug on this before it's too late."

"I can't do this on my authority," Galligan said, wavering. "I need to consult the mayor and the board of directors . . ."

"There's no time for that. For heaven's sake, man, you have a wife and family in town; their pictures are all over your office. Don't you realize their lives are at stake as well?"

More warning lights ignited on control panels and visual displays, as though joining in the debate. Spears looked up from her console in dismay.

"One of the dilithium crystals has fractured!"

Scott felt a chill run down his spine. The crystals were crucial to regulating the matter-antimatter annihilation reaction within the warp core. Damage to even one crystal gave them even less control over the runaway reactor.

"That's it," Scott said. "We're done talking." He edged past Galligan to get to Spears's console. "Step aside, lass. I'm making this call."

She surrendered her seat to Scott, while glancing apologetically at Galligan. "I'm sorry, sir, but I have friends and family outside too."

To his credit, the manager made no effort to stop Scott as he attempted to initiate the emergency shutdown protocol. Scott had just instructed the computer to begin the procedure when a power surge from the bollixed reactor caused the control board to crash. Precious moments slipped by as he waited impatiently for the system to reboot, which took much longer than it should have. One more reason why the old ship should have never been fired up again. The *Enterprise*'s computers could have rebooted three times by now.

"I don't understand." Galligan tugged anxiously at his collar. "Why is everything breaking down all at once?"

"It's like Spears said before," Scott explained, "one malfunction leads to another, setting off a chain reaction of minor problems snowballing into a major cock-up." He manfully resisted the temptation to say *I told you so.* "This whole setup was a house of cards just waiting to collapse."

The board finally lit up again.

"About bloody time," Scott said. Unhappily skipping over a couple of prudent preliminary steps, he attempted to disconnect the matter-antimatter injectors from the warp core in order to collapse the reaction.

At least that was the plan.

"Procedure incomplete," an automated voice reported. *"Shutdown unsuccessful."*

"What is it?" Galligan said. "What's happening?"

Scott wanted to know that himself. He scanned every readout in sight, called up every scrap of data from every blessed diagnostic program still running. They didn't paint a pretty picture.

"It's the injectors," he said. "They're not disengaging from the warp core the way they're supposed to."

"How come?" Spears asked.

"Hard to say without looking under the hood," Scott said. "Maybe the injectors are fused to their couplings. Maybe the bypass circuits are burnt out. Maybe it's a software issue. All I know is that we're not going to be able to shut down the reactor from here."

A countdown started in his head. At the rate the temperature was climbing within the warp core, they were looking at a major breach in at least two hours, assuming nothing else broke down in the meantime. At which point *Thunderbird*, the surrounding park, and several nearby blocks of shops and residences would become nothing but a radioactive crater. Jackpot City was facing a major catastrophe, just as Scott had feared.

Remind me to dig in me heels more next time.

"What now?" Spears asked.

Scott knew the options by heart. "If we're lucky, we can still shut down the reactor manually."

He peered through the EM shield grating at the warp power assembly beyond. Its usual orange glow suffusing the engine room had morphed into an infernal red glow, reflecting the increasing amount of energy being generated by the reactor. He briefly considered changing into a protective hazard suit before entering the chamber, but concluded there wasn't enough time. Radiation levels within the engine room were still within acceptable levels, at least for the time being. The place probably felt like the inside of an oven, but Scott figured he'd be okay if he moved quickly enough. And if the procedure took too long . . . well, radiation poisoning was going to be the least of his worries.

He procured a tool belt, complete with a multipurpose wrench and a phaser welder, from a supply locker and buckled it on. Spears handed him a tinted visor to shield his eyes from the glare inside the engine room, which he accepted gratefully. Galligan paced about the control room, wringing his hands.

"Do you think you can do it?" he asked Scott.

"If I can't, no one can," he replied, eschewing false modesty. *Aside from possibly Mister Spock.*

"No offense," Galligan said, "but I wish I found that more comforting."

"So do I," Scott admitted. "Just keep an eye on the situation and give me a shout if aught else goes amiss."

"Will do," Spears promised.

A metal gangway led to a Jefferies tube connecting the control room to the engine room. Scott crawled through the tube

and opened the hatch at the other end. Just as he was about
to clamber out of the tube, a loud metallic crack startled him.
For a second, he feared that the warp core had breached prematurely, but, no, he'd already be atoms if that was the case. He
saw instead that a plasma transfer conduit had cracked, jetting
radioactive deuterium gas into the engine room. The ruptured
conduit hissed like an angry serpent.

"Mister Scott, Mister Scott!" Spears shouted to him over an
intercom. *"We've got a radiation leak in the engine room."*

"Don't I know it, lass!" He considered, just for a moment, trying to make it to the injectors anyway, no matter the cost, but
realized that he'd just be throwing his life away without saving
anyone. Never mind the radiation; he'd be scalded alive long
before he succeeded in uncoupling a single nozzle. The flesh was
willing, but his fragile skin and bones could not withstand the
laws of physics . . . or basic biology. "I'm coming back!"

Klaxons blared and annunciator lights flashed red, their color
almost lost in the intense incarnadine glow from the warp core.
A force field slammed into place, sealing the engine room off
from the rest of the ship. Scott couldn't get past it if he tried.

He scrambled backward into the tube, yanking the hatch shut
behind him and making sure it was tightly sealed. He knew that
it was only a matter of time before the tube itself was sealed off
to help contain the radiation, so he raced to exit it as quickly
as he could. His tool belt caught on a rung, forcing him to dis-
card the wrench rather than waste vital seconds trying to work
it free. He tumbled out of the tube onto the gangway, landing
unceremoniously on his rump. A heartbeat later, a second force
field crackled into place, so that both ends of the tube were
blocked. He counted himself lucky as he closed the outer hatch
as well.

That could have gone worse, he thought, *but we're still deep in
the haggis.*

Between the radiation leak and the overheating warp core,

Thunderbird was in its death throes and poised to take many more lives with it. In space, he could just eject the warp core into the void, but that was not exactly an option in the midst of an overcrowded population center. Scott began to prepare for the worst.

"We need to evacuate all nonessential personnel immediately." He looked soberly at Galligan. "You should go too, for your family's sake."

Galligan shook his head. "This is my responsibility. If anything, you should save yourself by beaming back to the *Enterprise*."

"I've never walked away from a job in my life," Scott said firmly. "Not about to start now."

Even if the best he could do was try to delay the breach long enough for the surrounding areas to be evacuated.

"I'm not going anywhere either," Spears said. "I'm here for as long as it takes."

Scotty was moved by their dedication and grateful for their courage. He couldn't do this alone. He flipped open his communicator to notify Kirk of the crisis.

"Scotty to *Enterprise*. Put me through to the captain immediately."

Nineteen

Deep Space Station S-8

"You wanted to see me, Lieutenant?"

Sulu found Tilton in his office, peering vacantly out of the viewport. Knox and Johann were along as backup, not that the worn-down old station manager appeared likely to cause trouble. Then again, Sulu reminded himself, appearances could be deceiving.

"That's right, sir." Sulu declined to sit down. "It's about the saboteur."

Tilton didn't look at him. "Yes, I heard that you and Grandle apprehended someone. Good work."

"Thank you, but I'm afraid that was just an isolated incident. I have reason to believe that we still have a bigger problem, one that's been right under our noses all this time."

Tilton frowned. "I'm not sure what you mean, Lieutenant."

"Well, I've been aboard this station long enough to see that Mister Grandle runs a very tight ship, even under the present circumstances, which makes it highly unlikely that any serious saboteur could get away with it for as long as they have . . . unless they were uniquely positioned to do so."

That got a response from Tilton, who finally turned toward Sulu. "Excuse me, Lieutenant, what exactly are you implying? That Mister Grandle is the guilty party?"

"No, sir," Sulu answered. "Even Grandle has only limited access to this station's primary systems and controls. The only person on this station with the authority to disable or override any and all security measures, edit logs and registers, and have free run of the entire station, including its most sensitive areas, is . . . you, Mister Tilton."

Tilton's reaction was typically muted. There was no indignation or angry protestations of innocence. He didn't even look surprised by the accusation. His haggard face remained slack, his voice barely more than a monotone. He might as well have been discussing the weather in New Helsinki this time of year.

"An interesting theory, Lieutenant, but where is your evidence?"

"Honestly, it's the *lack* of evidence that's most provocative," Sulu said. "Take the incident in the shuttlebay, for instance. I've reviewed the engineers' reports; as far as they can tell, there was no obvious mechanical reason why the emergency vents and filters failed in the crisis. They didn't malfunction, they were deliberately deactivated in anticipation of the coolant leak, in which case there should be some record of *who* exactly entered that command, but that data appears to have mysteriously vanished from all the relevant databases." Sulu fixed a stern gaze on Tilton. "There's not many people on this station who could issue that command *and* delete all trace of it afterward. You covered your trail *too* well, Tilton. That's what pointed me toward you."

It wasn't exactly a smoking gun, and probably wouldn't hold up in a court of law, but Sulu felt in his gut that he was on the right track. He didn't need to prove it; he just needed to stop Tilton from doing any more damage. Not that a full confession wouldn't make this easier for all concerned.

"Is that all you have, Lieutenant?"

"Not exactly." Sulu crossed the room to examine the scale model of the *Shenzhou* on display in the manager's office. "I've been looking into your background. You've had an impressive career, mostly in engineering, including a stint as the deputy superintendent of the Tranquility Base shipyards back during the first Federation-Klingon War. You even received a commendation for preventing a matter-antimatter generator from exploding due to Klingon sabotage . . . which, ironically enough, proves you have the skills and the know-how to pull off this recent campaign of sabotage."

Tilton mustered a dry chuckle.

"Do you hear yourself, Lieutenant Sulu?" the man scoffed. "No evidence is evidence? Preventing sabotage proves I'm the saboteur? Sounds to me like you've gone through the looking glass and have this all backward."

Sulu feared that Grandle would feel the same way, which is why he had not included her in this informal interrogation. He hoped to present Tilton's guilt to her as a *fait accompli*.

"You have the means and opportunity," he insisted. "The only thing that still stumps me is the motive." He spun Tilton's chair around to face him and leaned toward the embattled manager. "*Why*, Tilton? Why sabotage your own station and the travelers depending on you?"

"I . . ." Tilton's blank expression buckled for a moment. Grimacing, he opened his mouth to answer, only to seemingly choke on his own words, producing nothing more than a strangled, inarticulate gargle. A muscle twitched beneath his cheek. "I . . ."

"Tilton?" Sulu was taken aback by the man's apparent distress. "What's wrong with you?"

"Is he all right, sir?" Knox asked, looking on.

"Beats me," Sulu answered. "Talk to me, Tilton. What's the matter?"

"Nothing," the man said. "Nothing, except—" He grimaced again, as though straining to get the words out, before abandoning the effort. The fit seemed to pass as his expression emptied out again, collapsing back into blank passivity. His voice drained of all emotion. "What do you want me to say, Lieutenant? I won't say it. I can't say it . . ."

"Tilton?"

"I'm so tired," he said, "so tired and alone . . ."

Sulu stepped back, away from the inert manager, who almost appeared to be having some sort of breakdown. He was tempted to summon Doctor M'Benga, but was reluctant to do so before he got the answers he needed.

"Talk to me, Tilton," he said again, more gently this time. "If you need help, we can get it for you. Just tell me what's wrong with you."

"Nothing," Tilton mumbled. His detached gaze returned to the viewport, looking out into space. "Nothing but emptiness, extending forever and ever . . ."

"I think he's gone, sir," Knox said. "Mentally, I mean."

"I don't get it," Johann added. "It's like he doesn't even care that he could get shipped off to a penal colony."

"More like a psychiatric hospital," Knox said. "Not that there's much difference these days."

Sulu froze. The young officers' chatter, along with this entire situation, teased his memory indistinctly. Something about all this felt strangely familiar, even if he couldn't quite place it just yet.

"What did you just say?" he asked.

Knox shrugged. "Just speculating about whether Mister Tilton belonged in a penal colony or a mental asylum, assuming he is the saboteur, as you suspect."

"Same difference," Johann said.

Sulu let their remarks echo in his brain, hoping the reverberations would shake the right memory loose. Tilton mumbled in the background, his face and voice empty of emotion, as though the man he'd been had been leeched away from him, leaving nothing but an empty husk . . .

"Great Bird of the Galaxy," Sulu whispered as it hit him like a phaser on stun.

It had been a few years ago, during the early days of the *Enterprise*'s five-year mission. A routine visit to a remote penal colony on Tantalus V had turned ugly when it was discovered that the Federation's most-celebrated psychiatrist, Doctor Tristan Adams, had been testing an experimental new mind-control device on the inmates under his care. Sulu had not been on the first landing party to visit the colony, but he'd beamed down later to help restore order to the asylum in the wake of Adams's defeat and accidental demise. He still remembered some of the brainwashed patients he'd encountered there, particularly a chilling young woman named Lethe, who displayed the same empty eyes and lack of affect that Tilton did now, thanks to Adams's insidious invention, which he'd called . . . what was it again? It took Sulu a moment to retrieve the name.

A neural neutralizer.

"Alert Doctor M'Benga," he ordered. "We need to get this man to the infirmary!"

Twenty

Yurnos

The smugglers' craft lifted off from the beach, its landing gear retracting. The unnamed vessel rotated 180 degrees before heading out over the bay, where it swiftly dived beneath the waves, disappearing from sight. The marmots harnessed to the wagon chittered at its departure, as the shuttle left Spock and Chekov alone on the beach with Eefa, who angrily cursed the smugglers in their wake.

"Faithless, murdering caitiffs!"

The men were still bound. She was still armed, and upset over Woji's sudden disintegration. Spock judged the situation volatile and hazardous. It required careful handling.

"No sudden moves or outbursts," he advised Chekov in a low voice.

"Understood, sir."

For the moment, however, Eefa's violent emotions were directed at the smugglers. Perhaps emboldened by their absence, she vented furiously into her communicator. "That's right, you cursed swine! Kill my man and just leave me here to deal with your enemies. I hope you choke on my tea!"

"My sympathies for your loss," Spock said.

"To limbo with your sympathies, you . . . Vulcan!" She glared at him and Chekov. "You're as much to blame as they are. I had a fine deal working here before you two came along. Now Woji's dead and it's all your fault!"

She waved the pistol at them, rage, grief, and a loaded firearm adding up to a dangerous total. Spock could not help finding the combination disturbing. His memories flashed back to that moment on Neural, two years, eight months, and fourteen days ago, when a bullet fired from a primitive rifle struck him in the back and passed all the way through his body to emerge from his chest, felling him. The weapon may have been crude by modern standards, but the pain and injury had been no less intense. His body still remembered the trauma even as he applied logic to put the memory in its place.

That was the past, he thought. *This is the present.*

"Your anger is misplaced. We did not harm your associate."

"But you started this!" she accused him. "You brought this on us!"

Spock regretted Woji's death, but, logically, he realized, it was the smugglers who chose to introduce homicide to the equation when any number of less violent responses were possible. He could not be held accountable for their crime.

"Your associates killed Woji without cause," he stated. "We did not force them to resort to murder."

He chose not to point out that Woji's execution had been in response to Eefa personally threatening the smugglers. It was difficult to predict how she would react to that observation.

"We are very sorry for what happened to your friend," Chekov said. "That was never our intention. What those criminals did was . . . unconscionable."

His palpable sincerity penetrated her shields, dampening her anger to a degree. She kept the pistol fixed on them nonetheless.

"You realize I can't let you go now. Not after what you've seen. Not with who or what you are."

Spock feared she was trying to talk herself into doing what she thought was necessary. He attempted to reason with her.

"We have no desire to interfere with your life or legitimate business affairs. Our only interest is in curbing the illegal activities of those who just departed. We have learned all we need from you."

"And I'm supposed to take your word for that?" she said. "A Vulcan . . . from Starfleet, whatever that means." She shook her head reluctantly. "You expect me to believe that you will just walk away after all this . . . and not want to settle scores?"

"Vulcans do not seek revenge," Spock stated. "That I can assure you."

"Same here," Chekov said. "No hard feelings, really. What's an involuntary wagon ride and a few bruises between friends?"

"No, no, I can't take that chance," she said. "You've brought too much trouble to my door already. I need to be rid of you for good."

The quaver in her voice belied her certainty. Her gun arm trembled.

"I am not convinced you are capable of killing in cold blood," Spock said. "Unlike those who took Woji's life."

"You don't know me. You don't know what I'm capable of." She glanced briefly at the bay. An idea seemed to occur to her. "Start walking . . . that way."

Chekov looked at her in surprise. "Into the bay?"

"That's right." She gestured in the direction of the surf. "Walk into the water and keep on going . . . all the way back to where you came from."

Chekov remained baffled. "But . . . we will drown first."

"I believe that is the intention, Ensign," Spock explained. It was evident Eefa saw the bay as a passive way to dispose of them that would spare her having to actually shoot her victims or look them in the eyes. "And yet she has not fully thought this through."

"What?" Eefa said. "What do you mean by that?"

Spock faced her calmly. Although the smugglers had taken

his phaser with them, he remained armed with his most potent weapon: logic.

"Your weapon," he pointed out. "I have had ample time to examine it and it is clear that it is only capable of firing one shot at a time, as one would expect from a flintlock pistol of that type. There are, however, two of us. Whichever one of us you shoot, the other will be able to retaliate before you can reload."

Eefa swallowed hard. Her eyes darted back and forth between the two men.

"You're both chained up. You think I can't handle a bound prisoner on my own?"

"A bound prisoner with nothing to lose and who has been trained in combat by the adepts of Collu S'Avala," Spock said. "Chained or not, we are both formidable foes. Rest assured that the surviving individual will be able to subdue you with ease, although the restraints may force your attacker to resort to more ruthless methods than they might otherwise employ. I cannot guarantee that you will not incur serious physical harm."

Eefa aimed the pistol directly at Spock.

"Won't do you much good if you're the one who gets shot between the eyes."

"Perhaps," he replied, "but I will be just as deceased if I drown myself at gunpoint. This way, one of us will survive to, as you say, settle scores."

Anguish contorted her face. She appeared on the verge of tears.

"You're just trying to confuse me!"

"Not at all," Spock said. "I am simply spelling out the incontrovertible mathematics of the situation. You cannot win here. Even if you pull the trigger, you will be defeated . . . and will have committed murder to no end. Where is the sense in that?"

"So what do you expect me to do?" she asked sourly. "Surrender? Even though you're in chains and I'm the one holding the gun?"

"Precisely," Spock said. "It is the only scenario in which you emerge unharmed."

Checkmate, he thought.

"My comrade is right," Chekov said. "You can kill one of us, but only one of us, or you can trust us to leave you in peace. Those are your choices." He shrugged. "I know which one I would pick."

A subjectively long moment passed as Eefa wrestled visibly with the dilemma. Spock wanted to think that the inexorable logic of his argument would sway her, but he had long ago stopped expecting non-Vulcans to behave logically while under emotional stress. There remained a significant probability that she would fire the pistol at one of them—and most likely him. He braced himself for that possibility.

"Curse it." She lowered the gun. "I guess the old saying is right after all. 'Sometimes falling is the only way to land on your feet.'"

Spock wished he'd known that saying. It might have rendered this tense encounter shorter.

"You win," she said. "What do you want?"

"Unchaining our hands would be a good start," Chekov said.

Eefa laughed bitterly. "Can't help you there. Woji had the keys to the lock . . . and they went with him."

"Terrific," Chekov said dourly. "Just our luck!"

"Do not abandon hope just yet," Spock said. "This presents a difficulty, but not, I think, an insurmountable one." He approached Eefa. "If I may have your communicator?"

"Communicator?"

"The device you use to speak with Mars and Venus and their gang."

The smugglers had taken their devices, so Eefa's communicator was the only one readily at hand.

"Oh, you mean the voice carrier." She contemplated the device in her grip. "What do you want that for?"

"It is difficult to explain in your terms. Suffice it to say that it has other uses." He turned his back to her, presenting his open palms. "I may be able to use it to engineer our release."

To his credit, Chekov grasped what he had in mind. "A sonic vibration?"

"That is the idea, Ensign."

Eefa snorted in exasperation. "The more you speak, the less sense you make, but if it will get you out of my hair faster . . ." She strode over and placed the communicator in his hands. "There! Work your marvels with it if you can."

"Thank you, madam. I hope to do exactly that."

Spock recalled the Capellan triblade found among the contraband collected by Jord and Vankov. Once, on Capella IV, he and Kirk had triggered a rockslide by using their communicators to induce a sympathetic vibration in solid granite. That feat had required two communicators working in tandem, but Spock was not attempting to bring down a cliff face here, merely to induce a sonic vibration sufficient to turn the tumbler in a primitive lock. He simply had to tune the communicator to a frequency capable of producing the desired resonance effect.

Granted, manipulating the communicator with his hands chained behind his back posed a challenge to his dexterity and concentration, but nothing beyond his abilities. That the controls on the simple communicator given to Eefa were quite rudimentary, lacking any specialized features, made the task somewhat easier.

"Let us attempt to undo your lock first," he said to Chekov. "Please bring it within reach."

"Of course." Chekov backed toward Spock, so that the men had their backs to each other. He raised his bound wrists so that Spock could get at the lock. "Excuse me, sir, but if you don't mind me asking: Are we quite certain this is safe?"

Spock had no intention or expectation of shattering Chekov's wrists. He placed the borrowed communicator directly against the lock to maximize the sonic resonance.

"You are in no danger, Ensign. You may feel a slight vibration, nothing more. Ask rather whether this experiment will succeed."

"I have faith in you, sir."

"This is a matter of frequency, not faith, but your vote of confidence is duly noted."

Spock activated the communicator, which transmitted the sonic vibration to the lock keeping Chekov chained. As it happened, a degree of fine-tuning was required to achieve the proper resonance, but he was soon rewarded by the click of the locking mechanism disengaging. He withdrew the communicator, being careful to make certain it remained tuned to the correct frequency, and tugged the lock open.

"You may proceed to liberate yourself, Ensign."

"With pleasure, sir!"

With the ends of the chain no longer secured to each other, Chekov swiftly managed to extract one hand from the bindings, allowing him to free his arms for the first time in hours. He appeared to take considerable satisfaction in unwinding the chain from around his wrist and hurling it onto the ground with some force.

"You did it, sir!" He grinned at Spock. "It worked!"

Eefa looked on in amazement. "Well, I'll be cursed. Seems you knew what you were doing after all."

"To do otherwise would be illogical," he replied. "Now then, Ensign, if you would kindly return the favor?"

"Aye, sir."

Chekov repeated the procedure with no difficulty and assisted in removing Spock's chains as well. Although his reaction to having his arms freed was less emotive than the young human's, Spock was also pleased to have a full range of motion again. He massaged his wrists to aid their circulation.

Eefa held out her hand. "Might I have my property back?"

"I'm afraid that is not possible," Spock said. The Prime Directive required that he confiscate the device lest it cause the

Yurnians to progress too quickly. "If it is any consolation, you will have no further need of it. Your smuggler friends will soon be out of business, at least if we achieve our aims."

"They're not friends of mine." She spat onto the beach to express her disgust with her former business partners. "Fine. Take my 'communicator' if you must. I'm sick to death of this whole cursed business."

Spock was glad to hear it.

"But how are we going to catch up with those murdering Cossacks?" Chekov asked. "They made a clean escape!"

"Not before revealing more perhaps than they intended," Spock said. "I believe I know how the smugglers plan to get the *nabbia* off the planet undetected, but we will have to move quickly if we wish to confirm this. We need to return to *Galileo* with all deliberate speed."

"But that must be kilometers away," Chekov said.

"Just so, which means we cannot linger here." He turned to Eefa. "I am afraid, madam, that we will have to commandeer your wagon for a time."

"Why not?" she said sarcastically. "You've taken everything else." She appeared too defeated to offer more than a token protest. "Would you care for the dress off my back as well?"

"That will not be necessary," Spock said. "Your wagon and livestock will be returned to you if at all possible." He glanced at the trail leading back up to the road. "Can you safely walk back to Wavebreak from here?"

"If I have to."

"That would be for the best," Spock said. "I apologize for inconveniencing you, but what comes next is not for your eyes."

She threw up her hands. "Serves me right, I suppose, for dragging you here in the first place."

Spock did not challenge that argument. "Live long and prosper," he addressed her, "by honest means."

The marmots grew restive as Chekov claimed the driver's

seat at the front of the wagon. Spock calmed them by stroking their ears as he had seen Jord do, then climbed onto a padded wooden bench beside the young navigator.

"Are you confident in your ability to control these creatures, Ensign?"

"Of course, sir. Russians have a natural way with animals. Everyone knows that."

"Perhaps, but these particular animals are far from Russian."

Despite his reservations, Spock unlocked the wheels. Chekov snapped the reins and the marmots started forward eagerly. He succeeded in steering them toward the slope, although how much of that was due to the young human's skill at driving the wagon versus the rodents' own heartfelt desire to escape from the cove was debatable. Spock opted not to question their progress as long as they were heading in the right direction.

The wagon rapidly ascended the trail, leaving Eefa behind. The route was just as bumpy as Spock recalled, but more easily endured now that they were no longer mere cargo in the back. They soon reached the larger road above, where the marmots vigorously attempted to turn toward Wavebreak. Chekov pulled on the reins and engaged the brake.

"Which way now, Mister Spock?"

"A highly relevant question, Ensign."

Time being of the essence, Spock did not wish to return to the mill by way of Wavebreak if a more direct route was available. He contemplated the starry night sky; it was theoretically possible that they could chart a course back to their shuttle by the stars alone, but their unfamiliarity with the local roads and byways complicated matters. He regretted that they could not risk enlisting Eefa as a guide without compromising Jord's and Vankov's secrets. He and Chekov would have to find their own way to the mill—and *Galileo*.

"Are we lost, Mister Spock?"

"Only to a degree," he replied. Perhaps the wisest course

would be to return to Wavebreak after all. Spock was confident they could retrace the route they had taken from the mill to the town. "We may need to let the marmots have their way—"

A thundering noise, as of many heavy paws pounding against the road a short distance away, intruded on their discussion. Spock turned to see several uniformed Yurnians riding toward them atop racing marmots. A warning shot fired loudly into the air.

"Halt . . . in the governor's name!"

Twenty-One

Baldur III

"What do you need from us?" Kirk asked from the *Enterprise*.

The captain's face was grim as it looked at Scott from the terminal in Galligan's office. Static and visual snow marred the transmission; Scott blamed the *Thunderbird*'s compromised circuitry, along with, possibly, any radiation leaking from the self-destructing engine room. He and Galligan and Spears, who were all that remained of the plant's meager skeleton crew after the rank-and-file workers had been instructed to evacuate, had managed to keep the engineering section sealed off from the radiation so far, but they had changed into protective suits just to be safe, not that the suits would save them when the warp core breached. The hood of Scott's suit rested on the desk as he conferred with Kirk.

"I thank you for the thought," Scott replied, "but to put it bluntly, I'm not sure there's much you can do for us for here at ground zero. We're doing our damnedest to delay the disaster for as long as possible, but we can't stop the warp core from melting down eventually. My advice, sir: concentrate on spreading the alarm and evacuating the city as fast as you possibly can."

A digital countdown on the screen, which Scott had set up on the off chance that he might lose track of the time, informed him that *Thunderbird* would be going nova in approximately one hour, twenty minutes.

"*Already on it,*" Kirk assured him, but Scott didn't need to be told that this was far easier said than done in the scant time available. "*Starting with the area directly around the park and* Thunderbird."

Scott understood that Galligan was in touch with his superiors as well.

"*We can beam down more technicians to assist you,*" Kirk suggested.

"No offense, sir, but that would just be throwing more lives in harm's way. In any event, we've raised *Thunderbird*'s outer shields to confine the radiation leaks to the ship, so no one is beaming in or out of here until this is over."

He left unspoken the obvious implication: that with the shields in place, they could not be beamed out. Not that Scott intended to leave his post; he didn't trust *Thunderbird*'s automated systems to manage the overheating reactor the way an actual flesh-and-blood engineer could. Countless lives depended on his postponing the breach for as long as he could.

"*Damn it, Scotty,*" Kirk said. "*This is insane. I can't lose you this way.*"

"Wasn't my plan either," Scott said with a fatalistic shrug. "But I knew the risks when I signed up . . . and have already made it out of more tight scrapes than the odds would favor. It's been an honor serving under you, Captain."

So much for retiring and buying a ship someday, he thought.

"*I should have listened to you,*" Kirk said. "*Never put you in this position.*"

"And if you hadn't, sir, this town might already be a crater." Scott didn't want Kirk blaming himself. "I'm where I need to be, under the circumstances. If anything, I should be apologizing to you for not preventing this."

"*Belay that kind of talk,*" Kirk said. "*Knowing you, Scotty, you did your very best and then some.*"

Scott kept an eye on the countdown. Galligan and Spears were keeping watch over the reactor at the moment, but now was no time for long goodbyes.

"Just one thing, Captain. There's a fine old bottle of single-malt Scotch in my quarters that I've been saving for a special occasion, and I'd surely hate to see it go to waste. I'd be obliged if you and Mister Spock and Doctor McCoy would raise a glass in my memory."

Kirk shook his head. *"Request denied, Mister Scott. I don't believe in no-win scenarios, which means you're not allowed to either. Find a solution, Scotty. Work another miracle. That's an order."*

"I wish I could, Captain, but we're already doing everything we can just to buy the city more time. We're trying to regulate, if ye can call it that, the reactor with our last remaining crystal, while bleeding off as much excess heat as possible by channeling the surplus energy into the ship's dormant systems, powering up everything from the deflectors to life-support to the long-range sensors and the artificial gravity, but the reaction is still building no matter what we do. It's only a matter of time before it's too much for the core to contain."

Seventy-eight minutes, to be exact.

"And there's nowhere else you can divert the heat?" Kirk asked.

"I don't think so, Captain. At this point, we've fired up practically everything except the old impulse engine—"

Scott slapped his forehead. He'd been so focused on keeping the warp core from exploding that he had missed one possible solution.

"What is it, Scotty? Do you have something?"

A sly grin crossed the engineer's face.

"Thunderbird is a ship, isn't she? Maybe she still has one last flight in her!"

Twenty-Two

Deep Space Station S-8

"You called it, Lieutenant. This man's brain has been tampered with . . . in a manner consistent with the application of a neural neutralizer."

Doctor M'Benga scanned Tilton in a private exam room in the station's overcrowded infirmary. His bedside manner was somewhat brisker than McCoy's, perhaps as a result of having interned on Vulcan some years ago; a specialist in xenomedicine, he spent much of his time aboard the *Enterprise* engaged in research rather than treating patients, while filling in for McCoy when necessary. At Sulu's request, M'Benga had installed Tilton out of sight of the other patients, no easy task, considering the shortage of available beds; the last thing the station needed was for word of the manager's condition to spread wildly before Sulu had a chance to confirm it. An opaque energy screen blocked light and sound from escaping the exam chamber, while Knox and Johann were posted outside the doorway to ensure that Sulu and M'Benga were uninterrupted. Tilton was stretched out on a diagnostic biobed, staring vacantly at the ceiling, as M'Benga continued to probe beneath the man's skull via a handheld medical scanner. Restraints held the stricken manager in place.

"Refresh my memory, Doctor," Sulu asked. "How exactly does

a neural neutralizer work, again? I've witnessed its effects first-hand, but I'm a helmsman, not a psychiatrist."

"I need to review the relevant literature myself," M'Benga said, "but basically the device employs a specialized beam that, as the name suggests, effectively neutralizes the subject's brainwaves, shutting down their thoughts and leaving them in a highly suggestible state. Depending on the duration and intensity of the treatment, the operator can erase or rewrite the subject's memories, alter their emotions, even implant powerful posthypnotic suggestions."

M'Benga put the scanner down on a counter after transferring its readings to the infirmary's main computer. His gaze remained fixed on the diagnostic panel mounted above Tilton's bed, monitoring the patient's life signs.

"Apparently the late Doctor Adams developed the device in hopes of 'curing' the criminally insane by editing their memories, but the potential for abuse was always there—and quickly corrupted his experiments."

Sulu nodded, remembering. Adams had ultimately employed the neutralizer on both his patients *and* his fellow healers, at the expense of their free will.

"Which is why Captain Kirk ordered the neutralizer destroyed," Sulu recalled, "and Doctor Adams's research locked up tight."

"The right call, to be sure," M'Benga said. "Alas, as history proves too well, once a new technology has been developed, it's all but impossible to put the genie back in the bottle. Backup copies of Adams's discoveries, some of them stored off Tantalus V, escaped into the wild and were traded by unscrupulous individuals who were quick to recognize its illicit potential." He shook his head ruefully. "Despite the Federation's best efforts to contain the technology, an illegal trade in neural neutralizers has sprung up in some of the more unsavory parts of the galaxy. They're scarce and, mercifully, very hard to obtain, but they can sometimes be had on the black market . . . as proven by the condition of Mister Tilton."

Sulu repressed a shudder as he contemplated the benumbed man on the biobed. Now that he understood what he was seeing, Sulu found the violation done to Tilton profoundly disturbing for reasons that hit far too close to home. At least twice in recent years, Sulu had been similarly brainwashed, robbed of his free will first by Landru on Beta III, then by those extragalactic "witches" on Pyris VII. He knew what it was like to be turned into somebody else's robotic pawn. Tilton deserved his pity, not blame for what he'd been forced to do.

"Somebody did this to him," Sulu said angrily, determined to track down whoever was responsible. Tilton may have been the saboteur, but the true criminal still eluded them. He looked at M'Benga. "Can I question him further?"

"You can try," the doctor said, "but I should monitor him while you do so."

"Understood." Sulu approached the biobed. "Tilton? Listen to me. Do you understand what's happening, what was done to you?"

"I have nothing to say," Tilton murmured, not making eye contact. "Nothing . . ."

"Just tell me who did this to you. Give me a name."

Tilton shook his head. "I . . . I can't say . . ."

"Look at me." Sulu took the man by the shoulders, earning him a cautionary look from M'Benga. "This station—*your* station—is under attack. Tell me who is responsible. Give me a name."

The urgency in his voice drew Tilton's gaze. He stared back at Sulu, who felt as though the man was truly seeing him, at least for the moment.

"I . . . it was . . ." Tilton struggled visibly to get the words out. An anguished expression twisted his face and his whole body tensed. Each word appeared to require a Herculean effort. "Want . . . to . . . tell . . . but . . ."

A groan cut him off in midsentence, much to Sulu's frustration.

"Who was it, Tilton? All I need is a name!"

M'Benga eyed the life-signs monitor with concern. "His blood pressure and heart rate are rising, Lieutenant. Neuro-synaptic activity is going critical."

"Just a few more moments!" Sulu realized that M'Benga was bound to shut down the interrogation at any minute. "The name, Tilton! You can do it. Spit it out!"

Sweat drenched Tilton's features, soaking through his clothing. His eyes bulged from their sockets. Sulu barely recognized the tired, soft-spoken manager he'd met when he'd first beamed aboard the station.

"It's . . . it's . . . I'm trying but . . ." Pain contorted his face. His body convulsed, struggling against his restraints. An agonized scream tore itself from his lungs, drowning out whatever revelations were trapped inside him. His head whipped back and forth. Warning lights flashed upon the diagnostic monitor as his life signs spiked dangerously.

"That's enough." M'Benga squeezed past Sulu to administer a sedative to Tilton. A hypospray hissed, and the manager's face and limbs went slack. "I'm sorry, Sulu, but the man was in obvious physical distress. I couldn't allow that to go on any longer."

"Understood." Sulu stepped away from the bed. He couldn't blame M'Benga for intervening, given his Hippocratic oath, but it was still frustrating. "He was so close to revealing the truth."

"But at what cost?" M'Benga watched Tilton's life signs ease back into the safety zone as he checked the man's pulse the old-fashioned way as well. "You want my instant diagnosis, Tilton's been conditioned to hide the identity of whoever brainwashed him. To even try to answer your questions caused him enormous pain."

Sulu had no reason to doubt the doctor's appraisal. He recalled hearing that the neutral neutralizer could have that effect while the *Enterprise* was cleaning up Doctor Adams's mess.

"Any way to get around that?"

"Short of a Vulcan mind-meld?" M'Benga didn't look hopeful. "Honestly, I don't know. We *might* eventually be able to pry the answers out of him, despite the conditioning, but who knows what toll that would take on his mind and body? We can't risk putting him through that, not in good conscience."

"I was afraid you were going to say that," Sulu said with a sigh.

Twenty-Three

Baldur III

". . . the situation at the Thunderbird *power plant is critical. All crew members currently stationed on the planet are directed to assist the local authorities as needed. Take charge if you have to. Kirk out."*

Uhura lowered her communicator. The emergency alert from the *Enterprise* had not been directed to her personally, but to every member of every landing party, so she was not obliged to respond. Instead she took a moment to process what she had just heard and go to red-alert status, which involved switching gears in a major way.

Only minutes earlier, she had been enjoying another evening at the Pergium Palace, where, in fact, she had just taken first place in a weekly talent show. She'd been celebrating her victory with Oskar Thackery and his crowd at their usual table, when she'd stepped away to take the call from the *Enterprise*. She glanced over at the booth, where her new friends remained still happily oblivious to the power plant's impending meltdown. A trophy cup, studded with cheap Spican flame gems, rested on the table in front of her vacant seat.

The power plant was only blocks away.

Scanning the crowded nightclub, she saw her fellow crew members also reacting to the news. Uhura pondered her next move. How to sound the alarm without starting a panic?

The decision was taken out of her hands when the subdued lighting of the club was suddenly dialed up and the music stopped playing. Mayor Poho suddenly appeared upon every entertainment screen, replacing a local bluegrass band which had been performing in the background. The mayor's grim expression instantly put a damper on the festivities.

"Attention, fellow citizens. An emergency evacuation order is in effect. All citizens are instructed to flee the vicinity of Jackpot City immediately. Proceed in an orderly fashion, but without delay. This is not a drill. I repeat, this is not a drill. Get going.

"May fate have mercy on us all."

The alarming message ended abruptly, leaving the screens blank and the club thrown into a state of confusion. Agitated voices clamored for answers or cried out in fear. Flossi, who had just brought a fresh order of drinks to the table, looked anxiously at Uhura. Other eyes turned in Uhura's direction as well.

"Nyota? Do you know anything about this?"

Uhura chose her words carefully. She had to strike the right balance between calm and urgency.

"This is for real," she said simply. "We need to move quickly."

She was debating how much to reveal about the danger to the city, when Levity trumped her by running up to the table.

"Listen to me, everybody!" she shouted too loudly. "I just heard from my cousin, who works at the power plant in the park. He says it's going to explode and take the whole city with it!"

Her voice carried across the club, adding to the panic. Customers and employees began stampeding for the exits, knocking over chairs and threatening to trample each other as they ran for their lives. Uhura saw Lieutenant Desai and several other *Enterprise* crew members try to bring order to the panicked exodus, but without much success. A few had drawn their inconspicuous type-1 phasers, but appeared hesitant to stun anyone for fear of creating even more bedlam. Uhura shared their reluctance.

"Calm down, everyone, please!" She jumped onto a table, spilling drinks and snack bowls, in hopes of getting people's attention, while shouting at the top of her voice. "Don't panic! I know you're scared, but people are going to get hurt if we don't keep our heads!"

Her voice was lost in the tumult. A fleeing stranger slammed into the table, almost sending her tumbling to the floor. She saw Desai go to the rescue of a server who had fallen and was at risk of being ground into the carpet; he snatched her up off the floor and hurled her into an empty booth to get her out of the way of the stampede, while blocking the rushing crowd like an offensive lineman. Elsewhere, bottlenecks at the exits were looking more like riots, with people pushing and shoving to force their way through doorways far too narrow to accommodate them all at once. Heated voices rose above the din, presaging violence.

"Stop this!" Uhura shouted. "Let us help you all get out of here safely!"

No one was listening, yet she had to do something to make her voice heard. Her gaze fell on her trophy, sitting forgotten at Thackery's table, then swung to the now-empty stage as a moment of inspiration came from out of the blue.

Maybe an encore performance?

With a dancer's grace, she headed for the stage, bounding from table to table to avoid the pandemonium packing the aisles. Cups and plates went flying. A high-domed Rhaandarite loomed in her way, and she leapfrogged over his head and shoulders to reach the next table before rushing up a short flight of stairs onto the stage, where, thanks to her advanced knowledge of communications technology, she swiftly accessed a manual control panel and switched the display function back on before taking her place center stage, which magnified her voice and image and projected it all over the premises.

It's showtime, she thought breathlessly.

Three stories tall, her holographic replica towered over the chaotic scene, even as her image also appeared on multiple viewscreens. Her amplified voice rang out over the chaos and panic, seizing people's attention, while the hologram's giant phaser was hard to ignore as well. Uhura fired a warning shot over the crowd, which was echoed on a much larger scale by her double, albeit only as an illusion. Gasps erupted from the mob.

That's more like it, she thought. "Do I have your attention now? Some of you know me already, but I'm Lieutenant Uhura of the *Starship Enterprise.* My comrades and I are here to handle this crisis and get you all to safety as quickly as possible, but we need your cooperation. Panicking is only going to make things worse."

Cashing in on whatever social capital she had built up over the last few days, Uhura was relieved to see the distraught patrons listening to her at last. She suspected this had less to do with her innate star power than with their understandable need for someone to take charge of the emergency and offer them hope and help when they were scared.

And, right now, that was her.

"Listen to the Starfleet personnel nearest you. Follow their instructions." She made eye contact with Desai and the rest, who nodded back at her, as they began regulating the desperate throngs streaming toward the exits. "We're trained to handle situations like this. Let us help."

Her words must have been convincing, as the evacuation became less frenzied and more organized. People were still visibly distraught, but they weren't a mob anymore. Bottlenecks turned into lines, which the Starfleet officers kept moving briskly. Uhura watched with satisfaction as the club began to clear out, but she knew there was much else to be done, not just to evacuate the Pergium Palace but the surrounding neighborhoods as well. Even in an era of mass communications, they couldn't count on every Baldurian getting the alert on time or being able to flee the city on their own power.

Too bad we don't have more manpower on site, she thought. "We need volunteers to assist with the evacuation. Anybody who can help, please report to me here at the stage."

Most of the civilians kept pressing toward the exits, but maybe a dozen new or native Baldurians broke away from the crowd to converge on Uhura, who was not surprised to see Flossi at the forefront of the group. Thackery and his crowd, including even Levity, scurried to join her. Uhura was impressed and touched.

"What can we do?" Flossi called out.

I knew she was Starfleet material, Uhura thought. *Remind me to recommend her to the Academy if and when we get out of this alive.*

"Round up the other club workers and whoever else wants to help. We need people to go door by door, house by house, business by business, to make sure everyone's got the word and has a way to get out of the danger zone. Secure whatever vehicles you can find and start loading them up with as many people as they can carry. Somebody who knows the area, chart the best routes out of the city."

On Earth or Alpha Centauri, job one would be getting people to emergency transporter stations and beaming them out of harm's way, but such stations were few and far between on frontier worlds like Baldur III, if they existed at all. They would have to make do with whatever resources were available.

"Desai, Lewis, Faust, Gonzalez, everyone else," she addressed the other crew members. "Break into teams, one Starfleet officer per group of volunteers, keep your communicators handy so we can stay in touch and coordinate our efforts. Check in frequently until we're sure the surrounding areas are cleared."

"Aye, Lieutenant," Pran Desai said. "We're on it."

Thackery raised his hand. "As it happens, I've got a ridiculously ostentatious sky-yacht parked on a roof nearby that can carry plenty of passengers."

"Perfect!" Uhura said. "You and Rixon start ferrying people out of the city. And contact your friends and associates. Enlist anyone else with a ready means of transportation."

"But what about people who can't be moved?" Levity asked. "My great-grandmother lives a few blocks from here. She's practically bedridden. She can't just clamber into a truck or flyer."

A valid concern, Uhura thought. "Your designated Starfleet team leaders will request emergency transporter rescues as required. Disabled and/or immobile citizens can be beamed up to the *Enterprise* on a by-need basis." She regarded the other officers. "Use your best judgment, but don't leave anyone behind."

"Hang on!" Levity protested. "Why can't you just beam all of us up right now?"

"I wish it was that easy," Uhura said. "But even the *Enterprise* can't transport an entire city's population in less than two hours."

Levity looked unconvinced, or maybe she was just worried about herself and her family. "But—"

"Leave her be," Thackery said, cutting her off. "I'm sure the folks on the *Enterprise* are doing the best they can, under the circumstances."

"Absolutely," Uhura assured him. "You can rely on Captain Kirk. I've trusted my life to him more times than I can count."

Flossi nodded. "What about you, Nyota? What are you going to do?"

"What I always do," Uhura said. "Work the comms and make sure the left hand knows what the right hand is doing."

———

"The first of the evacuees have been beamed aboard, Captain. Transporter room reporting many more incoming."

Lieutenant Elizabeth Palmer was manning the comm station with Uhura down on the planet. In a way, Kirk envied Uhura. He wanted to be there in the thick of things, getting his hands dirty, instead of being stuck on the bridge supervising the evacuation efforts from orbit. An unfortunate reality of command, however, was that sometimes you had to stand back and oversee matters while the people serving under you risked their lives on the front line. Kirk acknowledged that, even if he had never truly made peace with it. *If Spock was here to take the bridge,* he thought, *I'd be down there in a minute.*

"Good," he replied to Palmer. "Inform security to find temporary accommodations for them. Move them into the guest quarters, the shuttlebay, the storage holds, the bowling alley, the gymnasium, the botanical garden . . . anywhere we can set up cots and other necessaries."

"Even the VIP suites?" Palmer asked.

"Especially the VIP suites," Kirk said.

The *Enterprise* couldn't house an entire population indefinitely, but if Jackpot City was indeed destroyed by a warp breach, the survivors were going to need emergency housing in the aftermath, so there was no telling how long the *Enterprise* might have to accommodate them in the short term.

"And hail the other ships in orbit," he added. "Find out how many evacuees they can each accept. The more the better."

Not every vessel was equipped for surface-to-ship transports, but the *Enterprise* could always beam or shuttle any surplus civilians over to the other ships if necessary. First things first, he reminded himself. Getting people away from ground zero took priority. Finding shelter for them, either in orbit or on the planet, came later.

"Aye, sir," Palmer said. "I'm on it."

Kirk knew he was asking a lot of her, but he was confident she was up to the challenge; Palmer had served as the relief communications officer for years and never performed less than ably in all that time. Nevertheless, as Kirk glanced over the bridge, he couldn't help noticing all the missing faces: Spock, Scotty, Sulu, Uhura, and Chekov. Even McCoy was still down on the planet, assisting in the evacuation of the city hospital. Their absence troubled Kirk; Palmer and the others were good people and highly capable officers, but Kirk felt like he was facing this crisis on his own, missing his usual right-hand people.

What was a captain without his crew?

"Good news, Nyota. Another truckload of evacuees is on its way out of the city. That empties Zone F."

"Fantastic." Uhura drew a line through the designated area on a large paper map Flossi had procured for her. "That's one more block cleared."

Uhura had turned the Pergium Palace into an impromptu command center, only blocks away from ground zero. The map was spread out atop a table near the stage as she fielded reports from throughout the neighborhood. Teams of volunteers, each supervised by an officer from the *Enterprise*, were racing the clock to get any and all civilians away from the power plant and its dangerously unstable warp core. Uhura's personal communicator was getting a workout as she pined for her specialized earpiece back on the bridge, which would have helped her focus on the ceaseless stream of reports flowing into the club. She was half tempted to ask Captain Kirk to beam the earpiece down to her, but assumed that the transporters were fully occupied beaming shut-ins to safety.

"Here." Flossi offered her a steaming mug of hot *nabbia* tea. "You look like you could use this."

Uhura looked askance at the mug, but didn't turn it down. She needed to be at her best and the tea *was* supposed to be invigorating.

"Thanks."

Flossi winked at her. "I won't tell if you won't."

A priority hail from the *Enterprise* demanded her attention. She put the other chatter on hold as she responded immediately.

"Lieutenant Uhura reporting."

"*Kirk here,*" the captain's voice addressed her "*I understand you're overseeing evacuation efforts downtown?*"

"Affirmative, sir. I was in the right place at the right time." She glanced guiltily at the tea. "Or the wrong place, depending on your point of view, I suppose."

"*In any event, I applaud your initiative. I'm in touch with Mayor Poho and her people, but I wanted to hear from you first-hand. What's your situation?*"

Uhura concisely briefed Kirk on the status of her volunteer operation. "We're moving plenty of civilians away from the area, but whether it's fast enough or far enough remains to be seen. I have to admit, Captain, that I'd feel a lot better if I thought there was even a chance that warp core won't blow."

"*Scotty has a plan,*" he informed her. "*He's going to attempt to launch* Thunderbird *into space before the core breaches. But success is not guaranteed. One way or another, the fewer people in the vicinity the better.*"

"Understood, sir. And I'll take a risky plan over no plan any day, especially if Mister Scott has his hand in it."

"*My thoughts exactly,*" Kirk said. "*But I'm concerned by your own proximity to* Thunderbird. *I've instructed Palmer to keep a priority channel open in case you need to beam out in a hurry.*"

Uhura glanced around the Palace and at Flossi and the other locals she had come to know here. Her silly trophy cup still rested on the table, where it was being used as a paperweight to hold one end of the map down.

"Thank you, sir, but I'm going to stay here for as long as I can, and as long as I can do some good."

"*Message received, Lieutenant. Try not to call it too close. Kirk out.*"

Uhura put down the receiver, just to clear her mind before checking in with the volunteer squads. She took a sip of the tea.

Damn, that is *good,* she thought. *Sorry, Mister Spock.*

"Everything okay, Nyota?" Flossi asked.

"Here's hoping." She had faith that Scotty's mad plan would work. The only question was how much it would cost them. Peering across the club at the now-empty stage, she wondered if she should start singing "Nearer, My God, to Thee" and whether anyone would get it if she did.

It's not over yet, she thought.

Twenty-Four

Deep Space Station S-8

"What can I do for you, Lieutenant?"

The general store on the promenade was closed for the night, but Naylis admitted Sulu and Knox anyway, before locking the front entrance behind them. An actual steel door slid into place, as opposed to merely a protective force field. The lights were dimmed and most of the shelves and display cases were in need of restocking. Sulu had never seen the place so empty before.

"Just need a few moments of your time," Sulu said.

"I'm at your service, Lieutenant." Naylis stepped behind the central counter to straighten up a display of pocket-sized transponders. "Your timing is impeccable, I must say. I was just about to head to my quarters."

Sulu kept a close eye on the Troyian merchant. He had brought Knox along as backup while Johann remained posted outside Tilton's room in the infirmary, in part to keep anyone from seeing the manager in his present state, but also to guard Tilton from anyone who might want to silence him. Doctor M'Benga was hopeful that proper treatment could reverse the worst of the brainwashing. Sulu wanted to give Tilton a chance at recovery.

"Let me get straight to the point," Sulu said. "What do you know about neural neutralizers . . . and how to get your hands on one?"

Naylis stopped fiddling with the display. He looked up at Sulu with a quizzical expression on his face. If he was alarmed by this line of inquiry, he did a good job of hiding it. Sulu resolved to never play poker with the man.

"I assume you're asking in your professional capacity, Lieutenant. Please tell me you're not actually in the market for such an insidious piece of merchandise."

Sulu noted that Naylis didn't pretend to be unfamiliar with neural neutralizers, the existence of which was hardly public knowledge. Perhaps he judged that feigning ignorance would be unconvincing, considering his reputation for being well informed on matters of interest.

"Could you get me one if I was?"

"Goodness, what makes you think that?"

"Well, Grandle did say you could get your hands on just about anything for the right price . . ."

"Anything *legal*," Naylis stressed again.

Sulu recalled Grandle's skepticism regarding that claim. "That's right. You said that before."

And yet a neural neutralizer was apparently hiding in or around the station, and, from what Sulu gathered, Naylis was notorious for having his mint-green fingers in all sorts of pies.

"Look, Lieutenant," the merchant said. "I trade with dealers all over the quadrant, so, yes, I'm quite aware that the black markets exist, even for items banned throughout the Federation for very good reasons, but you have to believe me when I tell you that I would never stoop to such illicit dealings. I'm a legitimate businessman."

"Funny thing, though," Sulu said. "I asked the station computer to give me a rundown of recent imports and exports passing through this station, and it turns out that you recently received several large shipments from the dark side of Habah VIII, which is known to be a hub of illegal tech trafficking."

"Among other things," Naylis said. "If you look closer at the database, you'll see that those shipments are listed, accurately, as a large quantity of used antigrav lifters of the sort that will come in handy for prospectors on Baldur III." He gave Sulu a conspiratorial smirk. "What can I say? You can get lifters at a good price, and with considerably less red tape, if you're not too picky about whom you deal with, but it's not as though they're dangerous contraband. If anything, I was simply doing my best to lighten the loads of many a would-be miner."

Sulu glanced around the store. "Where are those lifters now?"

"Sold out almost instantly," Naylis said. "I made a handsome profit, if you must know, without having anything to do with a neural neutralizer."

"Then you won't mind if we look around a bit?"

"Must you?" Naylis said, sighing theatrically. "It's been a long day, and I haven't had my supper yet."

"All the more reason for me to get down to business." Sulu nodded at Knox, who stood by attentively. "Keep Mister Naylis company while I see what I can find, one way or another."

"Aye, sir," Knox said, watching his back. Her phaser remained clipped to her belt, but Sulu was confident that she could deal with Naylis if he tried to cause trouble.

Naylis's easy smile curdled. "Really, Lieutenant, I must protest. This borders on harassment. Perhaps we should see what Mister Tilton has to say about this?"

"Tilton is indisposed," Sulu said. "Just sit back and let me do my job."

Sulu walked the store, methodically scanning the premises with a tricorder in hopes of finding something suspicious. There was no guarantee, of course, that the neutralizer was nearby, or even that Naylis was indeed responsible for smuggling it onto the station—the case against the merchant was circumstantial at best—but it was a place to start searching for the neutralizer. The way Sulu saw it, an educated guess was better than no clue at all.

Wonder what Mister Spock would think of that logic?

The tricorder hummed as it surveyed the shop, finding nothing out of the ordinary at first. Then a blank spot registered on the display as the scans were unable to probe beyond what appeared to be a largish closet door located below an Employees Only sign. Fiddling with the controls, Sulu confirmed that the area behind the door was shielded against conventional scanners, which struck him as, well, excessive.

"What's behind this door?"

"Just a walk-in storeroom," said Naylis with affected casualness. "Nothing more."

"Then why the heavy security?" Sulu asked.

"Call me paranoid," Naylis said. "You can never be too careful in my line of work."

Sulu didn't buy it. Legal wares and supplies didn't require this level of secrecy. A control panel next to the doorway regulated access to the storeroom. "Care to open this for me?"

"I think not, Lieutenant." Naylis crossed his arms atop his chest. "I know my rights."

"And I smell a rat."

Sulu detached an all-purpose door opener from his belt, having come prepared to poke around where he wasn't wanted. The small handheld cylinder, which functioned as a high-tech skeleton key, was designed to circumvent both mechanical and magnetic locks via a combination of miniature tractor beams and signal emitters. This particular lock was a good one, much harder to pick than, say, the locks in that twentieth-century Air Force base he and Captain Kirk had burgled a few years back, but the device worked just as well this time around. A beep sounded as the door slid open to reveal far more than just shelves of unsold stock.

"Bingo," Sulu said.

The storeroom had been converted into a rough approximation of the neural neutralizer chamber back on Tantalus V. A reclining chair leaned backward beneath a circular beam generator embedded in the ceiling. A transparent partition, crudely assembled from what looked like repurposed materials, separated a freestanding control console from the actual neutralization chamber. Sulu repressed a shudder at the sight of the chair, which was presumably where Tilton's mind and memories had been tampered with.

"Ensign," he addressed Knox, "please ensure that Mister Naylis stays put."

"Aye, sir." She drew her phaser. "He's not going anywhere."

"Wait," Naylis cried out. "I can explain!"

"Really?" Sulu found that hard to believe. "This should be good."

"Well, you see . . . that is, you have to understand . . . it's merely that . . ." His voice faltered as he recognized the futility of trying to talk himself out of the hot water he had just landed in. "On second thought, I *can't* explain."

"I figured as much."

Sulu traded the door opener for his communicator. He flipped it open, intending to hail Grandle, when the store's front entrance retracted and the security chief strode in to join them. She arrived alone, a grim expression on her face.

Speak of the devil, Sulu thought. "Good timing, Chief. I was just about to page you."

"Got word that something was up," Grandle said. "What's going on here?"

Sulu wasn't sure where to begin, with the fact that Tilton was the saboteur, that the manager had been brainwashed by a neural neutralizer, or that Naylis had just been caught with a neutralizer in his possession? Probably the latter, he decided.

"There's something you need to see," Sulu said. "Take a look at—"

"Just a moment," Grandle said.

Without warning, she punched Knox in the head, knocking the unsuspecting ensign out cold. Knox slammed into the counter before crumpling to the floor. Startled, Sulu reached for his phaser, but Naylis got the drop on him by pulling a vintage Klingon disruptor pistol out from beneath the counter.

"Not so fast, Lieutenant," the merchant said. "Keep your hands where I can see them."

Grandle drew her own phaser as well. "Don't make a move, Sulu. We're taking this station back from you."

Outnumbered and confused, it took Sulu a few moments to grasp the truth.

"Naylis got to you too. You've been brainwashed like Tilton."

"Watch your mouth!" Grandle barked. "I don't have to listen to you. You don't belong here. You never belonged here!"

"That's right, Mister Grandle. Lieutenant Sulu is the real troublemaker here. He needs to be dealt with . . . for the good of the station!"

"That's absurd!" Sulu wondered how much conditioning had been required to turn Grandle against him. "Think, Grandle! Listen to what you're saying!"

"I told you to be quiet!"

A brilliant carmine phaser blast stunned Sulu.

———————

Dazed, Sulu woke to find himself in the neutralizer chamber, seated in the chair beneath the beam projector, as Grandle strapped his left wrist to an armrest. His right arm was already bound. Fear vaporized any last trace of grogginess from Sulu's brain as he realized what was happening. Naylis was about to brainwash him too.

No! he thought. *Nobody is going to make me a zombie again!*

"Listen to me, Grandle. This isn't who you are. You can fight this!"

"You're wasting your breath, Lieutenant," Naylis said. Turning his head, Sulu saw the Troyian standing by the control console, aiming a disruptor at Knox, who was back on her feet again, but who was also clearly in no position to come to his rescue. Naylis smirked at Sulu through the clear partition. "Mister Grandle and I recently had a long talk in this very room. She understands now where her loyalties lie. Don't think you can convince her otherwise."

Sulu wasn't so sure of that. Was it just wishful thinking, or could he make out a flicker of uncertainty on Grandle's face? She grimaced as she finished strapping him to the chair. A vein at her temple pulsed. She bit down on her lip as though fighting something trying to get out.

"Is he secure?" Naylis asked.

"Yes."

Sulu thought he heard a hint of strain in Grandle's voice. He tested his bonds; despite Grandle's statement to the contrary, the left one was actually a bit loose. Given time, Sulu figured he could probably work that arm free.

Provided Naylis gave him that time.

"Why are you doing this, Naylis?" he asked, stalling. "What's in it for you?"

"I could tell you," the smuggler gloated, "but you're not going to remember any of this."

"No harm in telling me, then. Indulge me. I'm sure you must have a very good reason for going to such lengths."

"Reasons," Naylis corrected him. "Plural."

"Such as?"

"For one, a consortium of tardy prospectors paid me handsomely to delay and discourage their competition. For another, I personally benefit from keeping as many travelers as possible stranded here at the station rather than moving onto Baldur III." He grinned mischievously. "It's a win-win situation, as they say."

"For you, perhaps," Sulu said. "From where I'm sitting, I'm not feeling the win."

"Give it time. Trust me, Lieutenant, you'll soon be seeing things my way."

That's what I'm afraid of.

Sulu tried to wiggle his left hand free without Naylis noticing. He watched anxiously as Grandle joined Naylis by the control console and took custody of Knox, who was surely next in line for the neutralizer. He shared an anxious look with the young ensign, whose arms appeared to be tied behind her back. Her phaser was nowhere to be seen.

"Don't do this, Naylis," Sulu said. "No amount of profit is worth sinking to these depths."

"Spoken like a true Starfleet officer," Naylis said. "It's ironic, though. You may recall that my home planet is positively awash in dilithium crystals, with fortunes just waiting to be seized. Alas, I'm afraid that I fell out of favor with the royal family—for reasons we need not discuss—which means that I've been forced to eke out a living as an exile. But who knows? I may soon be able to bribe myself back into the royals' good graces, which would certainly justify taking a few moral shortcuts." He smirked at Sulu. "Consider yourself lucky, Lieutenant, that I have better options than simply eliminating you and your ensign."

Sulu's arm was almost free. He just needed a few more minutes.

"But listen to me ramble on," Naylis said. "I hope I'm not boring you."

"I'm all ears." Sulu considered his options once he got his arm free. Could he manage to liberate the other one without Naylis catching on? And then what? He was still unarmed and at a severe disadvantage. "It's not like I'm going anywhere soon."

"True," Naylis conceded. "But let me ensure that I have your full attention."

He flicked a switch on the control panel, activating it. Sulu realized in horror that the time for stalling was over. A hum, growing rapidly in volume, signaled that the neutralizer was warming up. Desperate to avoid being neutralized, he yanked his left hand out from beneath the loose strap holding it in place. He reached frantically to undo the strap trapping his other arm, terrified that it was already too late.

It was.

The beam projector lit up overhead. Energy surged through the concentric circles defining the apparatus. *Don't look,* Sulu thought, attempting to avert his eyes, but an invisible beam overcame his resistance. He sank back into the padded seat, his gaze irresistibly drawn to the glowing rings of light, which exercised a practically hypnotic pull on him so that he couldn't look away. It was like a gravity well, seizing his concentration, dragging his thoughts into an inescapable vortex. His body tensed as he fought against the pull, but his mind grew sluggish, like an unresponsive helm, leaving him adrift and alone, barely able to hear his own thoughts, let alone hold on to them. The universe went away—except for Naylis's voice.

"Everything is as it should be. There is no sabotage, no saboteur, just a string of unfortunate accidents. You investigated the matter and found nothing. Naylis is innocent. You were wrong to suspect him . . ."

Sulu tried to tune the Voice out, but it was all there was, filling the growing emptiness inside his mind, so that it became harder and harder to distinguish his own thoughts from the Voice. His mind and the Voice were becoming one and the same.

"You can trust Naylis. You should listen to him, follow his advice. He and Grandle know what they're doing. They'll take care of everything. Just do as they say, believe what they tell you . . ."

Sulu couldn't look away. He couldn't stop listening. But he refused to surrender to the Voice, to have his will hijacked yet again. Captain Kirk had fought the neutralizer, so he could too. And possibly someone else as well . . . ?

"Grandle!" he shouted over the Voice. "Fight this! You can do it!"

Just stringing the words together cost him. Pain racked his body as he convulsed in the chair, gripping the armrests with white knuckles. His head throbbed as the lights spun faster and faster above him, the beam increasing in intensity. His jaw clenched.

"Hush. Relax. It only hurts when you struggle. Just give in and all will be well. Just trust Naylis and you'll be fine . . ."

Sulu bit down on his lip. Resistance was excruciating. In desperation, he latched onto a single image to anchor him in the emptiness: the helm of the *Starship Enterprise*. He clung to that visual even as the Voice buffeted his mind, trying to shake him loose from himself. He just needed to stay on course for as long as he could. He forced his jaws open one last time.

"Fight it, Grandle. Fight . . . !"

Ensign Peggy Knox was tortured by the sight of Sulu being tortured. She longed to go to his rescue, do her duty as a security officer, but Naylis and Grandle had the upper hand at the moment. Her hands were tied behind her back, her phaser had been taken from her, and Grandle had a tight grip on her arm and was watching Knox like a hawk.

Or was she?

Knox felt Grandle stiffen beside her. Tearing her anxious gaze away from Sulu's torment, the ensign saw that Grandle appeared to be showing signs of strain, as though Sulu's urgent appeals were getting to her. The security chief was practically vibrating with tension, her face betraying hints of some inner conflict. She blinked repeatedly and began to rock back and forth on her heels. Her hand tightened around Knox's upper arm, her fingers digging into the flesh beneath Knox's bright red sleeve to steady herself. Her head swayed as though she was feeling dizzy.

"Fight it, Grandle! Fight!"

Knox experienced a twinge of hope. She studied Grandle

closely, waiting for an opportunity. Sulu had explained to her about neural neutralizers earlier. He had also mentioned that some people had been known to push back against their conditioning, although never easily.

"No more words, Sulu. Just sit back and listen," Naylis said into a microphone at the control panel. Intent on brainwashing Sulu, he paid no attention to what was going on with Grandle, trusting the security chief to watch over Knox until it was the ensign's turn in the chair. He turned a dial on the control panel, presumably to increase the force of the beam. The hum turned into a high-pitched whirring. "You have nothing to fear. There is no saboteur. You've proven that already. You know that now . . ."

Sulu screamed in anguish, thrashing violently in the chair. Knox wondered how long he could hold out against the neutralizer. He was obviously going through hell to keep from surrendering to the device. His suffering tore at her heart.

"Give it up, Sulu," Naylis said. "You can't fight it. No one can."

"No . . . one," Grandle muttered under her breath. "No . . . NO!"

The security chief swung her phaser toward the neutralizer chamber. For a second, Knox feared that Grandle was about to put Sulu out of his misery, but then a sizzling red phaser beam struck the beam projector above the chair, disintegrating it along with a chunk of the ceiling. The blast triggered a fire alarm that wailed like a Hibernian banshee. The smell of burning cables and circuitry polluted the air.

Yes! Knox thought. *Sulu got through to Grandle, beam or no beam.*

"What the devil?!"

Naylis turned away from his console to stare in shock at Grandle, who was losing it, big-time. She waved the phaser, which was obviously *not* set on stun anymore, about wildly. Her eyes bulged from her sockets, as though she'd just received an overdose of cordrazine, and her face was flushed. Naylis

turned a paler shade of green, his own eyes anxiously tracking the business end of the phaser as it swung from side to
side. His voice quavered as he tried to talk the crazed security
chief down.

"Calm down, Grandle. Listen to me . . ."

"Shut up, all of you!" She reeled unsteadily, sweating pro-
fusely. "I can't hear myself think! My brain is tearing apart!"

She clutched her head, letting go of Knox's arm in the process. The ensign took advantage of the tumult to break away
from Grandle and charge at Naylis. Even with her arms tied behind her back, she still made a decent battering ram, slamming
into the corrupt merchant and knocking him backward into the
sturdy control console. His head smacked loudly against the
control panel, shaking the microphone, and he slid unconscious
to the floor. Knox kicked him in the ribs just to make sure he
wasn't playing possum.

Serves him right for taking my phaser, she thought. *Left me no
choice but to play rough.*

But she wasn't out of the woods yet. Grandle was still waving
her phaser around like a madwoman, posing an obvious danger
to herself and others. She seemed unable to distinguish friend
from foe.

"Make it stop!" she ranted over the blaring alarm. "You're
driving me insane!"

A frantic phaser blast fried the control panel, igniting a foun-
tain of white-hot sparks, as Knox scrambled out of the line of
fire. She realized that, ironically enough, she had possibly saved
Naylis's life by knocking him to the floor.

Not that he's likely to appreciate it.

"Take it easy, Chief," Knox said in the most soothing tone she
could muster under the circumstances. Trying to reason with
Grandle was possibly a lost cause, but a phaser and a mental
meltdown were a bad combination. She had to at least try to
de-escalate this crisis. "Let's just get you to the infirmary, okay?"

"Shut up! You're just trying to confuse me! You all are!" She swung the phaser at Knox, who found herself cornered in the refurbished storeroom. Spittle sprayed from Grandle's lip. "Why can't you leave me alone?"

In desperation, Knox threw a high kick at Grandle, hoping to knock the phaser from the other woman's grip, but the security chief had not lost her own fighting skills. She caught Knox's ankle with her other hand and twisted it, causing Knox to topple backward onto the floor. The crash knocked the breath out of Knox, who looked up to see Grandle's phaser aimed straight at her face.

"Um, mind setting that on stun at least?"

"Trespasser! Intruder! I'll make you leave me alone!"

Oh, crap, Knox thought. *I'm toast.*

Before Grandle could fire the weapon, however, Sulu suddenly appeared behind her. A karate chop to Grandle's neck worked better than a tranquilizer, causing her to crumple to the floor. Sulu stood over her, looking more than a little unsteady himself. Knox assumed that he had somehow liberated himself from the chair just in time.

"Thanks, Lieutenant! Glad to see you're still you!"

"Am I?" he asked uncertainly. He was blinking and sweating, too, although not nearly as badly as Grandle had been. He looked logy and confused, like someone only gradually emerging from a bad dream that didn't want to let go of them. His gaze swung back and forth between the fallen forms of Grandle and Naylis. Bewilderment was written all over his face.

"I'm . . . confused. I can trust Grandle, but . . . she was threatening you . . . but everything is fine, Naylis said so . . ."

He was clearly still feeling the effects of the neutralizer beam. Knox thanked her lucky stars that his first instinct had been to come to her defense anyway.

"It's all right, Lieutenant. It will make sense eventually, once Doctor M'Benga helps you through this."

She glanced over at Naylis to make sure he was still uncon-scious; even with the neutralizer trashed, she didn't want the unscrupulous Troyian to mess with Sulu's head any further. The sooner she got both him and Grandle under wraps the better.

"In the meantime, maybe you can help me back onto my feet?"

Twenty-Five

Baldur III

"Welcome to the bridge of the Thunderbird! *Have you ever wondered how your grandparents and great-grandparents first came to Baldur III? Today we're going to take an amazing journey into history . . ."*

What appeared to be an educational vid appeared on the reactivated viewscreen as Scott and Galligan hurried to reconnect ancient circuits and relays in order to get the bridge controls operational for the first time in decades. Galligan switched off the recording.

"Sorry about that," he said sheepishly. *"Up until recently, this place mostly hosted field trips."*

Scott recalled that *Thunderbird* has been preserved as a historical relic and museum before being pressed back into service as a power plant. At the moment, he was grateful that the colonists' old ship had been preserved so scrupulously. Aside from the historical plaques and signage now adorning various walls and consoles, the bridge looked much as it must have when the ship first touched down on the planet generations ago. He could only hope that *Thunderbird*'s vintage impulse engines had been just as carefully maintained.

Otherwise they were as good as dead, along with most of Jackpot City.

"*Approximately fifteen minutes to warp core detonation,*" the ship's computer announced in a calm masculine tone that only reminded Scott that he wasn't on the *Enterprise*, not that the update would have been any less alarming delivered by a more familiar voice. "*Please report to emergency escape pods.*"

"Fat lot of good those would do us here on the ground," Scott muttered.

He assumed that Spears had heard the announcement as well. The young technician was still in the control room, monitoring the feverish warp core, while Scott and Galligan worked on the bridge in their radiation suits. The cumbersome suits did not make a rush job any easier, so Scott was sorely tempted to shed it just for the sake of efficiency. As is, his gloves were tucked into his work belt. He figured he'd put them back on if his skin started burning.

"*You really think this will work?*" Galligan tossed a bronze plaque onto the floor in order to access a service panel at the bridge's main engineering station. A speaker in his hood allowed Scotty to hear him.

"It's our best shot," Scotty said.

As on the *Enterprise,* the impulse engines functioned independently of the warp propulsion system, which meant that, with any luck, they had been isolated from the cascade malfunctions that had turned the warp core into a ticking time bomb. The nuclear fusion reactors powering the impulse drive were already fueled and operational; Galligan and his people had prepped the reactors weeks ago, with an eye toward using them as a backup generator in the event the warp core failed. The challenge now had been to redirect the reactors' potential output from the colony's EPS grid back to the ship's long-inactive propulsion system, while bringing the helm and navigational controls back online as well, all the while hoping that *Thunderbird* could still take wing after her long slumber.

And before it was too late.

"When was the last time this ship flew?" he asked.

"*2168? 2169?*" Galligan guessed, suggesting that he was a better engineer than historian. "*Before I was born, certainly. It's been grounded for as long as anyone can—*" He froze as though suddenly placed in stasis. "*Oh, no.*"

Scott knew a worried tone when he heard one. "What is it?"

"*I just remembered! The landing struts were bolted to the ground decades ago. They're secured to concrete blocks!*" He turned away from the engineering station and started toward the exit at the rear of the bridge. "*Perhaps we can cut through the bolts with a laser torch?*"

"There's no time!" Scott said. Cutting through the bolts on all four struts would be an arduous, time-consuming task in itself, never mind dashing back and forth between them in the lower reaches of the ship. "We're just going to have to tear ourselves loose from them when we launch . . . and hope that it's only the bolts that snap."

Galligan swallowed hard. "*Are we going to have enough power to do that?*"

You tell me, Scott thought. *This is your ship.*

"If we can muster enough power to achieve escape velocity," he said instead, "I doubt a few bolts can nail us down."

Scott spoke more confidently than he felt, for Galligan's sake. The plant's manager was a good man, but life-or-death crises were new to him. In fact, Scott saw a bumpy launch ahead, assuming a massive matter-antimatter explosion didn't vaporize them all first.

"*Approximately ten minutes to warp core detonation,*" the computer said. "*Repeat: approximately ten minutes to warp core detonation.*"

"I heard ye the first time," Scott grumbled.

It was that "approximately" that preyed on his nerves. A few minutes plus or minus could mean the difference between disaster and deliverance, which meant they couldn't waste a single

second. Finishing up with the helm controls, he skipped rebooting the astrogator and other navigational aids. One way or another, this wasn't going to be a long voyage; they didn't need to
plot a course across the sector, just off the planet.

As fast as humanly possible.

"Spears," he ordered via the ship's intercom. "Get yourself to
the bridge, on the double. We're almost ready to take off."

In theory.

---

*"We're counting down to launch, Captain, while racing another
countdown."*

On the bridge, Kirk listened to Scott's voice intently. That he
was safe aboard the *Enterprise* while his friend and chief engineer faced imminent peril ate at Kirk; he had never been comfortable delegating danger to others.

"Understood, Mister Scott. Our sensors are locked on
Thunderbird. We are monitoring your situation and prepared to
offer assistance at any time."

*"Thank ye, Captain, but it's not just me ye have to worry about,
but the city as well. Even if we get the warp core off-planet before
it breaches, we're likely to cause a fair amount of damage blasting off from the middle of town. This isn't going to be like quietly
piloting a ship out of spacedock on impulse. We're going to have
to fire the engines at full blast to tear* Thunderbird *loose from her
moorings and escape the planet's gravity in a matter of moments.
All that superheated exhaust firing from the engines, propelling us
into space . . . it's going to leave a mark, sir. Not as bad as a warp
core explosion, to be sure, but tell me you've evacuated the area
around the park, sir."*

"The evacuation is underway," Kirk said. He trusted Uhura
and the other crew members on the planet to assist in every way
possible. "Leave that to us."

"And the orbits directly above the city, sir? We're going to be

coming up hard and fast, Captain, and I can't vouch for how well this old bird steers after all this time. Not sure how much helm control we'll have over this flight."

"We're clearing you all the room in space you need," Kirk said, "and have notified the spaceport to halt all arrivals and departures until further notice."

On the viewscreen, he saw a few stray vessels still in orbit above Jackpot City. He put Scott on hold and turned toward Lieutenant Palmer, who was still filling in for Uhura at the comm station. "Why haven't those ships broken orbit yet? Did they receive our emergency directive to clear that space?"

"They received it, sir," Palmer answered. "They're just . . . quibbling. They're asking questions. They want more information. They don't want to lose their places in line."

Kirk didn't want to hear it. He didn't have time for this. Scotty didn't have time for this.

"They want more details? Tell them that a self-destructing, radioactive, one-hundred-year-old starship with a melting-down warp core is about to rocket right up their backsides—unless they get the hell out of the way as fast as they can. And you can quote me on that, Lieutenant."

"Aye, sir," Palmer replied, with a hint of a smirk. "I'll do just that."

Kirk got back online with Scott. "That bottle you mentioned is waiting for you, Scotty. Come and get it."

"I'll drink to that, Captain. On our way."

———

Spears came rushing onto the bridge in her hazard suit. A door slid shut behind her. *"Are we ready for takeoff?"*

"As ready as we'll ever be," Scott said. Under ordinary circumstances, he would have insisted on running several more tests and diagnostics before launching an antique spacecraft on short notice, but life in Starfleet was seldom ordinary. "Take the communications station, lass, and strap in tight."

The captain's seat was empty, because everyone was needed elsewhere. Galligan was planted at engineering, the better to monitor the newly resurrected impulse engines *and* the dying warp core, while Scott had the helm, since he knew more about flying a starship than the other two combined. He wondered if either Galligan or Spears had ever been to space before.

Talk about diving into the deep end, he thought.

The viewscreen before him showed a nocturnal view of the park and the buildings beyond. The bright lights of Jackpot City were already flickering out as *Thunderbird* severed its connections to the colony's power relays. Backup generators and batteries were not going to be enough to keep the lights on, but that was the least of Scott's worries at the moment. Better a blackout than a blackened ruin, he judged.

"Approximately five minutes to warp core detonation," the computer said.

Scott used his communicator to keep Kirk apprised. "Scott to *Enterprise.* It's now or never."

"You are cleared for takeoff, Mister Scott," Kirk answered. *"Launch at will . . . and good luck."*

"I won't be refusing that, Captain. Scott out." He put away the communicator and faced the helm controls. It was a shame, he reflected, that Sulu was not at hand; the helmsman would have relished the opportunity to pilot the vintage starship—and was probably better suited to the task. "Brace yourself. This could be a rough ride."

"Engines powered and ready, Mister Scott," Galligan reported.

"Crossing my fingers," Spears added.

"You keep doing that, lass."

The push-button helm controls were less sophisticated than the *Enterprise*'s, which was a blessing in this case. No fancy flying was required; they were just going up and out. He vectored the director coils for a forty-five-degree-angle ascent, while thanking his lucky stars that Jackpot City had yet to erect any serious skyscrapers; even without Sulu at the helm, they should be able to clear the tops of the nearest buildings without *too* much difficulty.

"*Approximately four minutes to warp core detonation.*"

"I hear ye, I hear ye," Scott said. "On my count, three, two, one . . . engage!"

Thunderbird's impulse engines awoke from hibernation. Pure Newtonian physics came into play as the thrust of the engines' exhaust pushed against the planet's gravity, not to mention the sturdy steel bolts nailing it to the surface. The battle rattled the bridge even as the rumble of the old engines made Scott feel like an old-time astronaut riding a shuttle into a whole new frontier. For a few rapid heartbeats, the park refused to let go of the historic ship. Scott increased the intensity of the thrusters, hoping to melt or shatter the concrete foundation beneath the former museum. His efforts were rewarded as, with a bone-jarring wrench, *Thunderbird* broke its bonds and took off into the sky like its mythical namesake. Scott felt a sudden surge and affection for the dying ship.

There's a fine old gal, he thought. *Going out in a blaze of glory.*

Spears whooped in exhilaration or fear or some combination thereof. Galligan shuddered and closed his eyes, waiting for it to be over. Pressed back into his seat by the sudden acceleration, Scott held his breath as *Thunderbird* zoomed out of Baldur's atmosphere into space. On the viewscreen, thinning wisps of vapor gave way to the comforting familiarity of the empty vacuum Scott had traversed for most of his adult life. He eyed the screen anxiously, primed to take evasive action should another vessel suddenly appear in their path, but it appeared that Captain Kirk had indeed cleared the way for them just as he'd promised. Scott held to his course: out and away from Baldur III.

"*One minute to warp core detonation,*" the computer nagged, no longer hedging its bets. "*Warning: warp core breach imminent.*"

Scott breathed a sigh of relief. No matter what happened next, Jackpot City was safe.

"Eject warp core!" he ordered Galligan. "Now!"

The other man did not hesitate. He pounded on the engineering buttons like a concert pianist building to a crescendo. *"Ejecting!"*

There was a split second of suspense as Scotty half expected the emergency ejection procedure to malfunction as well, but for once the crucial safety measure functioned exactly as it had been designed to do: the bridge vibrated as, several decks away, *Thunderbird* vomited its combusting entrails into the void. The ejection was not visible on the viewscreen, but Scott could easily visualize the blazing warp core lighting up the dark as it tumbled through space in its final moments of existence.

"Warp core ejected," the computer confirmed. *"Alert canceled."*

"I don't believe it!" Galligan said. *"We did it. I'm going to see my wife and kids again. Just wait until they hear about this!"*

"Did my job just get sucked into space?" Spears joked. *"'Cause if not, I want a raise!"*

Scott was too busy to join in the jubilation. He ramped up the engines, wanting to put as much distance as he could between *Thunderbird* and the disgorged warp core before—

A shock wave struck *Thunderbird*, sending the ship tumbling end over end.

Twenty-Six

Deep Space Station S-8

"Are you certain you're up to this, Lieutenant?"

Doctor M'Benga eyed Sulu watchfully as he escorted his patient out of the examination room where Sulu had been recovering from his ordeal in the neutralizer chamber. Knox, who had been sitting outside the door, rose to join Sulu, who was glad to see that she appeared none the worse for wear after being sucker-punched by Grandle hours ago. As Sulu understood it, he had been out for some time, while Grandle remained under sedation. According to M'Benga, the security chief's violent rejection of her brainwashing had taken its toll on her system; she needed an induced rest to recover from the physical and psychic trauma. Sulu could believe it.

"I have to be," he replied.

Truth to tell, he was still feeling shaky. Fighting the beam had been excruciating, and his grip on his mind and memories was not as firm as he might have liked. The Voice kept echoing inside his skull, undercutting his resolve and reality, making him question his every thought.

Everything is fine. There's nothing to worry about . . .

No, Sulu thought, *that's a lie.* The sabotage was real, committed by Tilton, under the control of Naylis, who was now cooling his heels in the brig, while the trashed neutralizer equipment was locked up tight as well. *But, wait, that can't be right . . .*

There was no saboteur, Naylis said so. Trust Naylis.

Sulu grimaced. He shook his head to clear it. *Get out of my brain!*

"You all right, sir?" Knox gave him a worried look. M'Benga looked concerned as well.

Sulu was tempted to tough it out and pretend he was back at one hundred percent already, but he owed Knox and M'Benga more honesty than that. He lowered his voice and glanced around the crowded infirmary to make sure no one was listening in.

"Just feeling a few aftereffects from my session in the chair." Sulu liked to think that the Voice was gradually fading away, as though disappearing into the distance, but it wasn't quieting fast enough for him. He paused to confer with Knox. "You have a new duty, Ensign. Until I'm fully myself again, you're my reality check. I start to get fuzzy on our mission, or look as though I'm not entirely certain of my facts, your job is to remind me that the echoes in my head can't be trusted. You think you can do that?"

Knox gulped. "Yes, sir."

"Thanks," he said. "Sorry to dump this on you, Knox, but that beam did a number on me. Going to need a little time to get over it, that's all."

"I understand, sir."

"Sulu," M'Benga said, frowning, "if you feel you're not ready to be discharged—"

"Appreciate the thought, Doctor, but taking it easy is not an option right now."

He strode decisively through the infirmary, weaving his way through the bustling waiting area until they reached the private examination room where Tilton was recuperating. Johann remained posted outside, ensuring that the manager's condition stayed on a need-to-know basis. The security officer acknowledged Sulu's arrival.

"He's been asking to see you, Lieutenant."

"So I hear." Sulu hoped Tilton had some more answers for him. "I need to talk to him too." He turned to M'Benga. "What shape is he in?"

"Better," the doctor reported. "Over the last few years, modern medicine has made significant progress when it comes to treating victims of neural neutralizers. We've found that a careful regimen of neurosynaptic therapy, augmented by certain specific medications, can eventually reverse the effects of the beam in all but the most severe cases. Brain scans indicate that Tilton was more extensively programmed than either you or Chief Grandle, possibly over repeated sessions in the chair, so he's going to require ongoing treatment to fully recover from what was done to him, but he's already much better than how you last saw him."

Sulu was glad to hear it, and not just because he had to interrogate the man further. He recalled that Captain Kirk was back on his feet in no time, despite a close encounter with the neutralizer, which Sulu found very encouraging.

If the captain can get over this, so can I.

The door slid open to admit Sulu and his companions to the room beyond, where he found Tilton sitting up in a biobed, sipping on a drink. The older man still looked rather haggard, but he appeared considerably less apathetic or deranged than before, while the diagnostic monitor above him also painted a less dire picture of his health. He looked up as Sulu and the others entered. A pained expression hinted at the guilt he had to be experiencing now. Sulu didn't envy him.

"Lieutenant Sulu, I'm so sorry!" Tilton put aside his drink. "You have to believe me, I would have never betrayed my duties to this station, endangered so many ships and people, if Naylis hadn't—"

"No need to explain or apologize." Sulu held up a hand to cut off the man's apologies. "Trust me, I understand. You weren't responsible for your actions."

Sulu's reassurances failed to assuage Tilton. "You don't understand. If you knew all I've done—!"

"About that." Sulu took pains to avoid an accusatory tone. "How much do you actually remember about the . . . the . . ."

He struggled to complete the sentence, the words eluding him. The more he tried to complete his thought, the more slippery it became. What did he want to ask Tilton about again?

"Sabotage," Knox prompted. "We need to find out more about the sabotage."

There was no sabotage. You proved that. Everything is fine.

Negative, Sulu thought, trusting Knox more than the Voice. "Right." He grabbed on to the word and forced it out through his lips. "Sabotage. Tell me about it, Tilton. What did you want to see me about?"

"It's not over," Tilton said, visibly distraught. "Before you caught me, before Doctor M'Benga helped me, I sabo . . . *interfered* . . . with another ship that was undergoing maintenance here at the station. Abusing my privileges and access, I . . . tampered . . . with various replacement parts before they were beamed over to the ship to be installed aboard the vessel." He snorted ruefully. "Did quite a clever job of it, actually. My . . . alterations . . . were all but impossible to detect unless you knew what to look for."

He buried his face in his hands. "What have I done?"

Tilton's life signs reflected his agitation. M'Benga shot Sulu a warning look.

"What ship?" Sulu demanded anyway. He felt his own pulse speed up, despite the inner Voice assuring him there was nothing to worry about. **There is no sabotage.** "Which ship, Tilton?"

"The *Ali Baba,*" the manager said, his voice cracking. "A repurposed Coridian scout ship out of the Talbot system." He grasped Sulu's arm, desperate to get his warning across, no matter the strain to his system. Cords bulged in his neck. "They're not safe, Sulu! Not the crew, not the passengers!"

His diagnostics climbed toward the yellow zone.

"Steady there, George." M'Benga stepped forward to calm the man, applying his best bedside manner as he gently pried Tilton's fingers away from Sulu's arms. He eased the man back down onto the biobed. "We hear you. Mister Sulu will see to it, won't you, Lieutenant?"

"Right this minute," Sulu said, and not just to humor Tilton. He crossed the room to the nearest intercom. "Sulu to Starfleet Security Team B. Secure a vessel called the *Ali Baba*. Evacuate the crew and passengers immediately."

A voice, which Sulu recognized as belonging to Carlos Alvarez, another crewman on loan from the *Enterprise,* answered immediately.

"Sir, Ali Baba *departed for Baldur III hours ago."*

Sulu didn't understand. "Despite the lockdown?"

"Rumor has it that you and Mister Tilton and Chief Grandle are . . . otherwise occupied," Alvarez said diplomatically. *"A few ships, like the* Ali Baba, *saw a chance to defy the lockdown and break orbit . . ."*

Sulu kicked himself for not being on top of this, even though he'd been out cold in the infirmary for hours. Then again, the Voice kept telling him that he had nothing to worry about, that the station was perfectly safe. No wonder he hadn't seen this coming.

Everything is fine.

"Hail *Ali Baba*," he ordered. "Inform them that we have reason to believe that the ship's systems are compromised. Instruct them to turn back immediately, as their lives may be in jeopardy."

"Aye, sir," Alvarez replied.

"Keep me informed. Sulu out."

He stepped away from the intercom to return to Tilton's bedside. Exhausted by his confession, Tilton rested against the biobed, which was tilted upward slightly so that he could main-tain a sitting position.

"The *Ali Baba*?" he asked. "Safe?"

"We're taking care of it," Sulu said, "but is there anything else we need to know? A danger to another ship or the station?"

"I . . . I don't think so. But my memory is . . . confusing. Parts of it are missing, or don't match up with other memories. It's still hard to tell which are real . . . and which were beamed into my brain, tricking me, making me do things I'd never do if only I knew what I was thinking . . ."

Sulu knew the feeling, but he had to keep pressing Tilton. They couldn't let another impending disaster slip through the cracks in the manager's skewed memories.

"Try to sort them out," he urged. "I know it's not easy—believe me, I know—but we have to know everything you did while under the neutralizer's influence. Not to blame you or prosecute you, but simply to ensure that there are no further threats to avert."

"I know!" Tilton was getting worked up again. "I'll never for-give myself if another person gets hurt . . . or worse. I want to fix this, but . . . my brain . . . I can't trust my brain!"

"Sulu," M'Benga interrupted. "That's enough for now."

"I appreciate your concern for your patient, Doctor, but this is a matter of security. More lives may be at stake."

"I understand that, Sulu, but I can't in good conscience put Mister Tilton's health and recovery at risk simply because of a hypothetical risk. Tilton's mind and body both need time to heal. I'm sorry, Lieutenant, but I'm putting my foot down. You'll have to resume this interrogation later. Doctor's orders."

M'Benga had clearly made up his mind, so there was no point in arguing. Sulu wondered if Captain Kirk ever found Doctor McCoy just as stubborn.

All the time, I'm guessing.

"Your call, Doctor," Sulu conceded, while deciding on his next move. He didn't intend to sit back and wait for Tilton—or Grandle, for that matter—to be up to talking. There were still measures he could take in the meantime. "Mind if I borrow the computer station in your office?"

The office Sulu shared with Grandle was on the other side of the habitation cone and a few levels away. He didn't want to risk another emergency happening while he was en route in a turbolift.

"Help yourself," the doctor said. "I need to do my rounds anyway."

"Thanks." Sulu headed out the door. "Knox, you're with me."

"Aye, sir."

Relax, the Voice whispered. **Everything is fine.**

Sulu didn't believe that for one second.

M'Benga's temporary office, which he was sharing with the station's regular doctor, resembled McCoy's office back aboard the *Enterprise*, just a bit more cluttered at present. Sulu seated himself at a desk, facing a computer access terminal. Knox pulled over a chair to look over his shoulder.

"Computer," Sulu said. "How many vessels have defied the lockdown and departed the station today?"

"Five vessels have left the proximity of the station," the computer replied.

"List them."

"The vessels were, in order of departure, the Celestial, *the* Industry, *the* Gamma 337, *the* Ali Baba, *and the* Lucky Strike."

That last name caused his heart to skip a beat.

Helena's ship?

He was less concerned with the fact that she had left without saying good-bye than with the possibility that the *Lucky Strike* might have been compromised as well, endangering Helena and everyone else aboard her ship. And the same applied to at least three other vessels, not counting the *Ali Baba*, which was already known to have been sabotaged. Sulu fought the urge to demand that M'Benga allow him to run the names of the other ships past Tilton, no matter how fragile the recovering manager might be.

Don't worry about it. Everything is fine. No ships are in danger.

If only, Sulu thought.

"Sir?"

Knox's voice broke his reverie. "Yes, Ensign?"

"I wasn't sure, but, with all due respect, you looked like you might be zoning out again."

"Less so than before, I think, but good job keeping me on my toes." He fully realized just how awkward a situation he had placed Knox in; it couldn't be comfortable having to babysit a superior officer whose mental faculties weren't entirely up to snuff. "Thoughts, Ensign? Am I overlooking anything?"

"The lockdown, sir? Should we reinstate it?"

"Absolutely," he decided right then and there. A lockdown was possibly unnecessary now that the saboteur had been, well, neutralized, but Sulu was inclined to play it safe until he was certain that there were no more unpleasant surprises ahead. He needed to interrogate Tilton further once M'Benga judged it safe to do so, and Grandle as well as soon as her memories could be relied upon with confidence. Was there any point in trying to get Naylis to talk? He could threaten to extradite the man back to Troyius, where he was apparently none too popular with the powers that be.

The office intercom chimed urgently.

"Sulu here," he said in response. "What is it?"

"*Bad news, sir,*" Alvarez reported. "*We managed to hail the* Ali Baba . . . *and they're in trouble, sir. Their artificial gravity is out of control, powering up at an accelerating rate so that they can barely move. They can't disengage the gravity, they can hardly operate the ship, and, at this rate, they're going to be crushed to jelly if we can't get help to them in time."*

Damn, Sulu thought. Tilton's guilt-ridden words came back to him: *"If you knew all I've done—!"*

"Inform them we're dispatching emergency assistance immediately," Sulu said. "Stand by for specific orders."

"Aye, sir."

Switching off the intercom for the moment, Sulu turned to the computer terminal in search of relevant data.

"Computer, show me *Ali Baba*'s current location relative to station."

"Processing."

A star chart appeared on the terminal's visual display. Sulu winced at the picture it presented. Even if a rescue mission departed at once, the *Ali Baba* was three hours away. That might be too late for the endangered crew and passengers, but perhaps there was another ship closer to the *Ali Baba* that could be drafted into service?

"Computer, identify nearest other vessel to *Ali Baba*."

The answer came in a matter of seconds. "Allegra, *currently patrolling border of Antares Maelstrom.*"

Sulu hesitated. He was reluctant to divert *Allegra* from guarding the border, lest an impatient vessel risk the Maelstrom in hopes of getting out ahead of the competition, perhaps counting on finding the mythical Passage. The last thing they needed right now was another ship in jeopardy.

"Lieutenant?" Knox asked.

"Nothing to be concerned with, Ensign. Just taking a moment to weigh our options."

But a moment was all he could take if they wanted to save the lives aboard the *Ali Baba*. He made the only possible choice and switched the intercom back on.

"Sulu here. Hail *Allegra*. Inform them of the situation and order them to set course at maximum warp to render assistance to the *Ali Baba* as fast as prudently possible."

"*Aye, sir,*" Alvarez said. "*Hailing* Allegra *now.*"

"Keep me informed. Sulu out."

He assessed the situation. As he recalled, crew members Finch and Kumar were presently assigned to border patrol. They were good people, but the task before them was a tricky one. They would have to find a way to repair or disable the sabotaged gravity plates from outside the ship or else somehow evacuate the *Ali Baba* without also getting trapped by the super gravity aboard the ship, as well as administer whatever emergency medical treatment might be required. Sulu made a mental note to alert the infirmary that they could be expecting casualties.

Everything is . . . fine? There is . . . nothing . . . to be concerned with?

Even the Voice wasn't buying that line anymore. Its soothing assurances lacked conviction. Sulu chose to take that as a good sign.

"What now, sir?" Knox asked. "Do we just sit back and wait?"

"As Mister Scott likes to say, we can't defy the laws of physics, Ensign. Even today, with our warp drives and transporters, we can't be everywhere at once."

He understood her frustration, though. He was used to being at the helm of a starship, heading into the unknown, not being stuck in an office far from the action. He expanded the star charts on the terminal display, watching intently as *Allegra* sped away from the Maelstrom, leaving its border worryingly unguarded. He tried to reassure himself that this opportunity wouldn't tempt any reckless travelers. Surely nobody would be so rash as to brave the Maelstrom just to find a shortcut to Baldur III?

"Computer, display the positions and courses of the other vessels currently en route from the station to Baldur III."

"Processing."

The charts shifted on screen. Colored lines tracked the progress of the other vessels. All but one were wisely taking the long route around the Maelstrom. The *Lucky Strike*, however, had just abruptly altered course—and was now heading straight for the Maelstrom.

Twenty-Seven

Yurnos

"Halt, in the governor's name!"

Wearing matching uniforms dyed forest green, the riders charged down the road toward Spock and Chekov, who were still paused at the intersection above the hidden beach. Spock assumed these were the revenue agents Eefa had worried about earlier; it seemed her fears that they were abroad hunting smugglers were well founded. The secret cove was no longer as secret as she had hoped.

"Mister Spock?"

"Evasive action, Ensign."

"Aye, sir!"

Chekov released the brake. The alarmed marmots needed no urging to speed away from the charging tax agents, who were less than half a kilometer away and closing fast. Chekov gave the frightened animals free rein as they took off to the right, sprinting down the main road ahead of their pursuers. They screeched and chittered as they ran, their bushy tails waving wildly.

Escape was imperative, Spock realized. They could not allow themselves to be apprehended by the authorities. Exposure of his Vulcan nature, green blood and all, could fundamentally challenge the Yurnians' understanding of their place in the universe, centuries before they were prepared to cope with the reality of intelligent life and civilizations beyond their world. Spock was acutely aware that he had lost both his hat and his bandanna over the course of their captivity; at the moment, only distance and darkness shielded his ears from scrutiny, but neither would suffice if and when the riders caught up with them. His brain sorted through possible explanations he might offer, none of which struck him as particularly convincing.

"Hold on, Mister Spock! We're in for a rocky ride . . . for as long as it lasts!"

Their headlong flight was indeed turbulent. Bumps and ruts in the unpaved road impeded their speed while jarring the wagon and its passengers. A wooded slope, congested with brush and shadows, rose up to their left, while the right shoulder of the road dropped away sharply toward the crashing surf below. A crescent moon provided barely enough illumination to navigate by. Under ordinary circumstances, he would urge Chekov to slow down for safety's sake—it would not do to lose control of the wagon—but that was obviously not an option. Adrenaline flooded Spock's metabolism, priming his heart and muscles for action, yet his Vulcan training prevented it from overwhelming his judgment. He held tightly to a rail to avoid being thrown from the bouncing wagon.

"Do not worry about me, Ensign. Simply concentrate on keeping the wagon on the road, and ahead of our pursuers."

A pistol fired behind them, rather too close for comfort. Spock heard the bullet whiz over their heads. A frown marred his stoic expression; he'd had quite enough of firearms being directed at them.

"Halt, or find yourselves targets!" the lead rider hollered at them. A plumed hat, dyed bright red, possibly signified that she was in charge of the squad. "You can't escape us!"

"Don't shoot!" Chekov shouted back at them. "I've lost control of the marmots! They're running wild!"

Spock looked at Chekov. "A deception?"

"An exaggeration . . . sort of."

Spock did not ask him to elaborate. Instead he let go of the rail long enough to tune Eefa's communicator to a different, more familiar frequency. He lifted the device to his lips, hoping to be heard over the tumult.

"Attention: this is Commander Spock. We are in distress and require immediate assistance. I repeat: we are in immediate distress."

In a worst-case scenario, Jord or Vankov were not on hand to receive his signal at present, in which case his odds of escaping capture were extremely limited. He briefly considered throwing himself off the cliff if need be, but considered that an option of last resort, particularly since there was no guarantee that his body would not be recovered by the authorities afterward. Any adequate examination of his remains would swiftly turn up anatomical deviations exposing his non-Yurnian origins.

"We read you, Spock," Jord responded almost instantly. *"We've been standing by, wondering what happened to you and Chekov. It's been hours—"*

"A full account of our experiences will have to wait," Spock said. "We have a more pressing situation." He concisely briefed them on their current predicament. "Despite our best efforts, it is unlikely that we will be unable to evade our pursuers for much longer."

"Understood. What do you need from us?"

"Galileo," he replied.

If he and Chekov could not get to the shuttlecraft, Spock reasoned, *Galileo* would have to come to them, preferably in a timely manner.

"Home in on us by this signal, but do not delay. It is to no one's benefit for the authorities to have a Vulcan in custody."

"Gods, no!" Jord agreed. *"That would be a disaster. You mustn't let them catch you!"*

"That is precisely what we are endeavoring to prevent . . . for as long as we can."

"We're on our way! Jord out."

Spock lowered the communicator, clipping it to his simple leather belt, but kept the frequency open so Jord and Vankov could track the signal. He hoped their piloting skills had not grown too rusty during their long sojourn on Yurnos.

"Help is on the way," he informed Chekov. "We need only prolong the chase until aid arrives."

"Easier said than done, Mister Spock."

He was not wrong in his estimation. Peering back over his shoulder, Spock saw that the riders continued to gain on them, so that they were now less than ten meters behind the wagon. As the Yurnians' mounts were not burdened by pulling a wagon behind them, he saw little chance that he and Chekov could pull away from them. It was only a matter of minutes before the riders caught up with them.

More bullets flew past their heads, accompanied by loud shots and the distinct odor of gunpowder on the wind. It was unclear if the riders actually intended them harm at this point or if the shots were simply meant to encourage their surrender. He and Chekov ducked low to present less tempting targets.

"Please, no more shooting!" Chekov called out again. "I can't slow down! My rodents are out of control!"

His performance, if it was a performance, was most convincing, but was it enough to deter the riders from further gunfire? Spock feared that each agent was armed with multiple single-shot pistols. How far were they willing to go to apprehend a pair of likely smugglers? It occurred to Spock that the only actual contraband remaining in the back of the wagon was a single crate of Antarian glow water.

An idea struck him.

"Do not slow down," he instructed Chekov. "I will attempt to delay our pursuers."

Despite the roughness of the ride, he clambered into the bed of the wagon. Keeping his head down, he tore open the wooden lid of the crate with his bare hands, exposing a dozen bottles of the luminous beverage. The effulgent green radiance that gave the glow water its name and novelty shone in the shadows, illuminating Spock's features. Beyond Yurnos, where it was certainly rare and exotic, Antarian glow water was an inexpensive soft drink of little economic or nutritional value. Spock had never seen any purpose to it until this very moment.

Not exactly stun grenades, but I will have to make do.

Crouching in the bed of the wagon, he seized a bottle by its neck and hurled it overhand into the riders' path. It arced through the air before crashing into the road, where it shattered in a spray of broken glass and incandescent liquid that glowed all the brighter in the dark of night.

"What under the stars?!" the lead rider exclaimed.

The radiant spray startled both the riders and their mounts. The marmots reared up on their hind legs, all but throwing their riders, who had to urge them onward. Angry shouts and curses and confusion accompanied the screeches of the skittish rodents, which gave the spilled glow water a wide berth even as they reluctantly dropped back down onto all fours to resume the chase. Theirs tails twitched unhappily, while some of the riders struck Spock as more hesitant as well.

"It's just a trick," the lead rider shouted to rally the others. "Keep after them!"

Spock kept up the barrage. His intent was not to strike the riders or their mounts, but to slow them down sufficiently. Bottle after bottle smashed into the road, agitating the marmots while creating an obstacle course of glass shards and luminous green puddles, the latter of which yielded a distinctly unearthly effect.

"Bane-fire!" a rider cried out with what sounded like genuine superstitious awe. "These are no mere smugglers!"

"All the more reason to bring them to justice!" the leader shouted. "After them!"

Spurring her marmot onward, she chased after the wagon, with the rest of her troops close behind her. Both riders and rodents were obviously well trained and disciplined, as Spock concluded to his regret. Within minutes, the leader was only a few meters behind the wagon. Spock reached for another bottle to discourage her pursuit, only to come away empty-handed.

He was all out of glow water.

It was a measure of how frenetic the chase was that he had actually lost count of the glowing bottles. In a last-ditch effort, he hurled the empty wooden crate at the oncoming rider, but her agile marmot deftly avoided the missile and kept on coming until it was practically gnawing on the end of the wagon.

"That's far enough!" The rider leapt from her rodent into the back of the wagon, where she nimbly sprang to her feet and drew a fresh pistol from a bandolier across her chest. She menaced Spock with the pistol as she held on to one side of the wagon to keep her balance. "Halt this wagon!" she ordered Chekov. "Lock the wheels at once!"

"With all due respect," Chekov called back, "I do not think that would be wise."

"He is correct," Spock said. "Considering our current speed and momentum, braking too abruptly would likely flip this wagon end over end."

"Use the reins, then!" she barked. "Do whatever you have to, but bring this wagon to a halt. And you," she addressed Spock, "what gives you the audacity to—"

She got her first good look at Spock and his ears. Shock and bewilderment registered on her face.

"What manner of man . . . ?"

"Ill met by moonlight, it appears," Spock said, not expecting her to recognize the quotation. "I could attempt to explain, but—"

A blinding white spotlight enveloped the wagon. Spock's inner eyelids protected him from the glare as he squinted up to see *Galileo* swooping down from the sky. Its landing lights pierced the night.

Jord and Vankov had arrived—and none too soon.

The shuttlecraft's dramatic entrance awed the riders, who gasped and gaped in amazement as they struggled to control their panicky mounts. The shocking spectacle proved too much even for their determined leader, who suddenly lost interest in capturing two unusually troublesome smugglers. Abandoning her mission, she threw herself out of the back of the wagon in her haste to get away from *Galileo.* She hit the ground, rolled, and scrambled to her feet a few meters ahead of the other riders, some of whom opened fire on *Galileo,* peppering it with lead, which bounced harmlessly off the shuttlecraft's deflector shields. *Galileo* flew over the speeding wagon toward the riders, who turned around and fled in disarray, scampering away as fast as their terrified rodents could carry them. A single rider maintained the presence of mind to swing around to pick up his fallen commander before taking off after the others.

"Retreat!" the leader shouted unnecessarily. "Retreat!"

Spock watched them ride away into the night. He was pleased to see them depart.

"You may slow down, Mister Chekov. Our pursuers appear to have had a change of heart."

Chekov struggled with the reins. "I may need a minute or so, Mister Spock."

Galileo did not pursue the riders. Once it became obvious that they had been routed for the time being, the shuttlecraft turned around in midair and headed back toward the wagon. Spock used Eefa's communicator to hail the shuttle.

"Spock here. Your timing was impeccable. You have our gratitude."

"We aim to please," Vankov's voice replied. *"Just glad we got here in time."*

As it happened, Chekov needed more than just a few moments to bring his team of screeching marmots under control, or perhaps the galloping rodents simply wore themselves out. Either way, the wagon eventually slowed to a stop. Chekov sighed in relief as he locked the brake.

"For the record, sir, I think I would like to go back to navigating a starship, if it's all right with you."

"All in due time, Ensign. We still have a mission to complete."

Galileo touched down on the road several meters ahead, far enough away from the exhausted marmots so as not to excite them. Vankov exited its main door and sprinted toward the wagon. Spock glimpsed Jord at the helm within the shuttle.

"Mister Spock, Ensign Chekov! Are you all right?"

"We are unharmed." Spock climbed out of the wagon and onto the ground. "And in considerably better circumstances than we were mere minutes ago, thanks to your prompt intervention."

"But, Mister Spock," Chekov said, "those Yurnians saw the shuttlecraft. Is that not precisely what we sought to avoid? What about the Prime Directive?"

"That they beheld *Galileo* is regrettable," Spock said, "but vastly preferable to taking us into their custody. Instead of having an actual alien in their possession, they have only an isolated, inexplicable incident occurring on a lonely road late at night."

"My thoughts exactly," Vankov agreed. "I wouldn't be at all surprised if many of those revenue agents opted to keep quiet lest they be judged insane. At worst, this will become a tall tale few will believe."

"Supported by no physical evidence other than a dozen broken glass bottles," Spock said, perhaps as much to himself as to Chekov, "and scattered puddles of an effervescent liquid that will soon evaporate."

"Jord and I can try to clean up the glass," Vankov volunteered. "If this encounter is remembered at all, it will be as an obscure, unsolved mystery buried in the back pages of history."

Chekov nodded in understanding. "Yurnos's first UFO sighting."

"And hopefully its last for some time," Spock said, "provided we can terminate the smuggling operation once and for all. Only one more piece of the puzzle still needs to be put into its correct place, but to confirm my theory we must take off in *Galileo* at once. Time is of the essence."

He started toward the shuttlecraft. Chekov hurried after him.

"Why is that, Mister Spock? Where are we going?"

"I will explain on the way, Ensign. Suffice it to say that, like Mars and Venus, we have an appointment to the north . . . and a window we cannot afford to miss."

Twenty-Eight

Beyond Deep Space Station S-8

"Hailing *Lucky Strike*, please respond. I repeat: please respond!"

Sulu feared he was wasting his breath. He had been hailing the errant ship for what felt like forever, ever since it had first veered toward the Antares Maelstrom, but to no avail. He had to assume that Captain Dajo was receiving his transmissions—Helena would never set off into deep space without making certain the ship's communications array was in tip-top shape—so Dajo had to be deliberately ignoring Sulu's urgent attempts to contact him.

"Blast it, Dajo," he muttered under his breath. "Answer me."

Sulu was at the helm of *Fleetness*, a high-speed Zephryte shuttle he had commandeered back at the station. In hot pursuit of the *Lucky Strike*, he was flying solo, having left Knox and the rest of his officers behind at the space station in order to take on as many people as possible if, in a worst-case scenario, he needed to evacuate Dajo's ship. In addition, he was reluctant to risk any of his crew if he had to dive into the Maelstrom after Helena and the others.

Helena . . .

"Sulu to *Lucky Strike*. Resume your original course immediately. Do not attempt to cross the Maelstrom. If you survive, you will face prosecution for reckless endangerment upon your arrival at Baldur III."

Sulu told himself that this suicidal stunt had to be Dajo's idea and that Helena was just following orders. She had always played fast and loose with the rules, which was why she had chosen the private sector over Starfleet, but he couldn't imagine that she thought this was a good idea.

Listen to me, he thought, *even if you can't or won't respond.*

The *Lucky Strike* was nearing the outer fringes of the Maelstrom. Sulu hoped that his words were reaching Dajo or Helena or someone, because, in all honesty, he wasn't sure what he could do besides sternly issue orders and warnings. The borrowed shuttle was no match for the *Lucky Strike* if it came to phasers or tractor beams; all Sulu truly had going for him was his authority as a Starfleet officer, which appeared to carry little weight with Dajo and his crew. Even if he caught up with the *Lucky Strike* before it entered the Maelstrom, Sulu could hardly pull the other vessel over and issue Dajo a ticket. His best and pretty much only bet was to somehow persuade the other ship to turn back before it was too late.

And if the *Lucky Strike* did plunge heedlessly into the Maelstrom . . . ?

Sulu hoped it wouldn't come to that.

"*Hailing* Lucky Strike. *Think of the safety of your passengers. Do not enter the Maelstrom. That's an order.*"

Dajo rolled his eyes. "Persistent fellow, isn't he?"

"You have no idea," Helena said.

The bridge of the *Lucky Strike* was maybe a third of the size of, say, the bridge on a *Constitution*-class starship, but the basic layout aped Starfleet's. A mere handful of crew members manned the bridge controls, with a few more stationed in the engine room at the rear of the ship. Helena occupied her usual post at the communications station, while Dajo stood off to the side, listening to Sulu's messages along with her. At her captain's request, she kept the volume low enough that only she and Dajo could easily hear Sulu's warnings and admonitions. The ship's passengers, who were stowed away in the passenger compartments, couldn't hear a thing.

Probably just as well, she thought. "He's not going to give up, Mirsa."

"Just keep giving him the cold shoulder." Dajo smiled slyly. "We can always claim afterward that we didn't receive his hails. 'Technical difficulties' and such."

"If there's an afterward," she said in a low voice, "after the Maelstrom."

"Now is no time for faintheartedness, First Officer. The die is cast and the Passage awaits us. We know the way through the storm."

In theory, she thought, although she kept her doubts to herself. This was all her fault, in a way, since she was the one who had alerted Dajo to the opportunity. Having picked up a weak distress signal from the *Ali Baba,* she had been covertly monitoring the urgent communications coming to and from the space station, which was how she'd found out that the *Allegra* had been diverted to deal with the emergency, leaving a path to the Maelstrom open. *Perhaps I should have thought twice before informing Dajo of that development.*

"He's gaining on us, Captain," Buzuz called out from the sensor station. The insectoid Kaferian employed a shoulder-mounted vocoder unit to address his more mammalian shipmates.

Dajo returned to the captain's chair. He stroked his thin mustache thoughtfully.

"How long until he intercepts us?"

The navigator ran the calculations. "Approximately five minutes."

"And how long before we reach the Maelstrom?"

"One minute."

"Well, there you have it." Dajo relaxed into his chair, draping one leg over an armrest. "He'll turn back once we enter the Maelstrom."

Helena doubted it. "You don't know Sulu."

Nevertheless, she hoped Dajo was right—for Sulu's sake. She fought the temptation to respond to his hails so she could try to talk him out of pursuing them.

Don't do it, Hikaru. Don't risk yourself.

———————

"Listen to me. It's not too late to turn back. Don't throw your lives away just for a shortcut!"

The Maelstrom loomed ahead, dominating the horizon, as Sulu came within visual range of the *Lucky Strike*. The gold-plated passenger ship was dwarfed by the Maelstrom, the sight of which would give any sane captain or pilot pause. As a helmsman, Sulu had flown through ion storms, asteroid barrages, minefields, and even time itself; nevertheless, the Maelstrom sent a chill down his spine. The sheer size and turbulence of it reminded him somewhat of the galactic barrier enclosing the Milky Way—and not in a good way.

You don't fly into something like that unless you have a very *good reason.*

Sulu's heart sank as, undaunted, the *Lucky Strike* accelerated toward the Maelstrom without hesitation. Eyeballing the distance between him and the other vessel, Sulu didn't need a navigator at his side to realize that he wasn't going to be able to catch up with the *Lucky Strike* before it entered the Maelstrom, let alone get between it and the border. Not for the first time, he wished he was at the helm of the *Enterprise* instead. He would have a lot more options in that case.

"Sulu to *Lucky Strike*. This is your last chance. Think about what you're doing!"

The Maelstrom's border was not clearly defined, being thinner at its outer fringes then deeper within its churning depths.

For a short time, Sulu was still able to make out the *Lucky Strike* before it vanished into the Maelstrom as though disappearing into a dense, colossal fog bank. The shuttle's sensors could still track the other ship, despite the volatile energies surging within the Maelstrom, but for how much longer?

This is it, Sulu realized, *the moment of truth.*

He was not required to follow the other ship into the Maelstrom. He could simply cross his fingers and pray that Dajo knew what he was doing. Having done his best to dissuade the foolhardy travelers, Sulu could return to the station where he was still sorely needed.

"Who am I kidding?" he muttered.

Throttling up, he plunged into the Maelstrom.

Twenty-Nine

Yurnos

The planet's polar aurora was quite striking.

Seen from orbit, it appeared as a shimmering ring of light, hundreds of kilometers across, circling Yurnos's northern pole. Green shades predominated at the highest altitudes, reminding Spock somewhat of the Antarian glow water he had splashed over the landscape many thousands of kilometers to the south. Shifting ribbons of pink, green, and orange added to the luminous display, which was caused by solar winds exciting ionized particles in the planet's upper atmosphere, where they had been channeled by Yurnos's powerful magnetic field. The charged particles expelled the excess energy in the form of photons, producing the aurora, with color dependent on the elements and atoms affected. Periodic fluctuations in the magnetosphere caused the brilliance of the colors to wax and wane per a predictable cycle.

He observed the phenomenon through *Galileo*'s forward ports as they sped toward the arctic region at the top of the planet. Sensor displays monitored the intensity of the aurora, which generated powerful electromagnetic currents in the atmosphere.

"Are we in time, Mister Spock?"

Chekov manned the helm beside Spock. Like Spock, he was

still clad in his borrowed Yurnian garments, there having been neither time nor opportunity to change back into their uniforms. They'd traded Eefa's wagon for *Galileo,* leaving the wagon and its team with Jord and Vankov, in order to fly north toward the planet's higher latitudes in hopes of confirming Spock's theory regarding the smugglers' secret route on and off Yurnos.

"I believe so, Ensign." Spock carefully studied the sensor data while performing the necessary calculations in his head. "In theory, the auroral activity should reach peak intensity in approximately five point three-seven seconds." He peered out the window directly in front of him as he counted down. "Four, three, two, one . . ."

No obvious sign of the smugglers presented itself. Spock frowned. Was it possible that his conjectures were mistaken? Had he misinterpreted the imprudent remarks he had overheard on the beach, regarding the smugglers' plans to head north for a light show? He had been certain that he deduced the nature of the "window" they had vaguely alluded to, but what if he was mistaken?

"Mister Spock! Look!" Chekov gestured excitedly at the view through his viewport. "Rising up through the atmosphere, at two o'clock!"

The young human's keen eyes were not mistaken. Spock suppressed a flicker of excitement as he spied a spacecraft launching into space from the arctic sea hundreds of kilometers below. He increased the magnification on a globular visual monitor positioned at eye level above the instrument panel; the augmented image confirmed that the departing vessel was indeed the submersible shuttlecraft employed by Mars, Venus, and Mercury.

"It appears my calculations were slightly off," he observed.

"Or perhaps not everyone is as precise as you, Mister Spock." Chekov's smirk landed on the right side of not being irritating. "Few people are."

Spock conceded the point.

His broader theory had certainly been validated. As he'd suspected, the smugglers had been using the planet's intense polar auroras to mask their comings and goings from conventional sensors. Spock suspected that they scheduled their arrivals and departures in conjunction with predictable cycles of sunspot activity, the planet's position relative to the standard main-sequence star it orbited, as well as periodic fluctuations in Yurnos's magnetic field to ensure that the auroras were sufficiently strong enough to interfere with conventional sensor scans. It was, he had to admit, a rather ingenious stratagem. Small wonder they had managed to elude detection for so long.

"Do you think they have spotted us, Mister Spock?"

"I doubt it, Ensign. The aurora will likely mask our presence from their sensors, and they have little reason to be on the lookout for *Galileo*."

Chekov chuckled. "What's good for the goose, eh, Mister Spock?"

"Precisely."

The smugglers' craft deployed its retractable nacelles and sped away from Yurnos, heading out of the system. They were wasting no time or fuel in making a clean escape from this region of space. Spock saw its image recede in the monitor.

"Stay after them, Mister Chekov. We do not wish to lose them."

"Aye, sir."

Chekov opened up the throttle and *Galileo* pursued the smugglers' unnamed spacecraft. The shuttle's ion drive propelled them out of Yurnos's orbit and across the solar system, quickly leaving the planet's sole moon behind as well. *Galileo* proved a match for the shuttle, whose streamlined, aerodynamic contours provided little advantage in the vacuum of space. Spock watched with satisfaction as they gained on the smugglers, finding this pursuit rather more pleasing than the one they had so recently escaped. Given a choice, he preferred chasing to being chased.

As was only logical . . .

The shuttle exceeded light speed as it exited the system, proceeding into the dark between the stars. *Galileo* accelerated to keep pace.

"They are heading in the general direction of Baldur III," Chekov said, consulting the shuttlecraft's astrogator. "No surprise."

"Bring us closer, Ensign."

It was unclear if the other craft was aware that they were being followed. Spock took advantage of their proximity to conduct a thorough scan of the shuttle, recording its surface details, configuration, and energy signatures. The invasive scan yielded valuable data, but also provoked a hostile response.

"Weapons batteries charging," Spock said sharply. "Raise shields. Raise blast shutters."

"Aye, sir!"

Chekov flipped a switch, and sturdy duranium shields slid into place above *Galileo*'s ports. The shutters blocked their view, but Spock and Chekov could still see out of the shuttle via the display globes, which relayed visual data from *Galileo*'s external sensors. Between the shields and the shutters, the men were armored against most attacks short of a high-grade photon torpedo, which Spock judged unlikely to be found in the arsenal of common smugglers.

A crimson flash of disruptor fire lit up the rear of the other vessel, an instant before the blast slammed into *Galileo*'s shields, rocking both the vessel and its passengers; fortunately, the shuttlecraft held up against the disruptor beam better than Eefa's unfortunate henchman had back on Yurnos. A digital display on the instrument panel reported that *Galileo*'s shields were down precisely 17.862 percent after the assault.

"That packed a punch, Mister Spock." Chekov kept *Galileo* on course despite the impact. "I don't think they like us following them."

"Prepare to return fire, Ensign."

Chekov grinned wolfishly. "Music to my ears, sir."

Spock activated the shuttle's communication circuits. He hailed the smugglers via the same frequency Eefa's simple communicator had been tuned to.

"Attention: individuals calling themselves Mars, Venus, and Mercury. This is Commander Spock, representing Starfleet and the United Federation of Planets. Your actions on Yurnos are in violation of the Prime Directive. You are directed to terminate all such operations immediately and turn yourself over to face criminal charges."

Spock was a realist. He had little expectation that the smugglers would readily surrender to justice, but propriety demanded that he give them the opportunity. If nothing else, he hoped to make it clear that their days of flying below Starfleet's radar were over.

"Right," Venus responded to his hail. *"Like that's going to happen. Go jump in a singularity."*

"Mister Chekov, please demonstrate how seriously we take this matter."

"Aye, sir."

Galileo fired on the smugglers. Twin phaser beams converged on the aft section of the ship, producing bright cobalt bursts of Cherenkov radiation where they intersected with the other vessel's deflector shields. The intent was not to actually destroy the other ship or endanger the smugglers' lives, but merely to bruise their shields enough to demonstrate that *Galileo* could and would defend itself if necessary.

The smugglers retaliated with another disruptor blast that rattled the shuttle. The fiery red flare briefly filled the globe displays, blinding *Galileo,* before dissipating into the ether. Spock observed that the shuttle's shields were now down another 20.008 percent, suggesting that the smugglers had upped the force of their disruptors. They clearly had no intention of surrendering without a fight.

"*That you, Vulcan?*" Venus asked. "*Should have known Eefa wouldn't have the guts to dispose of you properly. What did you do with her anyway?*"

"Eefa is not your concern," Spock replied. "It is the actions of you and your accomplices that are of relevance at the present moment."

"*Don't even think you're taking this tea. We bought it fair and square, and have customers waiting for it.*"

"One particular shipment of *nabbia* is of no consequence," Spock stated. "Your reckless involvement in Yurnian affairs is the crux of the matter. Understand that Starfleet will not allow this to continue."

"*And you're going to stop us?*" she said. "*Get off our tail, if you know what's good for you. I'm in no big hurry to pick a fight with Starfleet, but I'm sure as hell not going to end up in a Federation rehab colony because of your high-and-mighty Prime Directive.*"

"Not to mention the cold-blooded murder of that man on Yurnos," Chekov retorted, joining the exchange. "He was no friend of ours, but it was his planet, and you killed him on it. Rehabilitation is the least you deserve."

"*And we have the Russian too, it seems,*" Venus said. "*Thanks for reminding me that you two are witnesses to that little altercation. Guess we can't have you running back to Starfleet to squeal on us, can we?*"

The smugglers' craft executed a loop, coming around to challenge *Galileo* head-on. A disruptor blast, much stronger than those previous, nearly threw Spock from his seat. Warning lights began to blink urgently upon the instrument panels. Shields were down to 36.408 percent; that they were now at less than half strength boded poorly for the shuttlecraft's continued chances of survival if they prolonged the encounter. Spock completed his scans of the smugglers' vessel.

"Evasive action," he ordered. "Break off pursuit."

"I'm trying, Mister Spock, but I think they are pursuing *us* now!"

Galileo reversed course while returning fire. The shuttlecraft wove back and forth in space, executing a zigzag flight plan to make it harder to target. Disruptor blasts continued to scrape away at their shields, however; Chekov was doing his best, but a percentage of the smugglers' blasts struck home with varying degrees of accuracy. A glancing blow tilted the shuttle hard to port before the artificial gravity compensated for the angle and stabilized their orientation. An environmental control panel in the passenger cabin overloaded, spraying sparks onto empty seats and crackling loudly until automated circuit breakers kicked in to cut off the flow of power to the damaged panel. An acrid odor lingered after the sparks ceased erupting.

Spock took control of *Galileo*'s weapons, retaliating with their phasers. He briefly entertained the hope that the smugglers would choose retreat as well, but evidence suggested they intended to finish the fight. He suspected their motives were as much emotional as they were calculated, but it was the nature of emotions to provoke violent behavior. His own people's history had proved that millennia ago.

A disruptor blast struck the underside of the shuttlecraft. The sensation was not unlike a marmot-drawn wagon hitting a bump at high speed. A schematic of *Galileo* appeared upon a display screen; a portion of the schematic flashed scarlet, relaying bad news about the ship's structural integrity.

"We've lost the starboard landing pad," Chekov said, reading the schematic. "I hate to say it, Mister Spock, but I'm afraid we are outgunned."

"So it appears," Spock agreed. Their shields were holding— barely—at a mere 26.021 percent of their desired strength. "Nor do our opponents seem inclined to let us withdraw from the field."

He assembled the data he had already accumulated regarding

the smugglers, their vessel, and their operations and transmitted it in a packet back to the Federation observers on Yurnos. It was imperative that the results of his and Chekov's investigation survive even if they and *Galileo* did not.

"*Feeling the heat, Vulcan?*" Venus hailed them to gloat. "*Bet you wish you'd stayed out of our business now. We gave you a chance to back off, but you just had to give us a hard time for trying to make an honest-ish living. This is all on you. But don't feel too bad. Maybe your precious Starfleet will award you both medals . . . posthumously.*"

Chekov switched off the comm, which Spock had little objection to. Venus and her cohorts clearly had no desire to engage in a meaningful dialogue.

"Mister Spock," Chekov whispered urgently, even though no one could hear. "Take the helm. I have an idea!"

He quickly explained his brainstorm to Spock, who deemed it worth attempting. He took control of the helm from the co-pilot's seat. "Proceed, Ensign."

Chekov opened a new channel on a specific frequency.

"Hailing *U.S.S. Enterprise*. This is *Galileo*. Do you read me? This is Ensign Pavel Chekov, hailing *Captain James T. Kirk*." He placed unusual stress on the captain's name. "Please respond, *Captain Kirk*."

"Chekov?" Vankov responded from Yurnos. "I don't understand. What do you—"

"Good to hear your voice, *Captain Kirk*," Chekov said hastily. "We have good news to report to you and *Enterprise*."

Chekov's scheme depended on Vankov swiftly grasping and playing along with the ruse. To his credit, the anthropologist caught on quickly. He lowered his voice an octave and assumed a more authoritative tone.

"*Kirk here, Ensign. What is your report?*"

"Your plan is succeeding, Captain. We have engaged the smugglers, who have taken the bait. We are leading them toward you now. You may emerge from hiding behind Yurnos's moon. Come and get them!"

"Affirmative, Ensign Chekov! We are on our way. Keep them busy until we get there!"

"Don't worry, Captain. We've got them right where we want them."

Spock did not know whether to be impressed or appalled by Chekov's mendacity. He was clearly developing a talent for it, perhaps in emulation of a certain James T. Kirk, who had been known to bluff his way out of a difficult situation. Chekov had evidently been paying attention to his captain's tactics.

The deception had the desired effect. The barrage of disruptor beams terminated abruptly as, according to Spock's sensors, the smugglers abandoned their pursuit of *Galileo* and took off in the opposite direction. It appeared that even the possibility of facing off against a *Constitution*-class starship was enough to make them lose their appetite for combat.

Spock could not fault their logic in that regard.

"Well done, Ensign. A creative solution."

"Thank you, Mister Spock." Chekov watched the smugglers' craft speed out of sensor range. "I have to say, though, I hate letting those villains get away, after all they have done."

Spock understood how the young man felt, but he kept his focus on the larger picture.

"Apprehending the actual smugglers was never our priority. Halting their activities on Yurnos was our mission, and I believe we now have enough information to make that possible. We discovered who and where they were getting the *nabbia* from, we determined how they were smuggling the tea off the planet, and, perhaps, we convinced them that Starfleet is no longer blind to their activities, which may be enough to discourage them from returning to Yurnos altogether. In addition, we now have full scans of their spacecraft, including their energy signatures, so it is unlikely that they will be able to elude Starfleet for long. In short," Spock concluded, "there is no logical reason why they must be captured at this particular point of time."

"I know, I know, Mister Spock, but it still goes against the grain." He gave Spock an apologetic look. "It is an emotional thing. You wouldn't understand."

"You might be surprised, Ensign, but as we explained to Eefa on the beach not too long ago: sometimes the most logical thing to do is to step away from the fight." He turned the helm back over to Chekov, confident the young officer would not be so foolish as to take off in pursuit of the smugglers. "For the record, Chekov, I do not fault you for possessing human emotions, but I do commend you for having the discipline and maturity to control them."

"Thank you, Mister Spock. That is high praise, coming from you."

He raised the blast shutters to permit them a better view of vast depths of space before them. The smugglers' craft was nowhere to be seen.

"Shall I set course back for Yurnos, sir?"

Spock shook his head. "I think not, Ensign. We have accomplished enough there for now. Set course for Baldur III . . . and the *Enterprise*."

Thirty

The Antares Maelstrom

Entering the Maelstrom was not like crossing a line in the sand. The turbulence was fairly mild for the first one hundred kilometers, but increased dramatically the farther *Fleetness* flew into the roiling plasma currents, which tossed the shuttle back and forth as Sulu struggled to keep it on course despite the violent forces buffeting the vessel and threatening to carry it every which way. Seated at the helm, Sulu was grateful for the safety harness holding him in place during the increasingly rocky ride even as he eyed the status reports with growing concern. The engine and thrusters were already straining; the shields were being battered by contact with the supercharged plasma, working overtime to protect the ship (and Sulu) from lethal amounts of heat and radiation, not to mention random energy discharges. The temperature was already rising within the cockpit, as if he wasn't already working up a sweat just trying to stay on the *Lucky Strike*'s trail. An obnoxious crackling noise penetrated the shields and hull, abrading Sulu's nerves.

No wonder no ship has ever crossed the Maelstrom, Sulu thought. *Calling it hazardous is an understatement.*

And this particular vessel didn't help his odds any. True to its name, *Fleetness* was built for speed, not endurance, typical of the Zephrytes, who, as a culture, were notorious for their impatience. The shuttle was fast, enabling him to catch up with *Lucky Strike*, more or less, but flimsy by Starfleet standards; certainly, it was not designed to stand up to these extreme conditions. As a sudden swell of plasma jolted *Fleetness*, accompanied by a blinding electromagnetic flash, Sulu resolved to never again take for granted the *Enterprise*'s sturdy construction, multiply redundant backup systems, and top-of-the-line engineers.

Where is Scotty, now that I need him?

The view beyond the shuttle's front ports was a seething, prismatic vortex that was psychedelic enough to give a Medusan a headache. Sulu dialed up the filters to protect his eyes from the glare. Unable to establish visual contact with the *Lucky Strike*, he could make out only a vague silhouette on the sensor display and try to maintain a fix on the other ship's warp signature. There was no point in attempting to track its ion trail, as any residual particles would be immediately swept away by the fast-moving currents; it would be like trying to follow a trail of bread crumbs in a hurricane—while trying to survive the hurricane at the same time.

Warning lights flashed on the shuttle's board, signifying that the shields were already on the verge of collapse. The Maelstrom was too much for *Fleetness*, which was succumbing to the tempest even faster than Sulu had anticipated. Once the shields went down, other systems were bound to fail as well, leaving nothing but the shuttle's hull between Sulu and oblivion. The only question was what would kill him first: a hull breach or a life-support failure?

Exiting the Maelstrom was not an option. At the rate the shields were crumbling, he wasn't going to make it back to regular space before *Fleetness* was torn to shreds. Forget saving Helena and the other people aboard the *Lucky Strike*. The rescuer was now in need of rescue, with only one chance remaining to him.

"Sulu to *Lucky Strike*. Mayday!"

"Sulu?"

The SOS was faint and difficult to decipher, given all the interference from the Maelstrom. Helena had to turn up the volume
and adjust the settings on her customized earpiece to make out
what Sulu was saying, but once she fully grasped the danger he
was in, she immediately broke subspace radio silence to reply.

"Hikaru, this is Helena. Stand by for rescue."

"Come again?" Dajo called out from the captain's chair,
which pivoted toward Helena. Seat belts kept them both from
being tossed by the turbulence. "I told you not to respond!"

"Sorry, Captain, but this is an emergency!" She tersely informed him of Sulu's desperate circumstances. "That shuttle's
not long for this universe. It can't stand up to the Maelstrom."

Not that the *Lucky Strike* was having an easy time of it. Bigger
and more solidly built than whatever secondhand shuttle Sulu
had scrounged up, the *Lucky Strike* was faring better than Sulu's
ride, at least so far, but Helena wasn't going to breathe easy until
they were safely through the Maelstrom, especially since the
fabled Passage was proving more elusive than expected, considering the absolutely "authentic" and "reliable" charts Dajo had
discreetly acquired back at the station. Helena had her doubts
about those charts, and the Passage in general, but she would
have to worry about that later, after Sulu was safe. Rescuing him
took priority, at least as far as she was concerned.

"That's not our fault," Dajo protested. "Nobody asked him to
follow us into the Maelstrom!"

"It's not about assigning blame," Helena said. "A man's life is
in danger. That's all that matters now."

"But what are we supposed to do about it? We don't have a
shuttlebay."

"Which is why we have to beam him aboard before it's too
late."

Dajo reacted in alarm. "But that would mean dropping out of warp and lowering our own shields . . . in the middle of the Maelstrom!"

"Just for a few seconds." Helena couldn't believe they were wasting time debating this. "For Athena's sake, are you seriously proposing that we just fly on and let Sulu die?"

"I'm simply thinking of the safety of this ship and our passengers," Dajo insisted, a trifle defensively. "Look at where we are. We're already taking our lumps from that murderous tempest outside. Even dropping the shields for a moment is going to take a bite out of the ship and its systems, when we might need everything we've got later on."

"That's a risk we have to take." Her temper flared. "I *defended* you to Sulu, Captain. I told him you couldn't be a saboteur, that you weren't the kind of man who would deliberately harm people. Was I wrong about that, Mirsa? Are you going to prove me a liar?"

They glared at each other across the bridge, while the rest of the five-person bridge crew looked on uncomfortably. She wondered whose side they'd take if she had to stage a full-on mutiny for Sulu's sake. Was she the only one willing to stand up to Dajo over this?

Don't make me do it, Mirsa. Prove to me that you're just a scoundrel, not a sociopath.

"Fine," he caved. "But you owe me one, Helena."

"Put it on my tab." She sighed in relief as she got straight to work. "First Officer to Transporter Chief. Prepare for emergency transport, pronto!"

The shuttle's deflectors were holding on by a thread, while vital circuits were burning out at a rapidly accelerating rate. Noxious fumes polluted the atmosphere inside the cockpit, forcing Sulu to resort to a breathing mask again. The artificial gravity wobbled erratically, making his stomach do flip-flops. Thrusters fought against the plasma currents to keep the shuttle from being swept away from the *Lucky Strike*. Sparks exploded from an overheated sensor panel; Sulu threw up an arm to shield his face. White-hot sparks scorched his sleeve. Groaning metal confirmed that the hull's structural integrity was failing.

"Sulu to *Lucky Strike*," he said. "Sooner better than later, if you don't mind."

"*We're on it*," Helena responded. He could hear the worry in her voice despite the static. "*Not going to lie to you, Hikaru. This is going to be dicey. I can't guarantee that we'll be able to lock onto you through all the interference between us, let alone beam you through the soup.*"

"Understood." Sulu winced at the thought of his atoms being strewn across the Maelstrom. "Not much choice about it."

"*Nope*," she agreed. "*Grabbing your shuttle now. Hold tight.*"

The ship shuddered as a tractor beam from the *Lucky Strike* seized hold of *Fleetness* in order to keep the shuttle in a fixed position relative to the larger ship. The bump was difficult to distinguish from the general turbulence, but Sulu thought he felt the difference. That the beam's grasp put more strain on the shuttle's much-abused hull was something he chose not to think about. The abused metal was more screaming than groaning now. An unnerving vibration passed from the floor to his own frame, rattling his bones.

"*Got you.*" Helena spoke quickly as though worried about losing contact with Sulu. "*We're going to need you to boost the transponder signal from your personal communicator as high as it will go, while we do the same with our transporter's confinement beam.*"

He flipped open his communicator and set the signal for maximum. "Done."

"*Good. I'm already patched into our transporter chief. Schultz, are you ready?*"

"*Just waiting on your order*," a masculine voice answered.

"Ready to drop shields?" she called out to somebody else aboard her ship. *"We need to do this in synch. Split-second timing!"*

Her signal was breaking up, but Sulu made out a hasty assent in the background. A quick glance at a cracked status display revealed that the shuttle's shields were at 0.46 percent and falling fast; they were dropping whether Sulu was ready or not. Bulkheads buckled noisily. Microfractures in the hull started to suck the smoky atmosphere into space. He gripped the communicator tightly, holding on to to it for dear life. He shouted over the whistling wind and shrieking metal.

"Helena! Now or never!"

Without waiting for her prompt, he reached out and shut down the shields.

What was left of them, that was.

Sulu staggered onto the bridge of the *Lucky Strike*, escorted by a guide from the ship's transporter room. Despite Helena's fears, he had arrived with all his atoms in place, as far as he could tell, but the turbulence shaking the ship made it difficult to keep one's balance, so he occasionally had to brace himself against a wall or doorway to stay upright. His legs felt a little rubbery as well.

Could be worse, he thought. *A few more moments and—*

"Hikaru!" Helena greeted him from her post. "Thank Olympus we got you in time."

"I was just thinking the same." He made his way across the lurching bridge, grabbing onto rails and consoles to keep from stumbling. "The shuttle?"

"In pieces," she reported. "Carried away by the currents."

Sulu felt a twinge of guilt regarding *Fleetness*'s destruction. Starfleet would surely compensate the Zephrytes for the loss of their shuttle, but he'd hoped to return it to them in one piece. He couldn't help feeling that he'd abused their trust to a degree, even if lives had been at stake.

"And yourself?" she asked.

"All here." He patted himself down, realizing as he did so that he was hardly looking his best. He was sweaty and disheveled; his uniform reeked of soot and smoke. "Not that I've been fully checked out by a medic, mind you, but I appear to be fully operational, if a bit worse for wear. Thanks for that."

"Welcome aboard," she said warmly. "Sorry I can't give you the grand tour, but this is not exactly a good time."

"So I can see."

He took a moment to survey the bridge. It was hard to miss that the *Lucky Strike* was taking a pounding. Sulu wondered how much more it could take before going the way of *Fleetness*. Was his narrow escape merely a temporary reprieve?

"Another rain check, then?" she said.

"Story of our lives," he replied. "If it's not one thing, it's another."

She smiled wryly. "The lengths some guys will go just to have a drink with a gal."

"At least you returned my call, lucky for me."

"You're welcome," Dajo said sourly, breaking into their banter. "Sorry to interrupt, Lieutenant, but if you're through distracting my first officer, we've got a Maelstrom to cross. Find yourself a seat and stay out of the way."

Sulu bristled at his tone, but let it pass. The *Lucky Strike* had just saved his life after all. That earned its captain some leeway.

"Don't be ridiculous," Helena said. "Sulu is a decorated Starfleet officer and one of their very best helmsmen. We'd be fools not to take advantage of that, under the circumstances."

"We already have a helmsman," Dajo groused. "And your friend the lieutenant has already complicated matters enough."

Sulu appreciated Helena's endorsement, but didn't want to make waves on an already stormy sea. He also decided that there would be time enough to confront Dajo about recklessly venturing into the Maelstrom if and when they reached

Baldur III. He took an unoccupied post at an auxiliary sensor station near Helena and fastened his seat belt.

"I'm ready to pitch in as needed."

"Don't hold your breath," Dajo said before turning his chair toward his own helmsman, a young male human, around Chekov's age, wearing civilian attire like the rest of Dajo's crew. Sulu noted that the helm and navigation stations had been combined into a single unit so that they could be operated by just one crew member. Dajo tapped his boot impatiently against the floor. "Talk to me, Perez. Where's the Passage?"

"I don't know, Captain Dajo, sir." Perez wiped sweat from his brow. His taut voice and body language betrayed the pressure he was under. "I'm following the course you provided, but I'm not finding anything resembling a safe passage." He gestured at the seething kaleidoscope of colors on the viewscreen. "Just kilometer after kilometer of . . . *that*."

"That can't be right," Dajo insisted. "Recalibrate your instrumentation to make sure we're at the proper coordinates. Maybe a swell nudged us off course without you realizing."

"I've already tried that, Captain. Trust me, we're precisely where we're supposed to be. It's the Passage that's a no-show."

"That's impossible!" Dajo pounded his fist on an armrest. "He gave me a money-back guarantee that those charts were the real deal!"

A sudden suspicion crossed Sulu's mind.

"Excuse me, Captain. Who exactly sold you those charts?"

"Naylis, if you must know." Vexed, Dajo apparently saw no reason to protect the current object of his ire. "I paid a hefty price for them too. That greedy Troyian drives a hard bargain."

I should have known, Sulu thought. "I hate to break it to you, Captain, but Naylis played you, along with the rest of us. He had his own agenda that didn't involve you or anyone else getting to Baldur III anytime soon."

He quickly briefed both Dajo and Helena on what Naylis had

been up to, leaving out only the part where Naylis had subjected him to the neural neutralizer; there was nothing to be gained by calling his own loyalties or capacities into question. And, come to think of it, the Voice did seem to be finally fading away at last. It was still there, whispering at the back of his mind, but it was getting fainter and easier to ignore.

Everything is fine. There is nothing to worry about . . .

Circumstances begged to differ. Nothing like coming within seconds of being destroyed along with your spacecraft, Sulu surmised, to focus the mind on the here and now. He almost had to admire, however, the way Naylis had shamelessly worked every angle: getting overeager skippers like Dajo to pay to put their ships in danger while simultaneously getting paid by their rivals to keep them from reaching Baldur III soon or ever. Harry Mudd would be proud.

"That perfidious green reprobate!" Dajo raged. "Is there no honor left in this benighted galaxy? No integrity?"

Sulu refrained from commenting, choosing to familiarize himself with the short-range sensor controls instead. That struck him as a better use of his time.

"Nobody deals false with me." Dajo slammed a fist into his palm. "When I get my hands on him—!"

"You may have to take a number," Sulu said. "But the point is, I wouldn't trust any information provided by Naylis, of all people. The Passage is a pipe dream that's just going to get us all killed."

A tremor shook the bridge, punctuating his assessment.

"He's right, Mirsa," Helena said. "Now that we know the truth, that we got swindled, it's crazy to keep looking for a passage that may not even exist. We need to cut our losses and get out of the Maelstrom while we still can."

Dajo hesitated, obviously reluctant to give up on his daring ploy. "But I promised our passengers that I would get them to Baldur III as quickly as possible."

"I'm guessing you also promised to get them there alive," Sulu said. "We all know that's not going to happen if you persist in trying to cross the Maelstrom. You took a gamble, Dajo, but it didn't pay off. Don't double down on a bad bet."

"Listen to him, Mirsa," Helena urged. "We need to be smart about this."

"I know, I know," he said with a sigh. "I just hate to let common sense spoil a properly audacious plan. Playing it safe goes against my grain, not to mention being bad for my image."

Sulu could sympathize to a degree. He also liked to see himself as something of a swashbuckler, within reason. "But—?"

"Take us out of here, Perez," the captain ordered. "We gave it our best shot, but the Maelstrom got the better of us. Hightail it back to normal space."

"Not going to be that easy, Captain," the young helmsman said. "That last big bump knocked us off course and the astrogator is getting screwy on me, so I can't get any proper bearings. And the Maelstrom makes it impossible to navigate by any known celestial landmarks. We're surrounded by constantly shifting rivers of plasma in every direction: ahead, behind, above, below, you name it. To be honest, sir, I can't even retrace our route, Captain."

Dajo frowned. "What exactly are you saying, Perez?"

"We're lost, Captain. Plain and simple."

A hush fell over the bridge as the full implications of the helmsman's announcement sunk in. Sulu experienced an unpleasant flash of déjà vu; this was like being stuck on *Fleetness* all over again. The *Lucky Strike* couldn't survive the Maelstrom indefinitely.

"Shield status?" Dajo asked.

A Trill woman at a tactical station responded. Like Perez, she was dressed more casually than a Starfleet crew member. A tank top, sweat pants, and headband made her look off duty by *Enterprise* standards. A bare midriff exposed her bilateral spotting, at least in part. "Fifty-eight percent, sir, for now."

"I see," Dajo said. He didn't have to spell out what that meant; that the shields were already down nearly forty percent was not a good thing. The clock was ticking and they had no idea which way safety lay. To his credit, Dajo tried to put up a brave front. "More than half strength? That's better than I expected. Don't lose heart, ladies and gentlemen, et cetera, things could be worse."

Then they came under attack.

A dazzling sapphire pulse lit up the viewscreen even as a powerful jolt caused the lights in the bridge to flicker and the screen to blink out. Sulu glanced down at the scanner display at the station he had appropriated. His eyes widened at what he saw on the screen.

"What in Hades was that?" Helena said. "That didn't feel like turbulence."

"Because it wasn't," Sulu said. "Heads up. We've got company!"

Rebooting, the forward viewscreen confirmed his pronouncement. An unfamiliar life-form glided past the screen, only meters away from the prow of the ship. Sulu caught a glimpse of a delta-shaped creature that looked like a cross between a manta ray and, ironically enough, the Starfleet insignia. It was roughly the size of a photon torpedo and its smooth iridescent hide glowed sporadically in places, with the radiant areas shifting constantly along the entity's surface.

Some sort of natural bioluminescence?

"Reverse that image and freeze it," Dajo ordered, leaning forward in his chair. "Give it thirty percent of the screen."

"Got it," a random crew member said informally. "Here you go."

A freeze-frame of the creature took over roughly a third of the screen, leaving a real-time view of what lay directly ahead on the bulk of the viewer. Sulu and the others gaped at the unfamiliar life-form.

"Anybody have a clue what exactly that is?" Dajo asked, possibly rhetorically.

"One of the mysterious life-forms rumored to inhabit the Maelstrom," Sulu assumed. His knowledge of extraterrestrial flora and fauna was not quite as encyclopedic as Mister Spock's, but Sulu felt confident that the entity on the screen was largely unknown to Federation science. At best it was the stuff of xenocryptozoology—until now. "Beyond that, your guess is as good as mine."

"Watch out!" Helena said. "It's coming around again!"

Looping about, the entity swooped out of the churning plasma to smack against the ship's shields again. Another sapphire pulse jolted the vessel, causing the lights and circuitry to sputter. Sulu moved quickly to power down his sensor controls to keep them from burning out during the surge.

"Shields down to fifty-six percent," the spotted crew member reported. "Those pulses pack a punch."

And that was on top of the pummeling the ship was already getting from the Maelstrom, Sulu realized. Their situation had suddenly become even more precarious, unless they could repel the creature.

"Just what we don't need," Dajo said. "Energize phasers, Fass. Let's give that beast a taste of its own medicine."

"Way ahead of you, Skipper," the spotted woman said. "Phaser batteries ramping up."

Sulu frowned at the prospect of immediately firing upon a hitherto undiscovered life-form, but he couldn't really fault Dajo for taking action to protect his ship and everyone aboard. With any luck, the phasers would only discourage the creature, not damage it.

"Acquiring target," Fass said. "Opening fire."

A bright yellow beam sliced through the Maelstrom to strike the underside of the creature as it banked away from the ship, possibly gearing up for another run at the *Lucky Strike*. The beam hit the life-form head-on, but only seemed to jar it. Its luminous segments flared brightly before dimming back to their original intensity. Sulu squinted at the flier, half relieved, half concerned, that the phaser burst hadn't impacted the creature more. If anything, the entity appeared to be slightly . . . larger?

What exactly were they dealing with here?

"Don't look now!" Helena pointed at the upper left-hand corner of the screen, which was partially obscured by the inset image of the life-form's first appearance. "Our new friend's not alone!"

Two more of the gliders emerged from the Maelstrom, swooping aggressively toward the ship. Taking initiative, Fass fired the phasers at the new arrivals, who appeared to shrug off the blasts as easily as the first creature. They slammed into the *Lucky Strike*, delivering jolt after jolt, or maybe sting after sting?

"Increase power to the phasers!" Dajo ordered. "Show them we're not playing around!"

"I'm trying, Skipper!" Fass said. "They're not getting the message!"

"Hit them harder, then!"

"Not so fast!" Sulu said. "I wouldn't do that if I were you."

"Why is that?" Dajo asked. "And who asked you anyway?"

"I'm running a scan on them," Sulu said. "As nearly as I can tell, they're composed of both matter and energy, in ever-shifting proportions. That's what those glowing patterns are, flowing all over their bodies; every part of the gliders can transition from matter to energy and back again."

"To what end?" Helena asked.

"Possibly to help them steer through the Maelstrom?" Sulu speculated. "By redistributing or altering their mass as necessary, like an old-fashioned submarine adjusting its buoyancy. In theory, they can make themselves heavier on one side than the other, tilt forward or backward, pitch and yaw, while gliding through the plasma currents."

It was just a theory, but it made sense to the helmsman in him.

Dajo snorted. "And that means we shouldn't defend ourselves because . . . ?"

"Don't you get it?" Sulu asked. "Those creatures can apparently convert energy into body mass at will or by instinct. Blasting them with energy beams isn't going to hurt them. If anything, it's only going to fuel them or heal them or even enlarge them!"

"And you got that from a quick, short-range scan?" Dajo challenged him. "Correct me if I'm wrong, but you're just a pilot on the *Enterprise*, not a science officer."

"I started out in the astrosciences division, with a sideline in botany," Sulu said. "I know my physics and biology, and, in my estimation, those gliders are not going to be stopped by phasers, no matter how high powered."

"Gliders?" Helena echoed. "Is that what we're calling them?"

Sulu shrugged. "Less of a mouthful than Maelstromites."

"Works for me," she said.

Triple shocks rocked the bridge, while further chipping away at the shields.

"Captain?" Fass inquired. "Should I keep firing back?"

Dajo glared at Sulu before shaking his head. "Belay that, Liddia. Let's try to outrun them instead." He nodded at the helmsman. "Hit the gas, Perez."

"Which way, sir?"

"Anywhere but here," Dajo barked, "and away from those things!"

"Yes, sir!"

The *Lucky Strike* picked up speed, accelerating into the Maelstrom, which made for an even choppier flight. Sulu tracked the gliders, hoping to see them fall out of range of the sensors as the ship left them behind, but saw the opposite instead.

"Are we losing them?" Dajo asked.

"Negative," Sulu answered. "They're hot on our trail, at warp speed, no less, and that's not all. There's more converging on us . . . from all directions."

"Evasive action!" Dajo commanded. "See if you can shake them!"

Easier said than done, Sulu thought. They were in shark-infested waters, so to speak; they were bound to encounter glid-ers whichever way they fled for as long as they remained lost in the Maelstrom. *We're in their domain.*

"Why are they attacking us?" Helena said. "Are we on the menu, or what?"

"I doubt they're predators," Sulu answered, although he couldn't say so for certain. "Hard to imagine that they evolved to feed on the infrequent flesh-and-blood space traveler. Where are their natural prey? I'm not picking up any other organic life-forms on the sensors."

He wondered if the gliders fed on the Maelstrom itself, or perhaps sustained themselves on some specific kind of particles or radiation found within the coursing plasma streams. Spock would surely have figured that out by now, but Sulu had more urgent matters on his mind.

"So what's their beef?" Helena asked. "Why won't they leave us alone?"

"Aggression, territoriality, fear of the unknown?" Sulu could think of plenty of possible motives. "Who knows?"

"I don't care why they're after us," Dajo said crossly. "I just want to save my ship . . . and our passengers, of course."

"Speaking of which," Helena said, "those passengers are get-ting agitated, understandably." She fingered her earpiece while manipulating the communications controls, which were lighting up like a swarm of Denebian glowflies. "I'm getting flooded with anxious queries over the intercoms. Want to try calming them down?"

"If I must," Dajo said grudgingly. "Patch me in shipwide."

She flicked a switch and gave him a go sign. "You're on."

He cleared his throat before hitting the speaker button on his chair. His voice dropped an octave to sound more authoritative.

"Attention, passengers. This is your captain speaking. As you may have noticed, we are experiencing a high degree of turbulence, but there is no cause for alarm," he lied. "Please keep your seat belts fastened until notified otherwise. Thank you for your cooperation."

He clicked off the intercom.

"Seal off the bridge and all other essential areas, and close all portholes in the passenger compartments. Restrict turbolifts to authorized personnel only." He paused to consider his options. "And pipe soothing music into the passenger areas as well."

Sulu doubted that would be enough to calm the restive passengers. Chances were some of them had already caught a glimpse of a glider or two.

"They're not buying it, Captain," Helena said. "They're scared and angry."

A dangerous combination, Sulu thought, *as if we didn't have enough problems.*

Matters escalated quickly. Within moments, fists and bodies pounded against the sealed entrance, adding to the clamor generated by the Maelstrom and the attacking gliders. Muffled voices could be heard demanding entrance and answers. Sulu could readily imagine the upset civilians on the other side of the sturdy duranium door.

"I was afraid of this." Dajo sounded as though he'd possibly dealt with irate customers before. "Fass, initiate antihijacking protocol B-2. Public areas only."

"You got it, Skipper."

Sulu looked away from the sensor controls, uncertain what Dajo was attempting.

Antihijacking protocol?

Puzzled, he heard the pounding and shouting outside die down, replaced by what sounded like bodies slumping onto the floor. Ominous possibilities flashed through Sulu's brain, some more appalling than others.

"Excuse me! What just happened?"

"Nothing too dire," Dajo assured him. "We merely flooded the passenger areas with anesthizine gas. A sensible precaution against pirates and other unwanted visitors, but it works for unruly customers too."

"Did the trick." Helena took out her earpiece to give her ear a break. "The lines have gone silent, and none too soon."

Sulu wasn't sure what he thought of this. Certainly, the *Enterprise* had similar security measures in place, but that was for dealing with the likes of Khan and equally serious threats. Then again, he had to admit that gassing the rioting passengers gave the crew one less challenge to deal with. Better perhaps to let the tranquilized passengers sleep through the emergency and hope there would still be a ship for them to wake up to? Sulu had no idea how many escape pods the *Lucky Strike* was equipped with, but until the ship was clear of the Maelstrom, abandoning ship was just another death sentence.

"Incoming!" Fass shouted. "They're swarming us!"

Despite the ship's high-velocity attempts to evade the gliders, the *Lucky Strike* came under attack again. Sulu's sensors registered at least nine gliders laying siege to the ship, resulting in a nonstop barrage of high-energy shocks. Based on his scans, he theorized that the gliders were converting subatomic portions of their own mass into energy to power their attacks. And, unluckily for the *Lucky Strike*, Einstein's famous equation worked in the gliders' favor. They could get plenty of firepower from very little mass.

"Oh, hellfire!" Perez exclaimed as sparks erupted from the back of the helm console. Unbuckling his seat belt, he scurried around to address the issue. Removing a rear panel, he hastily inspected the damage while muttering unhappily. "No, no, no. Don't give up on me, princess."

"How bad is it?" Dajo asked.

"Give me a moment!" Perez yanked back his hand after getting a mild shock. He blew on his fingers before diving back into the console's innards. He squinted in concentration. "I think I can bypass the toasted circuits . . . there!"

A triumphant expression lit up his face as he replaced the panel and sprang to his feet, just as a massive plasma swell spun the ship on its axis, hurling him into the ceiling and then dropping him back onto the floor, where he lay groaning.

"Carlos!" Helena shouted.

Automatic gyros righted the ship, but the helm was still vacant. Unbuckling his seat belt, Sulu scrambled across the shuddering bridge to take the controls. To his relief, he found that Perez's improvised repairs had been effective; the helm controls were responsive, even if the Maelstrom was still fighting the ship every kilometer of the way.

"Somebody get that man a medic!" he ordered, unconcerned with preempting Dajo. Did the *Lucky Strike* even have a doctor aboard?

Helena broke from her post, producing a medkit from a storage compartment beneath a nearby station. She rushed to Perez's side, managing the turbulence as best she could, and checked him out with a handheld medical scanner.

"A couple broken ribs, a possible concussion." She prepared a hypospray. "To help with the pain."

The hypospray hissed as she administered the dose.

"Chen, Yoder!" Dajo said. "Help Perez to his bunk, then hurry back here." He glanced at an indicator on his armrest. "Don't worry. The knockout gas has been vented."

"That's not necessary, sir," Perez protested. "I can manage—"

He tried to sit up, then winced despite the analgesic in his bloodstream. He clutched his side, gasping, as Helena eased him back onto the floor.

"Your spirit does you proud, lad," Dajo said, "but you've done your part. Fate's taken you out of the game for now. Retire to your berth. That's an order." He shifted his gaze to Sulu. "Seems you've got the helm after all, Lieutenant. Let's see how good you are."

I'll be better once we get out of the Maelstrom, Sulu thought. He resumed evasive maneuvers, throwing in a few well-honed tricks of his own, but knew too well that he could only buy the *Lucky Strike* some extra time at best; if the gliders didn't destroy the ship, the Maelstrom would—eventually. "I'll do what I can."

"That's somewhat less than reassuring." Dajo surveyed the battered bridge. Scorch marks defaced various surfaces, while a whiff of ozone hung in the air. "I just replaced that helm console a month ago," he lamented. He glanced back over his shoulder toward the sealed passenger compartments. "You don't suppose we can tack on an additional charge for wear and tear?"

"Just hope they don't sue you to the highest court in the quadrant." Helena packed up the medkit and made her way back to her usual post, while a couple of her fellow crew members removed Perez from the bridge. She watched him go with obvious concern. "Assuming we ever make it out of this maelstrom."

That's a big assumption, Sulu thought. *Unfortunately.*

"Shields down to forty-nine percent," Fass said. "We're stretched thin."

"Divert more power to the deflectors, from wherever you can find it." Dajo ran a hand through his mane. "Any and all non-essential systems."

"I suppose I can tap into the phaser batteries," she replied. "Not doing us much good anyway."

Sulu knew that was only a stopgap measure. Between the gliders and the Maelstrom, the *Lucky Strike* wasn't going to make it on its own.

"We need to send a distress signal to the *Enterprise*," he said.

"From inside the Maelstrom?" Helen balked at the notion. "Are you serious?"

"If anybody can do it," he said, encouraging her. "You're the second-best communications specialist I know."

"Only the *second*-best? Is that a challenge?"

He shrugged. "If you want to take it that way."

"And I don't suppose you have any suggestions as to how exactly to go about it?"

"Not exactly, but—" A possibility popped into his brain as he thought of Uhura. "Come to think of it, back on the *Enterprise* a few years ago, our communications officer managed to get a signal through what seemed like an impenetrable barrier, using a subspace bypass circuit."

He left out the part about the Greek god Apollo so that she wouldn't think he was feeding her a fairy tale.

"A subspace bypass circuit, you say?" Sulu could practically see the wheels turning inside her head as she sparked to the idea. "That just might work, if we can divert enough juice to the comms to boost the signal sufficiently."

"Just a minute there!" Dajo said. "We need every bit of available power for the shields. We can't waste it on some wild experiment!"

"You have a better idea?" Sulu said. "Shoring up the shields for as long as possible is not a long-term solution, and you know it. Sending out a distress signal may be a slim hope, but it's better than none at all."

Dajo couldn't argue with that. He spun his chair toward Helena. "Do you really think you can do this, Helena?"

"No guarantees," she said. "The ionization from the Maelstrom is going to seriously mess with the harmonics, but Sulu is right. It could be our best shot."

Dajo gripped the armrests of his chair as the bridge rocked beneath him. He stared glumly at the viewscreen where more gliders could be seen joining the swarm. A sapphire pulse forced him to avert his eyes.

"Go for it," he said. "And make it snappy."

Thirty-One

Baldur III

Thunderbird exploded in the vacuum of space.

"Target destroyed," Ensign Vance said. The navigator had fired the photon torpedo that had obliterated the derelict vessel now that Scotty and his associates had been beamed off it. Kirk watched as the spectacular explosion briefly lit up the void, sending sparks and ashes flying in all directions before dissipating completely.

"Never thought I'd be sorry to see that old deathtrap go," Scott said, "but she did us proud in the end."

The engineer stood beside Kirk's chair, still wearing the hazard suit he'd donned during the crisis, minus the hood and gloves. Kirk had suggested that Scott get checked out by sickbay before reporting to the bridge, but Scott wouldn't hear of it. In the meantime, his companions from the *Thunderbird* had joined the many other refugees flooding the ship both before and after the power plant's devastating lift-off from the planet.

"Had to be done, Scotty," Kirk observed.

The decrepit, irradiated vessel had barely survived the shock wave from the ejected warp core. Irreparably damaged, it had posed a significant hazard to navigation, given the amount of traffic headed toward Baldur III. Kirk had judged it best to consign *Thunderbird* to history, particularly since they had any number of more pressing issues to cope with.

"Oh, I know, sir," Scott said. "And don't think I'm not glad to be back where I belong."

"The feeling is mutual," Kirk assured him. "The *Enterprise* hasn't been the same without you."

Unfortunately, there was no time to toast Scott's return. As feared, *Thunderbird*'s volcanic departure had not left Jackpot City unscathed. There were major fires to be put out, both figuratively and literally.

"Mayor Poho for you, Captain," Palmer said.

Kirk had been expecting her call. "Onscreen, Lieutenant."

"Yes, sir."

Mayor Poho appeared on the viewscreen, looking understandably stressed. Kirk didn't recognize the furnishings in the background; as he understood it, the mayor and her staff had abandoned Town Hall for a more secure location outside the city. He glimpsed tense faces and bodies going back and forth behind her. The susurrus of many terse conversations accompanied the image.

"*Hello, Kirk*," the mayor said. "*Have the brave souls aboard* Thunderbird *been recovered?*"

"Mister Scott is standing beside me as we speak and his associates are safe as well," Kirk answered. "What's the word from where you're sitting?"

The mayor sighed. "The good news is that Jackpot City is still there, thanks to Mister Scott's inspired idea to return *Thunderbird* to the stars. The bad news is that the launch left some serious collateral damage behind. Take a look at this."

She reached for an off-screen switch or button and her image was promptly replaced by an aerial view of the disaster. An enormous crater belching fire and smoke occupied the site of the former power plant. The flames had spread to engulf the surrounding park, consuming acres of trees and foliage, then leapt across tree-lined streets to attack buildings of wood and brick and glass and steel; the timber constructions ignited first, but the tremendous heat was also causing bricks and mortar to crack and crumble. No lights shone in the endangered buildings, since *Thunderbird*'s sudden absence had triggered a citywide blackout. Billowing fumes obscured the video, which caused Scott to flinch noticeably. The roar and crackle of the blaze threw a hush across the bridge until Poho returned to the screen, replacing the distressing sounds and images.

"As you can see, Captain, we have a full-scale inferno on our hands, in the heart of the city," she said. "Making matters worse, our ability to combat the fire has been severely compromised by the blackout. Automated pumps and sensors and fire-suppression fields are down, along with many other crucial systems. We're also getting reports of broken pipes and electrical fires, but these are difficult to confirm or locate without certain monitors up and running. And as for manpower . . . most of what was left of our volunteer fire company evacuated with their families, so we're even more shorthanded than before."

Kirk grasped the extent of the challenge. He almost regretted evacuating so much of the city's population in anticipation of an even larger catastrophe, but if the warp core *had* breached on the surface, instead of in space, they'd be looking at colossal loss of life now.

"Fatalities?" he asked grimly.

"*None that we know of so far,*" Poho said. "*Thank goodness.*"

Kirk was glad to hear it, but he was not about to let that lull him into a sense of false security. With the fire still spreading, it was far too early to congratulate themselves on saving the city.

"I don't need to tell you that the *Enterprise* is using every resource we have to cope with this crisis. People, equipment, supplies, and shuttles are already being deployed, with more on the way."

"*Thank you, Captain.*" Remorse bled through Poho's somber expression. "*I owe you and Mister Scott an apology. I should have listened to you when you told me to shut down that reactor.*"

"You did what you thought was best for your community." Kirk wasn't interested in assigning blame. He preferred to deal with the problem at hand. "Now it's up to all of us to fix things before they get any worse."

"Amen to that," Scott said.

Kirk recalled the aerial coverage Poho had just shared with them. He had no intention of saving Jackpot City just to let it burn to the ground.

"Oh, wow," Flossi said. "We're really on the *Enterprise*?"

"The one and only," Uhura said.

The teenager gaped at the transporter room, having been in the Pergium Palace only heartbeats before. Levity and a few others from the club shared the transporter platform with her and Uhura. The Palace was still intact, as of moments ago, but the flames had been getting closer so Uhura had made the executive decision to pull out of the ad hoc command center and transport her new friends and allies to the *Enterprise*. Not all of the club's regulars were present, however; the last she had heard, Thackery and Rixon were ferrying one last load of evacuees to his property outside the city limits. She hoped they and their passengers were safely clear of the conflagration.

"Please exit the transporter platform quickly," Lieutenant Kyle instructed the group. "We have many more parties to beam up."

Uhura could believe it. She couldn't remember the last time she'd seen the *Enterprise*'s main transporter room so busy. Kyle had at least two other technicians assisting him with operations, while additional crew members were on hand to escort new arrivals to where they needed to be. Uhura hustled her own party out of the transporter room into the corridor beyond, which was possibly even more hectic, with a slew of on-duty Starfleet personnel rushing about their business. She did her best to keep

Flossi and the rest out of the way. Ensign Henri Camus appeared to take custody of the visitors.

"This officer will take care of you," Uhura promised. "Just stick close to him and he'll make sure you're looked after."

"Wait," Flossi said. "I don't need a babysitter. I can still help you with whatever comes next."

"You've already done your share and more," Uhura said sincerely, while trying to pass her off to Camus without hurting her feelings. Flossi meant well, but Uhura needed to get to the bridge, and the captain didn't need any helpful teenagers tagging along with her at a time like this. "I'd appreciate the help and the company, really, but the bridge is likely to be off-limits to civilians for the duration. Nothing personal."

The girl looked disappointed. "Are you sure?"

"Captain Kirk runs a tight ship, I'm afraid." Uhura flashed an encouraging smile. "The best thing you can do for me now is keep an eye on your friends, listen to Ensign Camus here, and let the crew do their jobs. Can you do that for me?"

Flossi nodded. "Okay, I guess."

"Thanks for understanding," Uhura said. "I'll see you later."

Meanwhile, Levity had her own concerns. "I'm looking for my great-grandmother, Fenella Dandridge. She was supposed to be beamed up here a while ago. I need to find her."

Camus consulted a data slate. "We're processing a lot of people, ma'am, but let me see what I can do. What's your name again?"

Uhura left them in the ensign's capable hands. A data slate of her own was tucked under her arm as she hurried toward a turbolift while simultaneously registering the buzz of activity in the corridors. Concerned crew members escorted patients in wheelchairs and zero-g stretchers, presumably beamed up from evacuated medical facilities on the planet. Snatches of urgent conversations reached her ears:

"Sickbay is full up with folks from the city hospital. Put all but the most critical cases in the temporary wards in the rec rooms for now. More beds are being set up on deck nine, or so I'm told . . ."

"We need to get those portable generators down to the fire stations immediately. No, use the cargo transporters instead. The primary transporters are for receiving evacuees only . . ."

"That's right. We need blankets, fresh water, emergency rations, whatever you can spare. We can always replace them later . . ."

"Shuttle departing in five minutes for that Rigelian freighter. We still have room for eight more evacuees, maybe more if they have small children . . ."

All hands on deck, Uhura noted. She made it to the bridge, where she saw Captain Kirk conferring with Mister Scott, while Yeoman Landon stood by, taking notes. She couldn't help noticing that Spock and Chekov had not yet returned from the mission to Yurnos. Their presence was no doubt sorely missed in this crisis. Sulu's, too.

"Welcome back, Lieutenant," Kirk said, acknowledging her return. He was clearly busy, but she appreciated the gesture even if he quickly returned to managing the emergency. She saw that the main viewscreen was occupied by a map of Jackpot City, with the raging fire indicated by a red zone that expanded as the *Enterprise*'s long-range sensors tracked the spreading blaze. Yeoman Landon handed him a microtape disk, which he loaded into the reader in his chair. He scowled at the new data as though he found it unsatisfactory. "This isn't good enough. I need to know for certain which areas around the fire have been completely evacuated."

"I may be able to help you with that, sir." Uhura beckoned to Landon, who took her data slate from her. She had transferred the information from her own maps onto the slate before abandoning the Pergium Palace. "I charted the areas my volunteers cleared up until we pulled out of the area."

Landon passed the slate to Kirk, who quickly reviewed its contents.

"Thank you, Uhura. This is just what I needed."

She knew the captain well enough to know he was working on a plan. She was curious to know what it was, feeling somewhat as though she had walked into the middle of a play having missed the first act, but figured she'd catch up soon enough. Crossing the bridge, she relieved Palmer, who relocated to an auxiliary comm station over by the environmental and shipboard subsystems rather than taking a break. Uhura sat down at her accustomed post and reclaimed her earpiece for the first time in what felt like forever.

Home sweet home, she thought.

She took a moment to survey the standard frequencies, where she found various ongoing in-ship, ship-to-ship, and ship-to-surface communications underway. She sorted through them, efficiently assessing and prioritizing them as she'd been trained to do, before noticing something odd: a faint subspace signal of some sort coming from outside the solar system. The signal was weak and spotty; in the crush of transmissions flying back and forth regarding the crisis on Baldur III, the barely imperceptible signal would have been all too easy to miss if she hadn't paused to take an overview of the incoming and outgoing messages.

What have we here?

Subspace static rendered the fragmented signal difficult to decipher. Uhura had to run it through several advanced filters and restoration algorithms to clean it up enough to realize that it was in fact a distress signal . . . coming from inside the Antares Maelstrom?

Looks like I got back to the Enterprise *just in time.*

"Do you think it will work, Scotty?"

"It's our best option," the engineer replied to Kirk. "Sorry I made such a mess down on the planet, Captain."

"You already saved the city once," Kirk replied. "Now we just have to save it from the aftermath of that miracle."

Kirk studied the map on the viewscreen. His own proposed solution was also going to leave a mark on Jackpot City, but playing it safe was no answer at all. He could only hope Mayor Poho felt the same way.

"Lieutenant Uhura, get me the mayor—"

"Excuse me, Captain," she interrupted. "I've received a distress signal from Lieutenant Sulu. He's aboard a commercial vessel, the *Lucky Strike*, that's lost in the Antares Maelstrom. They're in extreme jeopardy."

The announcement caught Kirk off guard. "What? How did Sulu end up in the Maelstrom?"

"Apparently it's a long story, Captain. But the ship, the crew, and its passengers are in danger and requesting our immediate assistance."

Kirk didn't know what to do. His first instinct was to go to the *Lucky Strike*'s rescue, but Jackpot City was still burning on the screen before him. He was torn between wanting to save Sulu and the other lives at risk in the Maelstrom and his duty to protect the city below. He was also all too aware that the *Enterprise* was currently crammed with evacuees, and taking on more, all of whom would be in danger if he took the ship into the Maelstrom to answer Sulu's distress call. Could he in good conscience risk their lives in order to save others?

"Captain?" Uhura prodded gently. "How shall I respond?"

Spock would surely point out that there was only one logical choice. Kirk saw that, too, but that didn't make it any less agonizing.

"Inform *Lucky Strike* that the *Enterprise* is currently engaged with an urgent situation on Baldur III." Kirk's stony face and tone strove to conceal what his words cost him. "Tell them . . . we'll respond when we're able."

"Aye, sir," Uhura said. "I understand."

No one challenged his decision. He was grateful for that, although part of him almost wished for a compelling reason to choose the *Lucky Strike* over Jackpot City.

"Sulu is on his own, then, sir?" Scott asked. "For the time being?"

"I'm afraid so, Mister Scott."

Thirty-Two

The Antares Maelstrom

"So that's it?" Dajo said. "They're not coming to help us?"

"They're not coming *right away*." Sulu tried to put a positive spin on matters for the sake of morale. "The good news is that, against all odds, our distress signal got through to the *Enterprise*." He gave Helena an appreciative nod. "The bad news is that any help will be delayed, which means we just have to hold out until the crisis on Baldur III is dealt with."

"And how are we supposed to do that?" Dajo demanded. "We tried fight *and* flight. Neither is working."

Despite Sulu's ongoing attempts to evade them, the gliders were relentless in their attacks and growing in numbers as well. Constant brownouts, short circuits, damage reports, and flashing annunciator lights testified to their losing battle against both the gliders and the Maelstrom. Seated at the helm, Sulu was tossed from side to side by the ceaseless turbulence and the sudden, random jolts to the ship, neither of which made piloting the vessel any easier. Sapphire pulses flashed constantly on the viewscreen, tinting his view of the roiling chaos all around them. Inertial dampers strained to cushion the upheaval, but with limited success. Sulu suspected that the dampers were taking damage along with the deflectors.

"Shields down to forty-three percent," Fass said dolefully. "Stay tuned for more bad news."

"Too bad we wasted power on that distress signal." Dajo glowered at Sulu. "Any other brilliant suggestions, Lieutenant?"

Sulu racked his brain and came up with one last option.

"Try talking to them?"

"You're joking, right? Do those beasts look like they want to start up a conversation? And what makes you think they're even capable of that?"

"What makes us think they aren't?" Sulu argued. The more he thought about it, the more the effort struck him as worth attempting. If there was one thing he had learned during his years in Starfleet, it was that there was often more to new and unusual life-forms than met the eye, and that deadly misunderstandings could sometimes arise during first-contact situations, as with the Gorn or the Horta, for instance. "For all we know, they could very well be sentient."

Dajo wasn't buying it. "Then why are they attacking us like a school of Izarian fang-fish in a feeding frenzy?"

"Sentience doesn't preclude anger or fear, as galactic history demonstrates all too well, but history also teaches that communication can be the first step to resolving conflict, even if wildly different species or cultures have gotten off to a bad start with regard to each other," Sulu said. "The very existence of the Federation is proof of that."

"But even if that's true," Helena said, "and the gliders are sentient, how are we supposed to communicate with them anyway?"

"I don't know," Sulu confessed. "How do they communicate with each other?"

"That's somewhere to start, I guess."

She replaced her earpiece as she set about answering Sulu's question. He stopped talking, not wanting to distract her, as he kept trying to get the *Lucky Strike* clear of the swarm. Dajo left her alone, too, despite his earlier skepticism. Long, bumpy moments passed before she spoke up again.

"How about that?" She looked surprised by her own discovery. "I'm picking up subspace transmissions between the gliders, as though they're signaling each other. Took me a while to zero in on the proper frequency, but . . . listen to this."

She shared the audio with the rest of the bridge. Dissonant tones warbled over the speakers, bouncing off and overlapping with each other. It sounded like utter gibberish to Sulu's ear, but the back and forth between them suggested some degree of communication, although it was difficult to tell just how sophisticated the dialogue was. Were these the vocalizations of animals or sentient beings conversing?

"What in blazes am I listening to?" Dajo asked.

"Hard to say," Helena said. "If it's a language, it's not like any I've heard before."

"The universal translator?" Sulu recalled Helena snagging a new UT unit after that brawl at Naylis's general store. He was suddenly very glad that she'd managed to keep anyone else from walking off with it.

"It's having trouble cracking this lingo so far," she said. "It's possible that the translation matrix just needs more time to digest the gliders' speech, or it could be that the standard linguacodes don't apply to a language this alien, if it's even a language at all."

A thought occurred to Sulu. He plucked his communicator off his belt and lobbed it over to her. "Catch!"

She snatched it out of the air. "Nice toss. But what am I supposed to do with this?"

"Cannibalize it, consult it, whatever it takes," he said. "Its built-in translator function has all the latest Starfleet upgrades, including a new algorithm our Vulcan science officer devised specifically to assist in communicating with nonhumanoid life-forms."

Spock had instituted that upgrade himself, Sulu recalled, shortly after he and Kirk and a few others had escaped from an obscure planetoid in the Gamma Canaris region. Spock had judged it worth sharing with the rest of the crew and Sulu figured he had his reasons.

"No offense," he said, "but Starfleet-quality software surely beats whatever civilian version you bought off the shelf. Maybe you can upload the program into your own translator, or splice the units together to create more processing power?"

Helena flipped open the communicator. "Ordinarily, I would vigorously defend my own gear, simply as a matter of pride, but at the moment I'm not inclined to look a gift matrix in the mouth." She switched on the communicator while working the controls at the comm station. "Give me a few minutes to marry these two units."

"Make it a shotgun wedding, if you have to," Sulu quipped. "We don't have time for a long engagement."

Sapphire pulses and gushing plasma currents drove home his point.

"Damn," Fass blurted. "I really want to shoot something instead of just sitting here. I'm going to lose my lunch if this keeps up."

Sulu was more worried about them all losing their lives, but he knew where she was coming from. Good thing he had gotten his space legs years ago. It took more than rough sailing to make him queasy.

"I think I speak for all of us," Dajo said, "when I say we'd rather your lunch stay where it is for the time being. Consider that an order."

"Aye, Captain."

A high-pitched squeal came from the comm station, drawing Sulu's gaze back to it. He saw that his communicator was now patched directly into the console's emergency override panel, while its flip-up antenna faced the external broadcast controls.

"Sorry!" Helena silenced the squeal with the push of a button. "Just a little system compatibility problem there. Got it smoothed out now, hopefully."

"Forget the noise," Dajo said. "Is it working it?"

"Let's find out." She pressed a speaker button. "Hello? Can you read me?"

The same inhuman tones echoed across the bridge, just as incomprehensibly as before. Sulu wanted to have faith in Spock's software, not to mention Helena's communications know-how, but he couldn't help wondering if this was an exercise in futility. What if the augmented translation matrix couldn't decipher the gliders' "language" in time or at all?

"Hello?" she persisted. "Can you hear me? Please answer me if you can."

He noted that she was keeping her sentences short and simple, to make it easier for the translator and, perhaps, the gliders. They didn't need to conduct a philosophical debate with the gliders; they just needed to convince them to stop attacking.

"Talk to me, please. We only want to speak to you."

The "please" was possibly superfluous, but he couldn't blame Helena for erring on the side of courtesy. It would be bleakly ironic to actually make contact with the gliders, only to come off as rude and insulting.

"Hello. Can you hear me?"

Sulu was on the verge of declaring the experiment a failure, when the unintelligible tones transformed into English, albeit in a halting fashion.

"*Hear . . . you . . .*"

"Well, I'll be damned," Dajo said. "Patch them over to me, Helena."

"No offense, Captain, but I'd rather trade seats with Sulu and let him take it from here. He's had more first-contact experience than either of us . . . and is probably more diplomatic, to boot."

Sulu had to agree with her, especially when it came to bypassing Dajo. They needed to win the gliders' trust, not try to snow them with a fancy sales pitch. Honesty and diplomacy were what were called for. Sulu trusted his own instincts over Dajo's, when it came right down to it.

"*Et tu*, Helena?" Dajo's expression darkened. "I'm the captain here. This is *my* ship!"

"But our lives are at stake," Sulu said, "and your passengers'."

Ignoring Dajo's protests, he stumbled across the bridge to take the comm station from Helena, who scrambled to replace him at the helm. As first officer, she surely knew her way around the controls.

"*Talk . . . at . . . us?*"

Sulu didn't want to leave the gliders hanging. He wondered which or how many of the beings were taking part in the conversation.

"Yes. We hear you. We mean you no harm."

"*No . . . harm?*"

"Yes, but you are harming us. Please stop."

"*Stop . . . ?*"

Sulu wondered if the gliders realized that the ship was just a ship and that they were actually speaking to living beings inside the *Lucky Strike*. Was it worth trying to explain that distinction to them? Perhaps later, he decided, if and when the universal translator had a better grasp of their language.

"Captain!" Fass called out. "The gliders are backing off. I think they may be halting their attacks, at least for the moment!"

"Can't complain about that," Dajo said. "Keep talking to them, Sulu. Mind you, you're not saying anything I wouldn't have said myself."

Sulu shrugged off Dajo's attempt to save face. He was more concerned with what the gliders had to say. The bridge was still experiencing extreme turbulence, but Fass was right that the energy bursts appeared to have paused.

"Did you stop harming us? Thank you. We are not an enemy. We will not harm you. We can be friends."

"No friends . . . not belong here."

He chose not to press the point. Establishing relations with the gliders could wait for another day, when innocent lives were not at stake.

"We understand. This is your home, not ours."

"Yes. Go. Leave."

Their message was clear enough. He just wished he could give them an answer that would satisfy them.

"We want to leave, but cannot find the way. We are lost."

"Lost . . . ?"

"Yes, we do not know the way."

A pause ensued, during which Sulu worried about the current limitations of the translator. Did the gliders truly understand what he was saying? If all they understood was that the ship could not leave, they might decide to finish what they started and destroy the *Lucky Strike* anyway.

"Can you show us the way to leave?"

Another nerve-racking pause, this one shorter than before.

"Yes. Show you the way. You go."

Sulu felt like cheering, but simply grinned at Helena, who gave him a thumbs-up.

"Thank you!" he said to the gliders. "Please show us."

"Follow . . . now."

On the viewscreen, the gliders turned away from the ship and fell into formation, all heading in the same direction. The luminous patterns shifting throughout their anatomy served as beacons through the foggy plasma streams.

"Follow that swarm," Dajo ordered, somewhat unnecessarily. "Don't lose sight of them!"

"Not a chance," Helena assured him. "I'm sticking to them like a magnetic boot."

The gliders set a demanding pace. They were clearly in a

hurry to show the door to their unwelcome visitors, which was just fine with Sulu. Even with the attacks on hold, the *Lucky Strike* was still being battered by the tempest outside, its shields were eroding, and gravity and life-support weren't going to be able to hold out much longer; the sooner they escaped the Maelstrom, the better chance they stood of escaping *Fleetness*'s fate.

They knew which way to go now. The question was: Could they make it back to normal space before the *Lucky Strike* became yet another lost ship, never to be seen or heard from again?

Thirty-Three

Baldur III

"Fire phasers, Mister Painter. Full power."

"Aye, sir!"

The *Enterprise* targeted Jackpot City. Twin beams, blazing azure, burned through Baldur III's atmosphere to converge on the surface of the planet. The rays sliced through buildings, pavement, foundations, and bedrock to carve a deep trench more than twenty meters deep and fifty meters across directly in the path of the voracious fire spreading across the city. The beams traced the perimeter of the blaze, racing to enclose an area several city blocks in diameter—and perhaps prevent the fire from spreading any farther.

Or so Kirk hoped.

He leaned forward in his chair, visualizing the phaser beams converging on the planet hundreds of kilometers below. As a young lieutenant posted to the *U.S.S. Farragut*, he'd once witnessed firsthand a phaser strike on a planetary target, so Kirk could easily imagine the sky-high plumes of vaporized matter rising up in the beam's wake, the pungent smell of ozone and burning rubble, and the fearsome sight of the immense beam itself, blasting down from the heavens like the wrath of an angry god, so bright and hot that you had to look away for fear of being blinded. Kirk didn't envy anyone still in the target zone, which cut through a swath of residential and business districts surrounding the burning park. He hoped Uhura was right about certain neighborhoods being thoroughly evacuated, and reminded himself that her data had gibed with official reports provided by Mayor Poho and her staff. Nevertheless he winced inwardly as he imagined the large-scale destruction being wrought by the phaser beams. Those were people's homes and businesses being disintegrated, along with familiar streets and landmarks.

Which probably would have been destroyed anyway, he thought. With the blackout and earlier evacuation still impeding the Baldurians' ability to combat the fire on the ground, Kirk's top priority had been to contain the massive blaze before it could grow any larger. The more of the city they could save now, the less they would need to rebuild later when the conflagration finally burnt itself out.

"Firing pattern almost complete," Painter said. "Closing the circle now."

Sensors tracked the path of the trench on the viewscreen. Despite the helmsman's announcement, the outline of the vast firebreak was no more a perfect circle than the blaze itself, which bulged and bended in places, reflecting the urban terrain. Kirk had to admire Painter's aim, however; the steady progress of the phasers matched up to the lines already charted on the map in anticipation of the operation. In other words, the beams were going where they were supposed to, plus or minus a meter or so.

"Keep at it, Mister Painter. You're doing fine."

"Thank you, Captain."

Within moments, the end of the firebreak met its beginning like a serpent swallowing its tail. The phasers stopped firing.

"Pattern complete," Painter said. "Phaser batteries powering down."

Kirk nodded in satisfaction, but did not relax just yet. The firebreak had been dug; it remained to be seen whether it would be effective.

"Current weather for Jackpot City?" he asked.

Unlike Earth and other more advanced worlds, Baldur III was not yet equipped with a working weather-control network. Although the trench had been carved wide by design, Kirk still worried that a heavy wind could blow flames, sparks, or cinders past the firebreak, allowing the blaze to escape containment. Even in these modern times, nature's whims could be a fire-fighter's worst enemy.

"Sensors report light winds blowing southwest away from the city," Lieutenant Lee Faust reported from the science station, which he'd been manning during the third watch. He had a solid scientific background, having recently transferred over from a research vessel, the *Pretorius*. "No appreciable effect on the fire predicted."

Kirk was glad to hear it. "About time things break in our favor."

"You can say that again, Captain," Scott said. He was posted at the engineering station nearby, the better to monitor the effect of the major phaser usage on the ship's batteries and power systems. "It's been one bloody thing after another, if you'll pardon me language."

A touch of profanity was the least of Kirk's worries. Contemplating the map on the screen, he deeply regretted having to sacrifice the portion of the city within the red zone, which had included the colony's historic Town Hall, among other structures, both old and new. Judging from the sensor results displayed on the map, however, the firebreak appeared to be working. The blaze was not spreading beyond the gaping trench. Kirk allowed himself to hope that the worst was over.

For Jackpot City, he thought, *if not for Sulu . . .*

"Lieutenant Uhura, are you still in contact with the *Lucky Strike*?"

"Affirmative, Captain. The ship is still holding together, but they're taking a lot of damage from the Maelstrom." Her worried expression and tone conveyed the severity of the situation. "They're running out of time, sir."

"Understood, Lieutenant."

Kirk gazed at the map before him, wondering when he dared turn his back on the fire to go to Sulu's aid. It could take hours or days for the blaze within the red zone to burn out completely, but perhaps it was enough to have the fire contained for now?

"We're being hailed by the mayor, sir," Uhura said, juggling frequencies.

"Pipe her through," Kirk said, "but don't lose that signal from Sulu."

"Not a chance, sir."

Poho replaced the map on the viewscreen. She looked tired, but perhaps somewhat less stressed than earlier.

"Good work, Kirk," the mayor said. *"At the risk of counting my chickens too early, our scouts and drones are reporting that we may have the fire under control at last. Shame we had to carve up the city to do so, but I'll take a few scars over cremation any day."*

"I'm sorry you lost Town Hall." Kirk recalled the historic wooden structure he had visited when he first beamed down to the planet. "There was no way to save it."

"It had a good long run," Poho said. *"We can rebuild it . . . after we finish dealing with more immediate priorities."*

"About that," Kirk said, "we've received an emergency distress call from inside the Antares Maelstrom. A passenger ship, caught in the vortex, is in immediate jeopardy. Now that the fire is contained, the *Enterprise* needs to respond as quickly as possible."

"Hold on there, Kirk!" Poho peered unhappily from the screen. *"We're not done here yet. We've got hundreds of people displaced, large portions of the city in flames or in ruins, little or no power, not enough security people or technicians, maybe even the possibility of looting, and you want to go flying off to rescue a ship that was reckless enough to try to take a shortcut across the*

Maelstrom?" She shook her head even as her voice softened to a degree. "*Look, I feel for those people, Kirk, I really do, but we still need your help here on Baldur III. If you fly off now, how are we going to manage on our own?*"

Kirk wished he knew. He understood the mayor's position, but the recovery effort on Baldur III was going to take time. Time that Sulu and the *Lucky Strike* did not have.

"I'm sorry, Mayor, but I can't simply ignore—"

"Excuse me, Captain," Uhura said. "I'm sorry to interrupt, but you should know that I'm getting flooded with hails from all the civilian ships in orbit and approaching the planet. They want to know what else they can do to assist in the disaster relief efforts." She beamed at Kirk. "Andorians, Tellarites, humans, Rigelians . . . they're all offering to help out. It's remarkable."

Kirk experienced a surge of hope and optimism.

"No," he corrected her. "It's what the Federation is all about. It's what we've built and are building together. Why we're out here in the first place."

Pergium fever may have obscured that for a time, even brought out the worst in some people, but humanity, along with many other species, *had* progressed since the gold rushes of earlier, more barbaric eras, as evidenced by the many shiploads of prospectors now volunteering to come to Jackpot City's aid. Doctor McCoy was currently tied up in sickbay, looking after all the new patients who had been evacuated from the planet, but Kirk wished that Bones was here on the bridge to experience this moment, if only to relieve his sometimes jaundiced view of humanoid nature. People today might not be perfect, but when push came to shove, they could still surprise you.

"Mayor Poho, Margery, it occurs to me that we've been thinking of all these new ships and new arrivals as a challenge, but they're also a resource. We have a veritable fleet on hand to help you through this crisis. You just have to take full advantage of that . . . and work together to everyone's benefit. After all, natives and newcomers alike, you all have plenty of incentive to get past this disaster and get the pergium flowing again."

The mayor looked uncertain. *"I don't know. I can barely get my own advisors to agree sometimes, although, come to think of it, there hasn't been any political wrangling since* Thunderbird *started melting down. We've been too busy trying to keep all our people alive."*

"Think of that as a silver lining," Kirk told her. "You have scores of new constituents in orbit with ships and resources to call upon as you need them. You can get by without the *Enterprise . . .* at least long enough for us to save a ship that is running out of time as we speak. Kirk out."

He cut off the transmission before Poho could prolong the discussion, while hoping that he was making the right call. Matters were not, in fact, quite as simple as he had made them out to be; the *Enterprise* still had to unload all the evacuees it had taken on before it could venture into the potentially perilous reaches of the Maelstrom, but now that Jackpot City was not facing total destruction, it would be safe to begin beaming refugees back down to safe havens outside the city or onto other ships.

"Damn it, Jim!" McCoy burst onto the bridge, exasperation overcoming Starfleet etiquette as he fulminated vociferously. "My sickbay is more crowded than a tribble's family reunion! Burstein and Chapel and I can barely keep up. I need you to reassign more personnel to sickbay just on a temporary basis." He snorted in annoyance. "Of all times for M'Benga to take a busman's holiday with Sulu."

Kirk had other ideas.

"Funny you should mention that, Bones. How fast can you relocate your patients to another ship or to the surface?"

McCoy's startled expression would have been comical under less dire circumstances. "Are you out of your mind? We just got all those patients stowed away. Why in blue blazes would I want to move them again?"

"To save Sulu's life . . . if it's not too late."

Thirty-Four

The Antares Maelstrom

The *Lucky Strike* was losing its race against time.

"Shields down to twenty-three percent and falling fast," Fass reported. "At this rate, our hull is going to be naked in no time."

Sulu recalled *Fleetness* crumpling around him as its shields failed beyond the point of no return. The *Lucky Strike* was larger and more solidly built, but he doubted that would make a difference in the long run. He wondered if the gliders were taking into account the conditions outside as, in theory, they guided the ship out of the Maelstrom.

"How much longer until we're clear of this gods-forsaken morass?" Dajo fished a flask from a compartment in his chair and took a restorative swig of spirits, not caring who was watching. "I hope our new friends aren't taking us on the scenic route."

"I doubt it," Helena said. She and Sulu had swapped posts again, putting her back at comms. "They're as anxious to be rid of us as we are to put them in our ion trail."

"Then ask them if we're almost there yet," Dajo said. "Are we getting close to the border or not?"

"I'll try." She hailed the gliders via subspace. "Hello? Are we almost out of your home? How much longer is the way?"

"Leave home soon. Quickly."

Was that an answer or a demand? Sulu couldn't be sure. The universal translator had yet to become fully fluent in the gliders' language, keeping their exchanges with the beings at a rudimentary level. Did they even grasp humanoid concepts of time and distance?

"*Quickly.*"

The gliders gained speed, making it harder for Sulu to keep up with them as he piloted the faltering ship. The helm controls were getting increasingly sluggish while the warp engine was losing power. He wasn't sure how much longer the *Lucky Strike* could maintain its warp field before it popped like a soap bubble.

"Speed up!" Dajo ordered. A translucent green beverage sloshed from the mouth of his flask. "We can't lose them! They're our only guides out of this soup!"

"Tell me about it," Sulu shot back. "But the speed's just not there. I can manage warp four at most."

"Blast it!" Dajo stabbed the intercom button on his chair. "Captain to engineering. We need more warp power!"

"Wish I could oblige you," a male voice answered. "But our circuits are all but fried at this point. We're running on backup systems as it is. If I push it too far, we could lose warp capacity altogether."

"*Faster!*" the gliders urged.

"Caution be damned!" Dajo said. "Give me warp five, Dawson. That's an order!"

"If you say so, Captain, but I have to warn you—"

"Just do it. Unless you want to live out the rest of a very short life being tossed like a salad!"

"All right," Dawson said. "But don't say I didn't warn you."

Sulu listened to the exchange, uncertain whom to side with. He feared that even warp five might not be enough to get them out of the Maelstrom in time. A status board announced an increase of available power to the helm, so he ramped up the speed to chase after the gliders. His unfamiliarity with the *Lucky Strike* troubled him; back on the *Enterprise*, he'd developed an instinctive grasp for just how far the ship and its shuttles could be pushed, and could always count on Scotty to make sure that the engines exceeded even Starfleet standards when it came to care and maintenance, but Dajo's ship was still a question mark. Sulu didn't truly know what the *Lucky Strike* was capable of.

"Warp five," he announced, "and holding."

Dajo grunted in approval. "That's more like it."

"Holding" proved to be overly optimistic. The ship managed at warp five for maybe ten minutes, tops, before the status board crashed and the ship fell abruptly out of warp, testing Sulu's seat belt as he was thrown forward by the sudden decrease in velocity. He hastily switched propulsion over to impulse, hoping against hope that they hadn't lost that too. The ship kept flying forward, albeit much slower than before.

"What the devil?" Dajo bellowed. "What just happened?"

"Looks like your Mister Dawson in engineering knew what he was talking about," Sulu said. "We pushed the warp engines too far."

He watched in dismay as the gliders pulled farther away from them, beginning to vanish into the churning plasma many kilometers ahead. It would be all too easy to lose them in the swirling polychromatic miasma.

"Quickly!"

The gliders had obviously noted that the ship was falling behind. Sulu hoped they wouldn't take that the wrong way. "Answer them, Helena. Let them know that we didn't slow down on purpose."

She nodded and addressed the swarm.

"We want to go faster. We want to leave, but we are too weak, too hurt, to go faster. We are very sorry, but we can only go slowly now. Please keep showing us the way."

"Quickly! Follow faster!"

"We are following as fast as we can," Helena replied. "We want to leave quickly, but we had to slow down."

"Not fast enough!"

The translator was granting the gliders' voices more inflection now, enough so that Sulu could tell they were losing patience. Were they about to resume the attacks again?

"Dawson!" Dajo reached out to his engineer via intercom. "What's going on down there? I need warp power back immediately!"

"Not going to happen, Captain," Dawson stated. "We barely shut the warp core down in time to avoid a meltdown. I even try to fire her up again, there's not going to be anything left of the ship . . . or the rest of us. You might as well ask me to go skinny-dipping in that boiling plasma outside. It's suicide either way."

Not a lot of wiggle room there, Sulu noted. *Or grounds for hope.*

Now what were they supposed to do?

"Hikaru! Captain!" Helena called out. "We're being hailed!"

Sulu looked at her, puzzled by the excitement in her voice. "The gliders?"

"No, it's the *Enterprise!*"

His mood instantly rocketed from bleak to jubilant. He should have known Captain Kirk would arrive in the nick of time. Defying the odds when all hope seemed lost was Captain Kirk's trademark move.

"Took his own sweet time about it," Dajo said, "but better than never . . . I hope!" He gestured at the main viewer. "On-screen!"

Helena shook her head. "Audio only, Captain. Best we can manage through the Maelstrom." She looked across the bridge at Sulu. "Captain Kirk is asking for you, Hikaru."

He imagined Uhura opening the channel and felt a pang of homesickness before addressing Dajo. "Mind taking the helm, Captain, while I answer this call?"

Dajo threw up his hands in exasperation. "Why not? It's not

like I'm the captain of this ship or anything." He unbuckled his seat belt and surrendered the chair to Sulu. "Make yourself at home."

Don't mind if I do, Sulu thought. He turned over the helm to Dajo and claimed the captain's seat. He activated the intercom, not wanting to keep Captain Kirk waiting.

"Sulu here, Captain."

Kirk's voice rang out across the bridge, loud enough for all present to hear.

"Good to hear your voice, Lieutenant. Sorry to keep you waiting, but we're on our way to you. What's your current situation?"

"Not good, sir." Sulu quickly brought Kirk up to speed. "At the risk of plagiarizing Mister Scott, the *Lucky Strike* can't take much more of this."

"Understood," Kirk said. *"We're at the outer fringe of the Maelstrom now. Do you think you can hold out until we reach you?"*

"We can try, Captain, but can you tell us how long that might be? Not to rush you, but time is not on our side."

"I wish I could give you a firmer answer, Sulu, but I'm informed that tracking your signal through the Maelstrom is likely to be . . . challenging. We may have to search some before we can pinpoint your precise location."

Sulu considered the turbulence and interference lying between the two ships, not to mention the increasingly restive gliders.

"Reluctantly, I'm inclined to concur." The prospect of the *Enterprise* wasting precious time hunting for the *Lucky Strike* dampened some of his earlier elation at being hailed by Kirk. Another concern occurred to him, and he muted the intercom long enough to turn to Helena. "Alert the gliders that another ship is entering the Maelstrom, but only to assist us in leaving their domain. The last thing we need is for them to see the *Enterprise*'s arrival as a provocation . . . or evidence of ill intent on our part."

And for the gliders to interfere with *Enterprise*'s rescue mission.

"One more thing, Captain," Sulu said, reopening the channel. "I told you briefly about the life-forms we encountered here, which we've taken to calling 'gliders.' A word of advice: should you come under attack by them, do *not* fire upon them. They're energy-based entities, at least in part, and phaser beams only seem to strengthen them. Your best bet is to try to communicate with them. Our comms expert can send you the appropriate frequency and linguacodes."

"Much appreciated," Kirk said, *"but you said these 'gliders' were guiding you out of the Maelstrom?"*

"That's right, Captain, but I'm afraid we may not be departing quickly enough to suit them."

"Then perhaps they can speed matters along by leading us to you?"

"I was just thinking that myself," Sulu said. He blamed several grueling hours of being jolted and shaken nonstop, in the immediate wake of having been neurally neutralized, for not arriving at that plan earlier. His own circuits felt about as fried as the *Lucky Strike*'s. He glanced over at the comm station. "Helena?"

She shrugged.

"Couldn't hurt to ask."

"Entering the Maelstrom, sir."

Vance reported from the nav station, not that the monstrous vortex was hard to miss on the *Enterprise*'s main viewscreen. Kirk contemplated the perilous space ahead, where the *Lucky Strike* was in need of rescue, along with possibly the finest helmsman who had ever served under Kirk. The sheer immensity and violence of the Maelstrom convinced Kirk that he'd been right to relocate all the evacuees before setting out on the rescue mission; unloading the evacuees had taken longer than he liked, but he could not in good conscience take innocent civilians into the Maelstrom. This was a Starfleet mission.

"So I see," he said. "Full speed ahead, Mister Painter."

"Aye, sir."

Plunging into the Maelstrom, they hit serious turbulence almost immediately. Kirk didn't envy Sulu enduring such conditions for as long as he had, and in a significantly smaller and less formidable vessel than the *Enterprise*, no less. Kirk doubted that even the *Enterprise* could endure these conditions indefinitely. A plasma swell caused the bridge to briefly lurch to one side before stabilizing. Yeoman Landon, who had been approaching the command area bearing a data slate, stumbled and grabbed onto a railing to keep from falling. The slate clattered onto the floor.

"Sorry, Captain," she said.

"You're excused, Yeoman." He addressed the helmsman. "How are you faring, Painter?"

"We're riding the rapids, Captain," Painter said. "Currents and eddies are doing their best to carry us off course, but we're managing." His gaze darted back and forth between the viewscreen and the astrogator to maintain his bearings. "Wouldn't want to keep this up forever, though."

"I don't intend to," Kirk said. "This is strictly a rescue mission. In and out."

"Works for me, sir," Painter said.

Kirk turned toward the science and comm stations. "Have we located the *Lucky Strike* yet?"

"Only in a broad sense, Captain," Faust said. "We have a lock on their distress signal, but we're also getting interference and echoes from the Maelstrom, complicating our efforts to zero in on the source of the transmission. At present, we can only narrow down their location to a search area of approximately one cubic parsec."

Kirk frowned. That was too large an area to search in so short a time. He could only hope that Sulu had managed to convince the locals to give them a hand.

"Any sign of a reception committee?" he asked.

Faust consulted the short-range sensors. "Life-forms approaching, sir."

Kirk hoped that was a good thing. "Show me."

"Coming within visual range in three, two, one . . ."

A swarm of gliders appeared on the viewscreen, swooping out of the swirling depths of the Maelstrom. The creatures were as Sulu had described them; their nonhumanoid appearance made it difficult to gauge their intentions and mood. Kirk couldn't tell if these particular gliders were feeling hospitable or not.

"Lieutenant Uhura. Did you install that translation data the *Lucky Strike* sent us?"

"Aye, sir. The new matrix is loaded. In theory, we shouldn't have to reinvent the wheel when it comes to deciphering their language."

"Let's test that theory," Kirk said. "Hail them."

"Opening a subspace channel now, Captain. They should be able to hear you."

"Thank you, Lieutenant." Kirk took a moment to compose his greeting in his head. Despite the urgency of the emergency, he felt the same excitement he always experienced when making contact with a new life-form for the first time. "This is Captain James T. Kirk of the *U.S.S. Enterprise.* Thank you for greeting us. We appreciate your hospitality, as well as your generous assistance to our fellow travelers."

An inhuman voice, that somehow remained so despite the translator, replied:

"*Jamesteekirk? Enterprise? Hos-pi-tality? You are . . . difficult . . . to understand.*"

"The matrix is still very elementary, Captain," Uhura explained. "I recommend using simpler language."

"I see," Kirk said, feeling slightly embarrassed. "Thank you, Lieutenant."

"You're welcome, sir. It's a while since we've had to deal with a genuine language barrier."

How old-fashioned, Kirk thought, before trying again.

"We mean you no harm. We only want to help the others like us."

"Help them . . . leave?"

"Yes, if that is what you want. We will help them leave."

"What we want, yes. Follow us . . . quickly."

On-screen, the gliders reversed formation and flew deeper into the Maelstrom. Kirk was grateful that this first contact had not forced him to resort to phasers or photon torpedoes to defend his crew. *Thank you, Sulu, for putting in a good word for us.*

"You heard our hosts, Mister Painter. Follow those gliders."

"What do you mean, it's too late?" Dajo asked.

"Too late for your ship," Sulu said. "But not for the people aboard."

Led by the gliders, who were anxious to see both ships gone, the *Enterprise* had finally reached the *Lucky Strike* before its shredding shields gave up the ghost, but only just barely. The Starfleet vessel was now cruising on impulse directly above the *Lucky Strike,* its own shields and engines in much better shape despite its speedy voyage through the Maelstrom. A swarm of gliders lingered in the vicinity, watching over the proceedings.

"It's true, Captain," Fass reported. "There's no way our shields—or what's left of them—can hold up long enough for the *Enterprise* to tug us out of the Maelstrom, even at warp speed. We need to abandon ship. It's our only option."

Sulu agreed with the assessment. The bridge of the *Lucky Strike* already resembled the interior of a derelict ship. The lights flickered dimly when they functioned at all; the illumination had already gone into evening mode to conserve energy. The gravity was pretty much gone as well, so that loose objects, ashes, and debris drifted about as though wafting on phantom winds. Charred consoles testified to numerous malfunctions and short circuits. The hull groaned, reminding Sulu of the last minutes of *Fleetness*. The tranquilized passengers were rising; he could hear them shouting and milling about outside the bridge. Stale air reeked of smoke, sweat, and desperation.

"But . . . there must be another way." Dajo had reclaimed the captain's chair, giving the helm back to Sulu. "Can't the *Enterprise* extend its own shields to protect us as well?"

"Not in the Maelstrom," Sulu said. "Maybe that might be an option in normal space, but the *Enterprise* can't stretch its shields that thin in these conditions without risking both ships. The *Lucky Strike* is expendable. Our lives aren't."

"Easy for you to say," Dajo whined. "What happened to that famous Starfleet ingenuity I've heard so much about? Aren't you supposed to pull some brilliant solution out of thin air?"

"We're lifesavers, not magicians." Sulu had already consulted with Captain Kirk, who had reached the same conclusion regarding the best course of action under the circumstances. "You want miracles, find an Organian."

"You think this is funny?" Dajo gripped the arms of his chair as though he would have to be pried out of it. "I expected better of—"

"For Athena's sake, Mirsa!" Helena looked up from where she was efficiently downloading the ship's logs onto microtapes in anticipation of abandoning ship. "A few hours ago, we were as good as dead. Now we're escaping with our lives . . . and the lives of the passengers in our care. Show a little gratitude."

Dajo looked only slightly chastened. "But we're talking about my ship, Helena. My livelihood. My pride and joy."

"Which you acquired less than a year ago by fleecing that shady Orion smuggler in the Serpentine Belt," she said. "You're welcome to go down with the ship if you insist, but I wouldn't advise it."

"Ditto." Sulu had some sympathy for Dajo. He could only imagine what it would be like to abandon the *Enterprise*, let alone a ship of his own, but Dajo had brought this on himself by recklessly braving the Maelstrom in the first place. "And I suspect that Captain Kirk will be unwilling to leave you behind no matter what you decide, so you might as well get used to the idea of surviving."

"Well, if I have to . . ." Dajo said. "Under protest, naturally."

"Naturally." Sulu refrained from smirking. "We should begin beaming people over immediately, starting with the passengers. The less time the *Enterprise* has to lower its shields, the better."

"And our shields?" Dajo asked.

Fass snorted. "Barely worth lowering. We're practically down to bare hull at this point."

"All the more reason to hurry," Sulu said. "But don't worry, the *Enterprise* has more than enough room to take on everyone— crew and passengers."

"And our cargo and provisions and personal effects," Dajo added.

Sulu shook his head. "No time for that."

Dajo started to protest, but then Helena reopened the channel to the gliders.

"*Leave. Quickly. Now.*"

"Care to take it up with them?" she asked. "Sounds to me like we're wearing out our welcome."

"Not to mention our hull," Fass added.

"Fine!" Dajo said. "I'll inform the passengers that there's been a slight change of plans to their travel arrangements. But first, about my accommodations aboard the *Enterprise* . . ." He looked hopefully at Sulu. "I understand there are VIP suites available?"

"Don't press your luck," Sulu said. *We also have a brig, if it comes down to it.*

Helena packed up her microtapes and launched herself toward him. The lack of gravity actually made navigating the lurching deck somewhat easier. She grabbed onto the back of his chair to halt herself and whispered in his ear.

"Speaking of accommodations, how large are your quarters on the *Enterprise*?"

Sulu grinned.

"Large enough."

Thirty-Five

Baldur III

"Welcome to New Town Hall," the mayor said. "For the time being, that is."

Kirk, McCoy, and Landon met Poho and her advisors in a two-story log cabin on the outskirts of town. Her makeshift office was in a state of relative disarray, with maps and monitors and microtapes piled everywhere and overflowing storage containers stacked haphazardly in corners. As Kirk understood it, the cabin had previously served as the headquarters for a logging operation that had shut down once pergium fever hit. Tents and barracks outside the cabin provided temporary shelter to families and individuals who had lost their homes in the fire. They were not the only such shelters, Kirk knew, but he was grateful that even more were not required. Additional refugees had been absorbed into Jackpot City's many surviving buildings, which had generously opened their doors to the displaced. It was a few days past the disaster and the colony, although still recovering, was starting to get back on its feet again with help from the *Enterprise* and other ships in orbit.

"Glad to see you're making do," Kirk said, "after everything you've been through."

"We're a hardy bunch, Captain." She looked over the office. "The new digs lack the historical luster of the old building, but it beats working in a heap of ashes. We also managed to back up and preserve all important records before they went up in flames." She guided them to a cluttered conference table, at which they found room enough to sit down. "Mind you, we fully intend to rebuild the original town hall the first chance we get. We're just going to make it more fireproof next time!"

"Probably a good idea," Kirk said. "I applaud you for already looking ahead to the future."

Any bad blood about the *Enterprise* briefly abandoning Baldur III to rescue the *Lucky Strike* had apparently been left in the past in favor of planning for tomorrow. Kirk approved of the mayor's attitude; he had never been one to look backward when there were new worlds and challenges ahead.

"Speaking of which, Captain, I have good news for you. After thinking it over, my council and I have voted unanimously that it's past time Baldur III steps up and joins the Federation. The *Enterprise*'s invaluable role in saving Jackpot City, along with the crucial assistance those other offworlder vessels provided during the crisis, convinced us that we're better off with you than stubbornly hoeing it alone. 'No man is an island,' they say, and neither is a planet, it seems."

Kirk smiled. He was not totally surprised by the news, since he had known such discussions had been underway, but he was pleased nonetheless.

"That *is* great news . . . for everyone. From what I've seen, Baldur III is going to be a tremendous addition to the Federation, and not just because of your pergium. Your people's ingenuity, courage, and hospitality are right in line with the core values of the UFP. You're going to fit right in."

"Damn right, we are," Poho said. "And we can't wait to pay Starfleet's generosity forward by helping out the other worlds of the Federation whenever we can." Her eyes twinkled. "While still making a decent profit, of course."

Kirk grinned back at her. "I'd expect nothing less."

"It's true," Landon said. "He anticipated you'd vote this way. It's in his logs."

"Not to look a gift horse in the mouth," McCoy said, "but you said the vote was . . . unanimous?"

He gave Boyd Cahill a quizzical look.

"I know what you're thinking," the noted curmudgeon said. "And don't think I'm not asking myself the same question, but . . . well, my own house is downtown, on the lucky side of that firebreak you carved, and my granddaughter was evacuated from her school by somebody in a Starfleet uniform. If the *Enterprise* hadn't been here when *Thunderbird* started blowing its fuse, I don't want to think about what would have happened to this town and everyone I care for." He shrugged. "Maybe the Federation comes in handy."

"I like to think so," Kirk said. He respected Cahill for being willing to change his mind.

"Just don't think you're going to turn everything upside down overnight," Cahill insisted. "Or that we won't pull out of the Federation in a moment if you start throwing your weight around." He eyed Kirk suspiciously. "We can leave if we want to, right?"

"The Federation is an alliance, not an empire," Kirk assured him. "Unlike the Klingons or the Romulans, we don't hold on to planets against their will."

Granted, seceding from the Federation was not as simple as giving two weeks' notice; the mechanisms for arriving at such a momentous decision varied from planet to planet, and could have serious consequences, but it was possible. Membership in the Federation was strictly voluntary.

"I think you'll find, however, that the advantages of being part of the Federation far outweigh any imagined threats to your culture or identity. As Mayor Poho just sagely observed, we're stronger together than apart."

Cahill declined to agree too readily. "Well, we'll see, I guess."

"An open mind is the most we can ask for," Kirk said

diplomatically before turning toward Navvan. "What about your people, Navvan? Are the Troglytes and the other new-comers okay with Baldur III joining the Federation?"

"I'll be honest with you, Kirk. Back on Ardana, during the long days and nights of our oppression, the Federation seemed very remote and irrelevant. You were too far away to hear our cries or witness how cruelly we were being treated by the elites of Stratos, let alone do anything about it, but then the *Enterprise* arrived and things began to change, albeit too slowly for some. And here on Baldur III . . . I heard how you intervened when my people came under attack over that claim dispute in the hills. That could have ended very badly, had you not taken swift and judicious action." Navvan reached across the table to shake Kirk's hand. "So, yes, Kirk, thanks to you, my people are willing to give the Federation the benefit of the doubt."

"You won't be disappointed," Kirk promised. "In fact, I've been in touch with the brass back home, just in case you decided in our favor, and they're prepared to fast-track Baldur III's admission to the Federation, which will make it easier to dispatch more ships and personnel and resources to help you rebuild and recover."

"In exchange for our pergium?" Cahill asked.

"I won't lie," Kirk said. "Baldur III's value as a major source of pergium certainly makes it in everyone's best interests to ensure that you have everything you need to get up and running again . . . and to keep you thriving for years to come. On a practical level, that means more engineers and doctors and nurses and administrators and relief workers to help you cope with not just the aftermath of the fire but with your expanding population and interstellar importance as well. Once you're formally part of the Federation, the powers that be will move heaven and earth to make certain that Baldur III lives up to its full potential, for the mutual benefit of all concerned. You can count on that."

"Well, you've certainly done right by us so far," Poho said.

"And we can certainly use all the help we can get at the moment, particularly when it comes to our energy crisis."

Power shortages remained an issue, Kirk knew. Portable generators provided by the *Enterprise* and the other ships were helping to keep vital services operating, but severe conservation measures were in effect in the meantime. Sunlight poured through the windows of the cabin in place of artificial lighting, although Kirk heard the mayor's personal computer terminal humming. Power was being strictly rationed.

"I'm told the first hydroelectric generator should be able to go into limited operation soon," the mayor continued. "In the meantime, a passenger ship from Deneva has been drafted to replace *Thunderbird* as a temporary power plant. A local philanthropist, Oskar Thackery, shelled out a fortune to purchase the ship on behalf of the community."

"Another ship turned generator?" McCoy said. "Is that wise?"

"This ship is not the ancient relic *Thunderbird* was," Poho assured the worried doctor, "and your own Mister Scott is personally overseeing the conversion to make sure it's done properly. I understand that he's being quite demanding when it comes to insisting that no corners be cut and that every possible safety precaution be taken." She smiled ruefully. "After what happened last time, I've instructed our own technicians to see to it that everything is done to his satisfaction, which is apparently a very high standard to meet."

"That's our Scotty, all right." McCoy relaxed visibly. "If he's got his eye on things, you should be okay."

"I understand that you and Doctor Burstein have the city clinic operational again?" Poho asked.

"More or less," McCoy reported. "We're getting a welcome amount of help and supplies from the doctors and infirmaries on the arriving ships, but we're still stretched pretty thin, so if you folks could just avoid having any more accidents or disasters for a while, that would be dandy."

"We'll keep that in mind, Doctor," Kirk quipped. "Make a note of that, Landon. No more disasters, per the doctor's recommendation."

Landon smirked. "Duly noted, sir."

"Very funny," McCoy said. "Seriously, anything we can do to get more doctors, nurses, and medicine here needs to be done yesterday."

"Well, Starfleet frowns on time travel," Kirk joked, "but that's where applying to the Federation is going to solve a lot of Baldur III's problems before too long. The Federation is not going to let its latest member lack proper health care facilities. It will be taken care of, even if Starfleet Medical has to dispatch a hospital ship to the system."

"Still couldn't hurt to light a fire under some people," McCoy suggested.

"Consider it ignited," Kirk said. "I'll call in some favors."

McCoy smiled slyly. "Now we're talking."

Bureaucratic politics aside, Kirk had faith that better days lay ahead for Baldur III. The "gold rush" had pushed the planet and its people to their limits, but when disaster hit, most people's better angels had prevailed, despite the lure of riches and the heated passions they'd aroused.

He wondered if Spock would find that "logical" or not.

Yurnos

"Releasing final satellite," Spock announced.

Galileo orbited Yurnos, having returned to the planet after reporting back to *Enterprise* in preparation for this procedure. Spock watched via his display globe as the last of four defensive satellites was launched from a modular mechanism temporarily installed on the roof of the shuttlecraft. Like the launcher, the satellites had been procured from the *Enterprise*, where they had been prepared by Lieutenant Charlene Masters and her engineering team, per Spock's instructions. Sensors tracked the satellite as it fell into a polar orbit around Yurnos that would have it crossing over each of the planet's poles every 17.5 hours. Spock watched carefully to confirm the launch had been executed successfully.

"Satellite positioned," he reported. "Orbital trajectory verified."

"That's four for four." Chekov grinned from the helm. "We're on a roll."

"Simply a matter of applied physics, Ensign. No lucky streaks required."

Both men were back in their standard uniforms, as well as at their now-accustomed places in the cockpit. Despite his confidence in his calculations, Spock relaxed slightly as the final satellite came into view through *Galileo*'s forward ports.

Approximately 50.55 centimeters in diameter, the matte-black orb had been shielded against the oscillating electromagnetic interference from Yurnos's polar auroras and calibrated to compensate for the same. An automated phaser array gave the satellite enough teeth to defend itself and/or discourage any casual visitors, but, along with the three companion satellites *Galileo* had already launched, its primary function was to sound an alarm at any unauthorized attempt to trespass on Yurnos. The satellites also functioned as warning buoys broadcasting a very clear message regarding the planet: Do Not Disturb.

"Do you think the satellites will be enough, Mister Spock?"

"They will do for the present," he replied, "until stronger measures can be implemented."

Now that the Federation was establishing a larger presence in this sector, the long-term plan was to discreetly establish a permanent watch station on the dark side of the planet's moon, where the Yurnians would not be able to see it for centuries. In the interim, the satellites' opaque black exterior would suffice to hide them from whatever crude telescopes the Yurnians might develop in the immediate future. With Baldur III only a system away, Starfleet would be in a position to respond to any new incursions with relative alacrity.

"Shall we inform Jord and Vankov of our success?" Chekov asked.

"I am hailing them now."

The anthropologists appeared on the display globes, thanks to upgrades to their hidden nerve center on Yurnos, which would also make it easier for the pair to contact Starfleet in the event of another emergency. In addition, Spock had provided them with instructions on how to recalibrate their sensors in order to better contend with the camouflage provided by the polar aurorae. Between the automated satellites, the observers' new-and-improved sensors, and, eventually, the covert watch station on the moon, the odds of any spacefaring intruders arriving undetected had become vanishingly small.

"So, Misters Spock and Chekov," Vankov greeted them. "Is your task done?"

"Affirmative," Spock replied. "Yurnos is now fully under the Federation's protection, until such time as its residents are ready to venture out into the galaxy on their own."

"Thank goodness," Jord said with visible relief. "Talk about a load off our minds."

"And how are matters on the planet?" Chekov asked. "There has been no fallout from that incident with *Galileo*?"

Vankov shrugged. "The tale is making the rounds of the alehouses, and has a few of the more skittish folks on edge, but if there are no recurrences, it's likely to become nothing more than a colorful local legend, especially after a few generations have passed."

"Not ideal," Jord said, frowning briefly, "but not a disaster either."

Spock agreed with her assessment. He regretted adding to the planet's superstitions, but it would not be the first time that a stray alien had inspired a myth or two. Other worlds, including Earth, had weathered similar incidents.

"And Eefa?" Chekov asked.

"We quietly left her wagon and rodents outside her home in the wee hours of the night," Vankov said, *"with none the wiser. She's still dealing tea from her shop, but only to Yurnians as far as we can tell. No fresh contraband has surfaced since you chased those smugglers away."*

"Speaking of whom," Spock said, "you may be pleased to know that the individuals in question did not get far. Firing upon a Starfleet vessel is not something the Federation takes lightly, let alone brazenly violating the Prime Directive, so the entire fleet was on the lookout for their distinctive vessel, which had secured a place high on the quadrant's most-wanted list. Venus, Mercury, and Mars were apprehended by the *Potemkin* three solar days ago, while attempting to trade their spacecraft for a new vessel at an asteroid trading post near the Klingon border." News of their capture had reached Spock and Chekov on their return trip to Yurnos. "Unsurprisingly, it turns out that the smugglers' names were not actually Mars, Venus, or Mercury."

"Imagine that," Vankov said dryly.

"Given the severity of the charges against them," Spock said, "it is unlikely that they will be resuming their smuggling operations for some years to come."

"I hope they throw the book at them," Jord said, scowling.

"More like an encyclopedia," Chekov said. "With large print."

"In any event," Spock said, "they no longer pose a threat to the Yurnians' cultural development, and we now have measures in place to alert us should anyone attempt to emulate them."

"Works for me," Vankov said. *"With any luck, this world will never know what you did for them, so we'll just have to thank you on their behalf."*

"What he said," Jord added.

Spock saw no logical need to be thanked simply for performing their duty, but he accepted the anthropologists' gratitude in the spirit in which it was intended.

"You are most welcome. We are pleased to have brought this matter to a satisfactory conclusion."

"What about you?" Chekov asked the pair. "Are you still staying on here? We could give you a lift to Baldur III if you wish to return to modern times and technology."

Vankov shook his head as the couple put their arms around each other.

"We appreciate the offer, Chekov, but, unlike you two, our work isn't done here. History is still unfolding on Yurnos and we've got a front-row seat. Not giving that up anytime soon."

"I look forward to following the progress of your studies in the years to come," Spock said sincerely. He had found time to review their published work over the course of his recent travels. "Your insights into Hodgkin's Law are most intriguing."

"Just wait," Vankov said. *"We're only getting started."*

A few more pleasantries ensued before Spock and Chekov bid farewell to the scientists and terminated the transmission. *Galileo* turned back toward Baldur III and the *Enterprise*, leaving Yurnos behind.

"An interesting world to visit," Chekov said. "Do you expect that the Yurnians will someday advance so far that they will be ready to join the Federation?"

"That is difficult to predict with any certainty," Spock replied. "There are too many variables with regard to the future of both Yurnos *and* the Federation. Only time will tell, but at least the Yurnians can now forge their own future . . . without any outside interference."

The Prime Directive had been upheld.

———

Hanging lanterns and candles illuminated the Pergium Palace, adding to the popular nightclub's romantic atmosphere as Sulu checked the place out for the first time. A vocalist working a traditional piano was taking advantage of the building's natural acoustics to entertain the guests without any artificial amplification. According to Uhura, this was the local hot spot, with or without electricity. Unlike several other saloons and eateries, it had survived the fires with only some minor scorch marks and smoke damage. Sulu was not too disappointed to have missed that action; he'd had his hands full in the Maelstrom at the time.

"Sulu, over here!"

Uhura waved to him from a crowded booth where she was socializing with a group of locals. She beckoned for him to join them. "Come on over. We can make room."

"Another time," he said affably. "I'm meeting someone."

He found Helena holding a seat for him at a table for two. Candlelight suited her much better than the blinding energy pulses they'd endured in the Maelstrom. He wondered where she'd found such an amazing dress on this rustic frontier planet, but chalked it up to her usual ingenuity and talent for scrounging up whatever vital part suited her needs at any given moment. That she'd gone to the effort of dressing up for their much-delayed date both flattered and encouraged him. He was glad he'd changed into a fresh Starfleet uniform.

"Right on time," she said warmly as he sat down across from her. "So, are we finally going to have that drink at last?"

He glanced around the dimly lit club as though scanning for hostile life-forms. "Unless a Romulan bird-of-prey decloaks in the next five minutes, I think we're good."

"Don't jinx us," she said.

A pretty blond server approached. "Hi, there. My name's Flossi. What can I do for you? I'm afraid the ovens and protein sequencers are down until the power is restored, so our menu is limited, but maybe I can start you with some drinks?"

"You must be a telepath, 'cause you're reading our minds,"

Sulu said. "Maybe a bottle of a good local wine?" He looked at Helena. "That all right with you?"

"Perfect. Not too strong, though," Helena added. "This thin air already has me light-headed."

"You get used to it," the server said. "I'll be right back with that wine. And don't even think about trying to settle up afterward. Drinks are on the house for *Enterprise* crew and their friends. This place wouldn't still be standing if not for you folks."

Sulu considered pointing out that he hadn't personally been involved in saving the city. "Actually—"

"No 'actuallys,'" she insisted. "Your credits are no good here. Any crewmate of Nyota Uhura drinks for free." She leaned forward and whispered conspiratorially. "I'm going to be Starfleet myself someday, just you wait."

Uhura had obviously made a big impression on the girl. "I'll save a berth for you on my ship . . . when I'm a captain, of course."

"I may hold you to that," Flossi said. "Be right back."

The server wandered off, pausing to check on Uhura's booth, before disappearing from sight. Sulu returned his attention to Helena, who was well worth his regard. Since being rescued from the Maelstrom by the *Enterprise*, they had been too busy assisting their respective captains, crews, and passengers to have any quiet time together, let alone compare notes on how they'd been doing since.

"So what's new?" she asked. "Aside from the fact that, miraculously, we both survived crossing the Maelstrom."

"I touched base with the space station today," Sulu said. "According to Doctor M'Benga, Tilton and Grandle are both recovering from the effects of the neural neutralizer, although it seems Tilton is retiring from his post as station manager after everything that happened."

"Probably inevitable," Helena said. "I know it wasn't his fault, but there's no way he could stay on after being outed as the saboteur. Might be just as well too. The old guy looked like he could use a nice, long rest."

Sulu couldn't disagree. "Word is Grandle has the job if she wants it. She got her brain messed with too, but she broke the conditioning in time to save me and everyone else, so her career isn't likely to be hurt by the incident. It's just going to be an isolated blip on her record."

"What about you?" Helen asked. "How is your noggin doing after getting zapped by that gadget back on the station?"

"Honestly, I think I'm okay. Doctor McCoy has me scheduled for some follow-up exams and treatments, but I haven't heard any deceitful voices whispering at the back of my head since before we escaped the Maelstrom. Hard to concentrate on your brainwashing when you're being swarmed by hostile gliders in a deadly cosmic vortex."

He spoke more lightly than maybe the question warranted, but he wasn't lying. He was confident that he would get past his ordeal in the neutralizer chair. After all, he'd been mind-controlled before and kept on going afterward. And here he was, having a candlelit dinner with Helena, while Naylis was facing serious criminal charges back on S-8.

I can live with that, he thought.

"Meanwhile, the Maelstrom has been officially declared off-limits now that we know that it's inhabited by a sentient species that doesn't want us trespassing on their turf. Knowing Starfleet, we're going to want to try making contact with them again at some point, as we did with the Melkotians and other reclusive peoples, but only on their terms and at their own pace."

"I hope you're right," Helena said. "But you really think that people aren't going to dare the Maelstrom again?"

"After what happened to the *Lucky Strike*?" he asked. "For better or for worse, I like to think we debunked the notion that there's a safe passage through the Maelstrom, proving that it's still safer to take the long way around. Which means S-8 is likely to remain a major hub for some time, so the Federation is treating it accordingly by making plans to seriously expand the staff and facilities there. The *Yorktown* has already been diverted to relieve the *Enterprise* crew still stationed there."

Flossi arrived with their wine and two glasses. Sulu opened the bottle and poured for both of them. The fragrant bouquet of the wine promised a treat.

"But enough about Starfleet," he continued. "What's up with your crew, now that the *Lucky Strike* is history?"

"They're managing," she said. "Some have signed on with other ships already, some have found work helping to rebuild the torched parts of the city, while others want to try their hand at prospecting, but mostly they're all just glad to be alive. Our passengers were pretty pissed to discover that their cargo had been lost with the ship, and a few threatened to sue Captain Dajo, but given that he has no real assets to speak of these days, most of them figured out they were better off seeking their fortunes in the mines, just like they originally intended."

Makes sense to me, Sulu thought. "And Dajo?"

"Don't worry about him. He'll land on his feet. He always does." She glanced up at the gambling dens on the mezzanine. "Wouldn't be surprised if he's up there now, trying to raise money for whatever he's up to next."

"What about you?" Sulu asked. "What are your plans?"

"Not sure," she admitted. "Maybe I'll have a go at prospecting too, see if I can dig up enough pergium to make a down payment on a ship of my own. There's talk of newly discovered veins in the western hemisphere and elsewhere. Maybe it's not too late to stake a claim where nobody has dug before." She shrugged. "I wouldn't object to striking it rich."

"Prosperity would look good on you," Sulu said. "But you're sure I can't talk you into signing on with Starfleet? With your skills and experience—"

She laughed out loud. "Be serious. I'd be drummed out for

insubordination within a week. I'm a freebooter at heart; you know that. No commitments."

"I know," he said. "Figured it couldn't hurt to ask."

"Consider me flattered," she said. "That you consider me Starfleet material, I mean."

"Among other things." He raised a glass to her. "That being said, apparently it's still going to be a few weeks before any additional Federation ships and personnel arrive to relieve the *Enterprise,* so it looks as though we'll sticking around for a while."

She lifted her own glass. "That suits me just fine."

"Me too."

Acknowledgments

This is a book I've wanted to write for a while now, so I'm very grateful for the opportunity to finally beam it out to the world.

Many thanks to my editors, Ed Schlesinger and Margaret Clark, for waiting patiently for this manuscript while I recovered from two major moves; to John Van Citters and CBS for steering the franchise; to my agent Russell Galen for ably handling the business end of matters; and, as always, to Karen and Sophie for their support and encouragement every single day.

About the Author

Greg Cox is the *New York Times* bestselling author of numerous *Star Trek* novels and stories, including *Legacies, Book 1: Captain to Captain, Miasma, Child of Two Worlds, Foul Deeds Will Rise, No Time Like the Past, The Weight of Worlds, The Rings of Time, To Reign in Hell, The Eugenics Wars (Volumes One and Two), The Q Continuum, Assignment: Eternity,* and *The Black Shore.* He has also written the official movie novelizations of *War for the Planet of the Apes, Godzilla, Man of Steel, The Dark Knight Rises, Ghost Rider, Daredevil, Death Defying Acts,* and the first three *Underworld* movies, as well as books and stories based on such popular series as *Alias, Buffy the Vampire Slayer, CSI: Crime Scene Investigation, Farscape, The 4400, Leverage, The Librarians, Riese: Kingdom Falling, Roswell, Terminator, Warehouse 13, The X-Files,* and *Xena: Warrior Princess.*

He has received three Scribe Awards, as well as the Faust Award for Life Achievement, from the International Association of Media Tie-In Writers. He lives in Lancaster, Pennsylvania.

Visit him at: www.gregcox-author.com.